Mafia Star

The Mancinelli Brotherhood

Sabine Barclay

OLIVERHEBERBOOKS

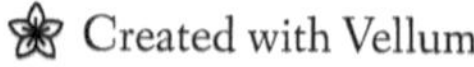 Created with Vellum

Thank you for joining me as we grew our love-hate relationship with the Mancinellis. Just wait until you see what's coming next.

Find me writing Historical Romance as Celeste Barclay.

Happy reading,
Sabine

Subscribe to Sabine's Newsletter

Subscribe to Sabine's bimonthly newsletter to receive exclusive insider perks.

Have you read *The Syndicate Wars*? This FREE origin story novella is available to all new subscribers to Sabine's monthly newsletter. Subscribe on her website. www.sabinebarclay.com

The Mancinelli Brotherhood

Mafia Heir

Mafia Sinner

Mafia Beauty

Mafia Angel

Mafia Redeemer

Mafia Star

Do you also enjoy steamy Historical Romance? Discover Sabine's books written as Celeste Barclay.

Chapter One

Marco

I'm standing next to my younger brother's new sister-in-law of four hours. The elevator doors shut as Lorenzo and Michelle make their escape for their wedding night, leaving the smoking hot Elizabeth and me alone. We turn toward each other.

"It was a beautiful ceremony."

Elizabeth doesn't seem to know what to say, but she beats me to saying something.

"Everyone seems to be enjoying the reception, too."

I offer her my arm to take her back to the ballroom. I suppose I'm trying to be charming. I did it as a joke earlier when I accompanied Elizabeth and Chelle back from the restroom. I'd extended my arm to Chelle, as the bride, to be gallant. Then I realized I'd be an ass to not do the same for Elizabeth. I say that now. But I think I was looking for an excuse to touch her.

I'd just like an excuse to touch her again. Chelle is definitely attractive, but not my type. She and Elizabeth look a lot alike, but her aura is completely different. Elizabeth's more like Chelle's best friend, Laura Kutsenko. Chelle's approach is more subtle while Laura and Elizabeth exude control. That's irony at its best since Laura is married to the head of the Russian bratva.

The reception is as much about our family celebrating this momentous occasion as it is our family and every other syndicate flexing their money, vying to be at the top of the New York underworld. The jewelry on both the men and women, the gowns the women wear, the general sense of affluence... All of us exude it to prove to the politer parts of society here that we are the ones they want to get into bed with. Nobody admits aloud that we're what the rest of the world likely considers the rich dregs— yes, an oxymoron —of society.

But we're the ones who make sure candidates we select get elected to public positions. We're the ones who ensure private financiers have the money to lend their clients. We're the ones who ensure the lower-level gangs and crime families understand their place and balance in this ecosystem where we— the Mancinellis —the Kutsenkos, the O'Rourkes, and the Diazes are the apex predators. Predators who left their guns at home tonight but are all carrying knives. We might not have a gunfight at a wedding reception, but no one wants to get stabbed on the way to our cars.

Elizabeth glances at my raised forearm before she takes it. If she weren't my sister-in-law's sister, I might try to get her drunk and take her home. So cliché, but like I said, she's smoking hot. It's been a long time since I've done a random hook-up or a one-night stand. I prefer to fuck women I know in the anonymity of my BDSM club. But I'd make an exception for Elizabeth if it wouldn't piss the fuck out of my entire family if they found out. Which they would.

I glance at her and still feel like I need something to say. How am I so fucking at a loss for words? Here goes nothing.

"I think I may sleep all day tomorrow. It's been crazy this week."

Four days ago, Enzo and Chelle decided to get married. This reception is a sign of just how much influence we have. The reception at the St. Regis, designer gowns custom fit for all the women in the wedding party, and the crème de la crème in attendance.

As we enter the ballroom, my gaze sweeps the room. I know where every member of the mob, the Cartel, and the bratva are. I know where my other brother, Luca, is along with his wife, Olivia, and their baby. Petra is the easiest child in the world. She sleeps or laughs. I know where my sister, Maria, is with my best friend and her husband, Matteo. I know where Gabriele and Sinead, and Carmine and Serafina are. I know where my uncles, my aunts, and my parents are. It's habit. I will never walk into a room without knowing my surroundings, and I will never enter a room where my family is without ensuring they're safe.

"Yeah. I don't think I'm going to last. I'm going to grab my purse and wrap then get an Uber."

That makes me stop so fast it jerks Elizabeth's arm.

"No, you're not."

She arches an eyebrow at me, and I realize how that sounded.

"I meant you can take one of our town cars home. We have enough, so you can have a driver. It's two in the morning in New York City, and you are dressed far too nicely and far too beautiful for someone not to notice. You're a target."

She stiffens, and now it's her turn to sweep her gaze around the room.

"I didn't mean any of the families. I meant some creep who'll try to mug you, or worse."

The families. She's vicariously a member now, so she

knows who I mean. I don't know how much Laura or Chelle have told her, but she's a smart woman. She's figured shit out.

"Thank you for the offer, but I can wait in the lobby until the car arrives. Then it'll take me straight to my building's driveway. I'll be fine."

My gaze roams over her body, lingering places her gown compliments far too well before I focus back on her eyes. It's my turn to cock an eyebrow. I purposely made my expression lascivious. I didn't expect her to blush. I expected her to glare. I soften my tone to the one I use when I'm scening with a woman at my club. The deceptively quiet one.

"Take the offer, Elizabeth. Otherwise, I will share that ride with you. You are not leaving here without someone I trust. Decide. Me or one of our drivers."

It surprises me when she hesitates.

"Thank you. Please ask one of your men to drive me home."

I admit I'm disappointed. Sharing the seat of some tiny Prius would have been better than going home alone in my own town car. But it wouldn't have come to anything physical. Everything about her draws me to her. Her bearing, her smile, her voice, the way her gaze can pin me in place. There are few women who can do the latter.

I escort her back to the head table, where she gathers her things. She says goodbye to her parents and brother before saying goodbye and thanking my family. I've already gotten Luigi's attention. I step next to Luca as she makes her rounds.

"Luigi's taking Elizabeth home."

I'm telling my brother for two reasons. As our underboss, he assigns the men to the family members they guard. Also, Luca prefers Luigi to guard Olivia and Petra, but since Luca is with his wife and daughter, I'm taking one of our most trusted men from his assigned duty. Luca stares at me for a moment before he nods.

"Don't read anything into it. She's practically our sister now, too. Would you let her Uber?"

That makes Luca glance over at her before he shakes his head.

"Hence Luigi."

"Fine."

"Thank you. Are you staying much longer?"

"No. Olivia is about ready to drop. We'll ride home with Mama and Papa. They can drop us off first."

Now that they have a child, Luca and Olivia bought a house in the same neighborhood as our aunt and uncle. It also happens to be the one where all the married Kutsenkos live. Irony at its best.

We all grew up in Queens— every syndicate family —but most of us moved to Manhattan after college. As the Kutsenkos got married, they started moving back to Queens to keep their family closer together. I suspect we'll all end up there or in our parents' community around the corner.

As Elizabeth says her last goodbye and moves toward the door, I scan the room for anyone who might be watching her. Motherfucking son of a bitch. Alejandro Diaz. He stares at her until she leaves the ballroom, then glances at me. He smirks knowingly before he heads for the door, too. If I follow him to keep him away from Elizabeth, I'll just confirm his silent accusation. If I don't follow, I won't know what the hell he says. Will it be something shitty about my family or me? Or will he try to seduce her? She's not related to anyone in his family. He sees her as fair game.

"All right. I'm headed out now. I'll see you tomorrow."

I hug Luca and make my way to the door, saying a couple brief goodbyes. I'm not getting drawn into some conversation with an old guard member who wants to tell me how they did things back in the day. I arrive at the elevators just as the doors close. I call for the next one, and it comes quickly. But neither Alejandro nor Elizabeth is in sight when I step into the lobby. Did he move that fast?

I make a beeline outside just in time to see Elizabeth get into the car and Luigi close the door behind her. I spot my driver and walk toward the car, but Alejandro appears. He's had this ability since we were kids. He'll skulk around in the shadows then show up right next to you like some fucking apparition.

"You look like a lost puppy, *cabrón*." Asshole.

I ignore him.

"Trailing after your owner who's leaving you behind. Did she leave you some food and water? Maybe give you a scratch behind the ear before she left?"

"Don't be shitty. She's Enzo's sister-in-law. I'm not hooking up with her."

"Maybe not, but you want to."

"That would be you. I didn't follow her out."

"No. You just followed me because I followed her."

"Or, all our cars are out here, and I'm ready to go home."

"Sure."

"*Fanculo*." Fuck off.

What more is there for me to say? He's an asshole just as much as I ever am. But I don't like that he noticed my interest in Elizabeth. I can justify it, but it's hard to hide something from someone who used to trade his lunch for mine in elementary school. His *bunuelos*— deep fried balls of cheese —and empanadas for my caponata— diced fried eggplant and a mix of carrots, celery, and whatever else I thought my mother was torturing me with —and bruschetta. One of many examples of our fucked-up childhood. We traded food back then. Now we trade bullets.

I pretend as though we weren't in the middle of a conversation and walk to my waiting car. I saw his driver at the other end of the block. Once I'm inside, I push him to the far corners of my mind. It's Elizabeth who occupies my thoughts. No surprise there. Why am I so drawn to her? We didn't really spend that much time together. I danced with her once since I was Enzo's best man, and she was Chelle's maid of honor. Laura was her matron of honor— no one made Chelle feel like she had to choose —but there wasn't a chance in hell Maks would allow anyone in my family to dance with Laura. She might gut one of us, and then Maks would have to pay us a shit ton and try to make polite society forget what they saw.

I've danced with plenty of women in nightclubs and the wretched fundraisers I've been attending since I was a teenager. No woman has ever felt so right in my arms on the dance floor as Elizabeth. Thank God I had to keep our bodies apart for proprieties' sake; otherwise, she would have felt my raging hard on. We chatted, but I could barely focus on the conversation. I was too busy trying not to picture her underneath me, on top of me, in front of me, in whatever fucking position— literally —we could manage. I've never had such a visceral reaction to anyone. At least not to someone I'm not about to kill.

It started last night at the rehearsal. She and I had to talk to the priest about our roles in the ceremony. Good thing my only actual job was to hand the ring over to Enzo. I barely paid attention to anything else. It's like she radiated this energy that made my body— mainly my cock —pulse. We sat beside each other at the dinner. I had the chance to pull out her chair, and our eyes locked just before she sat. Did something pass between us? Or was that something entirely conjured by my horny imagination?

Neither possibility matters. I'm not going to bang her. I can't even hook up with her without having sex. Papa would murder me after Enzo was done killing me. I'm not looking to settle down. I like my bachelorhood, even if it is getting lonely now that everyone else my age is married. I refuse to do what the others have done. I'm not bringing an outsider into the shitshow we call normal. I'm not having kids who are going to be the next generation of Mafia. When I want to fuck, I go to my club. When I want company, I go to the gym with the guys. When I want to be alone— well, I have plenty of time to do that now.

The six of us— Luca, Matteo, Carmine, Gabriele, Maria, and me —were inseparable as kids because our family is so close. As we got older, Carmine and Gabriele really separated themselves. Those shitheads. They caused a lot of trouble, and it's only been within the last year or so that we learned why. Now I feel bad for Carmine and his misspent and misunderstood youth.

Matteo and I have been close since we were three and were old enough to choose one another to play with. We've been practically fraternal twins since the day we were born. I'm two-and-a-half hours older. We used to share a crib when our mothers visited each other practically daily. Luca and Matteo's older brother, Emilio, were close until their falling out.

Once we really got into the family business, Maria sought her other friends because we could no longer involve her in the things we got up to. It was an adjustment back then— not having her around with her infectious laugh and ability to cause the most trouble and never get caught. I'm adjusting to this change in our relationships now that I'm the odd man out. Would it be nice to have someone to come home to? Someone to love and be loved by? Of course. Are my family members making it work? Definitely. Do I want to endanger a wife and children just because I might get lonely? Not a fucking chance in hell.

I don't fault the others for finding their soulmates. I just won't look for mine. I absolutely believe in them. My parents and aunts and uncles— except for Auntie Paola and Uncle Cesare —are proof they exist. I've known that my entire life. But that doesn't mean I need to find mine. However, that's small consolation as I climb into bed alone. I'm going to my club tomorrow night. I'll fuck this maudlin shit out of my system.

"Where are we at with those fuckers?"

I jerk my chin toward the two men strung up in the garage. This isn't some tandem residential space. This appears to be an abandoned commercial garage. It's where we deal with the unsavory parts of our jobs. It's where people walk in but never walk out. It's in an Italian neighborhood where we either pay people well for their silence, or they're smart enough to be too terrified to say anything. The guys are naked and hanging from hooks in the overhead door chains. We've been opening and lowering the doors a few inches to a few feet to coerce them. It must feel like their arms are about to rip through their skin. Not to mention the fact that I took pliers to their teeth earlier.

Matteo shakes his head and rolls his eyes.

"They've given up as much as they know. Now we're just punishing them."

We purposely don't grease any of the chains. The doors are the big metal ones that echo like thunder when they open and close. It drowns out the screams. As I look at the men, I know Matteo's right. We know the men who kidnapped Aunt Sylvia are all dead now. We know they were men Maks hired afterwards for an unrelated job, and he didn't know of their involvement. We don't know the mastermind.

We know the man who arranged the mercenaries was beaten to within an inch of his life for a completely unrelated issue. The Triad may operate in China, but they have no qualms about settling scores with individuals here in New York. It was a bit bittersweet, though. The man, Robert Simms, targeted Chelle for her connections to our family and the Kutsenkos. Simms attempted to wage his vendetta against Pasha Kutsenko through Chelle. We thought they'd killed him, but he survived. Motherfucker.

That's a prime reason why I don't want to bring an outsider into this world. There are Mafia daughters I could consider, but I've never been interested in anyone from the families who work for us. I've known the women my entire life. I even messed around with a few in high school. But if I were to marry, I'd want a life to come home to that's separate from work. Since work is family and family is work, there's no way to separate them. Hence why I won't marry.

But fucking hell. I'd still love to strip Elizabeth naked. Lick every inch of her. Make her beg to get off. Then thrust my cock into her and make us both scream. I need to focus on what Matteo's still saying.

"I can't help but think this is an inside job. How else would they know how to get into Uncle Sal's house? Do you think Pia and Natalia know about the tunnel?"

"No. Uncle Sal barely used the house before he and Aunt Sylvia got married. We may have played hide and seek there, but he didn't even remember about the bootlegger's door until Maria mentioned it. I doubt the girls are playing down there."

Our cousins are ten and twelve. Uncle Salvatore was in his forties when he married Aunt Sylvia. She was in her early thirties. Their marriage was an arrangement made in heaven. They got super lucky and have been head over heels for each other since she stepped off the plane from Sicily.

I keep playing Devil's advocate because this is the only plausible theory I can come up with right now. I think aloud.

"They might not play down there, but could they know about it? Did they mention it to some friend or classmate who told someone in their family?"

"I seriously doubt it. The girls go to private school. It's not like when we were growing up. They're zoned for the same schools we went to, but Uncle Sal and Aunt Sylvia don't want the girls to grow up like we did."

Matteo is right again. My generation went to high school with our nemeses. I continue to push back.

"Yeah, but there's no one in the other families who are the same age as them. It's not like us. They might not be going to school with the kids belonging to rival syndicates, but there are members of our branch who send their kids to the same school. It's expensive but not elitist."

That makes Matteo pause. He considers this and realizes I may have a point.

"Don't you think Uncle Sal has asked Pia and Natalia if they know about the tunnel yet?"

"I don't know. They were sleeping when the men broke in. Aunt Sylvia didn't fight them since she knew they'd take her, anyway. She didn't want to wake the girls and have them come investigate. We know they haven't told the girls what happened. Maybe they haven't brought any of it up. I'll ask Uncle Sal when I go over there later."

It would be easier to just call or shoot him a text. But when we're at the garage, we don't have our cells on. We turn them off miles before we get here and don't turn them back on until we're miles away. We don't need anyone tracking us. This place isn't on any city records. Just the opposite. Papers got destroyed when they took over the building.

It was abandoned back then, so it was easy to claim it and

then make it officially disappear. We don't need anyone following us or raiding us. We have a satellite phone in case of a genuine emergency here or with someone in the family. We've used it three times in the years I've been coming here. I walked through the door for the first time when I was fifteen. I'm now thirty-three.

Matteo looks at the tools on the table near us as he speaks.

"I can finish up here. Why don't you head over to Uncle Salvatore's now?"

"Thanks. Do you still want me to guard Maria tonight when she goes out with Veronica?"

My sister's husband grimaces. He's my best friend. I know what he's thinking, and his answer is far nicer than it could be.

"Yes. I can't stand her. How Maria finds anything redeeming about her is beyond me."

"I know. They've been friends since Gabriele moved here and started hanging out with Carmine. Fucking two decades. I don't think she's ever shut the fuck up since then."

"I'll owe you."

"I'll add it to your tab."

Chapter Two

Beth

It's been a week and a half since Lorenzo and Chelle got married and left for their honeymoon. I don't know why I've been so restless this entire time. For some reason, I can't focus. I can't think about anything other than that ornery man who was insistent I take a ride from his family's car service. Well, it wasn't actually a car service. It seems each of those men must work directly for the Mancinellis. I don't even want to think what their other duties must be besides driving the family around.

I've tried to think of other things, other people, and other men besides Marco Mancinelli, but he seems to have taken root — made a home —in my mind. I haven't thought of any other man besides him for the past week and a half, and it's totally driving me crazy. I've been to my club twice, hoping that scening with the guys I usually meet would be enough to distract me. But it's not. Every time one of them blindfolds me, all I see is Marco.

I don't see the man who I know. I don't see my dom. I see the man who won't leave my mind. The way he insisted I use one of their cars to get home. It was quiet, but oh so very dominant. It was clear he wouldn't accept any other answer. At the time, I'd almost called him Sir. I nearly bit the tip of my tongue off to keep from speaking that aloud.

All the men in the syndicate families seem to have that same quality about them. I've met several of the Kutsenkos through Chelle since she's best friends with the *pakhan's* wife. Never did I imagine little Laura Doyle would marry a member of the Russian mafia, but she did. And now my little sister has married a member of the Italian mafia. And all I can think about is a certain mafioso who makes my toes curl and my pussy ache.

I'm headed back to my club tonight. I'm in my own car. I'll park a couple blocks away. I'll wear a mask and dark clothing, hoping to maintain my anonymity. But the one thing I can't hide is how much I long to feel Marco's hands running over me. We didn't even spend that much time together at the reception. It was enough, though, to make me wonder what it would be like to be underneath him, on top of him, in front of him as his hand rains down on my ass and he pinches my nipples. I rarely fantasize so much about men. Why would I need to when I can have sex anytime I wish just by going to my BDSM club?

It's not like I have a sex addiction or anything like that. It's just convenient to know that if I want to get off, I don't have to just do it myself. I've been a member of this club for two years now, and I have a couple of men I see regularly. We never talk outside of our time there. We have a standing arrangement: if we happen to be there at the same time, wonderful. If we're not, that's okay too. If no one I want to scene with is at the club when I arrive, I simply watch. But I know both men tend to go on Thursday nights, and that's today.

My luck. Parking karma. I found a spot a couple blocks from the club. It makes it easy to slip through the door tucked along the side of the building, so no one will see me enter. I'm wearing regular street clothes, which is the rule. As soon as I get to the door, I put on my mask. There's a locker room where I can shed my jeans and T-shirt to show the lingerie I'm wearing beneath. I may not have the most confidence in the world, but I know women of all shapes and sizes belong to this club. And if the other women can be brave enough to saunter around in next to nothing, then I can find my huevos to do the same.

Once I'm inside, and I've stopped by the locker room and dropped my purse and my clothes, I make my way out to the main room. As I look around, I wish I could bring myself to wear just a thong and go topless. Or maybe even with pasties, but I'm not quite that confident yet. But I have on a cute pair of lacy panties and a matching bra.

As I look around, I search for either Jeffrey or Danny? Do I think those are their real names? Definitely not. After all, my name's not Amanda. But it works for us. Of course, I had to use my real name to sign up, but going under a pseudonym isn't unusual at a place like this. As my gaze sweeps the open room again, I notice both Jeffrey and Danny are here. They're already involved in a scene together with another woman. It's poor etiquette to go and interrupt them and say, "hey, do you wanna suck on me instead?" So, I bide my time and wonder if they'll finish soon and have any interest in starting a scene with me, or whether tonight will just be a night of watching and getting myself off.

That's not so bad. Getting myself off here doesn't seem as sad and as lonely as being at home and doing it every night besides the ones I'm here. And I haven't been like that in years, but ever since meeting Marco, it seems like I can't get my fingers away from my pussy. I can't seem to charge my vibrator enough. The man has been wreaking havoc on my horny senses, and I'm resentful and angry that I'm allowing myself to be like this. But I can't help it. Something about him is a magnet, and it's drawing me despite how I try to pull away.

As I round the corner, I slam into a man, forcing me to take three steps back, wobbling on the heels I'm wearing. Two strong but gentle hands shoot out and grasp my upper arms. I'm wearing a full domino mask, much like you would think was out of something like *Phantom of the Opera*. It's dark in here, so it's difficult to see my eye color, but it's obvious I have darker hair. The man's eyes that I look into are so dark they might be black. I wonder if they truly are that dark or if my green-brown hazel eyes look that way too. His wavy hair is thick, and I think a chestnut brown, almost so dark that it could be black. Like his eyes, I think it's merely the dim lighting in here.

When our gazes meet, my breath hitches. He takes a step back, even though he doesn't let go of me. We both take a moment to come to our senses. Then he pulls me to his chest and wraps his arm around my waist. His hand fists my hair. Quietly, he whispers against my ear.

"Beth, what are you doing here?"

It takes me not even two seconds to think of an answer.

"Well, what do you think I'm doing here? Isn't it rather obvious? The same thing as you."

I feel him tense under my hands now resting on his hips. He's wearing jeans with a tank top. I can't see his feet, but it wouldn't surprise me if he isn't in some type of designer Italian leather loafer. It seems like that would just fit. My tits are squashed between the two of us, and I can feel his growing cock pressed to my pussy. All I want to do is rub myself against him, knowing he's aroused just like I am. That I'm the one arousing him because he wasn't hard a moment ago. The hand that's around my waist slides down and cups my ass. It squeezes mercilessly, bringing me up onto my toes. He whispers again so only I can hear him.

"I don't think that's the right answer to give if you don't want to end up over my knee. Obviously, we're both here to do the same thing. What I want to know is why are you here at this particular club? Why are you even a member of a club like this?"

I respond to him with just as much snideness as he does.

"It seems to me like the answers to those questions are the same as the answers to your last set of questions. I think we're here for the same reason. This is an excellent club, and I came to get laid. Are you here for any other reason than that?"

I know I'm pushing it, and I know I want to keep doing it. That dominance I suspected— that I felt a hint of when I told him I would Uber home after the reception —is here in spades. I don't know if it's me, or if it's just being here in the club, that's making him act this way. I would hope it's the former, but maybe it is just the latter. I don't see this man being submissive anywhere. Definitely not in a place like this. Maybe it's just the persona he has when he walks through the door. Or maybe this is how he is even in real life, and I just don't know him well enough to tell.

But whatever the reason is, the longer he holds me, the tighter his hand grips my hair and my ass, the more I want to know. When he releases me, I almost whimper, unprepared to suddenly feel the cool air conditioning waft across my belly and my back after feeling his heat radiate into me. But he doesn't completely let me go. He grabs my hand and tugs me down the hall. I know where we're headed. I know what rooms are down this way.

I know what scenes people are enacting. There's a doctor's office, a classroom, a child's nursery, a formal dining room, a beach, and a few other themed places. You can tell which ones are occupied because a light glows beneath the door. It's a signal that you shouldn't knock or even try to open the door. We're almost to the very end before we come to a room that has no light underneath the door.

This room doesn't have a particular theme to it. Instead, I know what I'll find in there. There's a wheel, a Saint Andrew's cross, a spanking bench, and a sex machine— the ones that have the thrusting dildos. Marco doesn't think twice before opening the door. Pulling me through it then tapping my ass, he pushes me forward before slamming and locking the door. We stare at one another, and I'm sure he's waiting for an explanation, and I'm waiting to avoid giving him one.

When he prowls forward, he backs me up until my ass hits the Saint Andrew's cross. This is so fucking surreal; I don't even know what to make of it. I don't even know where to start. That I should run into my sister's new brother-in-law at a BDSM club that we're both members of, that we're both here at the same time, and both are half naked, locked in a room together where he could easily restrain me and fuck me all night, is both tantalizing and horrifying all at the same time.

I should be yelling at him, telling him no, telling him I want to leave, telling him I don't owe him any sort of explanation. But none of those things are coming out of my mouth. Instead, I'm trying to make sure drool doesn't leak from between my lips.

"Marco, what do you want? We shouldn't be taking up a room if we're not going to use it."

As soon as the words are out of my mouth, I wish I could grab them and swallow them back. The smile he gives me is pure seduction. He reaches back, pulls off his own mask. It surprises me that I recognized him, but I'd just known with certainty when I bumped into him. The mask is one that covered him from forehead to lip. The only things I'd been able to see that were unobstructed were his eyes and his lips. But now? I see all of him. Well, not all of him.

His fucking shirt and pants are still on, but what I'd really like is to see— other than his gorgeous face and chiseled chest — is just how big his cock is and to let myself guess what it would feel like with it shoved up my pussy. I don't know what to do, so I remain still. It doesn't take long before he grows impatient. He reaches around my head and unfastens my mask. I do nothing to stop him.

Now we're standing here, staring at each other, with nothing to hide. No way to pretend like we might not know each other. Nothing to help us pretend like we might be thinking of the wrong person. I'd say it's all laid bare, but yet again, we're still wearing clothes. I, far less than him. But neither one of us is as bare as my imagination or my aching cunt wishes.

"Elizabeth, you've already made me ask twice. You don't want to find out how I will handle things, *piccolina*, if you make me ask a third time. All I'll ask you is which place you want to go when I give you your spanking. So, answer me now, or go ahead and get on to one of these. And put your ass up in the air for me. My palms are already itching. Tell me now, what are you doing here?"

Trying to fuck you out of my system.

"I'm a member. I came here for the same reason everyone else does. I'm into this."

"Turn around, *piccolina*."

I don't budge. I know Enzo calls Chelle that, but it seemed too intimate to ask what it meant. Now Marco has called me that twice.

"What does that word mean?"

"Little girl or little one."

I have no response to that. He takes that as consent to do

more. It is. He unhooks and tugs off my bra then my bikini cut panties.

"Turn around."

His tone is gruff, and it makes me even wetter. If I step onto the cross, he's going to see the proof because my legs will part. That's humiliating as much as I want— crave —him touching me. I can't bring myself to do it. I consider shooting him a mutinous glare while I defy him. But instead, I go for impassive. I won't let him know how much he rattles me.

"Beth, you're naked in front of me. I've already told you I'm going to spank you. I suggest you do as I say only so I go easier on that fine ass of yours. If I have to make you get on that cross, I'll take more than my hand to it."

"You have no right to discipline me. I'm not losing my shit over you being here."

We're already practically pressed together, but he slides his hand between my back and the wood. He grabs my ass again, squeezing so hard that I go up onto my toes. It brings me flush against him. Fucking hell. He's harder. Not only that, the man is endowed. Very endowed. He leans into me, his warm breath against my neck, his lips just below my ear.

"No one watched me come out of the locker room in lingerie. I didn't have four men ready to approach me. Four men I know are into extreme shit. Men I know coerce women into rooms before they even realize they've submitted."

"And how do you know these men so well? Friends of yours?"

"Acquaintances over a long-time membership."

"While this may shock you since you have your cock pressed against my cunt and your hand on my naked ass, I don't go into rooms with strange men."

"I'm not a stranger to you, Beth."

First *piccolina*. Now Beth. It's the second time. No one has ever called me little girl in any language. No one calls me Beth. Ever. Liz or Lizzie for close friends and family. I'm Elizabeth to everyone else.

"You like it when I call you that."

It's not even remotely a question. He's right. Presumptuous ass. Speaking of asses.

I reach around him and grab his. It's difficult to do since it's fucking granite.

"I don't owe you any explanations— Daddy."

I cock an eyebrow as I try to squeeze harder. I infuse as much sarcasm into my voice as I can. But when I see the way his nostrils flair for a millisecond and the gleam in his eye, I know I've tested him one too many times. He'd leaned back after whispering to me. Now he nips my earlobe. I don't realize he's lifting me onto the cross until my feet land on the perches. Before I can do anything, he raises my right arm and fastens it. Then my left. I don't fight him because I'm too fucking curious. Next are my ankles. He squats to shackle me and remove my shoes. I force myself to look straight ahead.

I don't know what to expect, but it isn't him stepping away then grabbing the only chair in the room. He carries it over and sits right in front of me. He crosses his arms, and that's it. I don't want to look down to see how tight my nipples are, but I can tell they're sticking straight out. I can't see or touch my pussy to know how close to dripping I am. This is so fucking surreal.

A week ago, I thought he was hot and was wishing I could do this very thing with him. This week, I've been wishing I could forget how much I want to do this very thing with him. Now, I'm here, naked and at his mercy. For fuck's sake. He's the last man I have any business being anywhere near. That's why I haven't tried to get in touch with him. It's why I didn't offer anything at the reception.

Not only that. I've been here like twenty minutes. I barely looked around before literally running into him. There was no small talk about the coincidence. There was no awkwardness or embarrassment over both being here. No. He took control immediately. It's not something I'm used to. I'm not a Domme, but I am into power exchange. I like to switch. Sometimes I'm the top. Nothing about Marco— at the rehearsal dinner, the reception, or now —makes me think he would ever, ever, *ever* be a bottom or submissive. I don't think it's physically or mentally possible for him.

I had three siblings until one of my older brothers died in combat. Now I have an older brother, and Chelle's younger than me. Both drove me batshit bonkers when we were kids. They always called me the bossy one. Maybe. But I was also the one who got shit done and naturally led when we played. I also got us out of trouble more often than they ever did. I can wait him out.

I force myself not to wriggle. I want him to just say something to move this along. But it only takes a few minutes for me to realize he will never break first. That makes me think about how he has way more practice at this than I do. He's used to getting people to do what he wants. He's used to silent intimidation. I can and will hold out, but realizing why he has this skill dampens my mood. It doesn't turn me off per se. It definitely doesn't scare me— which it should. But it's just reality forcing its way into what is otherwise a fantasy.

He doesn't react outwardly, but I see something in his eyes when my mood shifts. He's getting a lesson in my obstinance. Part of me wishes he would crack first, so I can get that punishment. I want it way more than I should. I provoked him because I want it. But it's kicking me in the ass. And well he knows it. That's why he's doing this to control me rather than touching me. But one of us has to give, or else we'll be like this until the club closes in five hours.

We watch each other for what must be another ten minutes before some sort of silent truce happens. The moment he stands, I speak.

"Giving up already?"

"Little one, they say sarcasm is the lowest form of wit. I heard your toast. You're funny. They also say sarcasm is the protest of the weak. You're clearly not that."

I don't expect him to latch on to my breast and suck so hard my back arches. His tongue swirls over my nipple as he keeps working my tit. The moment my head falls back, he releases me. My head drops forward, but I force myself not to utter any complaint. It's the first truly sexual thing he's done to me. I wasn't sure he would do anything.

"You might have called me Daddy to throw my genuine term of affection back at me. But before tonight is over, you're going to call me that for real. Not because you're a little. You sure as shit are not that. You aren't bratty. You're openly defiant, so I think you're into switching. I am not."

No shit, Sherlock.

"But you haven't done a thing to protest my control. You might not have obeyed me like you should have, but you aren't asserting yourself either. You want me in charge. You want me to take care of your aching pussy. You want me to care about you coming someplace— probably for years —without a care for your safety. You assume everyone here always plays by the rules. You assume you can read people well enough to maintain control of any situation. But you aren't truly a Domme any more than I'm truly a Dom. But those men who followed you tonight, they are. So, you will never call me Sir or Master. But you will call me Daddy."

His fingers thrust into me without warning. Obviously, he

knows I'm wet enough for them to go in with ease. My eyes slide shut, and it's tortuous bliss having him stroke my g spot and rub my clit. I want to melt against him. This is the relief I sought with Jeffrey and Danny earlier this week and couldn't find. It's curing a restlessness I've never had before. A feeling those two guys never could have eased.

He releases my arms since he's tall enough to reach the cuffs with ease. He places my right hand on his shoulder, then reaches up to release the left and place it on his other one. He takes a step back, drawing me with him. I have no choice but to brace myself against him since my ankles are still restrained.

"*Piccolina*, the things I want to do to you. So far, you've consented by not saying no. But I would hear it now. Do you want this?"

"Yes."

"What's your safe word?"

"Something I never want to use with you."

That tumbles from between my lips. I want something that is only his.

"Chimpanzee."

I don't know why that comes to mind, but I can't imagine a reason for me to ever say that during sex unless it's my safe word.

He tilts his head back, so I can see his face. He grins.

"I don't know about that. I plan to have you wrapped around me like one."

While I ride your dick?

I'm not asking that out loud. I shrug my right shoulder. I'm unprepared for his teeth to tug my earlobe.

"You have a habit of that little shrug, Beth. I enjoy it because it makes me want to spank you. Dismissive and defiant. If you want to do this, then I will punish you for it. But only because we're roleplaying. In real life, I like it."

Before I can say anything, he snares me for a kiss that blows my mind. It starts out cataclysmically and ends that way. The beginning is purely lust. But it shifts at some point. It's still as passionate, but there's some type of genuine emotion to it. It's like kissing a boyfriend I've been with for months or even years. It feels completely natural to give myself over to it. It feels like I'm getting the same in return. He strokes my hair down my back. The way his hand rests on my ass is possessive but gentle. My hands roam over his back and through his hair. We're entirely equals in this.

When we pull apart, our foreheads rest together. We're both out of breath. He eases my arms from him, and I want to pull him back. But he squats to release my ankles. Then he's carrying me like a fucking chimp back to the chair. He sits with me straddling his lap. He cradles my head as he massages my breast. We're back to kissing, and this is purely vanilla.

This is way more disconcerting than winding up naked the third time I've met him. Way more disconcerting than his fingers in my pussy when he's my sister's brother-in-law. This feels like he cares. This feels like I care. The way he's holding me feels— good obviously. But it feels— protective and possessive without being controlling. It makes me feel like I'm his for more than a one-night stand or one scene. It makes me feel safe and cared for. I've never felt this type of safe and cared for at a BDSM club.

I've felt safe with the men I scene with. They've cared for me afterward as one expects a top to. But this is so fucking deep. This isn't we walk away and go our separate ways when we're done. This is we're a couple who came to play, and we're going home to snuggle in bed afterward. At least, to me it is. Who the fuck knows what he's thinking?

Chapter Three

Marco

What the ever-loving fuck am I doing? Besides trying not to come in my jeans, which is a Herculean effort considering Beth's pussy is pressed against my cock, and I've already sucked one of two of the most magnificent tits ever. I've never wanted to have a woman slide down my dick like I do this one who's driving me crazy.

It took everything in me not to freak the fuck out when I recognized her. From a distance, she was a chick with a banging body— curvy and soft in all the right places —and she had four shitbags eyeing her. I know them because I've been a member long enough to be acquainted with many of the regulars. Apparently, not Beth, though. Why do both of my pet names feel so damn natural even though I have no entitlement to call her either?

The moment our bodies touched in the main room, I knew it was her. Don't ask me how. Her perfume and eyes confirmed it. But instinct told me. Or maybe it was wishful thinking. But once I was certain, anger pulsed through me. She was completely oblivious. I noticed she recognized a couple of men, and I assume they're the douchebags she *used* to meet here. The fuck she's touching another man now. And I sure as fuck am not sharing her.

Protectiveness made me practically drag her away from anywhere those four could reach her. Possessiveness made me want to spank her, and it's why I can't stop kissing her as though she were my girlfriend not a woman to scene with then walk away. Not as a woman who might be a one-night stand. No. This is way different.

This is way more terrifying in its intensity.

I want to explain I'm not into domestic discipline. That's why I like her stubbornness and her steel backbone. But saying that implies we're in a relationship. We're not.

"Marco, what's happening?"

There's timidity in her voice now. And it matches mine, even though I'm fighting to keep it to myself. I don't like it. Not after the stubbornness of a moment ago. I don't want her scared around me. I don't want her doubting herself. And I don't know what to do about my own self-doubt. It's not an emotion I've felt in years.

"I don't know, *piccolina*. It's not anything I expected."

"This is— different."

I can practically hear her saying "isn't it?"

"It is."

That makes us both freeze. This shouldn't be happening. We look at each other before she stands, and I help her ease around my legs. It's a dose of shitty reality. I rise with her and wrap an arm around her.

"Beth, this is *not* a mistake. But this is a surprise. What do you want?"

She looks at me for a moment, and I know neither of us is going to tell the truth.

"I want this to be a surprising but good memory."

I give her a peck on her lips then release her. She looks around for her shoes I'm not sure she noticed me taking off. She reclaims them, along with her bra and panties. She fastens her bra and slides the underwear and heels back on. We don't avoid meeting each other's gaze, but neither do we linger. When I reach to unlock the door, I have the unsettling realization she might not be going straight home. She covers my hand and stops.

"Marco, I'm not staying tonight."

"Me neither."

I hadn't done anything before I ran into her. I actually stood someone up who I usually connect with when we're both here. I saw the woman when I came in. To be honest, I totally forgot about her the moment I ran into Beth. The idea of going to find her or anyone else feels wrong. The idea of coming back here to be with anyone else feels wrong.

After we both put our masks back on, I walk her out until she gets to the locker room. I'm done before her since I just slip my shirt on. I wait for her in the shadows since we already said goodnight. But I follow her out to make sure she gets in her car. I saw her pull out her keys before walking outside. I get in my car after she pulls out. I rest my head back and close my eyes. What the fuck did I just do?

All of us— my father, uncles, cousin, brothers, and friends —are in Uncle Salvatore's office. None of us is sure what to say. You can practically touch the anger in the room as though it were a breathing person we're all ready to execute. Every member of our senior leadership is looking at each other, including Uncle Cesare, who usually stays out of most of this shit but has been more present since Carmine and Serafina got together.

Uncle Salvatore is tapping his fingers in the unusual pattern he has. It's not pinky to index finger or index finger to pinky. It's more of what I'd call an arpeggio. He claims it's from the hours at the piano my *nonna* forced upon him. Each gets three taps. Ring finger then index finger then pinky and finally middle finger. He does it when he's thinking. Sometimes it heightens my rage or anxiousness. Other times it's reassuring. Today, it's the former.

"Are you really sure it's him?"

As I speak, I'm looking at Carmine, who was the bearer of the bad news. While Enzo is our hacker, Carmine is our intelligence gatherer. The man can find out the last time the Pope shat. He used to employ his skills to manipulate all of us. He'd discover little things and plant seeds that led to needless arguments that he would then quietly offer suggestions to resolve. He manipulated master manipulators. I understand now why he did it. A sense of survival when we were all kids. A need to feel relevant as a teenager. And deep resentment as an adult. We have our shared *nonno* to thank for that. But now that he uses his skills only for good, we all get along much better. He has the respect he's always deserved but trashed for years.

"Yeah. I can't believe it either. But we had him followed. We made sure one of our guys on the force was at the meeting. Cost a fucking fortune to get that cop to go along with it."

"But Luigi?"

I still just can't wrap my head around it. He drove Beth home after the reception. He's guarded Pia and Natalia for fuck's sake. We've trusted him to work at the garage. Now we find out he's a narc.

Uncle Salvatore stops drumming his fingers and looks at

Carmine again after staring out the window into the dark. I didn't make it home from the club before I got the call to come here. Discovering Luigi may have broken the omertà is one of the deepest betrayals in the Mafia. In our family. To me. He's a few years older than me, but we grew up together. We were friends. We've gone through some wild shit and saved each other's lives more than once. To learn he's been helping the cops, maybe even the feds, is the lowest blow.

A fundamental tenant of our code of honor is that no matter what, there is never a justifiable reason to involve the government, especially law enforcement. You just don't. And if you go away for a crime you didn't commit, oh well. You *never* share family secrets.

It hurts Matteo just like me since we were both close to Luigi. He speaks to the room, saying what we're all wondering.

"Why?"

Carmine releases an aggravated breath as he scrolls something on his computer before looking at Matteo.

"We don't know for sure, but it looks like NYPD is pressuring him to squeal about everything for immunity when the feds come after him for what happened in Kansas."

It's my turn to speak up again.

"Kansas? We haven't done anything there in ages except for the shit that just happened with Enzo. They can't possibly have figured out our involvement yet. The Rizzos wouldn't turn anything over. They'd take care of Luigi themselves if they were butt hurt about what Enzo did."

That was only a couple weeks ago. Enzo had an unexpected trip there while he and Chelle were still dating. We had some issues with the Chicago *Cosa Nostra* that spilled over to the Kansas City *Cosa Nostra*. Both the Rizzos and the Grassos — the ones in Chicago —both know— with absolute certainty — that nothing happens east of the Mississippi without our permission. And anyone who meddles, no matter where they're from, is dealt with swiftly and permanently.

Carmine scowls at his computer as he speaks, eyes still on his screen.

"That's what I'm still trying to figure out. Beside this threat against him— one we haven't substantiated —there's nothing to make us think he'd turn. He's never given us a reason to think he's anything but loyal. He's almost died several times to protect us. Is he tired of the risk? Did he get a better offer?"

I shake my head.

"They've arrested him before. He's done time, and he's never given up shit. He went away for five years for that robbery Pauly did."

That was a fuck storm. They didn't like each other to begin with, and the evidence rightly pointed toward Pauly. But Luigi was in the wrong place at the wrong time when they did the bust. But he didn't turn on Pauly then. He knew the code. He accepted the prison time rather than narc on any of us. He knew doing anything else was a death sentence. I can't imagine how he thinks anyone— including the feds —can protect him from us.

Luca looks at Papa then Uncle Salvatore before he speaks.

"Can we get that cop to wear a wire for us? We need to hear what Luigi is saying for ourselves. We need to know for certain. I don't want to lose a good man because someone's fucking him— and us —over."

Enzo's our accountant and usually runs the numbers to tell us how much we should spend on something like that. He keeps track of our bribes and the protection money businesses pay us. But he's away right now, so it falls to me.

"Hunter has been on our payroll for two years. I say we offer him ten grand to wear the wire."

Luca looks over at me.

"On top of the ten he's already getting every month? That's only one month's extra pay. Do you think he's going to demand more than that for a special job?"

"If he doesn't want me to put a gun to his head, he'll take whatever the fuck I offer him."

I shrug. He's a single beat cop with no real family. He has some connections within the force— his nose up his captain's ass —but he's nothing special. He wouldn't be that missed. It's what got our attention in the first place.

"What's burrowed up your ass?"

Gabriele leans over to whisper none too quietly. I didn't think I was being testy, but maybe I am. I want this meeting over with. I have other things to think about. Someone else to think about. I need to exorcise Beth from my brain. Best way to do that is to head back to my club tomorrow and spend the night fucking any other woman until I'm too exhausted to stand or sit. Even as I think that I know it's bullshit. I want her.

"Nothing. I just think he isn't worth more than ten grand. I'd rather pay him nothing at all and just make him do it, but I know we need to keep him happy."

Luca shakes his head.

"I say fifteen."

"For a wire? No. It's not like we're asking him to plant evidence or kill someone. Ten tops."

I dig my heels in. Enzo would make the same argument. The man parts with a penny like Cheron, the mythical Greek guy who ferried people over the River Styx. You'd have to pry it out of his cold, dead hands. But his strict accounting has made us prosper tenfold since the day he took over from Old Man Guglielmo. The guy was eighty-five when he finally handed over the ledgers to Enzo, who already had a master's in finance and his CPA license. Enzo quietly fixed the man's mistakes for four years until Uncle Salvatore eventually couldn't overlook them. He gave the guy a healthy pension and sent him to live on the Jersey Shore.

I don't need my baby brother coming home and blaming me for us overspending. I won't hear the fucking end of it. He's not a nag, but he is precise. He also gets what the going rate for shit is. He won't undercut the other syndicates with open contract men. But he also won't overpay for nothing. He doesn't waste money, and he won't set a precedent we don't want to pay later.

Gabriele offers his idea, and I like it.

"Why don't we tell him he's going to do whatever the hell we want. If he's smart, he does. If he isn't, we offer him the ten thousand. If he wants more, we make him do this last job for us."

Papa and Uncle Salvatore have remained quiet for a while. I watch my uncle, hoping we can decide and get on with things. I need some sleep, and I need to get some shit done before I figure out what I'm going to do besides jack myself off until I find someone to take my mind off Beth. I breathe a sigh of relief when Uncle Salvatore looks at Gabriele and nods. We have his decision.

Since I've been Hunter's contact, I speak up.

"Do you want me to give him the order tomorrow? Do we know the next time Luigi's supposed to meet with the NYPD?"

Luca scrolls something on his phone before he turns to me.

"He has Sunday night off. My guess is sometime then."

It's Thursday now. Perfect. I'll talk to Hunter tomorrow and gets things in place for the meeting. As long as that's not Hunter's day off too, we should be good. He's cozied up with enough people that he should be able to get close enough to overhear a conversation with no one questioning him. It would be great if he could be right there in the middle of it. But we have sensitive mics that pick up an ant sneezing. He just needs to be in the vicinity.

"I'll talk to him tomorrow. Anything else?"

My dad shoots me the same stare he's been giving me since I was a squirmy toddler in church. Normally, even in my early thirties, it's enough to make me freeze. But I'm over it today. I need to get out of here before I snap at someone. Uncle Salvatore's not looking any more pleased with me than Papa, but oh well. He wraps things up.

"Yes. We're done. Report back to me once you have things set up. I want to know time and place, so we're ready."

This has been the longest fucking week. Friday was just a regular long workday. Saturday was supposed to be my day off. I was getting changed last night into my jeans and tank top to head to my club when my phone rang in the sets of three. That automatically means it's a work call. I get calls from my family that just ring until I answer, or it goes to voicemail.

But three, then stop, then three, then stop until I answer means get my ass on the line. I had to change out of my tank top — which gives me plenty of freedom to wield whatever impact play device I want while covering my very recognizable tat of Italy on my left pec. We all have them. Our men have them on their forearms, but the don's family gets them on their chest, right over their heart.

I wound up at the garage all night and half of today. Enzo doesn't know it, but he just got another wedding gift. The *stronzo*— asshole —who was giving Chelle shit at work tried to back out of a deal we set up with him. We knew he would, so it gave us the excuse to deal with him. Part of our decision to bring him to the garage was for Enzo and Chelle's sake— he can't harass my newest sister if he isn't breathing. But most of it is because he tried to hire some of our guys to do a build for a Diaz connected project.

We let him take on two of our construction teams for cheap, knowing he bought the land he's building on from Enrique Diaz, the Colombian *jefe*. Enrique's a silent backer, and Simon Shapiro thought he was doing Enrique a favor by making us indebted to Enrique and him since he's employing our guys. Dumb fuck. He didn't get that it's the other way around. We control just how fast or slow, how expensive or cheap a build is when our guys work it.

But he did the unacceptable when he told Enrique he's paying us from money he's embezzling from a charity Chelle represents. It's one that's near and dear to her heart since she lost an older brother in combat. Trying to fuck us over was his first strike. Fucking over Chelle after harassing her was his last.

Things could have gone a lot faster, but drawing out his agony was the wedding gift. Chelle will never know what we did, but Enzo will. She'll just know he disappeared. She's smart enough to know we did it. She's also smart enough to know he must have done something more than just target her since Enzo didn't haul him into the garage after the fuck wad cornered Chelle in her office. He held off for Chelle's sake at work.

Shapiro sang like a little bitch, telling us several things about how Enrique was investing on the sly. He gave up the account information where Enrique deposited the money. Carmine isn't our hacker, but he's good at sleuthing shit out. He knew enough to backtrack and get into Enrique's account. He drained it. We are ten million richer, and that money is already in untraceable accounts all around the world.

Shapiro also told us about some other projects Enrique's nephew Pablo is planning. Shapiro intended to invest in those to reciprocate for Enrique's support. Pablo is Luca's equivalent as Enrique's heir and second in command. Unlike Uncle Salvatore who has two young daughters— their age and gender make them ineligible to inherit —Enrique has no children, so Pablo will one day take his place.

Shapiro reached the limit of his usefulness and he's now a pile of ash floating into nothingness in the Hudson. Since I finished at the garage, I'm now sitting in a van with headphones on while Carmine fine tunes the audio and video for the wire our cop is wearing.

"Yeah. We have something we gotta do. We'll see you tomorrow."

I watch as a cop bumps fists with Hunter. Not encouraging that he's getting the brush off before they've even stepped out of the precinct building.

"Looks like we're headed in the same direction though."

Hunter isn't giving up. Good. I didn't have to offer him shit to do this. He took one look at me as I approached him, and I knew I had him. He was only too happy to do what I said. I think he figured I'd off him right then and there if he didn't. My baby brother won't be kvetching at me over wasting money.

A second guy comes into view. I recognize him as someone else on our payroll. Interesting.

"Yeah— uh —we have something going on. We gotta hurry."

"I walk faster than the two of yous. I won't keep yous waiting."

Hunter steps past both of them and takes long strides down the street. When he passes a couple of women, he twists to let them pass. It allows us to see the other two officers are still following. He continues on until a man on a stoop comes into sight. Hunter stops when he comes even with the steps up to the building.

"Hey. I didn't expect to see you out here. How you doing?"

Hunter thrusts out his hand to Luigi, who's looking around.

"Great. Good seeing you."

Luigi definitely doesn't sound like he wants to strike up a conversation. Hunter turns again, so the camera picks up the two officers approaching. We observe them slowing down, and I can see them talking to each other. It's obvious they're debating whether they should change course, walk past like they don't see Luigi and Hunter, or stick with the plan.

Hunter decides for them.

"You guys know Luigi Delfino, right? Tommy, he grew up on the same block as us. What are you, like five years older than me and Tommy?"

"Something like that. Hey, Tommy."

"Do you know Ian Grady?"

It was O'Grady until his family came to America during the Potato Famine. The guy's up to his eyeballs in the mob. We've paid him for a few jobs, but he's sketchy as fuck. What the fuck is Luigi doing meeting with a guy who has known mob ties? This gets more and more interesting.

"Yeah. We've met."

Luigi offers nothing more, so the men just stand around. They're looking at each other, but I can't see Hunter's expression. He angles himself, so the camera is on Luigi, but I think he's looking at Ian and Tommy.

"I thought you guys had somewhere yous had to be. We won't keep yous."

Neither cop moves, but the camera is trained on Luigi, who's watching the two men. He's shooting one of them a look that clearly says "leave." But Tommy and Ian are too slow.

"Ah. This is your meeting. Interesting."

Hunter shifts, and now we can see Tommy and Ian, who appear uncomfortable. There's another pause before Hunter continues.

"I want in. Whatever this is. A Mancinelli man meeting a

cop on the O'Rourke payroll and another who'll take money from any outstretched hand means something."

Luigi slides his hand into his pocket, where I know he has a knife. But he won't brandish it. At least, not yet. There are too many people around. Tommy points to the door.

"Let's go inside."

He moves past Luigi on the steps and unlocks the door to a hallway that runs between two shops. There's a steep staircase to the right and a door at the end of the hallway. When Tommy takes three steps toward the stairs, Hunter crosses his arms.

"Uh-uh. You're not killing me in some room I can't get out of. Right here. Right now. What's going on?"

Ian gets in Hunter's face.

"We're not talking about this where anyone can walk in."

"Bullshit. It's ten o'clock. The stores've been closed for hours. There are no lights on upstairs, and Tommy had to unlock the door to get in. No one's coming in, and no one's around to hear us. Speak now."

Ian leans in.

"You're awfully fucking pushy. I wonder why? Someone paying you?"

"No. But someone is paying yous, and now that I know you're having a little powwow, I expect a cut. Yous ain't gonna kill me or even fuck with me."

Hunter may not have any family to miss him, but he is the captain's pet project. Tommy and Ian don't have the resources we do to make someone go poof. They'd leave a trail leading straight back to them. They know that.

Tommy pushes at Ian's shoulder, trying to intervene.

"We aren't getting paid. The feds chose us."

Hunter laughs.

"Right. Yous two? The feds? Bullshit."

"They know our ties. They knew we'd be able to get someone in the Mancinellis to talk."

Hunter turns to Luigi.

"Is what Tommy said true? The feds are pressuring you?"

"Yeah."

Luigi lifts his chin, his hand still in his pocket.

"I thought you were like besties with the don's nephew or something."

"No one outside the don's family is besties with anyone in it."

Hunter shifts. He must be doing something with his hands, but I can't tell what. Maybe into his coat pockets. But I doubt that since the others don't react. Hands on hips?

"What do the feds want with you?"

"What do they ever want? They want to know some shit about my boss."

"What the hell are they offering you that's good enough to believe Don Mancinelli can't get you?"

Luigi stares at Hunter, who turns toward Tommy.

"Fine. Whatever. Don't tell me. Tommy, what're they giving him immunity for? Where'd they say they'd set him up?"

Luigi takes a step forward, placing his hand on Hunter's chest. He shoves, and Hunter takes a step back. But he doesn't stay there. He gets into Luigi's face. Fuck us if this goes wrong. If they fuck him up, they'll find the wire and the camera. Luigi knows where to look.

"You ask too many fucking questions we aren't answering. I'll give you ten grand right now to fuck off."

Hunter isn't leaving there alive unless we go in and grab Luigi. Oh, well.

"You're giving me ten large, anyway. Like I said, you ain't touching me. But you are going to pay me. Since you can't do shit to me, you may as well answer my questions. Fifteen for my silence. I might even forget what you say for twenty."

Hunter holds out his hand and flaps his fingers. No one moves. He eventually lets his hand fall.

"I've got a long memory regardless of what you do or don't say. Maybe I'll be the one to feed the feds some info."

Luigi barks a laugh.

"You really do have a death wish."

"If the feds weren't offering you something good, then you wouldn't be so nervous about me going to them. They're offering you immunity and relocation. Why?"

"I saw some shit."

It's Hunter's turn to laugh with no humor.

"You've probably seen some shit since you were like five. Narrow it down. What shit?"

"Shit that happened recently."

"In the city? We all see shit every day. We just ain't say nundin."

Hunter's fucking Bronx accent gets thick sometimes.

"Nah. On a trip I went on recently."

Tommy turns everyone's attention to him when he speaks.

"We already know you went to Kansas and Chicago. The Rizzos and Grassos are running coke and meth between them. You told us some bullshit about your cousin being a Rizzo, but that doesn't check out. Why were you in Chicago, Luigi? We know you traveled with Enzo. Why was he out there?"

"Cubs versus the White Sox game. He's been a White Sox fan since he was a kid. Still collects baseball cards and wanted to get one signed. Puts them in glass cases once he does. The guy's got at least a million dollars in signed cards."

My brother couldn't give two shits about baseball and hasn't since we all played little league. Why's Luigi covering for him?

"There's no security footage of him in any of the boxes, and he sure isn't slumming it in the nosebleeds."

"We didn't go to the stadium. Private watch party. I was guarding the door at some guy's mansion. Enzo got the signed card delivered to him. I don't give a shit about baseball, so I didn't care enough to know more than that."

"Who's place?"

Luigi shrugs.

"You know they don't tell us shit like that. We find out that day where we're going and what the security is. What we don't know, we can't repeat. Obviously, there's a reason for that rule."

He looks pointedly at the other three men. He's usually right, but Luigi is senior enough that he knows where we're going and who we're meeting. I look over at Carmine. So far, none of this makes sense. He's lying for us.

Tommy's getting impatient.

"You had a shit ton more to say last time. Now you're clamming up."

"I had a shit ton more to say last time because I hadn't told you shit before that. There's nothing more to say. I asked to go along, so I could see my cousin. He told me shit about how the Rizzos are selling their coke to the Grassos because Don Edoardo's son-in-law thinks there's more money to be made in meth. The Grassos want to deal on college campuses and started with Grasso's son at University of Illinois. The Rizzos are getting their shipments coming in through Galveston. The Grassos are selling homemade meth. If you ask me, it's dumb as fuck. Coke still sells for more internationally. Meth is for modern day crack heads. It kills people too fast. Coke makes longer lasting customers. But I'm not a don, so I don't make those decisions."

"And your cousin told you all of this just cuz?"

Tommy sounds skeptical.

"We're close. At least we were."

"Were?"

"Yeah. Someone must have found out because they told Don Edoardo."

"And?"

Tommy's getting impatient. Luigi needs to hurry up and finish spinning this tale.

"Yeah. He was my cousin through my mom's side and was the don's nephew through his dad's. Don Edoardo found out Tony was telling someone what's going on. He put a hit on him and made it look like someone killed him while they robbed a truck full of coke. Left a bunch of stuffed animals all over the street from what I heard. Teddy bear massacre."

Enzo did that, but Luigi's making it sound like Edoardo just kept the coke. The drugs are now ours and coming in through New Orleans. Luigi's sending them on a wild goose chase.

Tommy keeps drilling him.

"How're you still alive?"

"Because I'm talking to you two numb nuts. That's why the feds are offering me immunity. I'm rolling on the Chicago don and the Kansas City one. You make sure you tell the feds exactly what I just told you. No more dicking around. I'm not looking to die for this shit. Not for knowing and not for narcing. I'm not going to prison either."

Ian nudges his chin up. Smug fucker.

"You've done time before. You'd be fine."

"I didn't do time for crossing a Mafia boss. My life's forfeit if I go in."

Hunter's been quiet for a while, but he speaks up now.

"How do we know you aren't just telling tales to protect the Mancinellis?"

"Because you don't tell the government shit about anything to do with the Mafia. It doesn't matter if it's another family or not. If Don Salvatore finds out I even looked in your direction, I'm dead."

Hunter presses.

"He'd put a hit on you?"

"I didn't say that. I said I'd be dead. I didn't say who or what would kill me."

"You trying to say you'd off yourself?"

Luigi just stares at Hunter. We might all be Catholic and suicide's a sin, but we murder without hesitation. Anyone who crosses us would be smart to die before we help them. He turns toward Ian.

"I told you what I know. Tell Agent Jimenez what I said. I won't talk to her directly until I see an immunity deal in writing. If I don't get one in the next twenty-four hours, the deal's off. I'll cry entrapment and coercion if they try to force me. I have a voice that carries."

Luigi turns toward the door, but Hunter catches his arm.

"You really think you can tell the FBI what to do."

"I know what they wish they knew. If they want the Grassos and Rizzos as much as they say they do, then they'll give me exactly what I ask for. If that's a fucking filet mignon every day until I die, then they better fucking buy a herd."

He yanks his arm away and walks out of the building. It leaves Hunter alone with Tommy and Ian. It's Ian who speaks first.

"If you fuck this shit up, Boon."

"I'm not fucking shit up. Not when I have fifteen grand coming my way. Pay me by the end of the week, and I'll suddenly have amnesia."

Tommy shakes his head.

"We need at least two for that kind of money."

"Ha. Is that the next federal payday? Waiting for this Jimenez bitch to pay yous, so yous can pay me?"

"Something like that. Don't think being up the captain's butt totally protects you. Maybe I'll tell Don Salvatore that you're in on this with Luigi."

"And how would you know how to do that unless you're on his payroll? Thanks for that little secret too. I'll add that to the list of shit to forget once I'm counting my money. Don't pay on time, and I'll go to the IG."

The Inspector General. That's the last thing any of them need. Having them and Internal Affairs snooping around means Tommy and Ian will be handing over their guns and badges until they're conveniently found innocent. Maybe a suspension without pay that somehow gets fixed when there's an accounting error. They might get their docked pay back, but it would take months.

"And have to explain to them how you got this info? No, you won't."

Ian sounds so certain. Hunter just laughs.

"Fifteen grand. Two weeks. Goodnight."

Hunter heads out the same door Luigi did. He turns back a couple times to see Tommy and Ian following him. He hails a cab, has the guy drive him around a bit before doubling back to where we parked our van.

"Yous get what yous need?"

He whispers as he climbs into the driver's seat. I look at Carmine, who looks at me. Neither of us says shit. Hunter doesn't need to know anything behind the scenes. I see him roll his eyes in the mirror. He eases out of the driver's seat and comes into the back of the van where I take off his wire and camera. While I pack that up, Carmine looks Hunter dead in the eye.

"You might be brown nosing the captain, but you don't have shit for family. You aren't fucking anyone. And you blow your money on cards and horses. No one will miss you. No one gives a shit now, so they won't give a shit if you're gone. Fuck us over, and you'll find out just how little anyone cares."

"I know, Carmine. I don't need the reminder."

"Good. If those fuckers pay you, you know it's ours."

"What? Why?"

Hunter splutters the two words.

"You're going to need someone to protect you one of these days."

Carmine grins, and if he weren't my cousin, it would chill my blood. But I'm pretty sure I already have ice in my veins. I toss Hunter his wallet and keys that we held as collateral.

"Get out."

Carmine and I watch him climb over the driver's seat and slip out of the van. I sit down in the chair I was in while my cousin and I watched our evening show. I look over at a guy I could barely tolerate being in the same time zone with until about a year ago. He still chaps my ass sometimes, but I don't hate him anymore. It's nice not having that animosity toward him. We got along super well when we were really little. We were both into trains and building tracks. We liked sailing remote controlled boats. We spent hours together. But that shit went south when he was about seven, and I was nine.

"What do you make of all this?"

Carmine looks back at the now turned off monitor as he answers.

"Luigi is covering for us. But why hasn't he told Uncle Sal or Uncle Massi that the feds are pressuring him?"

"I don't think he's told Uncle Sal or Papa because he's still violating the omertà."

Uncle Salvatore is the oldest, then Papa— Massimo —then Auntie Paola, Carmine's mom. We consider Papa the most relaxed of the three of them. Auntie Paola— the woman should have been both don and *consigliere*. There isn't a more loyal person to a family than my aunt. And that's saying something considering how her father fucked up her life by making her marry Carmine's dad.

She and Uncle Cesare were like oil and a match for eighteen years. Now that they have separate lives, they're practically besties. Papa and Uncle Salvatore defended her against their father and Uncle Cesare's. They couldn't stop the marriage edict, but they helped. For that, they have her unwavering loyalty. She's like a mom to all my siblings and other cousins.

She's in politics, and she's cutthroat. I seriously believe she's the deadliest person in our family. Cross one of us, and she will never forgive. If Luigi should fear anyone, it's Auntie Paola. She's trusted him to watch out for Carmine, her only child. If she believes the man ever endangered Carmine— or any of us —she'll demand her pound of flesh. She won't let any of us go easy on him. The only thing going for Luigi is that if she learns he broke the omertà for our sake, she won't let Papa or Uncle Salvatore touch him without having to live with her disapproval. She may be their baby sister, but her opinion means the world to them.

Carmine frowns.

"Do we give him a hint that he needs to talk to Uncle Sal before we do?"

"Yeah. But he better not let it slip. I'm not in the mood for Uncle Sal's temper."

Carmine scoffs.

"You aren't?"

I cock an eyebrow. Carmine's plot to fuck over the bratva nearly got one wife killed. Uncle Salvatore doled out Carmine's, Gabriele's, and Luca's punishments personally. Something he has never done before, but he was that enraged.

Then he exiled them to Sicily for six months. He needed that long to cool off.

He looks down at where my phone is on the counter that's built into the van. It's where we have all the receivers and monitors.

"Call him. Get him over here."

It doesn't take long for Luigi to get to us. He knows before he climbs into the van that we've been running surveillance. He's worked in this van before. His expression is wary to say the least. Carmine and I stare at him for a couple minutes before he sighs and unloads everything to us.

Then it's a trip to Uncle Salvatore's for him to repeat the entire story about how the feds thought they could intimidate him by threatening to tell his wife who he is and have their kids taken away. The woman's *Cosa Nostra* on all sides of her family since they were all in Sicily. His wife took the kids on vacation to Switzerland, which has no extradition treaty with the U.S.

Uncle Salvatore is the woman's godfather in truth. Luigi got a slap on the wrist because he didn't come forward to tell any of us. But Uncle Salvatore didn't punish him for breaking the oath since half of what he told the NYPD— and therefore the feds —was bullshit. What he said benefits us if the Grassos and Rizzos lose their markets. We can take them.

I may have tied up two loose ends this week, but I'm still restless. I took out a lot of my frustration on Shapiro by beating him senseless. But now that there's no reason for my anger at Luigi, thus no outlet for anything, I'm back to where I was earlier this week.

Craving a woman I shouldn't want.

Chapter Four

Beth

I'm clenching my jaw to keep from snapping at the movers. I don't know how much clearer I have to be about which sofa goes in which room as we stage the model home. I've only said it like sixty trillion times, motherfuckers. I told them as they loaded the truck at the warehouse. I told them before they opened the truck door at the Manhattan high rise. I told them as they brought the first two pieces inside. How is this so fucking complicated?

I know I tend to be a frustrated perfectionist— today is proving that —but my job is to make everything just right, so properties sell for more millions than they're worth. The decorating is truly the bow on wrapping. I work really fucking hard as an interior designer to create functional spaces where people can envision themselves living or working. I want the furniture placed to emphasize that. Is that so fucking hard? Really?

It's not entirely these guys' fault. It's actually barely their fault. I'm frustrated with myself. Sexually and mentally. I haven't gone back to the club because I can't move past thinking about Marco. I now associate him with the place, and it's a major turnoff. What we shared— I don't know what that was. It was a jumble of emotions that I both want to repeat and avoid at all costs. I have never had a man steal so much of my damn focus. I've had crushes before. I've been in lust before. I've even been in love a couple times. But I've always been able to set those thoughts and emotions aside for school or work. I can't with him, and I'm pissed at myself because of that.

"Ms. Russo, that's the last piece. Is it where you want it?"

"Thanks, John. It looks great." –ish.

I'll fix a few things, but the heavy stuff is where they should be. I hand over the check and watch the guys file out of the residential loft on the Upper East Side. As I look around, I realize I wouldn't mind if this place was mine. I don't think that about all the spaces I design. But this one has massive windows that let in a ton of light. Their angles allow for a cross breeze you can't get in most places in the city. The rooms flow well, but you can close off each one. It's open concept until you don't want it to be. Sometimes it's wonderful to fill a home with cooking smells. Other times, they're too pungent. You can shut kitchen doors here, and I'm jealous.

I turn at the sound of male voices, stunned to see both Marco and Matteo Mancinelli walk through the door. Matteo smiles, and I force one in return. But Marco stares at me, and I feel naked. He knows exactly what I look like without clothes, making me feel even more vulnerable.

"Hi, Liz. What're you doing up here?"

Matteo walks over to where I was standing near one of the open windows. Marco's slower to follow.

"I was just going to ask you the same thing. I just finished staging the model."

"We came to see how it looks. I'm always interested in seeing the final product of buildings I design."

My brow furrows.

"I didn't realize you were the architect on this project. I didn't think it was a Mancinelli holding."

"It's not. I was hired to do the design. Someone else did the build."

I dart my gaze to Marco, who's remaining silent.

"Well, I love it. I was just thinking I wouldn't mind if this were my place. You gave me a lot of options to work with in here."

"I'm glad you like it. You've turned it into a gorgeous space. Far better than I left it as a sterile, vacant loft."

Marco finally pulls something out of his ass to say.

"Did you design all the units?"

"Yes."

Now I'm the one who's gone mute. Both men wait for me to elaborate. I can't string a thought together as I fight not to stare at Marco. He's in perfectly tailored trousers, and a polo shirt that is clearly not off any rack. The sleeves are tight where they end around his biceps, and it stretches taught over his pecs. But you can tell there's some room around his ribs down to his tapered waist, even though the shirt is tucked tightly into his pants. Gorgeous. Just fucking gorgeous.

"I designed the retail space on the first two floors then did all the residential units up here. One of my colleagues did the floor of office suites."

Marco steps next to Matteo, so now I could touch him if I dared. His voice is like smooth bourbon. It's rich but still burns as it goes down.

"You do retail and residential interior design but not other types of commercial?"

"I do. But this was a massive project, so I asked for help. I work on all sorts of urban designs, but I specialize in retail. Residential is just a personal enjoyment that I'm good at too."

Marco smiles, and it's like a wolf grinning before it devours a lamb.

"Good at many things, I'm sure."

Matteo doesn't seem to notice any innuendo there, so maybe I'm just reading into it. Instead, he twists to look around.

"Are you leaving? Is there time for me to be nosy?"

"Definitely. The door locks when you pull it shut. Take your time."

I want to escape. Matteo goes in one direction, and I go in the other. I try to walk past Marco, but his hand lands on my ass and squeezes. When I try to take another step, his hold tightens mercilessly. He doesn't let go, but he steps behind me.

"Are you being more aware of your surroundings when you're at the club, *piccolina?*"

He releases my ass, now just cupping it. My heart races, and I'm torn between leaning back against him and wanting to bolt. I opt for taking two steps forward then whirling around.

"I've been just fine. Like always."

He grins at me but says nothing else. I don't know what I'm supposed to do. If his cousin weren't here, would he make some kind of move beyond what he just did? Would we be fucking by now? I know I wouldn't say no. Chelle's due back in three days from her honeymoon. I don't know if that makes me want to hurry up and bang him before she returns. Or do I not even care? I'm leaning toward the latter.

I've gone from a lamb to the slaughter to a deer in headlights again. He moves until his right shoulder presses against my right shoulder. His right hand is on my left hip.

"Be more careful there, little one. Don't let your luck run out. I will know if someone bothers you. And I won't ignore it.

So pay better attention to who's watching and following you, Beth."

He presses a kiss to my lips that's so brief I have no chance to respond. Then he's walking past me to join Matteo in the dining room. What the ever-loving fuck does "and I won't ignore it" mean? I don't know the specifics, but I already guessed what type of family my little sister married into. Does that mean he'd whack someone for me? Is that fucked-up or sweet? It's fucking sweet, I guess. Something is seriously wrong with me.

I grab my purse and call out a goodbye before I shut the door behind me. I don't let myself rest back against it like I want. I'm too thrown to wait around. I work from home most days, so I head back to my place in Brooklyn. I get another three hours of distracted work in before I make myself a rather pathetic dinner for one. But I couldn't care less.

I intend to exorcise Marco from my system tonight. I slide into a sleek black and sapphire teddy that I haven't worn before. I snip the tags before I step into my heels. I grab the same coat I wore last time, and I'm off. This time, I hail a cab. I don't need my destination in my Uber or Lyft account.

It only takes me five minutes to drop my coat and purse in my locker. Then I'm double checking my mask's in place before I head into the main room. Chelle knows I'm a member here, and she's expressed curiosity about BDSM. If Enzo is anything like his brother, then she's probably learning all about it on her honeymoon. Good for her.

"You have plans for tonight?"

I recognize Danny's voice as he steps behind me. His tone is neutral since he doesn't know what kind of mood I'm in. When I stiffen, he takes the cue.

"Ah, you're ready to do exactly what I want, aren't you?"

"Yes, Sir."

This is *not* what I thought I wanted. I thought I wanted to be a top tonight. I thought I wanted to have control, so I could push Marco from my brain. Maybe I want to be a bottom and submit to someone else. Let someone else take his place.

"Turn around, whore."

"Call her that again."

Oh, fuck.

"Dude, back up."

"Call her that again."

Marco's voice is purely menacing, and Danny gets the message this time. The hand that just clutched my hair releases it. I haven't turned around. Not because no one's commanded me to. But because I don't want to face Marco.

"Amanda didn't realize I would be here tonight. She has a new arrangement now. Move."

How the hell does he know that's the name I go by here?

"Amanda?"

"He's right."

How did those words just leave my mouth? I don't recall thinking them, but that was my voice.

"Why'd you just agree to me?"

"It's a new arrangement, and I didn't know he'd be here tonight. But now that he is..."

"But—"

"Move."

Marco doesn't sound like he's going to say it a third time. I spin and reach my hand past Danny. I step around him until Marco can wrap his arm around my waist and pull me against him. I go more willingly than I should considering he just unilaterally decided I'm not pairing with Danny tonight.

"I hope you enjoyed your time with Amanda because she's not available anymore."

Danny blinks at me from behind his mask. I know Marco's

declaration stuns him. I've always been adamant that I wouldn't enter into any kind of exclusive relationship. It's also obvious there won't be any power switching with Marco, which has always been a requirement for me.

"Danny, thanks for everything. I've had fun. But this opportunity came along, and it's the right fit for me for now."

Marco's fingers dig into my waist with my last two words. Danny's pissed, but he won't make a scene. At least not an angry one. He stalks away, and I'm ready to lay into Marco. Who the fuck does he think he is?

"*Piccolina*, you and I are going to talk. And we are having that talk in private. Argue with me or be awkward, and I will take you to that spanking bench and bend you over it for everyone to watch."

When my only reaction is to look in the piece of furniture's direction, Marco leans down and nips my earlobe.

"Is that what you want? Do you want people to watch me spank you? Watch me fuck you for the first time?"

"Fuck me? I didn't agree to any of this."

"Yes. You did. You did when you stepped into my arms. You did when you sent Danny away. You did when you didn't argue with my suggestion. You know you could have said no at any point, and I would have respected that. But you haven't."

He turns my head toward him, and I put up minimal resistance. When our gazes meet, he lowers his mouth to mine. His kiss is possessive, and I relinquish control immediately. His hand slides between us and cups my pussy. I press my hips forward, but he does nothing more. I whimper with need.

"Do you want people to watch us, Beth? Do you want other women to see my cock as I fuck you?"

"No."

My answer is immediate. I don't want that at all. Normally,

I don't mind some exhibitionism. But I'm suddenly feeling territorial in a way I never have before. I have my own question.

"Would you allow other men to see me?"

"If that's what you want. Since I'm the only man who's going to fuck you from now on, let them see what I have. What they'll never have."

"From now on? Marco, you don't decide that."

"I know. But you've been here since we ran into each other, yet you've only watched. I've done the same. Neither of us has fucked someone else. We've messed around, but no dick has entered your cunt, and I haven't put mine in any. Why is that, Beth?"

I close my eyes. I don't want to admit this aloud. Instead, I lean into him. He kisses my forehead and releases me to take my hand. We walk side-by-side to a stairwell. This leads to private rooms I've never gone into before. I look up at Marco, who's staring at someone else. I follow his gaze and recognize the owner of the club. The guy nods to Marco, and we head up the stairs. He seems to know where he's going, but the first door we stop at has the light glowing underneath. We move to a second, and he opens that one. The lights automatically flick on.

He follows me in. His hand goes to my nape as the door clicks closed. He pulls me back and past him until my back hits the door. His hold slides to my throat and isn't tight, so I don't fight it. I could break away if I wanted. We come together for this kiss, and I can't get enough. All my pent-up desire and frustration from the past week and a half pours forth. We nip and suck at each other's lips and tongue. His hands massage my tits while mine roam over him. But the moment I'm done reaching everything I can, he snags mine and pins them over my head. I'm stretched against him, my back arching to push out my tits.

"Did you really want to scene with Danny tonight?"

His warm breath beside my ear is so fucking erotic that I almost don't understand the question.

"No."

"Did you want to find Jeff and scene with him?"

"I would have."

"Answer my question, *piccolina*. Did you want to?"

"No."

"Who did you really want?"

"You. Did you want to scene with someone else?"

"No."

"Would you have?"

"Yes."

I don't like that answer. Not in the least. Especially not after he said he hadn't fucked anyone since we ran into each other. I know it makes me a hypocrite, and I'm fine with it.

"Do you know why I would have?"

"Because—"

"I want to fuck every thought of you out of my brain and my balls."

He speaks over me, not interested in any answer I might come up with.

"But I know it wouldn't have worked. Not when I'm pressed up against you with a cock ready to come in you with the first thrust."

"Do it."

"Do it, what?"

"Do it, Sir."

"Try again."

"Do it, Master."

His grip on my wrists tightens, and he presses me so hard into the door that I can't move. And I don't think he'd let me.

"Never call me that again. You are not my slave or anyone else's. I was ready to beat the shit out of that twat for calling you a whore. You are to be praised. Worshipped. Not shamed or degraded. If that's what you're into— what you need —then tell me now, and this is over because I will never call you that or anything else like it."

"I— I like it when you call me *piccolina* and little one or little girl. I don't mind the others, but I don't think I want to hear them from you. Not when you..."

Make me feel special.

"Not when I show you I care."

"Something like that."

"So, try again. Do it, what?"

I remember back to last time. I press a kiss to the very end of his jaw and whisper to him.

"Do it, Daddy."

He lets go of me and leads me to the enormous bed in the center of the room. It's a luxurious room with silks and satins on the bed, chairs, and sofa. But there are also cuffs attached to the wall across from the door. There's a rack on the wall that has various implements for impact play. I see the tray for things that need disinfecting, so it wouldn't surprise me if the dresser in the corner has a collection of butt plugs, dildos, vibrators, clamps, and a variety of other insertables. I refuse to use any here because ew. But I admit curiosity wouldn't make me say no to Marco if we were somewhere truly private with nothing shared.

Instead of sitting on the bed or even better yet, lying on it, we walk past it to the sofa. He gestures for me to take a seat, and once I have, he sits. I noticed at the wedding reception that the men in all the syndicates waited until the women at their tables sat. They also stood whenever one got up. That's some old-world manners drilled into them. Clearly, with Marco, it's not just because his parents were watching.

We both take off our masks, I run my hand through the underside of my hair.

"Beth, I want to explore this with you. I can't stop thinking about you or the other night. But I won't share you."

Okay then.

I wait, but he says nothing else. There wasn't a question, so I'm uncertain if he expects a response. It was a declaration that sounded pretty unequivocal.

"You've been straightforward so far. I figured you'd tell me what you want, but you haven't. What do you want, *piccolina?*"

"The same thing. But it can only be here. And we don't tell anyone. Your brother and my sister would freak if they found out we're fuck buddies."

"Agreed to that. What about the no sharing?"

"I sure as fuck won't share you. If you want me— want this —that badly, then I'm the only one."

He picks me up and places me on his lap. I clutch his arm to steady myself, but I know he would never let me fall.

"What are your limits?"

"Anything super taboo. You know. Fluids and what not."

He nods, and I'm glad I don't need to spell it out for him.

"What else?"

"Anything that will leave marks that last more than two weeks."

His expression hardens, and he glances toward the door. I cup his jaw and tug it toward me. The back of my other fingers brush his cheek.

"Marco, you don't have to avenge me. No one's ever done that, and I trust you to know your own strength. If I say that's a hard limit, I know you'll respect it. But I also know that if I wanted it, you're strong enough to do it."

"Even if you wanted it, I wouldn't. I will never leave marks that last longer than a couple days. I don't want to see those types of bruises on you, Beth. I won't inflict them, and I won't tolerate them. If it's a hard limit for you, I won't be pleased to see them."

"You won't. You told me you won't share, and I won't either. No one else is going to touch me, so no one else will leave any marks. I didn't think you were joking when you gave that command, and I definitely wasn't. I can't do this if you're going to be with other people."

I wasn't territorial with Jeff or Danny or any previous BDSM partner. I've been in exclusive romantic relationships, but even then, I never felt the streak of possessiveness I have now. I don't want to share something this intimate with him and know that he's off sharing it with someone else. When this runs its course, then he can do as he pleases.

"I get the impression you're into fluid power exchange."

I grin before I respond.

"And you're not."

"Not particularly. No."

"There might be times when I'd like to push you down on a bed and be on top. There might be times when I strip for you, and I decide how fast or slow I go. But I have no interest in anything else a Domme might do."

"You wouldn't miss it?"

"No. Controlling impact play or having guys wear plugs or rings is something I can take or leave. I enjoy restraining guys, but I don't feel right thinking about doing that with you."

"Why? Do you think I wouldn't relinquish that control?"

"I don't. And..."

"Beth, I don't want you to ever be frightened to share your thoughts with me. I don't want you to be embarrassed either."

"I don't want to do anything that might be like work."

I rush to say that, and now I'm mortified since I just made a huge assumption.

"What did Chelle tell you about our family?"

It could sound accusatory, but it doesn't.

"Nothing. But I've heard the whispers since I started working in the city. People know who the Big Four families are, and all of them were at the reception."

"Big Four? Is that what we're called?"

That seems like confirmation of sorts.

"I mean, that's what you are, aren't you? I don't know if that's an official name anyone else calls you. But it seems fitting."

"Beth, what do you know or think about us?"

"I know that when the Mancinellis or Kutsenkos walk into any room, they command it. I know I've been to a couple events when I was a kid where the O'Rourkes were, and they were the same way. I know the Diazes through Chelle who knows them through Laura. They're no different."

Laura Kutsenko— née Doyle —grew up next door to the *jefe's* younger brother's family. Laura was best friends with the *jefe's* nephew Juan since they were toddlers. No one ever called Enrique that in front of us, but we knew.

"There are a lot of businessmen and women in New York with just as much presence."

"Ha."

It's somewhere between a derisive snort and laugh.

"Marco, you know that's bullshit. Chelle has never told me — even alluded to —specifics, but I can guess. I don't know what's been done to you, and I don't want to know what you have to do to others. But tying you up just doesn't feel like something you'd be into."

"But you let me restrain you."

I did, and it was before I gave it much thought. But now that he points it out, I won't stop him if he wants to do it again. I enjoyed having him hold my hands above my head. I enjoyed having him pin me against the door.

"Beth, if you want to restrain me from time to time, I won't say no. Just know that when I openly take back control, you won't doubt that I always had it."

"You mean you'd let me cuff you to that bed tonight if that's what I wanted?"

"Yes. You can edge me and fuck me. But the moment I'm free, I will fuck you until you're sore."

"Are we really going to have sex?"

"Yes. Several times tonight and then several more times tomorrow night. And as often as you want it after that."

"And it just stays between us here?"

He hesitates for a heartbeat before he nods. Does he want us to fuck somewhere else? He couldn't mean that he wants something more than just an arrangement, could he?

"Beth, when you want this to end, then tell me. If that's tomorrow or six months from now or whenever, I won't trap you."

"Same."

His hand cups my ass while the other fists my hair. His kiss is rougher than any of the others. He's in complete control, and I can't keep up as he ravishes my mouth. His teeth tug on my lower lip before he leans back.

"I'm not going anywhere, little girl."

That statement sounds so absolute.

"Beth, in all seriousness though, you know who we are. Can you live with that? With being with someone like me?"

As I gaze into his whiskey-brown eyes, I realize what my sister must have. These men are good. They must do horrible things. They must have committed the worst crimes. But they don't do it for kicks. They do it because in their hearts, they're honorable. They just live by a different moral code than most. I can live with it while I fuck him. And I think— I know —I could live with it beyond just sex. I wish I could live with it beyond sex.

"Daddy, I don't want the details, and I don't think you'd ever give them. But I accepted Enzo as my brother and believe he's perfect for my sister. If I'm not passing judgement on him, I won't do it to you. I'm comfortable with you, and I feel safe. I trust you."

"That's all I want. I will take care of you, *piccolina*."

This kiss is like that last we shared the other night. It's tender and about more than just lust and kink. It's the kind that scared me shitless because it makes me want so much more than we have. It's the kind that drives me to want lovemaking not fucking.

I feel the straps of my teddy sliding down my shoulders, then my breasts are bare. He's toying with my nipple, and I just want to get closer to him. I tug at his tank top. When I have it free of his pants, he yanks it over his head and drops it on the sofa. Holy fuckballs. I can't help but run my hands over his chest and shoulders. I could tell he was chiseled before he removed his shirt, but now. Was Adonis Roman or Greek? Whichever the Roman one was, that's Marco.

"Keep looking at me that way, and I won't last past that first thrust like I said."

"Hmm?"

I'm kissing along his neck, enjoying the feel of the cords in his neck straining as he speaks. He eases me off his lap and onto my feet. He unhooks the catches down the front of my teddy before he pushes it to my waist and eventually to the floor. I gasp when he sweeps me into his arms then lays me on the bed. He tosses my heels behind him and quickly moves to fasten the restraints around my wrists and ankles. I watch him move to the dresser and pull out a satin sash and a packet of fresh earplugs.

"Marco, that's a hard limit for me. I can't do audio deprivation."

He turns to me and nods. He drops them back into the drawer with no questions asked. I don't think it's disinterest. I think he's respecting my privacy and my boundaries. But I want him to know.

"I had a lot of ear infections as a kid, and they were scary. Not being able to hear reminds me of that."

"Then we'll never do anything where you can't hear what I'm going to do."

He places the sash at the foot of the bed and kneels on one knee before he leans forward and drops a soft kiss on my lips. Then he's gone again. I want to mull over that moment of affection, but he's at the rack on the wall, deciding what he wants to use. He takes down a crop and a flogger. I wait to see if he's going to get anything else, but he seems satisfied with those. At least for now.

He says nothing as he moves toward me, but I can hear his footsteps. I watch him set the crop and flogger on the bedside table. This really is a decadent bedroom by any standard. He holds up the sash, and I nod. I assume it'll be a blindfold. He confirms my suspicions as he carefully ties it behind my head. He makes certain he doesn't catch any of my hair and that it will rest comfortably when I put my head down.

"What's your safe word, *piccolina*."

"Chimpanzee, Daddy."

I don't know why that word feels so natural now. I said it to be patronizing and condescending. I sure as fuck don't see him as a father figure. I don't have daddy issues or some kind of female Oedipus complex. I just think it's kinda sexy, and I've said more than once that I feel safe with him. I feel protected too. He made sure those guys that I honestly didn't notice didn't follow me the last time we were both here. I didn't love hearing Danny call me a whore tonight. It didn't feel right. But having Marco interrupt— even rescue me from it —was nice. I felt protected. I know I'm not a little. Not when I usually like switching. But it doesn't feel like age play when I say it. Maybe it's sort of like how Latin American cultures use *papi*.

"Pull on your restraints for me."

I tug my arms and legs, but there's very little give. He's a stealthy bastard because I'm not prepared for the crop to come down on my breast. He slaps the top of my left one four times before he nails my nipple dead on. My back arches off the bed and into his fingers. He pinches and twists, and I yelp. He eases off the pressure.

"You surprised me. That's all."

"Use your safe word when you need it."

"I know, Daddy. But I don't. I like it."

And I do.

My abs flex when the crop comes down just above my belly button. I shiver when the smooth leather thongs of the flogger sweep down between my tits and over my belly. As he trails them back up my right ribs, the crop smacks my right breast.

"Oh!"

These slaps come in a staccato rather than the slower ones he gave the other side. There are six before he brings the crop down the hardest on my nipple. I'm focused on the sensation there, so I'm not prepared for the flogger to land across my middle. He sets a swishing rhythm that makes the thongs land across my belly, ribs, breasts, and mound. I picture his wrist making a figure eight. Just when I think I'm getting a reprieve because the flogger stops, his mouth wraps around my left nipple. The moment he applies suction, the crop lands along my pussy.

"Marco!"

I scream in surprise and with the flash of pain.

"Are you all right, Beth?"

"Yes. Just unprepared."

"Good."

If this were a true Dom/sub deal, he wouldn't allow me to use his first name. It doesn't seem to faze him that I did. I also didn't respond to his question with Daddy. He may dominate this scene, but he isn't my Dom. I'm not quite sure what to make of that. I have no time to think about it as another wave of searing pain shoots through my cunt. But it's soon soothed when he sucks my other nipple. I receive a series of quick slaps on my clit that make me moan and squirm. My mind and body don't know if they want to escape or beg for more.

Then it all stops. He's gone. All I hear is my breathing, but I know he's still here. I can sense it even without knowing the door hasn't opened. I picture the layout of the room, trying to guess what he's going to do next.

"Fuck!"

How the hell is he so fucking silent? His mouth on my clit makes me claw at the air. There's nothing for my hands to grasp since they're bound, palm up. His tongue dips into me before he laves my clit over and over.

"I'm close. Please, may I come, Daddy?"

As soon as the two sentences leave my mouth, I know I've just asked to be edged. It would have been better to just come without permission and dealt with those consequences. He pulls away and nips at my inner left thigh. With his hand wrapped under my leg and over my hip, he presses just below my belly button as three fingers from his other hand slide into me. I tremble when he hits my g spot. The internal and external pressure feels amazing. His thumb rubbing my clit is bringing me back to the edge. This time, I'm keeping my fucking mouth shut.

But he must feel me straining toward my orgasm because he stops right when I'm on the cusp. I shudder with need as I strain to wrap myself around a body that isn't there. He's still between my thighs, but I want to wrap myself around him as he fucks me. I want to feel him inside me. Maybe chimpanzee wasn't the right word. Maybe he was right that I would want to curl around him like one.

"*Piccolina*, you don't come until I say you can."

"When will that be, Daddy?"

Chapter Five

Marco

I'm in over my head.

This is the most sensual, most erotic experience of my life as I bring Beth to the edge then pull her back over and over. And she's the last woman I should be with. It was bad enough that Enzo fell in love with the best friend of our enemy's wife. Now I'm falling head over heels for my brother's new sister-in-law. Sister. We don't use qualifiers in our family. It would sound incestuous if people didn't know.

"I'll decide when you come, and tonight it won't be without me inside you."

"Could that be soon, then?"

I chuckle as I go back to sucking her clit. I watch her body as she writhes while my fingers and mouth work her. She's growing desperate to come, and I don't know how much longer I can last. I thought going down on her would give me a chance to calm down, so I don't embarrass myself by coming too soon. But everything about her makes my lust grow exponentially.

While I used the flogger, I'd toed off my shoes and dropped my pants. As I walked to the end of the bed, I'd stripped off my socks. I'm in my boxer briefs now, and they're fucking cutting off my goddamn circulation to my balls. I use the hand that was pressing on her belly to work them down my hips. I probably look ridiculous wiggling my hips to get them to drop. Good thing she can't see me. But I'm finally naked. Halleluiah.

As I work her pussy and clit, I press my pinky against her asshole. She tilts her hips, so I can ease the tip in. She doesn't shy away, so I lock that nugget away for later. But that's not what I want right now. I climb onto the mattress all the way and crawl over her body, stopping to suck each nipple. When I'm resting on my left forearm, I slip the blindfold off. I want to see her expression when I enter her.

"Do you want to switch to vanilla and have me release you, Beth?"

"No, Daddy."

"You want our first time to be me fucking you."

"Hard."

I cup her cheek. I make sure our gazes lock.

"*Piccolina*, I have never desired any woman as much as I do you. I'll fuck you hard to show you, but I hope you don't need me to prove it. I don't want anyone but you."

And I mean that. This is a fuck buddy arrangement that's going to stay here at the club. But I wish it were more. And that shocks the shit out of me every time I think it. I can fucking hear every man in my family say I told you so. I can see every woman in my family smirking at me. They all said my turn would come. But Beth isn't the right woman. If she were, we wouldn't be in this situation. We'd be in one where we could actually pursue this.

"I don't like admitting it, but I think I do need more than you just showing me."

I appreciate her honesty. This is a lot we're rushing into. I've already admitted I was here, hoping to fuck her off my mind. Why? Because she's the only one I want. As I think about it, I want to prove it and not just show her.

I reach into the drawer beside the bed where I know there's a plethora of condoms. I grab one I know fits after digging a little. I shift to kneel, and she watches me rip the foil. Her gaze rivets to my dick, but as I roll the condom over the tip, her eyes dart to mine. I'm watching her. She returns her attention to my cock as I continue to cover it. I toss the wrapper in the trash next to the bed. Then I position myself, the head rubbing between her pussy lips. I didn't even need to use my hand to get me there. My cock found it on its own.

I flex my hips and surge into her as hard as I dare. Her neck arches as her head sinks farther into the pillow. She moans, and my cock twitches. I pull halfway out, then thrust again.

"Yes!"

"You want more?"

"You know I do."

I don't correct her that she didn't address me with a title. If I were a Dom, I would care. I don't. I just want to know she's enjoying it. From the way her legs keep trying to bend to cradle my hips, I would say she's into it. Her hands are in fists since she has nothing to cling to but air. I pound into her, rubbing her clit with my pubic bone each time I'm balls deep.

"I need to come. Please."

"Do it."

I add more force, making the bed shake. I know she's trying to dig her heels into the mattress to meet my thrusts, but her restraints make it difficult. I'm fucking her, and she's taking it. It feeds some caveman part of me, and I can tell she's reveling in it. I hope there's no doubt in her mind just how much I want her. I want to consume her. Control her body in this moment and bring her more pleasure than anyone else ever has. To be the only man she thinks of when she wants to fuck.

"Fuck, Daddy... I'm coming... Don't stop!"

Her entire body contracts beneath me. I kiss her, and she sucks my tongue. She doesn't want to let me pull away. She whimpers when I withdraw, but she sees I'm reaching to unfasten her legs. Once her ankles are free, I release her wrists. I grab her hips and thrust balls deep. Before she knows what's happening, I roll us, so I'm on my back.

"Fuck me, *piccolina*. Show Daddy how much you want this."

"Want you."

She moves on me, setting her pace. She bounces, rocks, and circles her hips. Each rhythm changing just as I feel like I'm about to come. She's edging me now since the sensation shifts and pulls my orgasm just beyond my reach. I'm clinging to a bunch of the sheets in each hand, determined to let her be in control. I want to dig my fingers into her hips and move her the way I need to get off. But, fuck, she's gorgeous as she rides me. Her honey-brown hair is loose down her back. Her hips are broad, and while her belly is toned, her ass is soft. Her tits aren't huge, but they're full. Every part of her feels like it was made to be just what I crave.

"I'm going to come again, Daddy. And I'm going to make you come too."

She can think that. But I now have a different plan.

"Oh, God... Marco... Fuck. That feels so good... I'm coming."

Her fingers squeeze my pecs as she braces herself, leaning forward. Her cheeks are flushed as her eyes drift closed. She's exquisite. When her eyes open, and she sucks in a deep breath, I lift her off me. She reaches for me, but I'm quick to place her on her belly. I hover over her, wrapping my left hand over her wrists at the small of her back. I rest on my elbows, and my right hand pulls back hair from her left shoulder. I nudge her legs wider until I can enter her again.

"You are mine, Beth. Mine to pleasure and deny. Mine to watch as you come on my tongue, my fingers, my cock. I will claim all of you just like you've claimed all of me."

There's more truth in that statement than I wish to examine. I thrust four more times before I feel my cum fill the condom. I release her wrists and start to lift my weight from her. She pulls her arms free, but her hands search for my arms. She wraps hers around mine.

"Don't go yet. Please."

I settle back, so my forearms bracket her head. I feather kisses on her temple and cheek. I don't rest all my weight on her, but I give her most of it. I feel her body sink farther into the mattress beneath mine as she sighs. Her eyes are closed as she slides her hands up to cover mine. We lace our fingers together, but neither of us speaks.

We just had rough sex, but this feels much more like basking in the bliss a couple would share. This isn't how I've felt during regular BDSM aftercare for someone I dominated. The emotions are so much more genuine. And that scares the ever-loving fuck out of me.

I kiss along her shoulder until she tries to twist beneath me. I rise enough for her to roll over. Her kiss is as soft as mine have been, and I wrap her in my arms as I roll over again, putting me on the bottom. I like how she feels sprawled across my chest. I like the way her silky hair feels under my fingers as I run my hand up and down her back. I like how her ass fills my palm as it rests there. I especially love the feel of the pecks she's giving my neck as her head rests in the crook of my shoulder.

But neither of us says anything. Neither of us acknowledges that this is more than just fucking. We're both close to drifting off when we, by silent mutual agreement, get up. She slips her teddy back on along with her heels, while I gather and put my clothes back on. But her hand rests over my outline of Italy. She does nothing for a moment then pulls away. We reach the door and look at each other.

"Tomorrow night?"

We speak at the same time. Then we nod in unison.

"Marco, if something comes up, please let me know. I don't want to come here without you."

"Same."

I lean in and kiss her. We have each other's number from coordinating things for the wedding as maid of honor and best man. I walk her back to the locker room and duck into the men's to grab my stuff. I put my button down back on. My keys, wallet, and phone were always with me just in case. I hang back until I see Beth walk outside. She glances back, maybe hoping to see me. I slip out but stay in the shadows as I watch her hail a cab. The cab pulling away without me in it is probably the saddest metaphor of my life.

BETH

I'm so sorry. I have to cancel tonight. My brother wants me to meet his girlfriend at dinner, and they arranged a date for me. I don't want to go.

My fucking luck.

"Marco?"

I turn toward Luca's voice as he walks into my living room. I shove my phone in my pocket, wishing I could respond right then and there. But I don't want to deal with Luca's questions.

"Yeah. What's up?"

"We have a problem."

"What's new about that? Can you be more specific?"

"What's crawled up your ass lately? You're being pissy with everyone."

I didn't think I was, but maybe. I'm fighting to hide my disappointment over not getting to see Beth tonight. Last night was the most earth-shaking experience of my life, and I thought I was going to get round two tonight. I know I can't get her out of my system yet, so I figured I wouldn't fight the current anymore. I finally allowed myself to indulge, but here I am having my hand slapped away from the cookie jar.

"I'm not being pissy with anyone. I'm just frustrated that shit keeps cropping up that we can't completely resolve. It's a bunch of fucking Band-Aids instead of resolutions."

"Maybe so, but you need to fix your attitude."

"Is that an order, big brother?"

I'm being a total ass right now, and Luca doesn't deserve it. He shoots me a look that says he won't respond to that now, but he'll remember it later. Most likely when we're boxing. I inhale, forcing myself to calm the fuck down and stop being a douche.

"What's going on?"

My tone is more normal, and I can see Luca appreciates it.

"Turns out Shapiro was into some deeper shit than we realized."

"Like what?"

"Like insider trading with Niko and Pasha."

"So?"

If it were someone not in the bratva Elite Group, maybe we would turn them over to the feds and let the idiot do some time at a white-collar crime country club. But the fact that we're dealing with the *pakhan's* brother and cousin complicates things. It makes it something we have to overlook.

"So, their little insider trader was to quietly buy the bulk of the publicly traded shares in Publius Genomics. Niko and Pasha now have forty-nine percent between them."

Motherfucking pieces of shit-eating douchebags. I don't even know what the fuck that phrase means. But those fuckers just came after my company. I own fifty-one percent of the corporation I started. It's named for Publius Cornelius Scipio Africanus, known as possibly Rome's greatest and undefeated general. We may not be the largest company, but we've been on the cutting edge and are growing quarterly. I sure as fuck won't be defeated by these *testa di cazzos*—dickheads.

"How'd Shapiro get involved?"

"He used the money he was embezzling from the charity he was supposedly the biggest patron of. He bought the shares just as the bell rang the night before we grabbed him. He sold them for pennies to Niko and Pasha and got a kickback for it. He knew Davidson was ready to sell his shares because Davidson and Shapiro have the same broker. The broker convinced another person, Helen Peters, to jump ship. He said it must be a sign if Davidson was bailing. Davidson and Peters sold for less than market price, thereby, devaluing all the stock. Niko and Pasha don't plan to sell. Just the opposite, they want the board to cast a vote of no confidence to boot you off."

"They want a hostile takeover."

"Pretty much."

"Why? Why that company and why now? This is a distraction but from what?"

"Carmine's working on it. But Sergei and Anton have put up firewalls and every other block they can conceive of. We need Enzo's skills to hack it. They know he's away. That's why they're striking now."

I run my hand through my hair. Of course, my brain circles back to Beth. It's a blessing in disguise that she cancelled. I have this shit to figure out. I would have had to be the one to call it off.

"All right." My left hand goes to my hip as my right hand runs through my hair again. "We know Misha and Pasha just got a big shipment in from Jamaica. We both know it's not just sugar in those sacks. They're running Bolivian coke through Negril. We also know Bear Imports/Exports also just brought in a shipment of Bahamian rum in those standard containers that came off the ship last week. I want the coke, then our guys bust up the rum crates in the warehouse and torch it. We need the coke filtered from the sugar. We send the sugar sacks by big rig up to Canada, but we fly the coke to Iceland. From there, we get it in baggies and into fucking fish— whatevers —and sail them to the Netherlands. Let them chase their tails up to Montreal."

Iceland has among the lowest drug use in any European country, so they won't search as thoroughly as other places. The people we have there will shove the baggies into whole fish that're being exported and even into bottled fish products. Once it's to our people in the Netherlands, it's not our problem anymore.

"When?"

"Give it two days. If we retaliate tonight, they'll know we found out."

"That might get back at them, but what are you going to do about the shares they own?"

I grin.

"There's a Czech biotech company looking to expand. I'd be willing to take a loss for Niko and Pasha to wake and discover the Czechs own the majority stake in a company they just tried to takeover. I'm certain Karolina Svoboda will be happy to let those Russian fucks know they can't do shit without her permission."

While Czech-Russian relations aren't too bad right now, there's no love lost on the Czech side after being forced into the Soviet Union back in the late 1960s. The woman's father was like a national hero in the Velvet Revolution that overthrew communism in 1989. The Kutsenkos may have next to no ties left with their motherland— though Misha and Pasha named their company Bear Exports/Imports —as in the Russian bear —but they can't change who they are just like a leopard can't change its spots. They can fuck all the way off.

"Once we have the coke out of the warehouse, I'll make sure the bank transaction goes through. The time difference will work in our favor. I'll talk to Karolina in the morning."

Luca returns my grin and rolls his eyes.

"Always one step behind us. Poor little boys."

They're neither little nor boys, but what-the-fuck-ever. Fuck around and find out.

"Is there anything else Shapiro got up to that we need to deal with, or can he finally rest in peace?"

"Nothing that I know of. What's going on with you? Do you need to get laid or something?"

This again? Hell. I thought we'd moved on.

"My sex life is just fine, thank you very much."

"Not with the way you've been acting. You're like a coiled spring under pressure."

"Luca, I don't need advice on when to fuck."

"Then maybe you need a vacation."

That brings to mind images of Beth in a string bikini on some beach where I can yank the bows and watch it fall off her.

"Who the fuck are you picturing?"

"What?"

I look blankly at Luca. Shit. Can he tell I was daydreaming?

"You are definitely thinking about someone specific. I didn't think you had any significant arrangement. At least, not one with a woman you'd travel with."

"I don't. I was thinking about hooking up with someone wherever I go."

Luca just stares at me. None of us do— did— now that I'm the last unmarried guy —random hookups. Too many possible complications with someone we haven't run a background check on. Luca, Gabriele, and Lorenzo might not have snooped into their wives' history, but the background checks were run. I already know Beth's because it came as part of Chelle's.

I might have done a little late night studying after the rehearsal dinner. There wasn't much to read. I knew we belonged to the same BDSM club, but I didn't think I would run into her so soon after the wedding. We've both been members for years and never encountered one another. I know she has a near perfect credit score and hasn't had a speeding ticket since she was twenty.

"Fine. Keep your thoughts to yourself."

"You were always a nosy fucker, Luca. I think Carmine learned it from you."

"Bullshit. Mama expected me to keep an eye on you heathens. I had to make sure I knew what you were up to."

I roll my eyes. We're eighteen months apart, and that's the furthest apart my parents had any of us. Enzo came almost a year to the day after me, and Maria came almost a year to the day after him. They didn't have three boys then tried for a girl. They would have been just as happy with another boy as they would have been with four girls. They said they stopped before the number of kids outnumbered the parental hands.

The men of my dad's generation— so Uncle Salvatore, Uncle Domenico, and Uncle Cesare —have all been hands-on fathers. There were plenty of times when Papa had four kids' meals being passed through the car window after soccer practice. If Mama was working, he chopped the orange slices and took them to the matches. Uncle Domenico is the musical one and taught all of us the piano. How he's not deaf is beyond me.

None of them are anything like *Nonno* Vicenzu, Papa's father and our last don. He would give Papa and my uncles shit, but none of them cared. People may have feared *Nonno*, but they didn't respect him. He believed those were synonyms, but Uncle Salvatore has shown they aren't. Men both fear and respect my uncle. I'm grateful I've only ever worked for Uncle Salvatore.

"Hello to la-la land."

Luca snaps his fingers in front of me. I bat his hand away.

"I have shit to coordinate now that I have a plan in place. Sorry that I'm not listening to you babble more than your daughter."

Luca's grin softens into one full of pride. He's a huge softy at any mention of Petra. He and Papa are ridiculous together with the faces they make and the songs they sing.

"Shouldn't you be home in time for Petra to wake up from her nap? I thought you had the night shift."

"*Vaffancullo*." Fuck off.

But my brother shows me a photo Olivia must have sent a little while ago of Petra in a bouncy swing.

"Go home to your wife and kid. Let me figure out how to run the world."

We hug, and then I'm back to being alone in my place. Blessedly alone. I pull out my phone and realize we'd been talking for almost forty-five minutes. I must have been staring off into space a lot more than I realized. Luca was definitely more patient than I realized.

ME

No worries. I'm bummed. But I get it.

I glance at the time on my phone, and I bet she's already at dinner by now. I stare at the screen, wishing for a response, but nothing comes. I drop my phone into my pocket and make my way into the kitchen. I pull out a couple things of leftovers and reheat them. I'll deal with setting up the plan in the morning. I'm about to flip on the TV when my phone vibrates.

BETH

I need a favor

Chapter Six

Beth

Oh, thank God. This is the worst fucking date ever. What was Steve thinking? His girlfriend, Chasity, is really nice. But her cousin, Derik, is a douche. He and I have nothing in common. At. All. Like he already said I play with pretty pillows every day. He said I play dress up with houses. He even acted surprised that there are college degrees in interior design. I don't know what his deal is.

I'd asked him what he did first— HVAC repair —and asked if it took a lot of training. I listened to him drone on and on and on some more about shit I didn't understand or care about. But I tried to be polite. It was Chasity who asked what I do. Then fuck face launched into his comments. Steve finally had to step in because he was pissed, and he didn't trust me not to slap the asshole.

ME

> Are you near Bella Vita by any chance?

It's one of Lorenzo's restaurants. Chasity wanted to try it out after finding out our sister is married to the owner. Derik's been acting like a dick about how rich Chelle must be now.

MARCO

> I can be. What's wrong? What happened?

I can hear him in my head. His calm but firm voice. The one that demands I answer his questions. The one I loved hearing— thus taunting him —the first night at the club. Right now, it calms me.

ME

> Steven and Chasity want to go to Ivy. I don't want to be stuck dancing with this guy. I'm over it. But I can't go home yet because I promised Steve I'd stay out the whole night and give this guy a try.

MARCO

> Did he do something?

Oh, fuck. I don't need Marco scaring the shit out of Derik. I just want an excuse to leave.

ME

> No. He's just not my type. He's kinda obnoxious, but he didn't do anything wrong. Can you come and rescue me? Please. I'd ask Chelle, but...

But Chelle doesn't get home until tomorrow. And even if she were home, she just got married. I wouldn't ask her to come

84

out to make excuses for me. I guess I'm willing to ask Marco, though.

MARCO

Give me twenty minutes. Where will you be?

ME

Ivy

There isn't an immediate response like before. Is he getting ready to head out the door? I can't hide in the bathroom forever.

MARCO

I'm on my way, piccolina.

Thanks, Daddy.

ME

Thanks!

I head back to the table just as Steve hands his credit card to the waiter. Derik doesn't look like he even offered to pay any of it. No one here doesn't know we're now related to the owner. But it's not like there was a friends and family discount. If I'd realized the check was coming so soon, I would have waited to text Marco, so I could offer to pay part of it. It's not like Steve, the stockbroker, can't afford it. It's the principle of at least offering.

I slide into my chair and take a fortifying last gulp of wine. Derik's arm is draped over the back of my chair, and I stay leaning forward a little. I don't want to give a single hint that I want him touching me. The moment Steve's done signing the receipt, I'm practically leaping out of the chair. But it isn't until I smile at Misha at the door to Ivy that I realize what I've done.

Fuck me. Fuck me. Fuck me.

This is a bratva owned club, and I just asked Marco to

come all the way inside. There's no way he's getting past Misha without being seen. Pasha's over by the dance floor, and Bogdan's walking toward the back with Christina. There're probably some other family members working tonight too. No wonder Marco didn't respond right away.

I fumble for my phone after I say hello to Misha.

ME

> I just realized. You don't have to come. I'll say a friend called and needs me.

His response is almost immediate this time.

MARCO

> I'll be there in five.

ME

> You really don't have to.

MARCO

> I'll be there in five.

Did he even retype that? I think he must have copy-pasted.

"Hey, Steve. I'm going to go back and ask Misha how Laura and the twins are doing. Be right back."

Before he, Derik, or Chasity can say anything I squeeze through the crowd.

"Misha."

"Hey, Liz. How're you?"

"Good. You?"

"Hot but good."

That he is. Blond hair and blue eyes. But not my type. I like dark and brooding. Shit. I'm having second thoughts about this. It's just going to cause talk. Not that it'll matter when they see me leave with Marco.

"Marco Mancinelli is going to be here in a few minutes."

I watch as Misha stiffens and looks toward Pasha. I notice Anton's with his younger brother.

"Misha, he's not coming to cause trouble. He's coming because I asked him to get me out of a shitty date. He lives near here, and I thought he might get here quickly."

"What happened? Did the asshole do something to you?"

It's the same immediate protectiveness I got from Marco's text. It's sweet, but it does nothing for me like it does when it's Marco.

"No. He's just a jerk, and I'm not interested. I didn't think about you guys owning this place when I asked him. I know he isn't welcome, but he's coming as a favor to me. Please let him in."

Misha presses his earpiece and fires something off in rapid Russian.

"Fine. The others know."

"Thanks. Can you point him in my direction? See the two guys and the woman halfway down?"

I point along the bar, leaning a little to the left to see. I know Misha's tall enough to have an unobstructed view.

"Yeah."

"The guy with the maroon shirt is my brother Steven. That's his girlfriend. The other guy is my date."

"Got it. Liz, if you need to get away before Marco arrives, just signal any of us."

I look around and realize Anton, Pasha, and Sergei are now looking at me. I didn't even notice Sergei at first. He's up on the mezzanine level looking down. Quite the entourage I seem to have gathered.

"Thanks. I better get back to them. I said I came to ask about Laura and the twins."

"Got it."

He says something else into his earpiece as I walk away. It's Steve who greets me when I join the others.

"How're they doing?"

"Well. Apparently, Konstantin and Mila decided to redecorate their playroom while Maks ran to the bathroom the other day. They pulled every book and toy off the shelves in like three minutes flat."

"Oh, no." Chasity's eyes widen. "Were they okay?"

"Oh, yeah. Apparently, Maks wasn't. Laura made him clean it up alongside the twins. You'd never guess it, but those toddlers have their dad wrapped around their little fingers. Laura's the strict one."

I know all this because I chatted with Laura a couple days ago. She has the top tier of Enzo and Chelle's wedding cake, and I got Chelle's dress preserved. She offered to grab the dress and take everything over to them when they get back. At least, I'm not entirely lying. Maks is a complete softy with his kids. Bogdan's the same way with his son. My guess is Galina, Maks and Bogdan's mom, is babysitting Lev— Bogdan and Christina's six-month-old son —tonight.

"Who're you talking about?"

Shit. That's a legit question. I don't know if Chasity knows about Laura, but Derik definitely doesn't.

"Our sister's best friend. She has twin two-year-olds."

"Sounds like her husband's pussy whipped."

I don't even know what the fuck to say to that.

"I'll be sure to let his brother know that. He's walking this way."

Marco's voice comes from over my right shoulder. I see Steve's brow furrow, then he smiles.

"Hey, Marco. How's it going?"

Steve reaches out to shake Marco's hand as he steps beside me. It forces Derik to take a couple steps away while Marco's free hand rests on my lower back. Steve doesn't know what to make of that. Chasity frowns.

"Chasity, Derik, this is Marco Mancinelli. His brother Lorenzo married our sister Michelle."

"Hold up. Your sister married a Mancinelli?"

Derik's grinning like a jackass. He didn't know who owns Bella Vita just that we're related to them now. I glance up at Marco, but his expression remains relaxed. However, his arm slides around my waist, and I take a step closer. Derik's smile drops as he sees the possessive gesture. Now he's scowling at me, then his sister.

"You said she was available."

Chasity doesn't know where to look, so she shifts her gaze to Steve. My brother rolls with the punches a little better, but I know I'll be explaining shit in the morning.

"I didn't know it was more than a date or two."

Derik sneers at me before turning his glare on Marco.

"What're you doing here, anyway?"

Marco shrugs.

"I figured it's close to ten. Your evening was probably going to be over soon, so I decided to take Beth home."

"Beth? Her name's Liz."

Derik's the one who speaks, but I can tell Steve's thinking the same thing.

"Marco calls me that. He's the only one."

Steve looks like he's locking that little nugget away for later.

"Are you ready, *piccolina?*"

Marco's voice is barely more than a whisper against my ear. I nod before I step forward to hug my brother.

"I'll talk to you tomorrow." I give him a pointed stare. "It was nice meeting you, Chasity. Goodnight, Derik."

Rude. I know. But I don't give a fuck. I turn toward the door, and Marco wraps his arm around my waist. I move to do the same for good measure, but his arm adjusts, so I'm forced to hold mine higher. It's awkward since I'm shorter, but it still makes us look like a couple. He nods to Anton and Sergei, who are now at the door. I mouth "thanks."

There's a town car waiting for us, so I slide in first. Marco walks around to the street side door and gets in. The driver closes mine, and I notice the privacy glass is up. The car pulls away from the curb, but neither Marco nor I have given the driver an address or directions. When I look over at Marco, I realize he must already know it and told his driver before he walked in. His family probably ran an extensive background on all of mine. Did he already know I belonged to the club? Fuck. That's embarrassing.

"Marco, I'm sorry I made you go in there. I told Misha why you'd be showing up. I know they'll be talking about it, but I figured they would, anyway. I didn't want him to give you any shit."

"I know. He pointed you out, even though I'd already spotted you."

"You had? I didn't think I'd be easy to see."

"I will always find you, Beth."

"Thank you, Daddy."

I can't believe I just said that. He might call me *piccolina* wherever and whenever he wants. But Daddy is supposed to be just at the club. Not the real world. He picks me up and settles me on his lap just like he did last night when we sat on the sofa.

"You can call me that whenever you want, Beth. I think you felt really uncomfortable all night. And now that you're with me, you feel safe. That's why you said it."

"It is. But you know I'm not a little, right?"

He chuckles.

"Nothing about that teddy last night or the way you rode me makes me think you're a little."

"You let me be in control for a little bit. Or at least, you let me think I was. You took over just like you said you would."

"Does that bother you?"

"No. I thought it was— just right."

"What were you really going to say because I think it was a fuck ton more than 'just right?'"

"Really good."

"Beth."

"What?"

"Fine. I'll say it. It was damn well perfect."

"It really was. Thank you. It exceeded what I expected."

"Good."

He smirks at me before he gives me a soft kiss. I lean against his chest, wishing we had our masks. If we did, I would suggest going back to our original plan. We ride in silence for the next five minutes, and I don't mind. He sounds casual when he speaks first.

"Do you have plans to see Chelle and Enzo when they get back?"

"Not right away. Laura's taking the top of the wedding cake and the gown back to Chelle the day after tomorrow. I figured I'll let them settle in and get over their jetlag."

They went to the Dalmatian Coast in Croatia for their honeymoon. The photos I saw online look amazing. Apparently, Gabriele has a house there that they used. I suspect their family has houses all over the world. I know they have a family jet.

I think about what my sister said their plans are when they get back.

"Chelle said Enzo wants them to live in her place. Did he tell you that?"

"Yeah. He says her place is way homier than his."

"My sister's place has to be way smaller than his. She mentioned a penthouse."

"True. But Enzo is a bit of a minimalist when it comes to his place. His furniture is comfy, but he never made it feel like a home. He has nothing on the walls. He has plenty of books, but half of them are about accounting and shit. He said Chelle's place is more welcoming."

"It is."

I want to ask if his place is like Enzo's. He thinks of something to say before I do.

"Did you bring your work home with you?"

"Do you mean do I have work to do tonight?"

He laughs and shakes his head ruefully.

"I meant did you bring your interior design skills to your own place? Is it showroom perfect?"

"Hardly. I'm way more frugal than my clients. I don't feel the need to have name brand everything when I can get almost equal quality somewhere else. But I did knock out a couple walls. A man must have designed the place. Too much wasted space."

I shoot him a teasing grin and waggle my eyebrows.

"I'll be sure to let Matteo know."

My smile falters for a moment.

"He didn't design my building. It's been around since before any of us were born."

"I know. But Maria complained the house he designed for them has too many nooks for dust to collect with no practical purpose. He said she has too many ornaments that need to be out of sight. I'm pretty sure she bruised a couple ribs with her elbow. It's super pointy."

I love hearing how they tease one another. My family was like that before Sam died. We're slowly getting back there, but it's not the same. He was the jokester. Hearing Marco makes me miss Sam, but it also fills a hole that's been there since the day the Marine and Navy chaplain showed up at my parents' door. The Doyles were over, and we were watching the Super Bowl. I haven't watched that game since.

"What's your aesthetic? That's what it's called, right?"

"Or just style. I like Cape Cod meets Miami. Mostly soft colors with a lot of white, but a few punches of bright color here and there. I have a balcony with two white Adirondack chairs on it. They have neon green pillows. I have coral Havana shutters on the bedroom windows. I don't know if you can picture it, but it works."

"I'm sure it does. I saw all of the loft. You have impeccable taste."

"Thanks. It's easy to do with the budget I had."

"From the sounds of it, it could have been completely gaudy and gauche. But you made it very elegant."

"That was the goal. What about your place? Is it purely functional like Enzo's?"

"Don't get me wrong. His is comfy, but it's just not homey. It actually sounds like our tastes run very similarly. I have colonial shutters instead of Havana, but they're sort of close."

Close enough. They both are affixed to the sides of the windows, as opposed to Bahamas shutters, which open like an awning.

"Since I live on the top floor, mine are interior shutters."

"I live in a walk-up in Brooklyn. Mine are interior, too."

I know both are rather unusual, but my guess is he has them for the same reason as me. They're practical, but they also personalize the space in a way you can't do from the outside of an apartment or condo building.

"I have a few Miami-esque Art Deco pieces, but mostly, it's Cape Cod comfy."

"Overstuffed sofas with throw pillows? Blankets perfectly laid over the backs?"

I laugh since I can't picture him like that at all. But he pulls out his phone and unlocks it. He taps a couple things before he pulls up a photo of his entire family there watching a soccer game. Maria and Carlotta— I think she's his aunt —both have their hands out in front of Gabriele.

"He lost a lot of money to them that day. Everyone else was way more conservative with their bets. He took a gamble betting against them. We warned him."

"Are they avid soccer fans?"

"Maria played in college and even on a co-ed team during med school. Auntie Carlotta coached Maria's high school team to state championships the four years she played varsity along with the two before and one after. So yeah, they're fans."

"Wow."

"Did you play sports?"

"Yes. Laura and I both swam. Michelle dove. All three of us played water polo."

"Your sister really is more competitive than she comes across, isn't she?"

"Yes. She can make Laura and me look like pussycats. She hides her claws until a second before she sinks them in."

He presses his lips behind my ear, his warm breath making me shiver when he whispers to me.

"I intend to make you purr, little one. Are you free tomorrow night?"

"Mmmhmm."

It was more of a moan than a hum to confirm. Just as I'm about to turn my head to kiss him, the car rolls to a stop. I glance out the window and realize we've gotten to my place. Why couldn't we just be at a stoplight? Or better yet, why didn't we get stuck in any traffic on the bridge? Oh, that's right.

It's eleven o'clock at night. There's never traffic when you need it.

"Come on, *piccolina*."

He places me beside him, then opens the door. He steps onto the sidewalk and offers me his hand. When I get out, I'm prepared to say goodnight, but he puts his hand on one of my favorite spots. My lower back. I don't know why it does this thing to me where my pussy aches, but it does. I lead the way in, and we're quiet until we get to my door. He doesn't invite himself in, but I can tell he's sweeping every inch of my apartment that he can see.

"Would you like to come in?"

I want him to, and it seems like the polite thing to do. But he hesitates. And that crushes my soul.

"Beth, would I be coming in as your friend or something else?"

"I— I —my friend." *I guess.*

"You said you want to keep things to the club."

"I do."

I rush to answer because I feel like that's what I'm supposed to say. But it's not what I mean. Not what I want.

"Then, I think I better go."

"You don't want to be friends?"

I thought I was crushed before.

He holds the door open for me to walk through, then he follows me and shuts it behind him. I put my stuff on the dining room table and kick off my heels. His hands touch my waist for a moment before he pulls away, and I turn around.

"Of course, I want to be your friend. I can control myself, Beth. As much as it might kill me, I can. But you are every temptation I could ever imagine."

"And you once caught a fish this big."

I hold my hands apart.

"I'm not exaggerating. It was a struggle to not touch you more at the loft, and it's a struggle now. I didn't want the car ride to end."

"Me neither."

We stare at each other, and it feels so sad. Like we both want to say and do more, but we can't. Is it really because our siblings got married? Is it really because we agreed to keep everything at the club? No. I think we're both too chicken-shit to do anything in case the other rejects it.

"Tomorrow, *piccolina*."

"Okay, Daddy."

He kisses my cheek, then he's walking out. The door shuts softly behind him. Why did I let him leave?

Chapter Seven

Marco

Adulting blows. Like massive chunks. Enzo and Chelle are back— which is great because I missed my brother. But they're busy moving in together, and he's just dumped the responsibility for all our strip clubs onto my lap. They've passed hands as one guy after another has gotten married. None of us are into them as patrons, but they're mainly cash businesses. They make it easy to launder money, so that's a main reason to keep them. They're also unofficial offices for us. It's where we hold a lot of business meetings with men who don't want to be seen walking into the Mancinelli Developers' building and definitely don't want us walking into theirs.

But when are strip clubs the busiest? At night. What does that mean for my plans? They're fucked. It was my turn to cancel on Beth the night after we had the most mind-blowing sex I'd had up till then. I didn't want to tell her where I had to be instead of with her, but if she found out I lied, it would ruin everything. I'm certain she wasn't thrilled, but what could I do?

That was three weeks ago, and we've met at the club four out of seven nights each week. Each time we've talked a little longer during our post coital bliss. Neither of us suggests meeting outside the club, and neither of us hints at something more or that this is something more.

We've been helping our siblings move today after three weeks of splitting their time between here and Enzo's penthouse, and it's pure torture seeing her but not being able to touch her, talk to her alone. I'm fucking over it and doing something about it right now.

"What type of salad do you want, Enzo?"

"Greek. Chellie, what do you want?"

"Mmm. Cobb, please."

"Liz, why don't you come with me? I could use a hand carrying everything since I'll have the pizza too. Would you mind?"

I caught myself before I called her Beth. She looks surprised for a second. Was it by the name or the fact that I invited her to come with me? She glances at Chelle and Enzo before she nods. She leans over to Chelle and whispers none too quietly.

"We'll be back in thirty. We'll be sure to be nice and loud when we get back."

I hadn't thought about that, but my brother looks like he's ready to devour his bride. I pray I've been hiding my desire for Beth better than Enzo hides his for Chelle. The moment the elevator doors close, we're stuck together like magnets. I fumble but find the stop button. I press her into the corner, my hands sliding down the front of her shorts.

"You're awfully wet, *piccolina*."

"That's your fault."

"Mmm. Do you want me?"

"As much as you want me."

She cups my dick, which has been at half-mast since I saw her walk through the front door. Thank God these are looser jeans than some of mine.

"I'm going to make you come, but you're going to beg first."

I dip my fingers into her pussy, and she coats them. It's easy to slide them all the way to the base. Her hips rock as I stroke her velvety cunt. All I can think about is how badly I want to fuck her right now. Kinky. Vanilla. Whatever the fuck we can manage as long as I'm inside her. She's running her hand over the top of my jeans and driving me crazy.

"Take me out."

She tugs at the belt, the button, and the fly before drawing me out of the opening in my boxers. I knew I wore these for a reason.

"Would it shock you to know I want you to titty fuck me then suck you off?"

Her voice is soft, but it's not a whisper. She might have phrased it as a question, but it's a declaration that nearly brings me to my knees. I fist her hair and hold her head in place.

"I'm going to take you up on that offer the next time I have you naked. I'm going to watch my cock slide past those plump lips."

She knows I don't just mean the ones on her mouth, but she licks those to tease me. I dive in for a kiss and work her cunt faster. She squirms, trying to ride my fingers harder. She reaches between us to press my hand deeper, but I pull out.

"Marco."

She whimpers my name.

"Who decides, little one?"

"You, Daddy."

"That's right. If you need to come, ask."

"Will you make me come, please?"

"Not yet."

I work her until she's close again. Her hand feels divine on my cock, but I'm forcing myself to concentrate more on her than what she's doing to me. If I don't, I'm going to come before I let her get off. That's not what I want. I push her to the edge one more time before I pull my hands out of her shorts and lick my fingers.

"Marco!"

She clutches my shirt as she trembles with unspent lust. I push myself back into my pants before starting the elevator again. She stares at me stunned. I pull her against my chest as we ride down to the ground floor. She's pissed, and I can feel her frustration and disappointment pulsing through her. She turns to pull away and head down the street. We could walk to the restaurant, but I steer her toward my town car. Normally, Luigi would be my driver today. But we're still deciding what to do with him. We need to be certain he isn't fucking us over. We believe him to a point. He still got in bed with the feds.

Pauly opens the door, and Beth looks up at me. She gets in, and I'm certain she's confused since the place is only three blocks away. But I have other plans. I trust Pauly's discretion more than just about anyone's.

"We're headed to Michelangelo's, but take the long way."

He nods, and I know he'll give me at least twenty minutes before he pulls up. He won't open the door until I tap on the window. We're on each other again the moment we're alone. I lift her to straddle me, and she presses her tits together through her shirt, but it isn't enough. I rush to unbutton it, tempted to unfasten her bra. She beats me to it.

"Daddy, may I take my bra off?"

"Mmhmm."

It's a front clasp, so she releases it. I reach both hands up to fondle her as I lick and suck. This position isn't what I want—

need. I lie her back on the seat, and she wiggles down her shorts. I narrow my eyes as I watch Beth peel off her panties.

"Wear panties again, and I'll light a fucking fire and burn them. Then I'll toss in every other pair you own. When I want your pussy, nothing is getting in the way. Do you understand, little girl?"

She shivers, but I see the excitement in her eyes.

"I asked a question. Do you understand, little girl?"

"Yes, Daddy."

I waste no time settling between her thighs, her legs hooked over my shoulders. I brush my thumbs over her nipples until they're hard. I capture them between my thumbs and forefingers and pinch mercilessly as I practically swallow her clit. She can't help but scream. I don't stop, instead pinching harder.

"Please, may I come?"

"Mmm-mmm."

I shake my head and twist her nipples tighter. It's painful, and she loves it. I know she does from the sounds she's making. Then I'm rubbing the sensitive nubs as I kiss the insides of her thighs. I push up to rest one knee on the seat. One of her legs falls to the floor. The other rests at my waist.

"Unfasten my pants, *piccolina*."

She looks all butterfingers, but she rushes to undo the belt and button before she pulls down the zipper. She sees my cock pressing against the front of my boxers. She grabs the waistline and yanks out and down.

"Do not wear these fucking things again. Daddy."

She tacks that on as an afterthought.

"You think to give me orders?"

I pick her up and turn her over like a rag doll. I place her onto her hands and knees. My hand crashes down on her left ass cheek, then the right. Then it lands across them both. I lean over her and whisper.

"I like it when you think to give me commands. I like you possessive like that. But don't think you'll always get what you want. I ultimately decide, *piccolina*. Can you live with that?"

"Yes—"

"What were you going to say?"

"Nothing."

The spank that lands across her horizontal crack almost shoots her into the door. My arm wraps around her waist and pulls her back.

"Do not lie to me, Beth. Say you don't want to tell me. I'll respect that. Your thoughts are your own. But lie to me, and we stop. There are going to be enough of those already if we're keeping this a secret. I don't want more."

"I'm sorry, Daddy."

I pull her up, so her back is against my chest.

"This is something serious. No dominant/submissive play. I mean this as Marco and you as Beth. Don't lie. You can always tell me you don't want to share your thoughts. I hate that it's not fair of me to demand that. I know it's not fair because I'm sure you know there are parts of my life I can never tell you. But I don't want lies when there don't have to be."

"Yes, Marco. I'm sorry."

"It's all right."

I kiss her neck and ease her down to the seat, turning her onto her back again. I return to sucking her tits as she digs her fingers into my shoulders. She needs more, and I know it. I need it too. My cock is sliding along her pussy, and I'm flexing my hips like I would if I were pumping my dick into her.

"I have a condom in my purse."

I glare at her. I hate the idea she has it for someone else. When I pull out my wallet and get my own, she returns my expression. She doesn't want to think about me fucking someone else just as much as I don't want to think about that with her. She wraps her hand around my wrist.

"Wait a second."

She digs in her purse and grabs her phone and unlocks it. She scrolls through what appears to be her personal email until she finds what she wants. She turns her phone for me to see. It's lab results from two weeks ago. It shows she's clean. I haven't been with anyone without a condom since grad school.

I reach into my pocket and pull out my phone, scrolling until I find what I want. It's the same thing she showed me. We must be on the same schedule for Lab.Oratory. We have to provide quarterly proof of STI testing.

"I have an IUD."

"Are you saying you don't want me to wear a condom?"

"If you're okay with it."

I shove the condom and wallet back into my pocket before I push my pants and boxers down my legs. My hands come to rest at the end of the seat beside her head. I thrust into her and sigh.

"You want to feel me bare, *piccolina*. But what you really want is to feel my cum on your thighs."

"You're right. It feels better for you, doesn't it?"

"Fucking perfection, little girl."

I move, and her eyes drift closed as she concentrates. She grasps my ass and pushes me deeper. I reach back, grab her wrists, forcing her hands over her head. I guide them to wrap around the end of the seat, mine covering hers. She splays her fingers, and I lace them. She does what she can to push her left leg against the floor and her right against the seat to lift her hips in rhythm with my thrusts.

"Open your eyes. I want to see you as I make you come. I want you to see what you do to me, Beth. You make me want to lose control, but I won't."

"I want you to. Please."

"No. I'll never lose complete control. I'm too much bigger and too much stronger. I'd hurt you and never forgive myself."

"Then just harder. So much harder."

I oblige, slamming into her, my pubic bone rubbing her clit. I press my chest to hers as we kiss. My fingers flex over and over as the need to come creeps into my core.

"Come for me, *piccolina*. Let me take care of you."

"I want that, Daddy."

"Call me that again, *piccolina*."

"Daddy."

Saying it seems to push her closer to coming. She strains beneath me.

"Come."

The single command detonates something within in us. Pleasure and a hint of my coming release floods me as she cries out my name.

"Marco!"

I pick up the pace, pounding into her even harder. I love her calling me Daddy. I want to hear her call me that again.

"I'm going to make you come again before I fill you with my cum. When I do, you will take it all. Your greedy little pussy is going to suck it all in."

"Yes, Daddy!"

The dirty talk. It often annoys me and seems so stupid when it's forced. But when we do it, it's a massive turn on. It's because it's Beth. If the women I scene— scened —with said that shit about me doing it to them, I'd roll my eyes and tune it out. Since I've never gone bareback with any of them, I've never uttered those words before.

I release her hands and pull her hips up. She wraps her legs around my waist as I keep thrusting into her.

"Fucking hell. That feels so good, Daddy. Don't stop. Yes... I'm coming... I'm coming."

One elbow comes to rest next to her ribs, and I slide that forearm under her shoulder to fist her hair. Then I feel it. I close my eyes for a second before snapping them open. I want to watch her as she comes. Not where my cock enters her pussy. I want to watch her face. We are those magnets nothing can separate.

"Beth!"

I'm still shooting my cum into her when I scoop her up and sit down with her in my lap again. She flops forward, resting her head against my left shoulder. I pin her against me as we both pant. Her left hand goes to my opposite cheek, and she nudges me to look at her.

"Kiss."

It's once again gentle. So tender that it makes my heart ache. We keep doing something that could upset our siblings. We both know that. Neither of them would approve of me bringing Beth into our world just to be a friend with benefits. We sit together, neither wanting to ruin the moment. I know I don't know what to say. I don't think she does either. Every time we come together, it becomes more and more intimate. I don't have the same detachment I usually do. From the way her hand rests on my cheek, her fingertips brushing my stubble, I don't think she's indifferent either. We aren't keeping this at the club, I guess.

But we can't dawdle forever, and we've already been outside the pizza place for at least ten minutes. We make ourselves presentable, and I open the door. I help her out, and we go in. Twenty minutes and a chat about our favorite childhood books later, we opt to walk back to Enzo and Chelle's. We shift to talking about our favorite family vacations. Pauly follows in the town car, which puts me at ease since I'm not carrying my gun. I have my knife in my left pocket since I'm left-handed.

"You were gone for ages."

Chelle takes the bag of salads Beth carried, and Enzo grabs the bag of sodas and pizza I had. It's cute to watch them in the kitchen together as they get our plates and glasses. I slide my gaze over to Beth, thinking how nice it would be if that was us one day. These daydreams are getting me nowhere but Blue Ballsville. When our eyes meet, I think she might be thinking the same thing.

We weren't at Enzo's long this morning since he had so little to move. It doesn't take us long to finish up here. Chelle and Beth work in the master bedroom to get the closets and bathroom organized. I help Enzo set up his computers in the third bedroom. Now Chelle and Enzo each have their own office since it's a three-bedroom apartment. The square footage is about three-quarters the size of Enzo's four-bedroom penthouse, but I agree it's a much nicer place for a couple.

"What's going on between you and Liz?"

I'm unprepared for Enzo's question, so it takes everything in me not to react.

"What do you mean?"

"I saw you two glancing at each other. Are you interested in her?"

"I—"

"Don't lie, Marco. I already know the answer."

I scowl at my baby brother who's as tall as me and weighs about five pounds more.

"She's attractive and intelligent."

"She is. But that doesn't answer the question."

"She's your sister."

"But she isn't yours. You are interested."

I say nothing, instead pretending to pay attention as I plug a cord into his computer tower. What the fuck do I say?

"Dude, if you're into her, ask her out."

I nearly slam my head into the desk as I look up at him. We don't just casually date. That's why this shit is so complicated. If she and I go out, it's because I'm truly ready to bring her all the way into this world and keep her here. I won't string her along romantically. I won't date her and remain emotionally closed off, only to hurt her. She might be fine with her sister marrying a Mafioso, but I don't know if she'd even consider it for herself.

"I'm not ready to propose."

"Don't be an ass. A date isn't a proposal. You might not be compatible, so it wouldn't even be an issue."

I know we're compatible in one area.

"And if it doesn't work? I don't want to make anything uncomfortable for you or Chelle."

"And if it does work?"

"You and I both know there is a far greater likelihood she won't want any part of our life when she learns what it really means. Chelle will shelter her from it because you'll shelter your wife."

That's what I really fear. I can tell myself every which way from Sunday that my hesitation comes from not wanting to rock the boat with Enzo and Chelle. But it's really the possibility that Beth might reject me. That I'll open myself up to her, and she'll walk away. And I would let her. None of that fucking TV bullshit about sleeping with the fishes or now you know, I'll have to kill you. There's so much she would never know.

That's another issue. The other men in my family might be fine telling half-truths and full-on lies to their wives, but I don't want that. I don't want to lie by omission, and I sure as shit don't want to look Beth in the eye and know that what I tell her is full of crap. It would only be to protect her, but I hate the idea that I would spend the next five decades deceiving her. She deserves better than that. I don't want to be that type of man. I'm not looking down on my dad or the others. I just don't think I could live with it. I sure as fuck couldn't live with telling her the truth. She'd never see me as anything but a monster.

And that boils down to another truth I don't want to examine. I am a monster. I do fucked-up things in the name of family. I don't regret any of it. I won't stop, and I have no interest in changing. It means the people I love and the people who depend on me are alive. I have absolutely no limits to what I will do to protect them. And that makes me completely depraved and indifferent to human life. I don't think I'm a psychopath who kills indiscriminately. I don't get any kind of rush or thrill from it, though it is fulfilling at times.

That moral void in me isn't something I want Beth sucked into. I don't want to taint her with the underworld's stench. I know the women in my family— by birth and by choice —navigate this shit. I know they love the men in my family and would do anything for them and for all of us. But the one thread or spark of conscience I have screams loudly enough that I can't ignore it.

Keep Beth out of this!

"Earth to Marco."

"Huh?"

Fuck.

"Sorry. I was thinking about the plumbing crack at T&A. I think there's a slab leak."

"Bullshit. You were not thinking about a strip club, though you might have been thinking about tits and ass."

"I got bored with your rambling. Thinking about work was more interesting than you talking about something that doesn't exist."

"Liar."

"Fucking ask Vincente about the leak."

There is a leak, but I was thinking about a certain set of tits and ass.

"Whatever. They aren't my problem anymore."

I know. I don't want the trouble of dealing with the women there. We have managers who are good at what they do, but one of us still oversees the payroll and liquor inventories. We don't trust anyone outside of our family with ultimate control of any of our businesses. At one point, all the men in my generation were single *and* rich. I'm the only one left that's true for. Some dancers and waitresses care a little too much about that. I'm not in the mood to fend off false interest. I'm not into arm candy, and I prefer to play the stock market than the gold digger one.

"Don't remind me. I'm going in the morning before any of the women arrive. I'm not in the mood for any bullshit. I want to deal with the plumbers and go."

"What? You don't want Denise trying to swallow your tongue again?"

Motherfucker.

I look up to notice Beth and Chelle in the doorway just as Enzo finishes speaking.

"I didn't want it near me the first or last time, and I don't want it near me now. Who the fuck knows where it's been."

Well, shit. That just made me sound like a dick. But I don't want Beth thinking I fuck strippers. That I fuck employees.

"Maybe—"

"I'll deal with the leak and any damage. Carmine can send a crew over to deal with any plaster or baseboard repair. I can order new furniture if it's as bad as we think. The guys can be there to receive the shipment when it comes in. I'm not wasting my day there."

I plug in the last cord and stand. Beth doesn't know where

to look, and I can tell Enzo is being a smug bastard. He was testing me, and in the process made Beth feel crappy. But if I point that out, then I'll confirm there's something between us.

Chelle looks at Enzo, then me, then Beth.

"Are you doing a remodel or something?"

I glance at Beth before settling my gaze on Chelle.

"Hopefully, it won't come to that. It's just one of the back rooms. We might need some new tiles and chairs."

"If it's a bigger job, you know an interior designer."

Beth's stomach sucks in at her sister's comment, but her expression doesn't change. She doesn't move, and she doesn't look at me. At least not in the eye. I think she's looking at my right shoulder. She knows there's an ace of *bastoni*— clubs — there. She doesn't know it means "boss" or that I got it when I became a *capo*. My tank top strap always covers it since it's as unique as the map of Italy is large.

She probably guessed what *A vita o a morti*— life or death in Sicilian —means when she saw the small print on my right ribs. I got that after my first mission. I hid it from my mother for eight months because I was fifteen. My dad found out the day I did it, and that was horrible. But it was my first tattoo, and Mama cried. She said she'd made a perfect little person, and I'd defaced her creation. Guilt from a Sicilian mother rivals any in the world.

"I know how big Liz's high-rise project was. I don't know that she has time for something so boring."

I try to get her off the hook, but now she meets my gaze and cocks an eyebrow. Is she challenging me? Does she think I'm trying to keep her away for any other reason than I don't want her to go somewhere I don't want to linger? I'm happy to pick shit from an Ikea catalogue and order that.

"Do you?"

I give her the option, expecting her to turn me down.

"If it's not that big a project, I'm sure I can squeeze it in. What time should I drop by?"

She sounds casual, but I recognize the hint of stubbornness from the first time we encountered each other at the club. My gaze hardens, and her lips twitch. She is testing me. She wants to play a little game— a private little game. Very well.

"Be there at eight."

"Sounds good."

As she and I walk out of the building half an hour later, she whispers to me.

"I take pole dance classes instead of swimming these days. Maybe I can practice before class tomorrow night."

Before I can say a word, she hails a cab and jogs to the curb. I'm left there standing slack jawed with my dick swinging in the wind.

Chapter Eight

Beth

So much for keeping things at the club. I've been replaying the car ride to the pizzeria over and over and over since yesterday afternoon. Who am I kidding? I'm like a kitten he petted once who now trails him everywhere. I want more than just hooking up at our club. I want more than just a quickie in the backseat of a car or a crazy kiss in an elevator.

Me and my dumbass mouth. I'm the one who said we had to limit it. But I said it before he could. I was worried he only wanted bootie calls, and I couldn't bear to have that suspicion confirmed. So, I spoke before he could. Was I wrong?

Maybe.

The way he came to my rescue at Ivy. What he risked by going into the lions' den. Did that mean anything more than he's a chivalrous guy? I'm reading too fucking much into it. I know he wants to fuck me, which is pretty fucking flattering in and of itself. He said I'm too tempting and that he wants me more than any other woman, but is that just dirty talk? Is it just physical? After three weeks of amazing sex and getting to know each other afterwards, I want to know if the pillow talk means something. But I don't want to find out my feelings are one-sided. Humiliating and heartbreaking. I'd rather exist in limbo than find out my feelings are unreciprocated.

"Excuse me."

I just put my foot on the sidewalk from the last step up to my building when a guy slams into me. The sidewalk is crowded but not so congested he couldn't move around me. I apologize, but he says nothing. He just pushes past and nearly knocks me off my feet. Luckily, I'm in flats.

"Asshole."

I mutter it under my breath and check my purse. It's zipped, so I know he didn't just pickpocket me. I dig around in my slim, black portfolio briefcase. It's old-fashioned by most standards, but I think it looks sophisticated and perfectly cliché for a New York interior designer. There's nothing in there that he could have dropped. I've lived in the city since I was twenty-three. I'm adequately suspicious of strangers.

I check over my shoulder, and he's standing at the end of the block on the phone, looking in the other direction. Marco texted me the address last night, so I head to the subway, taking the G Brooklyn-Queens Crosstown. The car is packed during rush hour, so it's elbow to elbow.

I keep my bags pressed against my front; shoulders rounded to keep from being bumped around too badly. But when we get to my stop, I have to muscle my way through the six people in front of me. I follow in the wake of a guy much bigger than me. But I'm jostled from the back and nearly stumble over the gap between the train and the platform.

As I change directions toward the stairs, I glance back at who pushed me. My nose is practically in the guy's chest. The temptation to shove my elbow into his gut is real. Back off, fuck sack. But I ignore him once I get onto the street. I look around to orient myself since I'm not familiar with this part of Queens. I see the cross street I need, having set my GPS before I left my place. I tap start and listen as it tells me where to go. I'm focused on that, but I'm always aware of what's going on around me. I know that guy is still way too close. I noticed the one I followed off the car is now moving slower, so I'm catching up to him.

I turn off the audio to my navigation, not needing to announce to everyone where I'm headed. I scan the surrounding area as the hair on my nape rises. Something is fucking off. Like super off. I want to take an unexpected side street to see if I'm truly being followed, but I don't know my way around well enough to do that. I look over at the road and see a cab letting a man out about fifty feet behind me. I dart to the curb and hail the car. I blurt the address as I watch out the window.

"That's like a block away."

"I know. I hurt my ankle. Thanks."

I don't owe him an explanation, especially since I'll give him like a seventy-five percent tip. Actually, it's better than that. It's four bucks, and I shove a ten at him. I scramble out of the vehicle, looking around. The man who bumped into me in front of my place is standing two buildings over from the strip club. I look back, and the two men from the subway are waiting to cross the street.

Please let the door be unlocked. Please.

I bolt for the strip club's front door and yank on it. Sweet Baby J. It's locked, but a guy turns around and pushes it open.

"Ma'am?"

"Marco. Is he here yet?"

"Beth?"

I look over and see him crossing the floor from the bar. I run toward him, and he envelopes me in his arms.

"Beth?"

"Followed."

"What?"

He's rubbing my back, but he tries to push me back when he realizes what I said. I shake my head and burrow closer. I drop my bags on the floor and wrap my arms around his waist. I freeze. It's like slow motion when I lean back. I know what I just felt at his lower back when my arms slid beneath his suit coat.

"Who followed you, Beth? Where are they?"

I blink, then gather my wits.

"There's three of them. One of them is two buildings to the left." I point. "And two more were about to cross the street."

Marco looks over my head and gestures his toward the door. I watch four guys hurry outside. He bends and grabs my bags, then I squeak when he sweeps me into his arms. It'd be fucking *Officer and a Gentleman* romantic if this weren't such a fucked-up situation. He carries me to an office and punches in a code. I hear it unlock before he pushes down on the handle. He hoists me a little higher, so he can put my stuff on the desk, then he sits with me on his lap.

"Tell me what happened, *piccolina*."

"In a moment. Why do you have a gun, Marco?"

His eyes bore into me, but he says nothing. I wait, but I know he won't be forthcoming.

"Marco, answer me. I'm serious. Why the hell do you have a gun in broad daylight?"

"Don't ask questions you already know the answer to."

My chin jerks back. I guessed what Chelle was getting into when she said she was with a Mancinelli. It was all silently confirmed at the reception. But it's now smacking me in the face that I've wound up in the middle of it, too.

"Those men followed me because of us."

"Yes."

"How do they— Do they know—"

"I can't give you an answer to how they know or if they know about the club because I don't have one yet."

Yet.

Is he going to use that gun to get it?

"Beth, I'm not going to walk out and shoot someone."

Am I that transparent?

"Lean back and let me hold you while I collect my own thoughts. Someone following you is rattling me."

He eases me against his chest, and I can hear his heart's racing. As fast as his heartbeat is, it's soothing to have it under my cheek. I put my palm next to my face. His left hand wraps around me to stroke my arm while his right hand strokes my back. He kisses the crown of my head. I sigh and melt against him.

"I knew I just had to get to you, Daddy."

I don't know if he heard me because my voice is so faint.

"I will always protect you, *piccolina*. Always come to me."

There's a knock on the door, and I curl into him.

"*Avete qualcuno?*" Do you have someone?

"No."

"*Ti troverò più tardi.*" I'll find you later.

"Marco?"

"Shh. It's all right. They didn't find anyone, but I'll talk to them in a bit."

"Shouldn't we get to work? You made it sound like you didn't want to be here long today."

"I'm not done holding you, *cuore*."

That sorta sounds like heart in French. Who am I to argue?

I'm feeling calmer every moment he's holding me. Finding he has a gun freaked me out after being followed. Now I find it reassuring. And honestly, not that surprising now that I'm not terrified of being attacked or kidnapped. But it leaves me thinking about something I never planned to bring up with him because we're supposed to be friends with benefits. I sit up, but I don't try to get off his lap.

"Chelle confided something in me when she slept at my place before the wedding. It's something I'm certain you already know."

I watch him, and his expression grows wary.

"She told me about our family's ties to the O'Rourkes. Marco, I already knew. I'll tell you how if you want, but is your family the same as theirs? Tell me the truth. Are you in the mob?"

"No."

I start to pull away. I knew the answer. I just wanted to hear it from him, but he's lying to me.

"Wait, Beth. Stop. The mob is *the* Irish. The O'Rourkes. *The* Russians are the bratva, and that's the Kutsenkos along with their Andreyev family. The Diazes are *the* Colombian Cartel. My family are *the* Italians. We are the Mafia with a capital M. *Cosa Nostra* to be exact. Mob and mafia are tossed around interchangeably, but in our world, we know who's who. We aren't the same."

Aren't the same? I'm pretty sure they're a fuck ton alike.

"Are you saying that if I hear about those countries in reference to American organized crime, those are the families you're talking about?"

"Yes. Technically, we're Sicilian. But no one on this side of the Atlantic seems to get the difference. That's not the hill we die on."

That does nothing to reassure me when I know he has a

gun strapped to his back. I once called them The Big Four when I mentioned them all at the reception. Apparently, I wasn't so far off.

"Chelle told me about our family history with the O'Rourkes. I never told her or anyone else that I already knew. I'm the same age as you and Dillan, but I dated Shane for nearly a year in high school without anyone knowing. I went to a Christmas party with my grandparents when I was a junior, and he was a sophomore. We hit it off, and I didn't know about his family. We dated for two months before I noticed how secretive he got about stuff. I mentioned his family offhand one day to my parents, and they clammed up. I tried to a dig a little with my grandmother, and she warned me to stay away from the little reprobates. Neither of us lied about it, but neither of us did anything to draw attention to our relationship. But I broke up with him about ten months in because he got into some big fight at a party, but he wouldn't tell me why."

"I know exactly what party you're talking about, and I know exactly how badly he got beaten up."

Oh, shit.

"You do?"

"I do."

We stare at each other for a long time, then I finally say it.

"You did it, didn't you?"

"Most of it. Misha finished what I started."

"Misha? He was there?"

"Beth, my life is so far past fucked-up I don't even know what to call it."

He closes his eyes and tilts his head back. I don't know what to do since I think he's going to shut down. But a moment later, he looks at me.

"The four families all lived close enough in Queens that we were zoned for the same high school. We used to play little league and peewee sports together. One night in high school, we all wound up at a party together. Usually, we steered clear and had our own sets of friends. But that night, Juan and Pablo's cousins insulted Maria when she stuck up for a friend who had a crush on one of the *Tres J's*. One of the three called Maria a bitch, and I overheard him. When Luca and Matteo saw me rush Javier, they came over. Maria knew to get out of the way and pulled her friend out, too. Pablo and Juan, along with their other cousin Alejandro, came to help the *Tres J's*. Carmine and Gabriele heard the noise and us yelling in Italian to one another. Once they joined in, the O'Rourkes decided to stir the shit up even more by egging us on. Pasha asked Maria what happened, and she told him. That family has absolutely no tolerance for anyone mistreating women. They jumped in to defend Maria, which only pissed my brothers, cousins, and me off because they said we couldn't defend her properly. Long story short, it turned into a melee when the O'Rourkes did more than just shit talk because Luca accidentally punched Cormac instead of Niko. People fled, and Maria got out of there with her friend. Shots were fired, and knives stabbed and slashed. It was bad."

"You have an old scar near your right kidney. It's round and sort of puckered."

"Yeah. That was courtesy of Alejandro. Fucker shot me from behind."

I sit dumbfounded. What the hell do I say to that? We're the same age, so he was sixteen when that happened.

"Wait. What were Carmine and Gabriele doing there? They were only fourteen."

"They were freshman."

As though that explains everything. As I stare at him, I guess it does in his world.

"What happened?"

"We heard the sirens, so we all fled. The house we were at backed up to woods, so we spread out into our families and hid. I was so sure all the blood would lead them straight to us. I found out later Maria recognized a cop from where she hid in the neighbor's backyard. She went and whispered to her who was there. The woman's dad worked directly under Papa. Once the family names got out, the cops packed up and took off. Uncle Salvatore had never been as angry before as he was that night. He yelled at us in English, Italian, and Itanglese."

That must be like Spanglish but with Italian.

"As bad as that was, it was worse facing Auntie Carlotta. She's a surgeon and had to patch us all up. We all thought we were so grown up after that fight and had balls of steel. Since we were men, a few of us thought we could swear while we got our stitches. Hell. She made us *all* limp into the kitchen and handed out bars of soap. I seriously thought she was going to go through with it. I really thought she was going to make us wash our mouths out. She has the least tolerance for profanity. She didn't care that we were in pain or half doped out of our minds on the meds she gave us."

I shouldn't laugh. And I'm really trying not to. But the image that conjures makes me nearly choke as I hold back.

"I got the feeling Shane got in a bunch of trouble, too."

"We all did. Liam was in charge back then, and this psychopath named Vlad ran the bratva. Enrique and Uncle Sal led our two families. All of them lost their shit. It would have been World War Three if anyone had been seriously hurt or killed. It would have set off a street war. We got so fucking lucky because some of the other guys were just as badly injured. We all learned a lot from that night."

I can't believe he shared that much with me. Maybe he could because it's from so far in the past, but it was a ton of insight into his world.

"Beth, what did Shane tell you back then about his family?"

"Not much. It was more about my family. I know both of my mother's grandfathers were high up. People even thought her dad would takeover instead of Liam. But he wanted out. I don't know the deal he made, but Shane said it had to be something big for them to let him out when he wanted to marry my grandmother. I guess they didn't totally release him until my mom and aunts were born. Chelle told me they've been watching out for my family as part of that deal. But my mom basically fired them when my parents accepted Enzo as their son-in-law."

"Did Shane tell you that his family was watching out for yours?"

"No. I had no idea back then. I haven't thought about him or his family in years, but it pissed me off to find that out from Chelle. He could have told me someone was watching me all those years ago."

"These men who followed you. What did they look like?"

"Nondescript. They didn't look stereotypically anything. Not Latinx, not Eastern European, not Irish, not Mediterranean. Just run-of-the-mill American."

"Did they say anything to you?"

"No. The first guy bumped into me hard as I was stepping onto the sidewalk outside my building. I checked my purse, which was still zipped. I felt around in my briefcase, but there was nothing missing and nothing extra in there. When I was getting off the subway, the guy behind me shoved me, and I nearly tripped. Then he was super close to me on the stairs. I noticed the guy I followed off the train was hanging back. I started walking here, then noticed a cab. I took it for the last block. When I got out, the guy from my apartment was two doors down. I have no idea how he got here ahead of me since he went in the opposite direction from the station after he pushed past me."

Marco reaches around me and turns on a computer then a monitor. I shift to make it easier for him to click and type. He pulls up security footage, and I see myself get out of the cab. He clicks around, and the view changes.

"There. That was the guy outside my building."

I look at Marco, but his face registers nothing. It's completely blank as though he wasn't looking at anything. He changes to another shot, looking down the block toward the light.

"Can you pause it?"

He does.

"Those two. The one right by the lamppost and the one next to the bus stop. They're the ones from the train."

I look at him again, but I can't read anything at all. He sits back, one arm on the armrest, and the other around my hips.

"Beth, I want to arrange a security detail for you. I don't know those men, but I know what kind of men they are. I don't want you going anywhere unless one of the men in my family is with you."

"What? I don't need babysitting, Marco."

His arm flies off the chair and grips my hip. The other goes up to my hair and holds me in place.

"No one is fucking babysitting you, Beth. You don't need someone to make sure you don't drink poison from under the sink or watch horror movies past your bedtime. What you need are trained men who can protect you from pieces of shit like those men who someone hired to do a lot more than just scare you. I will not budge even a millimeter on this. You will accept the bodyguards. You will not argue with me about this. Do you understand?"

He lets go of my hair, but his fingers bite into my hip.

"I understand what you're saying, but I don't agree."

"Why?"

"Because I want to know what the hell you mean by someone hired them to do a lot more than scare me. Is someone trying to kill me? Why does it have to be someone in your family? All the men are married. Won't their wives think that's inappropriate?"

"I don't know if someone is trying to kill you, but those men know how to. As for guards, it has to be someone in my family because no one else is good enough for you. I want at least one man I trust with my own life and those of the people I care about most to be with you. That means someone related to be my blood or by blood oath."

"Blood oath. What does that mean?"

He's pissed. Is it just because I'm arguing? Is it because he has to deal with this? Is it because he let something slip?

"You're about to get a lesson in our family tree. Matteo's father, Domenico, is my father's best friend. He's also Papa, Uncle Salvatore, and Auntie Paola's adopted second cousin. His wife, Matteo's mother, is Mama's best friend. Auntie Carlotta and Uncle Domenico are like second parents to me. I'm two-and-a-half hours older than Matteo. When we were twelve, we started carrying knives. Wonderful family tradition we have. We made a blood oath by slicing our palms. It was before we knew Uncle Domenico was adopted, so we thought we were already related. But we pledged to protect our families with our lives. Apparently, Carmine and Gabriele made the same sort of pledge when they became best friends about a month after Gabriele moved here when they were twelve. They'd just gotten their knives, too."

Chelle had already explained the family tree to me, so I knew who was related by blood, by marriage, and by long family ties. I had no idea about these boyhood oaths.

"Beth, ask Chelle. She'll tell you Enzo has the same rule for her. If she's going to work or some normal errand, then two regular guards go with her. But if it's anything other than routine, then one of my generation goes with her. That's the rule for all the wives."

"Wives, Marco. I'm—"

"More than my fuck buddy, and we both know it."

"I'm not."

His hand goes back to my hair, so he presses my head forward. He doesn't have to use any pressure. I lean into the kiss. He stands and leans me back on the edge of the desk, the keyboard digging into my right ribs. I shove it out of the way. His hand glides up my inner thigh.

"No panties, *piccolina*. Hoping I'd fuck you again?"

"You did in a car yesterday."

"And you ran to me."

"I was coming here, anyway."

"Beth, you got into a cab. You could have gone anywhere. You came to me."

I stare into his eyes, and there's no point in playing dumb.

"You're the only person I thought to go to. You're the only person who doesn't make me feel scared."

He eases his hold on my hair and smatters kisses over my cheek and the bridge of my nose.

"*Cuore*—"

"What does that mean?"

"Sweetheart. I'm more than a fuck buddy to you, and you are way more than that to me. We can pretend and waste time better spent together. I don't want to just meet to fuck at some club. I don't want to steal chances to taste you and pleasure you. And I sure as hell don't want to waste any opportunity to just hang out with you. Do you know how hard it was not to touch you at Enzo and Chelle's yesterday? To not be affectionate with you when they couldn't keep their hands off each other? Do you know how much I wanted to hold your hand while we walked back to their place? I want more than sex, Beth."

"Me too. To all of that. I felt the same way. I was too scared to admit it in case you didn't want it too."

"I was the same. But you coming here, you trusting me, gave me the balls to tell you what I want."

"Have you ever told anyone outside your family the stuff you just told me about your past?"

"Never."

"I thought so. Why did you?"

"Because I want you to know me, *piccolina*. I don't want to be closed off to you when I don't have to be. You've already seen that I won't let you know what I'm thinking if I don't want you to. You've already seen there are questions I won't answer. That will never change, and I hate it. But I will never knowingly endanger you, my family, or the people who depend on us. That means I have to keep things from you. But if it doesn't have to remain a secret, I don't want it to be."

I think about what he's told me, and it's a lot to take in. None of it is a turn off. Just the opposite.

"If I enter this world of yours— if I accept all of it —it's not just for a fling. If I let myself get close to you and all the danger that goes with it, then I want a real commitment, Marco."

"Beth, the only way I would let you into my life is if I believe we're in this for good."

For good? Now that makes my head spin a little.

"It was all or nothing for Chelle and Enzo. Is it like that for us?"

"If you ever want to walk away, I will never keep you from that choice. But I'm not going anywhere. I've thought about this non-stop since the reception. I didn't think I'd have the chance to get this close to you, but I knew if I did, I would be ready to commit."

"I told you Chelle hasn't told me everything, but I've guessed a lot. I accepted you and all that probably goes with you the moment I went into that room with you. *That* kiss that night. I knew I wouldn't walk away if you accepted me. It's been so bittersweet to think I might have something physical with you, but nothing more."

"Beth, I'll give you every bit of me I can. Some parts you'll never have. And that's just as well because that's not the man I want you to see. There's more I'll have to explain over time, and if it's too much for you, then you walk away with no questions asked."

"Marco, my sister is an excellent judge of character. She knew when she married Enzo, she was getting your entire family. I trust her. I know she's happy with the choices she made. I know there are other women who have married into your family over the years, and from what Chelle says, they're all happily married. That means something to me. It tells me a lot about your family and the man they must have raised you to be. That's why you're the only person I thought of when I got scared. I'm accepting who and what you are. I have no intention of walking away. You'd be the one to leave."

"There's no chance of that, *tesoro mio.*"

"What does that mean?"

"My treasure."

"*Mio?* Not *mia?*"

"*Tesoro* is fixed gender, so it's the masculine form even when said about a woman."

"I think I'm going to need a daily lesson in Italian."

"Mmm. I can think of plenty of ways to praise my best student."

"Your only student, Marco."

"I've been only yours since the moment we met. I fell for you immediately. Your rehearsal dinner speech was intelligent and witty. You looked so happy with your family. I couldn't stop staring. Then to dance with you at the reception was agonizing bliss."

"I don't think those two words go together."

"They do. I was so happy, but my body ached to touch all of you."

"When I got home, I couldn't stop thinking about you. Stop wanting you. I might have eased some of that while fantasizing about you. A few times."

I can't believe I just admitted that. He chuckles, and I cringe.

"No, no. I did the same thing. That's why I'm laughing. Beth, we have to go back to what we were talking about before. Will you accept a detail that includes a member of my family? We do it for all the women, so not a single wife will think it's odd if their husband guards you. They'll know what you mean to me the moment I ask."

"What do I mean to you?"

"My future."

Chapter Nine

Marco

Everything I've sworn since I became an adult flew out the window the moment I saw Beth's panicked expression. The moment she ran to me. Every pledge I made not to get involved and commit to a woman dissolved in a heartbeat. Everything I've secretly longed for with her rushed to the surface as I held her then carried her to the office. It's an exercise in futility to pretend I mean any of those promises anymore.

The woman in my arms is everything to me. I hate— loathe —that it took her being frightened for even a second for me to decide I won't ignore my feelings any longer. Certainly not now that I know they're reciprocated. Not now that I've let her in, and she's accepted me.

I reach between us and unzip my pants. I usually wear boxer briefs, but I wore boxers on a whim yesterday. I wore them with a purpose today. I guide my cock to her cunt and thrust. But I don't move more than that. She was leaning back on her elbows before, but now she sits up. She wraps her legs around me, and her arms are loose around my neck. We're just holding each other. We're close enough that she doesn't have to do more than whisper.

"Does this mean we're in a committed relationship? I want to see you as my future, too?"

"I think we have been since the beginning. Neither of us wanted to fuck anyone else. It just took us a little while to admit it."

I cup her cheek, and she leans into it. Her eyes close, and she sighs before leaning her head against my chest.

"Can we just stay like this for a moment? I just want to feel you inside me. I want to hold you too."

"I don't need to get off right now."

I lift her off the table and settle back in the chair. This is a connection unlike anything else. Our bodies are one, but that just feels like it's a demonstration of something way deeper. How is that possible? We haven't spent that much time together. We haven't gone out on dates and chatted into the wee hours of the morning. We've talked about things from our childhood, college, our careers, and we've talked about our family histories. But not a ton more than that.

I just know it in an elemental way. Something she radiates. Something about how she carries herself and the way she says things. It draws me, and I just know. My intuition keeps me alive nearly every day. Something will make my back tense, or some invisible thing presses against me. A nudge. Something will pulsate in my ear that my body absorbs. I don't know how to describe the intangible, but I just know in moments of danger that it's coming. It puts me on alert.

I don't have the sense of imminent danger with Beth. Just the opposite. It's all those sensations, but I feel at peace when it's her.

"Beth, will you stay with me tonight, please? I'd feel a lot better if you were within reach."

She sits up so she can see me.

"I'd prefer that too. Why would anyone take an interest in me? Did they see us getting the food yesterday and assume we were already a couple?"

"It could have been then. It could have been when we left Ivy together."

"It wouldn't be the Kutsenkos, would it?"

"No. If they had men following you, it would be for your safety. They would never let their men touch you. And they definitely wouldn't let their men intimidate you. They'd go after me instead."

"Would the O'Rourkes be pissed that another woman in my family is with another man in yours?"

"I don't think so. Your grandfather made their family swear to watch over yours. It was a condition of him getting out and agreeing to take the fall if he was ever busted."

"What?"

I can only sigh. She's about to get a lot of lessons in syndicate life.

"Every organization has the same principles. Our oaths might be called something different, but they boil down to the same thing. The organization comes before the individual. Always."

She stares at me for a moment before she nods. It's slow as though she's trying to wrap her head around it.

"For those of us in our leaders' inner circles, family comes before all else. Without us, the people who depend upon us are in danger. They're left vulnerable. The Mancinellis will always put the Mancinellis first. The O'Rourkes will always put the O'Rourkes first. Same with the Diazes and the Kutsenkos—plus their cousins' family."

Sergei and Misha are related to the Kutsenko brothers through their mothers, who are sisters. The only difference between the Andreyevs and the Kutsenkos— plus Pasha and Anton who are cousins through their dads —is the blond hair.

"If someone is arrested and convicted, they take our secrets to the grave. You never break your fealty."

"So, if they'd sent my grandfather to prison for a crime he didn't commit, he wouldn't have fought it."

"Yes."

"Does that mean you could wind up like that too?"

"It's a possibility. Beth, I can promise you I will always do everything in my power to come home to you. I can promise you I will always be faithful to you and that I want a long life together. But I can't guarantee anything other than my fidelity."

"You want a long life together?"

"I wouldn't let you anywhere near any of this if I didn't want to make a go of it like Enzo and Chelle. I'm certain he had a conversation very similar to this with your sister."

She takes a deep inhale before sighing.

"I'm certain too."

"About their conversation?"

"That, and I want that long life with you. I can't pinpoint what it is about you. We haven't known each other long, and there are tons about each other we don't know. Like I don't know your favorite color or band or movie. But I know that the — I don't know — I guess —aura you put out draws me like no one ever has. I can tell you're intelligent, hardworking, loyal, driven by duty, kind, funny, and you make me feel— right."

She shrugs and shakes her head. She doesn't know how to articulate it, and neither do I. Having her in my life feels as obvious as saying the sky is blue.

"Have you been arrested before?"

"Yes. More than a couple times. But I haven't been to prison. Papa is an exceptionally talented attorney, and now Gabe works for him, too."

I can guess what she's thinking. That we coerce people. That we tamper with evidence. That we eliminate complications. She isn't wrong. But she also isn't getting off my dick, which is staying surprisingly hard considering we aren't moving.

"What happens if you are arrested in the future?"

"If we're together, you leave. You get as far away from me as you can. You don't try to help, Beth. You get to my family as fast as you can. They'll know what to do. If we aren't together, they'll find you and protect you."

"What about if you get hurt? We're together— dating, I guess. I'm not family."

I run my hands up and down her arms. I don't want to scare her off by moving any faster than we already are.

"I don't know what you're going to want in the future. But the moment my family knows we're together, you become one of us. We don't date casually. We don't do flings. Until you, I swore up and down that I would never get involved with someone. It's selfish as fuck that I am. I didn't want to suck a woman into the hell hole that is Mafia life. But now that I know you, I can't let go. I don't want to. I wouldn't let you get this close to me if I weren't truly serious about the long life together. If I get hurt or something worse happens, my family will take care of you and make sure you know what's happening."

"Who'll decide what happens if it's life threatening or— or unreversible?"

"*Piccolina*, I have a health directive. Papa made sure everyone has a Power of Attorney that lists every member of the family as having rights to determine care. That way, whoever gets to the hospital first can decide. Wives always have the final say. The moment my family knows we're together, they'll know you have the ultimate say."

"What? I'm not your wife."

"No. Maybe one day you will be. But you're the person I'm choosing to make a future with. That carries weight in my family because it's not a decision made lightly."

She's silent for a moment, looking down between us. Our clothes hide where our bodies join, but I know she feels it. This is a fucking intense conversation, but a necessary one. I don't think it would feel as emotionally connected if we weren't physically connected.

"My parents have that Power of Attorney for me. I don't know that they'd agree to you deciding for me without being my husband. I can amend it, and I want to. I didn't know what was going on today. I still don't. But you're who I came to. You're the one I trust my life to. You were right. I got in a cab. I could have gone anywhere. I still came to you, even though they probably knew this is where I was already headed."

"There's one more thing along those lines. I know you're close to Laura through Chelle. If you absolutely cannot get to my family, go to the Kutsenkos first. Aunt Sylvia has a rule Laura adopted. Any syndicate woman— wife, mother, sister, daughter, girlfriend —can seek shelter with her. No questions asked. The woman is untouchable until her family can get her. It changes nothing among the men, but it's a truce long enough to get the woman out of danger. I'd like to think the O'Rourkes and Diazes would respect that and offer the same sanctuary, but I just can't be sure. Not even with your connections to them already."

"How often does that happen?"

"Not once since Aunt Sylvia joined the family. But it's a mandate we all obey."

"If Salvatore is your don, then what does that make Sylvia?"

"*La madrina.* The Godmother. I know that sounds cliché after the movie, but it's true. Luca is our underboss as Uncle Salvatore's heir. But Aunt Sylvia— any of the women in my family —could run things if ever something happened to the men. Don't doubt the strength of the women in my family. They're far less forgiving and far more protective than any of the men could ever be."

"You're like protective to the nth degree. I can already tell. How could anyone be more?"

"They're mothers."

That makes her smile, and it's like the heavens opened to let the sun through.

"Makes sense. But if you've never used the rule, why is it so important to Sylvia? You called it a mandate?"

That's a painful subject for everyone.

"Not long after Aunt Sylvia moved here to marry Uncle Sal, her younger sister got separated from her guards in Palermo. She was on foot, and men chased her. She passed three families who could have saved her, but she knew they wouldn't. The men assaulted and murdered her. She was visibly pregnant. Aunt Sylvia refuses to even consider that happening to another woman. God help any man who scares a syndicate woman enough to run to us."

Aunt Sylvia may be the most elegant woman I have ever seen, but she's made of sterner stuff than most would imagine. She grew up in Sicily, and her father heads her branch there. *Cosa Nostra* is all she's ever known. They raised her to one day marry an influential man, and she's the perfect match for Uncle Salvatore. I know he trusts her with more than he probably should, but he respects her opinions. She's an attorney trained in France, but she now handles our legal corporate ventures.

"I'm sorry for your family's loss. And I hope it never comes to any woman seeking shelter from your family or Laura's. But it is reassuring to know that I can go to them if it's dire."

"Only if it's dire. It has to be you're truly in fear of dying. Otherwise, you must come to my family. Your parents know more than we realized, and obviously Chelle does too. But I don't think your parents told your brother anything. I know Chelle hasn't."

"I don't think so either. But my brother has some questionable clients. He's a broker to some extremely powerful and wealthy people. It wouldn't surprise me if he's turned a blind eye to several things the FTC would want to know more about."

We already know from the background check run on Chelle's family. We know of the clients his firm represents, and we know he's clean but a little dusty.

"You already knew that, didn't you?"

The question isn't accusatory. It's as though she feels silly for stating the obvious.

"I did."

"How did your family run a check on Chelle and not know about my family's ties to the mob?"

"Papa and Uncle Sal did. They're the ones who had to tell Chelle. She confronted your parents, and the rest of it came out."

"Oh."

I wonder if that pissed her off. It doesn't seem like it, but I've already learned she can hide her emotions better than most. Maybe it comes from having to hide her thoughts from clients with abominable taste.

Another knock on the door interrupts us.

"*Chi è?*" Who is it?

"Gianni, *capo.*"

"*Dateci altri cinque minuti.*" Give us five more minutes.

"*Non può aspettare.*" This can't wait.

"*Le tubature?*" The pipes?

"*Si tratta della signora.*" It's about the lady.

When Beth's hands— which were resting on my forearms —clutch my sleeve, I know she understands this is about her.

"*Cinque minuti, a meno che qualcuno non stia morendo.*" Five minutes unless someone is dying.

"*Sì, capo.*" Yes, boss.

"We need to get going, don't we?"

"Yeah."

Neither of us wants to move. Our kiss starts off like a flicker, but it soon turns into a flame. I place her back on the desk, and she grips the edge with one hand and the back of my neck with the other. It's rough, and it's fast. Our kiss is sloppy as we swallow each other's sounds. Her fingers fist my hair as she comes. I'm right behind her.

"When we go out there, no one is going to know my cum is inside your pretty little pussy. But you will. You'll know that no matter what we find out, you're mine. No one comes near what's mine unless I allow it. You're safe with me, *piccolina.*

"Daddy, between the things you say to me and the sound of you speaking Italian. I don't give a fuck what's happening out there. Can you just fuck me for the rest of the day?"

From her smile, I know she's joking. But the look in her eyes— sultry as fuck —says she means it.

"One of these days, we're going to fuck all night, then the entire next day, then that second night, too. I won't let you out of our bed except to get a snack. Even then, I think I might prefer feeding you, so you can lick my fingers."

"Mmm. I'm more likely to suck them."

She grabs my left hand and brings it to her mouth. Her tongue flicks it but nothing more. Just as well since we're in a strip club. We keep it clean. It's just the thought of it. I think she must have the same one from the way she cocks an eyebrow. I pull out and help her off the desk. She looks at the box of tissues on the desk, then me. She pushes her skirt down and twists it back into place. She runs her hand through her hair as I tuck my shirt back in.

"You can leave your stuff in here if you want."

She glances at her bags and nods. I lead her to the door and hold it open. Once we're in the hallway, I slide my hand into hers.

"We're going to continue in Italian until I know what's going on. If it's something I can explain, I will."

"I know. I trust you."

She keeps telling me that. I pray I'm always worthy of it. Her grip tightens a little when we step out of the dim light into the main area with the center stage. There are three poles up there with tables surrounding what looks like a peninsula. I don't expect to see my father or Uncle Salvatore. I notice Uncle Domenico talking to a guy near the door. Fucking hell. Why are they here?

"Shh, *piccolina*. It's all right."

She tries to let go of my hand, but I keep hold of hers. They've already seen us. I'm not pretending this is anything less than it is. I won't look like naughty teenagers who got busted together. She curls hers back around mine, and I feel her relax. She needed to know I wouldn't dismiss her or us. She was prepared to for my sake, but she's glad I didn't.

"Papa, Uncle Sal, Uncle Dom. What's up?"

"We were on our way to a meeting and stopped by to see if you wanted to come."

My dad smiles at Beth and dips his chin. My uncles do the same.

"I have the leak to deal with. Carmine's men got here about twenty minutes ago."

It might be more than that because I don't know how long I was back there with Beth. Uncle Salvatore stands and buttons his suit coat.

"It's nice to see you again, Elizabeth."

"Liz, please. It's nice to see you too, Mr. Mancinelli."

"Same."

Papa and Uncle Domenico grin at her as they both speak. It lightens the mood.

"Please, it's Salvatore. And these two goons are Massimo and Domenico. There are too many of us to say Mr. Mancinelli without the busybodies answering, too."

Beth isn't sure what to do, but she laughs. I don't think she expected Uncle Salvatore to have anything resembling a sense of humor. Our family is hilarious and loves nothing more than to tease one another. We're shockingly normal outside of work.

"Liz came by to look at the damage and see if she thinks it should be redesigned."

Papa looks at me when he responds.

"Your brother told us."

Wonderful. Enzo and his big mouth. They're here to check up on me. Meeting my ass. But just as well they are here.

"Papa, someone followed Liz here."

The three older men swing their attention to Beth, and she tries not to shrink beside me. These men went from relaxed to Mafioso in a heartbeat, and she doesn't know they aren't directing their anger at her. I shoot them a pointed look, and the degree of menace shrinks.

Uncle Salvatore takes the lead even though Papa will probably call Beth daughter within a few months.

"What happened, Liz?"

"A guy bumped into me when I stepped onto the sidewalk outside my building. Then a guy shoved me off the subway and followed me way too closely up the stairs. The guy who was in front of me slowed down and followed me, too. I took a cab the last block, but somehow the guy who was near my place was already here. I guess traffic was light."

Uncle Salvatore keeps his attention on her.

"What about the other two?"

"When I looked back as I got out of the cab, they were waiting to cross the street. One of your men was near the door and opened it for me. Marco was already here."

"Uncle Sal, we looked at the security footage, and we spotted the men. Our guys headed out before Liz and I pulled up the feed, but they found nothing. I haven't talked to them yet, so I don't know the details."

Papa approaches until he's standing in front of us. His tone is softer than Uncle Salvatore's, but I know it. It's the fuck around and find out tone he gets when anyone steps a little too close to his wife and kids— never mind we're in our thirties.

"Has anything like this happened to you before?"

"No. That's why it's so disconcerting."

"Have you had any problems with clients, or anyone approach you since Chelle started seeing Enzo?"

"Nothing is different than it was two months ago." She looks at me. "Only my involvement with Marco."

The three men who have been role models to me my entire life are the quintessential swarthy Mediterranean men you see on Dior or Armani or Louis Vuitton ads. Silver foxes. They can be suave and debonair when they need to be. But when three sets of dark eyes are drilling into your soul, it doesn't feel so charming. Beth doesn't cower now that she knows they're kinder than their reputations would seem. She stands tall when most would wither.

"Marco, how long have you and Liz been involved?"

"Since just after the reception. We ran into each other and hit it off."

That's mostly the truth.

Those three sets of dark eyes pin me to the spot. I know they'll have more to say later about having Beth work on a strip club project. It won't matter that it wasn't my idea. It won't matter that they have no objections to women coming to the clubs. Their objection will be that this is hardly the best introduction to our family businesses.

"Uncle Sal, I'm going to speak to Luca about adding Liz to the rotation. Now that it's known we're together, I want her to have guards. But after today, I want someone from our family with her any time it's out of her routine."

"Of course. Dante, Frederico, and Carlo can stay behind with you. We'll be fine."

Each of those men is assigned to Papa or one of my uncles. They have a driver and at least one other car with two men following them. That's too much power in one vehicle for them to go anywhere with only one guard each. It's too much temptation for someone who thinks to make a point by going after the don, the *consigliere*, and the former *capo dei capi*— boss of bosses. That was Uncle Domenico before I was old enough to assume the position. I'm officially the head of all our *capos*— or lieutenants. It means I lead Enzo and our cousins and friends. But I've never seen myself as anything but equal to them. Well, I did think I was superior to Carmine and Gabriele for a long time, but now I see them as equals.

"Three guards?"

Beth looks at me, and I know that terrifies her. She's wondering just how bad things must be.

"That's for my sake, as much as it is yours. Uncle Sal knows I'll lose my shit if there isn't someone to guard each side of you. I'm the fourth."

"Okay."

She doesn't sound so convinced.

"Liz—"

"Stop calling me that now that your family knows."

Her voice is a whisper, but I'm sure the others hear her.

"Beth, until we know what's going on, I'm going to hover, and I'm going to be overprotective. I admit it. If I'm smothering you, tell me. But I won't back down on how many men guard you."

She shoots me a lopsided smile. I know I pretty much just contradicted myself. But at least I'm trying. Her free hand covers the forearm above where our hands are joined.

"Thank you."

Uncle Domenico— always the shit stirrer —finally pipes in.

"I haven't heard the name Beth in ages. It suits you. You said you go by Liz."

"I do. That name is for Marco."

She's polite, but there's that challenge in her voice that makes me go rock hard in an instant. I let go of her hand and wrap my arm around her waist, pulling her close. I kiss her cheek, and the men laugh.

"Now I understand."

Uncle Domenico grins at me, and I can hear the silent "attaboy."

Beth looks up at me, confused.

"They know you're going to fit in. You respectfully made your wishes clear."

Her cheeks flush, and she's not sure if I'm serious. Now she's wondering if she overstepped. I can read it all on her face.

"*Cuore*, remember what I said about the women in my

family? They know you'll fit in. You're no pushover, but you're also tactful."

Her eyes widen a fraction when I use the endearment in front of the others. I did it without thinking, just knowing not to say *piccolina*. But I want them to understand this is already serious. Uncle Salvatore elbows Papa.

"I'll tell Sylvia to set an extra place at Sunday dinner."

Chapter Ten

Beth

We're at Marco's, and I'm soaking in the tub. I don't remember the last time I gave myself time to have a bath. I'm a wash and go kinda gal. I don't use product beyond shampoo and conditioner. I don't buy fancy body washes or poufs. I'm happy with economy size, so I rarely have to remember to buy stuff. But this is pretty fucking awesome. I didn't realize it, but Marco did a rush delivery order while he walked to and from the office to get my bags. He ordered bubble bath, shampoo, conditioner, lotion, a terry-cloth robe, and a few other things that arrived five minutes after we got here.

He's in his office on the phone with I don't know who. I hear Italian drift to me from time to time, but I don't understand any of it. The little bits I can hear sound serious, but he isn't angry or frustrated or anything other than his normal tone. But that means nothing. He can regulate his voice and expressions like none other.

Then again, Chelle said the same about Enzo the night we

spent at my place before the wedding. Neither she nor Enzo loved the idea of being apart, but it was practical since they both had things to do before the ceremony. And it was fun having the sister time. Neither of us have ever been particularly girlie, but we used to have a lot of fun together when we were younger.

I've let out some water and refilled the tub with hot water four times already. Marco must have poured half the bottle of bubbles in here because they cover me all the way up to my chin. He has an enormous soaking tub, so I'm able to stretch out. I didn't take him for the bath type, but maybe. I'm enjoying the time alone. It's been a lot to take in since this morning. I insisted I look at the space and do some sketches after Salvatore, Massimo, and Domenico left. I spent an hour examining, measuring, and drawing before we left.

I didn't love having four men surrounding me since it felt excessive, but I did love feeling safe. I kept looking at Marco as we walked from the car to the restaurant he took me to for lunch. I could tell he was scanning the area, ever vigilant. I could also tell me being practically invisible gave him some level of comfort. Him relaxing meant I could relax. Lunch was really nice. It was our first date, and he made me laugh the entire time.

We swung by my office since I needed to gather some things for me to work from home for the next two days. Well, work from Marco's place for the next two days. The men waited outside my office suite, so I didn't have to explain. They're my usual days out of the office, so it didn't raise any eyebrows.

We're going to make dinner together, and it feels so perfectly domestic. Like we've been a couple since forever. That it's just a natural routine for us to grill meat and have some side dishes after a normal day at work. Except, nothing was normal about today. I wound up scared shitless, with a boyfriend who I'm now living with for an indefinite amount of time, and a Mafia family that's probably wondering what the next wave of trouble my family is going to bring to theirs will be.

Marco filled me in on the shit that happened with Chelle. I texted with her, and she apologized profusely for not telling me everything. But I get it way better and way easier than I would have before falling for Marco. Now it seems par for the course. All of that in the space of twelve hours. I thought Chelle and Enzo's relationship moved too fast, but I never shared my opinion with my sister. I didn't want to hurt her. I didn't want to push her away. But now I get it. These men are— intense.

I have a thing for cars. My older brother, Sam, and I used to watch *Top Gear* together. I thought the British guys were funny, and Sam liked the technical stuff. It was our thing. I remember the Koenigsegg Gemera was the fastest production car at one time. It could do zero to sixty in one-point-nine seconds. The Mancinelli relationships go from zero to sixty in one-point-eight seconds. Blink and you'll miss it. You'll miss how easily these men get into your blood. How easy it is to fall for them. How fast you develop feelings that are deeper than any you ever imagined. Flat out. Period. The depth is more shocking than the speed. I won't say I'm in love with Marco. I'm not. But I can see myself being there. That's why I can think about a long-term relationship with him. Why I didn't get cold feet when he said his future is with me. I feel the same.

I've had other relationships that took time to develop. I've felt lust at first sight like I did with Marco. I've been fond of guys I've dated, but it never went much further than physical attraction. I've even been in love. I'm certain I loved a boyfriend in college, even though we realized we weren't compatible. He can't help it, but he's patronizing as fuck. We're still friends.

I had another boyfriend after college who I was really serious about. I thought he was the one. He was going to be the one, but he just wasn't in the same place as me. He thought he was ready to settle down, but he didn't get what that entailed. That it meant our relationship needed to come before going out with his buddies. When I realized he meant more to me than I did to him, I knew our future wasn't together.

With Marco, I know I come first in everything that isn't Mafia. I can accept that because it's honor, duty, loyalty, and family that drive his decision. Those are admirable traits I respect. When he swore his fidelity, I believed him without reservation. Nothing about the men in his family makes me think they fit the Casanova stereotype. Just the opposite. I think once they commit to the woman they want, nothing could ever make them stray. They'd die before betraying the woman they love. Marco might not love me, but he would never betray that family value.

That's why I can do this. That's why I can put my faith in him. It's why Chelle loves Enzo and is making a life with him. Marco's said I can walk away if this doesn't work for me. I want it to. I plan to make it work. But there's a sliver of me that's relieved just in case.

I'm just leaning forward to reach for the pouf and body wash when Marco walks in.

"My Venus on a half-shell."

I'm pretty sure he's referencing the Renaissance painting about the goddess's birth and not the sci-fi book. I don't know about resembling the goddess of love, desire, and fertility, but I'll take the compliment.

"At least my Adonis returns my feelings."

I wink at him as he strips. I scoot forward, and he slides in behind me. Venus's feelings were unrequited since the mythical Adonis preferred hunting. There's something to that.

Marco puts me ahead of most things in his life, but he will always choose his family and hunting for whatever it is they go after. It's rather bittersweet to realize that.

"*Piccolina*, I will never prefer the things I have to do over being with you. I accept my obligations, but it doesn't mean they're what I want."

His mind reading skills are uncanny and unnerving. But it's what makes me wonder if we might be soulmates. How else would he know my inner thoughts so well?

I lean back against him, my eyes closing. He wraps his arms around me, and I feel my shoulders lower, and my body presses heavier against the bottom of the tub as I stop holding myself so stiffly. I thought I was relaxed while I was alone, but now my body feels boneless. He just holds me, but I feel myself twitch. I blink my eyes open as he laughs.

"I must have been dozing off."

"You've done that four times already. You were already asleep."

"What? No."

"You were. I could tell even without you twitching."

Fuck. Was I drooling? Was I snoring? Fuck. Was it some worse bodily sound?

"You're practically rolled onto your side. Your arm is around my waist."

I hadn't noticed. I twisted at the waist and draped my right arm around his waist. He adjusts me as he slides farther under the water. I'm lying belly to belly with him, my hips between his legs, my pussy just below his cock. He's hard, and it would be easy to mount him and fuck. There's plenty of room in the tub. But neither of us moves beyond breathing.

"Daddy, I'm so comfy. I could fall back to sleep like this."

Except it's probably only midafternoon. It's a little early to be thinking about sleeping the night away with me on top of him.

"We can add some more hot water, and we can soak as long as you want."

I raise my left hand out of the water. My fingers are already raisins.

"How long have I been in here?"

"Probably an hour by now."

I doubt I've taken a bath this long since I was a little girl with toys trying to do the backstroke in a traditional size tub.

"I have work I have to do."

I sigh with regret. I'd really rather take a nap with Marco. But I assume I'm sharing his bed tonight. He said he'd feel better with me here, and he doesn't want me out of reach.

"Fine. If you insist."

He sounds playfully beleaguered.

"I'm not such a fan of adulting, but I like my place and my car. My student loan company says they like my money."

I roll over and sit up. He tugs me back a little and massages my shoulders. Now I don't want to and can't go anywhere since he insists. Whether it's my back or my pussy, his fingers are magical.

"You can work wherever you're comfortable. My office. The dining room table. The living room."

It surprises me that he offers me his inner sanctum. I guess there's nothing there he worries about me seeing. He— oh! He hits a particularly tender spot. He feels the knot and works on it. He's better than any professional masseur or masseuse. I might keep him just for this. My mind goes blank as I enjoy the pain that leads to pleasure. The bath. The massage. The way he held me. I have never felt so taken care of in my adult life. This is what he's been promising me since the beginning.

"*Tesoro mio*, I'll finish the rest tonight. I plan to enjoy working your entire body. But I have a feeling you won't enjoy this a hundred percent— maybe ninety-eight —if you don't get your work done."

"How'd you know?"

"Because we're alike. Knowing the work is there will lurk in your mind until it's done."

Again with the mind reading. But it isn't some secret power. It's a connection because he said we're alike.

The tub's faucet is on the side, so the front connects to a walk-in shower. We don't linger as we rinse off, though I can tell we're both tempted. Our first bath and our first shower together and no sex. A bit disappointing, but in a way, it's nice to know we can be naked together without having to fuck. There's more to this than just sex. We dry off, and he offers me a t-shirt and a pair of boxers since his basketball shorts looked like they'd come to my calves.

The afternoon passes with the same speed as my bath. Emails, billing, drafting, ordering— it zooms by as I work at the dining room table. I didn't feel right taking over his office. He works at the opposite end except for when he had to take some calls. Most were in English, and they were related to some construction projects his family has. I didn't listen closely. A few were in Spanish, and I could follow along with those too. But I had no idea about the two in Italian. He stepped away mostly so he wouldn't interrupt me. I thought it was sweet.

We make dinner together, Marco and I sharing a bottle of wine on his balcony as we grill steaks and vegetables. It's so completely normal. Our conversation jumps around from our siblings to more about what we studied in college and grad school. Alcohol rarely gives me heavy head, but I think everything from this morning drained me more than I realized. I'm exhausted by the time we're done with dinner. I help do the dishes, but I'm drooping. Once we've cleaned up, Marco suggests we head to bed. He follows through on his offer to give me a full body massage.

Much to my dismay this morning, I realize I fell into a practical coma. I don't even remember Marco getting into bed next to me. I have a vague recollection of snuggling closer to him in the middle of the night. I wake to his shoulder beneath my head, and his hand stroking my back as sun filters through the curtains.

"Did you sleep well, *piccolina?*"

"Like the dead. I don't remember the last time I slept so deeply. I seem to have had the comfiest pillow."

"Same. I slept better than I have in years. Having you curled up beside me was perfect."

I sense he wants to say more, but he holds back. Dare I test the waters?

"I hope I keep sleeping that well."

The hand stroking my back cups my ass.

"You will because I'm going to be your pillow for a long time to come."

I gaze up at him, and I can't believe how happy and satisfied that makes me. I push up onto an elbow and give him a quick peck. But he cups the back of my head and pulls me in for something far more. The hand on my ass moves to replace the one cradling my head. His now free hand dives between my legs, inching inside me.

"This is how we're going to start our days, little one. I'm going to make you come by fucking you hard enough that each step you take reminds you I belong inside you."

When I know I'm wet enough for him to slide into me, I move to straddle him. I know he lets me since he could easily position me however he wants. I drop onto his cock, and we both groan. That moment. That feeling of him entering me. Fucking divine. His hands on my hips control how I move. He sets a pace I'm not sure I can keep up with as he thrusts into me over and over. I have to lean forward and press into his chest to hold on. His hand rains down a ringing slap on my ass.

It spurs me on. This is purely for our pleasure, and I love it. He does it again, this one louder and harder. I Kegel. He tries to lift me, but I clench my pussy and press my knees into the mattress. He can still do as he wants with my body since he's stronger. But he knows the game I want to play. He pinches my nipple until I scream. His smile pure sex appeal. I fight his pace now, slowing my body as best I can. Before I know it, he surges up, wraps his arm around my waist, and flips us. He uses his free hand to push up and brace himself. The hand that was around my waist is now around my throat.

"If you don't want this, safe word."

I shake my head since his hold is still light.

"More, Daddy."

He growls. Fucking growls. His grip tightens until it makes it hard to breathe. He's slapping his hips into mine. I am going to be sore. He's moving just how he knows I love it. Rubbing my clit just how I need it.

"Hands over your head, *piccolina*. Try to take control again, and I'll pull out and come on your tits. I won't let you come until tomorrow."

My hands fly up to grab hold of the top of the mattress. I'm not just lying there taking it, but his hold on my throat is decreasing the air getting to my lungs, making my body harder to move. I'm almost tempted to safe word or snap. I know he'd understand that too. But my orgasm crashes over me, and I scream. At first, it's silent, but the moment he releases me, my voice fills the room.

He rears back and grabs my hips. He fucks like a porn star the way he pistons his cock in and out of me. It's rough, and I marvel at how fast he can move. I practically salivate as I watch his six-pack flex into an eight— maybe even ten —pack. Is that possible? All I know is that every muscle between his shoulders and his hips strain. My legs are now bent, and my knees are against the chiseled grooves in his ass. Fucking hell. It's like fucking marble. I love his ass. I love all of his body. The sight and the feel push me close to the edge again.

"May I come, Daddy? Please?"

"Yes, *cuore*. Come because I can't hold on."

"Don't. Fuck me harder and come in me."

My wish seems to be his command. He loses as much control as he'll allow himself, and I'm gone. I can't keep my eyes open for a moment, but I don't want to miss it. I don't want to miss his expression when he shoots his cum into me. Me. Only me. Fucking territorial much? Yes.

He collapses forward but still careful how much weight he drops onto me. He rolls us again, and I curl my legs up as we kiss, his arms going in opposite directions across my back. He clings to me, but I can't imagine going anywhere, even if the roof were on fire.

As my mind settles, I realize this was something different for me. I thought we were fucking. If anyone watched us, they'd think so too. But it felt different. It was rough, and it was hard, but we filled it with emotions that make me realize I just made love to him. That's something I will not be sharing aloud.

"Beth, what are you doing to me?"

I don't know how to answer that. I want to say, "making you fall in love with me." But that doesn't feel right.

"Besides making my heart practically beat out of my chest, I've never felt that way before. *Cuore*, I said I wanted to be rough enough to make you sore. But did I hurt you? Was it too much? I couldn't stop myself. No. Not true. I could have the moment you safe worded or if you'd snapped. I didn't want to. I wanted to give you all of me. What are you doing to me?

He asks the same question twice. Maybe he does want an answer.

"Whatever it is, you're doing the same to me. And you didn't hurt me at all. It's never been like that before. I've never—"

I don't know what to say. This need. This connection. It's scaring me. It's too much, too soon. The bliss is dissolving fast, and it's freaking me out. It's too intense for someone I barely know. I can't do this.

"What's wrong? Something just changed in your body. You're tense. Did I say something? Do you not like it?"

I refuse to cry during sex or even after it. That'd be ridiculous. But the emotional tsunami is sucking me under. I can't sort through all of this since my brain is now mush.

Marco holds me and doesn't push for answers. I'm grateful. This future I've been imagining. I let myself get carried away. A life married to the mob— the Mafia. I don't want this.

Chapter Eleven

Marco

Beth's changed her mind. She's completely withdrawn from me in the matter of seconds even though I haven't pulled out of her. Whatever just caused the shift makes any arousal I might have left drain away. My dick doesn't cooperate, and I hate the feeling of my body leaving hers. But it seems to bring her relief. What the fuck just happened?

Whatever this is, I don't get the sense she wants to talk about it. She's slow to pull away, but she rolls off me. She kisses me, but it almost feels like she thinks she has to before she can make her escape. I watch her walk into the bathroom. I gave her a fresh toothbrush I happened to have. She shuts the door, and I hear the water run at the sink. Then it's the shower. I'd hoped to share that with her this morning since we didn't take advantage of it yesterday afternoon. We didn't stop by her place, so she has no fresh clothes. That's why she wore my t-shirt and boxers.

She's quick. I will give her that. I'm not sure what to do. Do

I stay in bed? Do I meet her at the door and get ready too? Do I make her coffee? This is why I never sleep over at a woman's place and don't have them sleep at mine. But I thought Beth was my girlfriend. Why the awkwardness?

I climb out of bed, and I'm making it as she comes out. I turn from her side and look at her. She's as naked as I am. I watch her eyes sweep over me, and I see the spark of interest. But I don't know if I should go near her. I choose to get her another t-shirt and boxers. When I hand them to her, I realize she's been crying. Her eyes are red and glassy. I take the boxers back and slip them on before pulling her into my embrace. She comes willingly.

"What's going on, *cuore mio*." My sweetheart.

"I don't think I can do this, Marco. I thought I could. I wanted to."

"Wanted? Not want."

"I don't know. I know you're going to have guards for me, and I know one of them will be from your family. But am I going to need them? Am I in danger now? Is Chelle?"

"Yes to all three. And you know Enzo and I would change that in a heartbeat if we could. Our world has changed in the last few years, and my family is regrettably part of why. Women and children used to be off limits. No one went near them. But things have happened, and now women aren't as safe as they once were. Children seem to still be untouchable."

I say that, but then I remember an incident Maks and Laura had with shots fired at them while their twins were newborns. I think about the men who broke into Uncle Salvatore and Aunt Sylvia's house. They took my aunt while my cousins slept right above them. This is why I'm selfish as fuck to have brought Beth into this. This is why I swore I never would.

But there's something else. It's not just the risk to her safety. The shift wasn't from that.

"Beth, what's really going on?"

I draw her back to the bed and guide her to sit next to me. My heart aches as the tears silently slide down her cheeks. She's quick to swipe them away, but they're just replaced by more. I cup her cheek and kiss the other side, the saltiness bitter on my lips. I don't want this. I don't want to hurt her, but I don't want her to walk away.

"This is moving too fast, Marco. It's not just what's going on outside your front door. It's what's happening between us."

"What do you need?"

"I don't know. We've barely been out a few times, and I'm already staying at your place. Last night felt like we've always been a couple. There's still so much I don't know. I don't even know your favorite color. Just now— for me..."

"It's royal purple."

That makes her pause.

"Really?"

"Yes. My parents got me a bath robe when I was eight, and I made sure my brothers and sister knew it was because I was meant to reign. I was a little shit. But I discovered I really love the color."

She offers me a watery smile. I'm slow, like she might flee if I make any unexpected movement, but I kiss her forehead.

"What was it about just now that upset you? Was what I said too possessive?"

"No. It was perfect. I love how you talk to me."

She freezes when she finishes, and I know why.

"This is moving too fast for you because our feelings are pretty fucking extreme for one another so soon. I didn't fuck you, Beth. We didn't fuck. You know that just like I do, and that terrifies you."

"Yes."

"I don't think you love me yet. And I don't know if I love

you yet. I'll back off if that's what you want. I'll sleep in the guest bedroom if you need more space to slow things down."

"No."

She blurts that answer. Then the tears start again. She's so conflicted, and I don't know what to do to make it better. I don't know how to control this situation, and it makes me want to crawl out of my skin. I don't like her pulling away from me. And I definitely don't like feeling like I can't fix this.

"Daddy, I don't know what I want. One minute, I feel like I need to retreat. But when you offer me that space, it's like a knife to my heart. All I want is to cling to you. It's humiliating to admit this. I'm not used to having such intense conversations all the time. I'm not used to revealing so much about myself. But I open my mouth, and I seem to just vomit my thoughts whenever I'm with you."

"I never want you to regret sharing how you feel. There are so many things we won't be able to discuss. So many things I can't tell you. It's unfair because I'll always have to hold back a part of me. And you're being vulnerable and open with me. I promise you I will always tell you the truth about how I feel. I don't want you to retreat, Beth. I want to move at whatever speed you're comfortable with, but I don't want this to end. Just the opposite. I might not show it, but it's fucking scary for me to feel so much for someone so fast. My family is different in so many ways from normal. My family is proof soulmates exist. I've seen it my entire life. I don't know if you're mine and I'm yours. But I'm willing to accept you might be because that's just how it's been in my family for as long as I can remember. I don't know if you even believe in soulmates."

"I think my parents could be. They still love each other after forty years, but I don't get the same feeling from them as I do when I see Enzo and Chelle together. But they're newly-weds. I believe Maks and Laura are the most perfectly matched couple I've ever seen, so soulmates must be real. Maybe I'll think that about Enzo and Chelle once I get to know your brother better. I keep thinking you might be mine. But what if I'm not? What if you change your mind?"

Now we're getting somewhere. I scoop her up and place her farther on the bed. I climb on next to her, and we sit facing each other. I lift her legs over mine and pull her closer.

"I have the same fear, *piccolina*."

"You do? You seem so decisive about everything."

"I am decisive because I've had to be. I rarely have the luxury of mulling things over. Sometimes I have to make quick decisions to be proactive, but more often than not, it's reactive. But I'm trying to navigate this just like you are. I haven't been in a relationship since my sophomore year of college. It just got too hard to keep girlfriends at arm's length. It shocks the shit out of me that I've let you get so close so fast. It's scary to feel so close to you when there's so much risk to letting you in. Your safety and my family's."

I don't think she would turn on me or my family now that her sister is a part of it. But she could. She could go straight to the feds. She could point them right to us and tell them everything I've told her.

"Marco, no matter what happens, I will not betray you."

I nod as I swallow the sudden lump in my throat. We're still dancing around things. We're not talking about what changed everything twenty minutes ago.

"We didn't fuck. We made love, and that scares the shit out of you, doesn't it?"

She blinks several times; the seconds passing by. Then she nods.

"We did or something like that. But I'm not sure I feel that outside of sex."

"Neither am I."

I don't know if that helped or not. Maybe?

"Daddy, some part of our minds understands what this is. But it's not our conscious part. I don't want to fight this, but I am scared. I don't want to end this, but I need it to slow down."

"That's fair."

She wiggles closer until she can wrap her arms around me. I pick her up, so she's sitting on my lap.

"I trust you to get what I need because you already always do. I'm sorry I'm being this way. I wish you could make it all better, but that's not fair to ask when I'm the one who's fucked-up."

"You aren't fucked-up, and I wish I could fix it too."

She sits back and looks at me.

"Me freaking out leaves you feeling out of control, doesn't it?"

I nod.

"I feel like things are out of my control too. I need you as much as I feel like I should retreat. I wish you could be in control of all this, so I didn't have to worry."

"I would if I could."

"I think you can, actually. Spank me."

"What?"

"You know what this dynamic is. You know submitting isn't actually handing over complete control. But it is letting someone else lead when you want to follow. It lets me focus on what's happening in the moment. You would feel in control of at least this situation since you'd be doing the spanking. I'd feel in control because I'm letting you. I need this, Marco."

"I do too. You know this is purely for getting us back to our equilibrium, right? This is not a punishment for you needing to sort out your feelings."

"I know."

"Come here, *piccolina.*"

"Yes, Daddy."

She shifts, so she's lying across my lap. I squeeze her ass. I love her tits, but her ass makes me— I don't even know because I want to fuck her no matter what. But her ass is a rush to me.

I bring my hand down, and it's not gentle.

"I'm going to spank you ten times on each side. You are going to count each one."

"Yes, Daddy."

My palm lands on her right cheek.

"One."

Now her left.

"Two."

"No. I said ten on each side."

"I know. I want to count to twenty. I want to know it's that many."

She turns her head to look at me. She's as into the push and pull of pain and pleasure as I am. This is our homeostasis. I alternate sides, sometimes spanking both cheeks at once. She does a double count for those. Other ones land across her horizontal crack, pushing her clit into my thigh. I feel her rubbing it. If this were some sort of punishment, I wouldn't allow it. But I want her to get off as many times as she can.

"Nineteen. Twenty."

Tears are falling again, and she's kicked her legs and grabbed the comforter several times. Relief fills her voice as she counts the last two. Her ass is bright pink. The moment it looked red, I made sure my hand landed somewhere new. I don't want her to be in pain past this. When this is over, it's over. I tug her right leg to bend and come near my hip. My fingers dive into her, my thumb rubbing her clit. She's so wet it coats my fingers before they can even find her g spot. I thrust two in at first, but now I'm at three.

"All of it."

"Does my little girl need me to fist fuck her?"

"Yes!"

I quicken the speed my three fingers work her as I guide her onto her hands and knees. My free hand slips beneath her as I shift to kneel behind her. I rub her clit as I keep working her cunt, sliding my hand each time I press in. I add my pinky as she moans over and over.

"Uh-uh-uh."

Each thrust elicits a breathy sound until my entire hand finally slides in.

"Uh!"

Her body trembles as I continue to work her. I don't let up on her clit as she pushes back against my hand.

"Safe word if I get too rough, Beth. I won't be pleased if I hurt you."

"Stop talking and fuck me harder."

I yank my hands from her clit and spank her the hardest I ever have. I fist her hair and pull her back off her hands as I thrust my fist as deep as I dare.

"I thought you wanted me in control. Do you want to order me around now?"

"No. I just need you, Daddy."

I change my tone, and I know she loves it when it gets deeper, and my words are slower.

"Are you desperate for Daddy to make you come?"

"Yes."

"Are you going to be Daddy's good girl?"

I'm pushing the edge of our dynamic. I won't call her little girl because neither of us wants her to be a little. But I will make her back down and accept that I decide. That's what she wanted, and this isn't a power switch.

"Anything you want as long as you don't stop."

"Ask me to come."

"Please, may I come?"

"Yes."

I go back to rubbing her clit. She falls forward, her hips riding my fist. She shakes as a powerful orgasm overtakes her. Before she's done, I pull my hand out and shove my cock in. I slam into her hard, making her come again. I look at my cock and my hand. My coated fingers move to her ass. I press into her there, working my way in as I stretch her. I smear her juices in and around the hole. Then I press the tip of my dick to her.

"Is this what you want? Do you want me to finally take all of you?"

"You can't take what I give. But yes. All of me. Make me yours."

I'm careful since I don't know her experience with this, and she hasn't worn any plugs with me. My cock is wet, but we aren't using lube either. I move millimeter by millimeter until I know she can handle it. I slide all the way into her ass, and it's so fucking tight I start to come. I keep my movements gentle and slow. I rock rather than thrust.

"Fuck, Beth. I'm coming."

"Good, Daddy."

I pull her down to sit on my lap as I fill her ass with my cum. I kiss along her shoulder as I wrap an arm around her middle. My dick finally stops as I slide my hands up to cup one of her tits.

"Are you all right, *cuore?*"

"So all right. Thank you, Marco. I feel a lot calmer than I did before."

"Tell me when you need this. Tell me when you need me to take control. I will give you everything you need. I wish I could promise to give you everything you want. But I will always make time for what you need. I will always take care of you."

"I know. Realizing that is part of what got a little overwhelming. But now that we've talked and now that we've done *that*, I feel way more at peace."

She pulls away from me, easing me out, and turns around. She cups my cheeks.

"You are a good man. You might do some bad things, but that doesn't make you a bad person. I've never thought you were, and no one will convince me otherwise. That's why I'm falling for you so fast and why I was scared. But I know without a doubt that whatever this is we feel, we feel it together."

"Absolutely."

As we gaze into each other's eyes, I think we're both accepting it's us against the world. We're in this together, and that's how we want it.

"I don't want this to be a one-way street, Marco. I want you to know I will give you everything you need, and I will do my damnedest to give you everything you want. I won't make you bear the weight of the world alone."

"I know. You gave me what I needed just now. You understood me."

She smiles, and all is right between us again.

"You did most of the cooking last night, Daddy. I'll make you breakfast."

"Mmm-mmm. I'm taking you out for breakfast. If we don't leave here for a while, I'm going to keep you in here all day. Neither of us will get a damned thing done but each other."

"And the problem with that would be?"

"I heard your call yesterday. You have designs due today. I won't get you in trouble at work."

She exaggerates her sigh of resignation.

"Fine. I suppose going out to breakfast is nice. But only if I get some afternoon delight back here."

"That you can count on." I waggle my eyebrows. "What are you in the mood for?"

Chapter Twelve

Beth

I'm ashamed of how I acted this morning. Maybe it was sub drop— the crash that sometimes happens after the euphoria ends and the endorphins decrease. It's why there's such a thing as aftercare in the BDSM world. But I usually don't experience it, and there was no reason to think I would have since it was pretty tame sex compared to what it could have been— what I hope it will become with Marco. Maybe that's part of it. Maybe the focus on sex wouldn't be such a bad thing right now. It would take us back to what we originally envisioned this being between us. What the fuck do I know?

I still feel like a fickle bitch. One moment I'm telling myself that meeting Marco and being with him is the best thing since — forever. Then I'm ready to run naked from his apartment. PMS? I don't want him to fear I'm going to bail on him when things are hard. I don't want him to think I'm going to shut down on him. Time. I think that's what we both need.

We're headed to a little bistro that apparently has an

amazing breakfast menu. It's a few blocks away, so we're walking. The guys guarding me today are a bit more spread out, letting Marco and me have some privacy. Marco's walking on the curb side as we hold hands. There's a guy about ten feet ahead of us and one about that far behind us. The one on my right is making it hard for anyone to pass between us, but he's leaving about a four- or five-feet gap when he can.

When we get to the restaurant, the lead guard— Pauly — goes in ahead of us. He comes out with an expression I can't read. I can't understand what he says either.

"*C'è qualcosa di strano lì dentro.*" There's something off in there.

We're standing in the doorway when I hear a scuffle. Marco and I look to our right, and one guy from the subway is fighting with Vinny, the guard who trailed us. Immediately, Pauly and Marco close in, putting me between them. I look to my left, and I don't see the guard we had in front of us.

"Where's Tony?"

Marco turns his head at my question. His arm goes around my waist and pulls me flush to his body as he twists to look around. I don't understand what's happening. It's obvious Pauly knows his job is to protect me ahead of anything else since he isn't going to help Vinny. *Pauly. Vinny. Tony.* With names like those, I was feeling pretty fucking immortal when we left Marco's place. Now? Not so much.

I glance back to my right, and I notice the man from the subway is out cold on the sidewalk. Vinny's rushing toward us, pushing through the crowd that formed to watch the unexpected show— two muscle-bound men wailing on each other.

"Over there, Marco. That's the guy who bumped into me in the street."

I point to where we expected to see Tony. How the hell did these men know where we were going? I get the subway guy might have been following us. But how is the other one always ahead of me?

"We gotta get Beth inside. Straight to the restroom, Pauly."

"I know."

He knows? Is this their crisis strategy? Get the woman into a space with few people and probably no windows and only one door?

Pauly turns on his heel and yanks the door open. Marco still hasn't taken his arm off me. He propels me forward so fast I almost lose my footing. It's a good thing he's holding me. Maybe that's why. It's crowded, so Pauly has to push his way through with a few "excuses me's" and some shoulder bumps.

"Check it."

We're almost to the hallway with the sign for the restrooms. Pauly hurries forward and knocks on the women's door. Nothing. I expect him to go in, but he rushes to the men's door and knocks there too. He inches it open as he draws a knife from his pocket. That makes me look down, and I realize Marco has a knife in his left hand. It's a switchblade— I think that's what they're called —and it's open.

"It's less noticeable than if I pull my gun. Neither of us will until we need to. They'll expect us to take you to the ladies' room."

All four men were in suits as I've come to notice is the norm. After finding the gun holstered at Marco's lower back, I get that means the other men are carrying too. I don't want to know if they're licensed. I don't want to know if they have permits. I just want to know they're there, and these four men will use them to protect Marco— and me. Mostly Marco. Whoever this is might hurt me, but I'm fucking certain they'd kill him.

Pauly nods, and Marco nudges me forward. We enter the restroom, and it's a single. Pauly flips the lock before they both back me into the far corner. They have their guns drawn now, and Pauly's speaking rapid Italian into an earpiece. He's looking at Marco and shaking his head. What the fuck does that mean?

"Beth, no matter what happens, you stay behind Pauly and me. If I tell you to get down, you curl into a ball and cover your head. Back to the wall, knees up, head down. Leave nothing exposed."

Exposed? Like vital organs?

I tuck my hand into his belt beside the holster. I have a death grip on his belt and pants. I don't realize it, but I tug him backwards. He takes a step back and completely sandwiches me between him and the wall. His shoulders are broad enough, and I'm short enough, that I can't see around him. I feel safer, even if this makes him a target. Wait. That's not what I want. I try to adjust, so I'm not leaving him entirely open to anyone who breaks in. He won't budge. Instead, Pauly shifts to keep me still protected, but he could step in front of Marco if he had to.

I know bodyguards are supposed to be willing to take a bullet for their client. But Pauly's commitment pulsates in the air. There's an element of silent rage to him. How dare someone threaten the don's family?

Marco pulls out his phone. I can't tell, but from the way his right arm moves, I think he's sending a text. Is he letting his family know something is wrong?

There's a thud against the door. Both men raise their guns. Then it's pounding as a man's voice comes through the door.

"Marco! *Sono i federali. Sono qui per te.*" It's the feds. They're here for you.

Federali? Federals? Feds? Shit. Are they going to arrest Marco?

"*Luigi, ti ucciderò, cazzo.*" Luigi, I'm going to fucking kill you.

"*Più tardi, capo. Devi far uscire la tua donna.*" Later, boss. You need to get your woman out.

I don't understand any of this. I only caught *capo*, which I know means boss. But I only knew that before meeting Marco because of the movies.

He turns his head and whispers to Pauly.

"*Non mi fido di lui. Aspettiamo.*" We wait. I don't trust him.

"*Lo faccio. Mi ha parlato della roba che vogliono i federali. Non ha fatto il filo alla tua famiglia. Non lo farebbe mai. Se dice che dobbiamo andarcene, lo facciamo. Devi credergli.*" I do. He told me about the shit the feds want. He hasn't crossed your family. He never would. If he says we need to get out, then we do. You need to believe him.

The fact they won't speak English in front of me terrifies me. They don't want me to know anything. Is it to keep me from learning anything that could implicate them? Is it because of family secrets? Is it because they don't want me to know their plans because— because why?

"Beth, we both learned Italian before we learned English. It's just habit to lapse into it. One of my family's men is out there, but we don't know if we can trust him. He says the feds are coming."

"Can't trust him? Why?"

"I can't get into that. If we have to leave, you stay between Pauly and me. You don't go with anyone but the two of us. Pauly's my mom's cousin's husband."

I peer up at Pauly. Marco's explanation is supposed to make it all clear, but I have no idea why he told me the family connection.

"Ms. Russo, Nicoletta Mancinelli scares me more than any

woman I have ever met. My wife is fierce about our children, but Mrs. Mancinelli is creative. If I let anything happen to her son or future daughter, I'd rather kill myself than face her."

With four children, I imagine she's protective to the fourth power. Somehow, though, I think he's likely terrified of every woman in the Mancinelli family. I know what my mom is like, and she's a better shot than most. I suspect Marco's aunts and sister are just the same.

Since we seem to be waiting, I suppose it's as good a time as any to explain something.

"Marco, you know my mom's history. You know Chelle can shoot. I still shoot trap competitively. I don't own a handgun, but I shoot at a range regularly. I'm a better shot than both of them. Do not doubt that I know how to and will shoot to kill. If you say Luigi isn't to be trusted, and it's your life or his, I won't bat an eye when I put a bullet through his head."

Marco looks over his shoulder at me as though I've sprouted a second head. He glances at Pauly before he looks back at me. What more can I do but shrug? It was something I did with my grandpa and Sam. My brother went into the military and was a sharpshooter. I stuck with shooting clay pigeons. I understand now that my grandpa encouraged it because of our not-so-distant family ties. I didn't know that back then. It was just a special connection I had to the two of them.

"We'll discuss that when we get home, *piccolina*. You stay behind me."

Marco whispers the endearment, but I'm sure Pauly heard. Right now, I couldn't care less.

"Marco! Come on!"

Luigi calls out in English. From the way Marco continues to watch me, I realize he let us chat to distract me. But time's run out. Either we go or we stay.

"Pauly, lead."

The man lowers his gun to his side as he unlocks the door. While he's doing that, Marco tugs me to stand behind it. He's wrapped his body around me as though he expects someone to storm in. When nothing happens, Pauly opens the door wider. He slips out, and Marco steers me to follow him. I'm unprepared to see Pauly with his arm around a man's neck, his gun to the guy's temple. He uses Luigi as a shield as he moves into the hallway. Marco's left arm goes around me this time. There's no way anyone can get to me if they approach from behind.

"Tony has the car out back."

Luigi rasps the words, barely able to speak with Pauly's arm strangling him. Is that where Tony disappeared to?

I can hear raised voices toward the front of the restaurant, but we're headed toward the fire exit at the end of the hallway. We creep forward, and I notice Pauly changes his hold on Luigi. He puts the gun to Luigi's kidney and clutches the other man's suit coat between his shoulder blades. He walks close enough to Luigi that no one can see the weapon.

The sign on the door says the alarm will sound. Luigi's slow as he reaches into his pockets. Neither Marco nor Pauly seem concerned when Pauly's captive draws a knife from each pocket. It shocks me to see how fast Luigi works as he uses the tip of his knife as a screwdriver. It's hardly ideal, but it's also obvious the man has done this many times before. The end cover of the bar on the door pops off as he pries it open the last half inch. Then he's severing the wires and pushing the cover back on. The entire time, Pauly has the muzzle to his back.

Luigi keeps both knives out as he pushes the door open. I freeze, waiting for the alarm to sound. But there's nothing. With his knives in front of him, he steps outside. I look around as it's my turn to walk through the doorway. There are more voices, and I see black sedans on the street. These aren't town cars. Marco herds me toward the back of the building.

"Stop!"

Marco shoves me into a run. I feel his body move away from mine, then I hear the soft whoosh of a gun with a silencer firing a moment before a bullet lands on the street two feet from my left foot. Pauly releases Luigi as his former captive pulls a gun from beneath his shoulder. I realize he could have drawn on Pauly or Marco at any time. He didn't. He would have been dead before the gun came out of the holster. But he could have tried.

Pauly moves to one side and Luigi to the other, both turning toward the direction we came from and Marco fired. There are more people yelling for us to stop. And I hear footsteps pounding behind us. Marco checks over his shoulder, and I'm certain he fires again.

"Up there. Is that Tony and Vinny?"

I see men ahead of us at the end of the alley.

"Yeah. Can you go faster?"

I could if I weren't in the ballet flats. I do my best without them coming loose from my heels. When Marco yanks me to the left, and I look over my shoulder to see him point his arm straight out to the right and squeeze the trigger, I find the strength to sprint. He's keeping up with me, but now I'm pushing against his arm. I don't want to see who he shot at or whether he hit them. Knowing Marco, he must have hit his target. He doesn't shoot again, and no bullets come near us.

"We're almost there, *piccolina.*"

He doesn't sound winded in the least while I suck in air through my nose. I can almost make out Vinny's and Tony's expressions when three officers step out in front of us. Marco doesn't think twice about reaching over my shoulder and shooting the officer on the right. I see the two guards bolt toward us. Marco swings me around and bends over me. I look up and watch Luigi and Pauly running toward us, aiming over us.

"Marco?"

Is he hit? He's totally exposed to the man and woman he left standing.

"*Andiamo!*" Let's go.

Luigi calls out as he passes us. Marco stands up, bringing me with him, as Luigi and Pauly fall in and now shield me as we rush forward. We just need to get to Vinny and Tony. I don't know who felled the two officers, but we pass them. It could have been Vinny and Tony from behind them or Pauly and Luigi from the front. I don't care. I truly don't. It's us or them. I'm not interested in dying or getting arrested because that would mean they get Marco too.

We're almost to the car. We emerge from the alley, and we just have to get to the door one of the men left open. So fucking close. Pauly and Luigi are back to being behind us, and Vinny and Tony are running to the front seats, Vinny on the driver's side. I don't know what happens, but I'm suddenly flying. Or rather falling onto my left side. I hit the concrete hard. I know Marco tried to land first, but there's someone on top of both of us. I'm disoriented as someone grabs my arms and tries to pull me from Marco, who's still holding onto me. I flail and kick out, striking anything or anyone close enough to hit.

"Ms. Russo, come on."

Pauly's voice permeates. I look up and realize he's the one trying to get me away from the fight Marco is now in. I scramble to my knees, seeing Marco's gun just past his head. I lurch for it, grabbing it and rearing back. I put the pistol to the man's head who's on top of Marco.

"I will pull it. Get the fuck off."

I lower it to his outer shoulder and put it against his sleeve before I squeeze the trigger. He howls and rolls away. I lift the gun again, ready to shoot him in the head as Marco grabs my wrists.

"Beth, no. Come on."

I let him pull me to my feet before I look up and see his bloody face. I still have the gun, and I throw my weight forward as I prepare to shoot the man who hurt my boyfriend. I have no idea what possesses me. There isn't a rational part of me right now. Flight has disappeared, and now I'm ready to fight. The protectiveness I feel is superhuman. He hurt Marco.

The man I'm willing to kill for is pushing my hands down as someone behind me pulls me toward the car.

"He hit—"

"I know, Beth. We have to go, Beth."

I hear my name, and it registers. Maybe that's why he said it twice. But I'm still in a haze. One man takes the gun from me as Marco herds me into the car.

"Step back. Hands up."

Vinny's already in the car. Marco shoves me in, and I fall forward. I scramble to right myself as someone slams the door shut. Vinny pulls away from the curb. I hear a barrage of pings against the car. Metal on metal. I realize people are shooting at us. I search for the button and lower the privacy glass. There are cars with lights surrounding us. There's no way for us to get past. There's a woman tugging on the door next to me, but it's locked.

"Vinny?"

"Stay down, Ms. Russo. This car has bulletproof windows. They're shatter proof too. The don has to be on his way."

Salvatore. How is that going to help? Won't the feds arrest him the moment they see him? I don't have a number for anyone in Marco's family.

"Vinny, what's Massimo's number? Or Gabe's?"

He rambles them off as my hands shake. My thumbs barely dial both numbers as I start a three-way call.

"Hello."

"Massimo, help! They have Marco."

I hear a second voice. It must be Gabe.

"Who?"

"The feds or someone. I don't know. They were shooting at us. Vinny's with me."

I put the call on speaker.

"*Signore—*"

"No. English."

I demand to know what's happening.

"Sir, they were waiting for us when we got to the restaurant. Luigi warned Tony. I got stopped when a guy attacked me. Pauly and Marco took Ms. Russo inside. Luigi followed. Tony found Afonso."

That's the first time I realize there's a man in the passenger seat. Where the fuck did he come from?

"He brought the car around. Tony and I were waiting for Marco and Pauly to get Ms. Russo to us. Shots fired and at least six officers dead."

What?! Fucking pull your head out of your ass. You watched three of them get shot.

"We got to the car. One of them tackled Marco and Ms. Russo. Afonso and I have Ms. Russo in the car, but we're blocked. They have Marco, Tony, Pauly, and Luigi."

"Luigi?"

I don't know which voice that is.

"Yeah. He tried to get us out. There's no way."

No way what? Is this what Pauly meant? Something about Luigi not crossing the family?

I have questions that won't wait.

"What do we do for Marco? Where will they take him?"

Massimo responds, sounding calm enough that I want to scream at him to get upset. They took his son.

"They'll take him to Federal Plaza. If it's anywhere else, we'll know. He has a tracker on his belt he already activated. He won't talk, Liz. He knows what to do until Gabe or I can get there. Sinead will come with us."

"Who's Sinead?"

Gabe speaks up.

"Sinead's my wife. She's a criminal defense attorney. She normally doesn't get involved in family business, but she defended me not too long ago. She knows what she's doing. Among the three of us, Marco will be home in time for lunch."

He sounds so damn confident. I want to believe him. I want to think he's right.

"What do Vinny, Afonso, and I do? We can't pull out. How do you know he activated a tracker?"

"All of us just got the text right before you called. Salvatore and Luca are on their way."

"No! The don and underboss can't come here. The place has cops and feds everywhere. They'll just get arrested too. Massimo, there's like fifty officers here. I can't even see all of them, but there's gotta be two dozen cars between what's behind the building and what I can see down the alley."

There's a moment's pause, and I'm sure Massimo and Gabe are wondering how I know Luca's position. Who Salvatore is, isn't a well-kept secret in New York.

"I'll send Matteo and Carmine."

Something rattles my door. I look up to see a man with a metal pipe or something in his hand and what looks like a wedge of something in the other.

"They're going to pry my door open."

"Liz, listen to me carefully. Do exactly what I say. If you tell the FBI anything, it's as good as testifying in federal court.

You do not have to answer a single question including your name. Remain silent. Nothing you can say will help anyone. Do you understand?"

"Yes."

"If they get you out of the car, comply with any orders they give you. If they forcibly move you, don't fight it. They will arrest you. If Marco sees that, he will try to get to you. Either maneuver so he can't or get him to look at you. You must convince him without a word that you're okay."

We read each other's thoughts, but do we have telepathy? Would he understand?

Afonso has been quiet until now, but he speaks up.

"*Signore*, they're working all the doors. They're trying to get in through the trunk too."

I spin in my seat to look out the rear window. The movement next to me had my attention. They're going to get in through the trunk and push the backseat down. If I panic right now, I will do no one any good. But the temptation to lose my shit feels like the weight of the universe pushing onto me. I hear the metal bar scratch against the metal of my car door. I look up and notice there's a sliver of light coming through above the hinge. I use my free hand to tug the door as though I could keep it shut. I watch as the officer moves to the other side closer to the handle.

"Massimo, I can see your men. They have them all in handcuffs, pushed face first into a wall. It looks like people are yelling at them, but I can see none of their mouths are moving. Tony's bleeding from his forehead. Luigi looks the worst. He must have been fighting them. They broke his nose."

Neither Massimo nor Gabe say anything. I shift my gaze to Vinny and Afonso. They're looking straight ahead. I focus on my phone and watch the seconds tick by on the call. I don't like the silence. The talking was keeping me calm.

"Massimo, are you sure they're really going to take Marco somewhere legal? They won't do anything to him, will they?"

"They won't hurt him. They know who he is. That's why they went after him."

"But—"

"Liz, you have to trust me. It's been a long time since Marco's been arrested and never by the feds. But he knows what to do. They won't make the don's nephew disappear. If the feds are involved, they know Marco's position. They want him because they think he's a rising star in our family. One day, Luca will be don, and Gabe will be his *consigliere*. But they already know Marco's title. They want someone high enough up that they think they can break him. They believe too high up— like Luca —would be pointless."

"What's Marco's title? What's his position?"

That's met with silence.

"Answer me, Massimo. I won't say a word, but I need to understand what they're going to ask me. I need to understand, so I can tell you. If Marco and I are in this for good, then I have a right to know who my future husband is."

I can't believe I said that. I can't believe I put that out there. Especially after how I acted this morning. That was about a million years ago.

"Marco is the *capo dei capi*. The boss of bosses. You're going to marry the third most powerful man in the New York *Cosa Nostra*. Unless Luca has a son, one day Marco will be the underboss."

Chapter Thirteen

Marco

I'm going to make every officer who got within a hundred feet of Beth wish they'd never been born. I can see the town car even if I can't see through the tinted window. I know Afonso and Vinny are in the car with her. Luigi whispered that to me. I'd arranged for a town car to follow us just in case. This wasn't the just in case I was fearing. I now know the three men who approached Beth were FBI agents. The one who shoved her is the one who tackled us.

I'd already beaten him badly enough his mom wouldn't recognize him, but Beth shot him. We are going to have to talk about her reaction to these types of situations. I'm proud she has the courage to shoot. But now we're going to have to make sure numb nuts doesn't name her. Who knows who else saw all of it? I was focused on getting her into the car.

The one thing I now know unequivocally is that Beth is just as protective of me as I am of her. If this weren't such a fucked-up situation, I'd feel loved. That's fucked-up in and of itself.

They have me standing by a car, so the fucking news crews they called can film me. Let them. As long as the guys keep Beth out of sight, then I don't give a shit where they splash my face. I watch a man walk to the side where Beth got into the car. I pray I didn't hurt my girlfriend when I pushed her none too gently into the vehicle. Fucking shit. The little bitch officer has a slimjim and wedge. The lock pick tool won't work on our vehicles because they're for older cars. But it will allow him to pry at the door frame. If he can get it open enough to slide the wedge in, then he'll get it open.

I watch in frustration as the piece of shit succeeds and gets the door to peel away from the frame. Three other officers are working on the doors, and one's at the trunk. I dart my gaze around to see which reporters are watching the car. Only a couple. The rest are still shouting questions at me. I make sure my attention doesn't linger any longer in case someone realizes there's an important person in the town car.

If there weren't so many officers— NYPD, FBI, and ATF — swarming the place and a few less cars, Vinny would have plowed through them without a second thought. That's why Afonso moved over. I'm certain of it. Vinny started out driving a tow truck for us as a repo man. He gives no shits about anything blocking him and his job. He'll ram anything and keep driving. He knows what our town cars can do versus the veritable tanks we've made our SUVs. But there's no way he could get through so many barriers without totaling the car.

"Who's the woman?"

I look straight ahead as a Bureau of Alcohol, Tobacco, and Firearms agent steps in front of me. He shifts, trying to force me to look at him. I'm taller than the fucker. It does nothing. He's a big guy, but not as big as Gabe. My cousin's best friend is two-forty-five on a skinny day. He's lean. He's not some chubby lineman for the NFL. He's a fucking beast. I can carry his ass if I have to, and I have. I've also knocked Gabe on his ass more than once when we've sparred. I'm the only one who enjoys boxing, but we all do it. We all train to fight. It's not like it's some skill we picked up as teenagers and hoped we kept. I didn't beat the shitbag almost senseless by chance.

"Who's the bitch?"

I don't respond despite how much I'd like to bash his brains in. At the very least, spit on him. But I keep my composure.

"She the bitch you're fucking these days? I thought you kept your fucking to that club of yours."

It doesn't surprise me they know something so private. It pisses me off, but it doesn't surprise me.

"Or is she some high-end hooker you fucked last night and took out to breakfast?"

He can keep talking. All he's doing is racking up a tally of shit I'm going to do to him in six months when he thinks I've forgotten about him. I can't touch him before then. It would be too obvious. But people are going to think he got shot in the line of duty. Let them think he's a hero. I don't give a flying fuck. What I do give a fuck about is the shit I'm going to do to him before I kill him.

"They're going to have her out and in front of all those cameras in a few minutes. Her face is going to be plastered across newspapers and TVs. People all around the world are going to know who she is. If we can't get anything out of her, someone else will. Does she like it rough? Some Colombian asshole or Russian prick will fuck her and leave her broken. And it'll all be your fault for getting close to her."

I wonder if these are the interrogation tactics they teach. He can try to mind fuck me until the end of time. I won't break. But that resolve is sorely tested when I watch the car door swing open, and a female officer yanks Beth out. Cameras pan in her direction. She doesn't turn toward them, but neither does she lower her head. She looks straight at me. I know she takes in the bruises forming on my face, my hands cuffed behind my back, and the officer breathing down my neck. With this douche watching me, I can't do anything but keep my expression impassive.

Beth shoots me a warning look, and I know she's telling me not to react to the officer cuffing my girlfriend. I know she's telling me she's all right. I need to wake up from this nightmare. I need to get Beth somewhere safe, then find out who did this. I saw the beating Luigi took, and I know it came from an FBI agent pissed that he lied to them about everything to do with us. One of the NYPD officers had to pull the guy off Luigi, who spat blood in the douchebag's face. Luigi already has a mouth full of dentures. He's not too worried about having a tooth knocked out when he took a fist to his mouth for that.

Another female officer joins the first one as they manhandle Beth, who is cooperating. But I can tell both women are rapid firing questions at her. Her mouth doesn't move once. As they walk her past me, she shoots me one more warning glance. She doesn't want me to do anything to defend her. She wants me to think rather than react. She doesn't know me in these situations. I won't do a damn thing that'll give these officers a reason to rough me up more, add to the charges, realize how important Beth is to me, or let them know I'm plotting their deaths. I have a memory for faces and names.

"They're going to take your girlfriend to central holding. They're going to toss her in with the dregs of New York society. You could protect her."

They won't put her anywhere except an interrogation room. Sinead, Papa, or Gabe will get her out long before they can put her in gen pop anything. She'll be out in less than an hour. I hit my tracker as I rushed Beth into the restroom. I'm certain Vinny or Afonso has called Papa. Beth might have even gotten the number from them.

I'm unprepared to see them take Beth into the restaurant instead of a squad car or SUV. Why?

"I bet you want to know what they're doing. Give us her name, and we'll let you talk to her."

That makes me want to laugh. Talk to her? So they can listen in? Uh, no. I don't like her being out of my sight. Out of the camera's sight, they could do just about anything to her. I'm worried they might rough her up to intimidate her. They won't do too much because they don't know who she is yet. Not really. I'm certain they know her name, but they haven't figured out who she is to me. They probably guessed a girlfriend, but they don't know she's going to be my wife.

Oh, that much is now a fucking given. Not just to protect her by giving her my last name. I'm marrying her because I have never met a woman I admire more. One who awes me at every turn. One who gets me on such an atomic level. One who makes me feel at ease when I'm with her and ready to burn down the world when I'm not.

I know there's more to my feelings than that, but I don't know how to describe them. They're too enmeshed in the others for me to explain them. But they're there. I won't rush her, but something about the way she looked at me makes me know she feels the same way. The resolve. This won't push her away from me. Just the opposite. God help anyone who ruffles another hair on my head. My vindictiveness may pale compared to what I saw in the look she shot me.

"Aren't you wondering what they're doing to her in there?"

Of course, I am. But I don't acknowledge the question any more than I have the others. Isn't this fuck nut bored yet? He can keep going on and on, but I won't break. I have two brothers and a sister. We used to hide each other's toys all the fucking time and lie our asses off to each other to keep them. Papa would make us answer to him, and we'd all go silent. We wouldn't lie to our father. We weren't that fucking stupid. Papa's father, *Nonno* Vicenzu, was terrifying. Luca and I once broke a plate while we were doing the dishes. It wasn't anything special, but the noise interrupted a phone call. I thought we were going to get a belt across our asses and soles.

Neither of us said a word. Neither of us ever contemplated turning the other over. We were in it together. We would sink or swim together. In the end, that dedication got us out of trouble. Our crazy grandfather commended us for our loyalty.

The only person with the power to break us is Mama. And that's only to confess to our own sins. We still stay tightlipped about each other. She might not have known the truth— or she probably did and just didn't expect us to tell her —but she still punished us as kids. Now she just gives us her most disappointed look.

So, the long and the short of it is: if I can survive my mother, there isn't a damn thing this *stronzo*— asshole —can do to break me. It's almost amusing to listen to him try.

"There's no way to protect her when you're out here, and she's in there. You can't know what she's saying. What she's telling those officers."

That touches a nerve, but I keep looking over the douche's shoulder.

"Who's in charge?"

I want to smile, but I don't. I know that voice.

A guy's voice is a little too rude when he responds. He'll regret it by the time she's done with him.

"Who are you?"

"I'm Sinead Scotto, and I represent Ms. Russo. Where is my client?"

"How do we know she's your client?"

"How do you not? What we both know is that you're a federal agent who might be obstructing justice by denying a detained person their legal right to counsel. Now, if you'd like to keep your pension and worthless health insurance, move."

I watch as Sinead walks past. She looks me over and nods.

"If you haven't read him his rights or put him in a squad car to take him to Federal Plaza, then get those handcuffs off him before I file a suit for unlawful arrest, intimidation, and harassment. Take him and charge him or let him go. I won't say it again."

She stares at a woman blocking the door until the NYPD officer moves aside. The woman's fear radiates from her expression, and that almost makes me laugh. Sinead disappears into the restaurant, but she and Beth are back outside in a couple minutes. My girlfriend no longer has handcuffs on. Dante and Alonzo greet them and escort Beth to one of our cars. I can tell Beth doesn't want to leave, but I nod as I look over my shoulder at her. It's the first time I've openly acknowledged her. She doesn't look happy, but she keeps walking.

"Why are Mr. Mancinelli and his colleagues still standing here since I'm certain none of you have Mirandaed any of them? Either take them downtown and file charges or release them. Since there are plenty of photographers here, it'll make it very easy for me to lodge complaints against each and every one of you for unlawful detention, intimidation, and harassment. I warned you already. Unless you'd like to be named individually and collectively in a civil suit, you follow the laws you swore to uphold."

She raises her chin and looks around. The feds don't know her from Eve, but it's obvious enough NYPD know her reputation as a litigator to whisper to each other. I watch as some speak into their shoulder radios. I don't know what they hear back from their supervisors, but it's not long before the NYPD clears out. Sinead looks around and spots the men who must be the commanders. She walks to them, and without yelling but with a voice that carries, she addresses them.

"Hello. I'm Sinead Scotto. I'd say it's a pleasure to meet you, but I have no need to lie. Why are you detaining Mr. Mancinelli?"

A graying man with a smarmy smile looks down at her. Dumb motherfucker. He's the one who initially asked who she was.

"How do we know you're actually his attorney?"

Sinead pulls her wallet out and hands several things over.

"Here are my driver's license, my ABA card, and my business card. You'll see my name matches the one I gave you. My American Bar Association card shows I'm a practicing attorney. And my business card shows I'm a managing partner at Mancinelli, Mancinelli, Mancinelli, Mancinelli, Scotto & Scotto. That would be Massimo Mancinelli, Salvatore Mancinelli, Sylvia Mancinelli, Michelle Mancinelli, Gabriele Scotto, and Sinead Scotto."

When Sinead joined the family, she left her position at her old firm. Papa, Uncle Salvatore, Aunt Sylvia, Gabriele, and Sinead incorporated. Uncle Salvatore never litigates anymore, but he's still a member in good standing with the ABA just like Papa. Don't even ask how they're members along with Gabriele. It's fucking expensive. While Chelle and Enzo were on their honeymoon, Papa filed to add Chelle to the corporation. The name is ridiculously long and not the company they all actively practice under, but it makes a point.

"Are you going to make a move? If not, then release them. If you are going to arrest them, then let's go. If you're thinking of waiting this out until the courts close, so you can hold them overnight, I will make your life so damn miserable, you'll quit or retire by this time tomorrow."

"Are you threatening me, *ma'am?*"

The man's tone makes me want to punch him.

"Why would I do that when you already know I'm right?"

"It sounded like a threat."

"Then you're awfully sensitive for this job. I have no need to threaten you. But I can promise you."

She pulls out her cell phone and unlocks it. I'm way too far away to know what she's doing. But a moment later I hear the phone ringing.

"Judge Hartman, this is Sinead Scotto. I have you on speaker."

"Hello, Ms. Scotto. To what do I owe the privilege?"

The man sounds even less excited to talk to Sinead than the ATF shithead.

"I'm taking a wild guess, but I think you signed the warrant for Marco Mancinelli. I'm standing here with Mr. Mancinelli and three of his colleagues. *Your* ATF and FBI agents have already shot at an innocent bystander then detained her in cuffs simply because they believed they could. Now *your* agents refuse to acknowledge me as legal counsel for Mr. Mancinelli and his colleagues. And *your* agents won't release the men or take them in for questioning rather than having them stand around for paparazzi to photograph. The only upside to that is I now have a record of pretty much every officer here today."

She stresses "your" because it's common knowledge Judge Herman Hartman is the one most apt to sign off on a warrant for any syndicate family. It must chap his ass something fierce since he'll sign the warrants, but none of the charges ever stick. He has a zero-win track record. He keeps hoping. He's convenient for law enforcement, but they're idiots to keep using him.

A wing and a prayer, I guess. That and he's the cheapest one to bribe.

"What're your names?"

Sinead asks the two commanders.

"Special Agent Sydney Waller."

The FBI agent responds first. The middle-aged, over-weight, bulbous-nosed ATF guy hesitates. I can just barely see Sinead cock an eyebrow.

"ATF Agent Mason Spegal."

The judge's voice comes through the phone.

"Get them downtown. Stop making this a circus."

Sinead grins. This is what she wants. She knows they won't let us go, but she wants us off the street. She also wants us where Papa and Gabe must already be waiting. It wouldn't surprise me if Uncle Salvatore and Luca are there too. It's a risk for either of them to go anywhere near federal law enforcement, but no one will touch them until they have a bulletproof case.

They won't waste an arrest and make Uncle Salvatore look like the persecuted martyr once he makes sure the right press is waiting for him to walk out of the building. He probably already has the members of the press corps we want waiting for us. They'll spin this shit like tassels on a stripper.

Spegal gestures, and a guy tugs on my right arm. He pushes me toward an SUV. I look back and see Luigi, Tony, and Pauly are all being taken to separate vehicles. They're probably terri-fied that having all three of them together would let them commandeer the car. Dumb fucks. Without a grate between us and the drivers, any of us could do that on our own. Hands cuffed behind our backs or not. I watched them with my men, and I know the cops dropped the ball. They might have gotten our guns, but their pat downs were shit. None of us lost our knives. They're flat enough that you wouldn't think they're anything but a money clip.

Sinead walks over to me and looks me over. She won't ask me anything since she knows there's nothing I should say. Even before she joined our family, she would have advised her clients to remain silent. I glance toward where the town car Beth got into used to be. Sinead's lip twitches. Beth will be safe. It's as close to a reassuring smile as she'll offer me in public.

I can only imagine how Beth must feel right now. She nearly walked away from me this morning. Or at least, she had a moment's temptation. What the fuck is today going to do to our relationship?

Chapter Fourteen

Beth

I've never had a reason to be in Federal Plaza before. I spied Carmine and Matteo as I walked in. They're inconspicuous; I only noticed because I was trying to take everything in, in case it would matter to Massimo later. He said he'd send them, and he did. I didn't expect Sinead to show up at the scene. She whispered to me she was in the same law school class as my sister and Laura Kutsenko. It made me wonder why Chelle didn't come instead. But she hasn't been a defense attorney in years. She works in the nonprofit sector.

"Ma'am, step this way."

I let a new agent take my arm as I pass through security. They've uncuffed me, but I'm still surrounded as though I might— could —make a break for it. I rode to the New York FBI field office alone. I saw Sinead talking to two men who looked in charge. One had an FBI jacket on, and the other had an ATF one.

What a lot of fuss for one man. Huh. My boyfriend must be important.

I can't help the snarkiness now that I'm not terrified Marco will "accidentally" die in custody. I look for any name or identifying piece of information on every agent who gets near me. I might not remember them all, but I will remember most. I suspect Marco is going to demand that information, and I have no qualms handing it over. Not for my sake. I'd rather he not do anything to them because of me. But I don't give a shit what happens to them after shooting at Marco, after having someone jump him, after subjecting him to the reporters and cameras. That makes me consider how easily I shot that agent in the arm.

That was about the stupidest, most short-sighted thing I've ever done. But I'd never felt that kind of blind rage in my life. I didn't know I possessed it. If I feel that way about a threat to Marco, what the fuck am I going to do if we get married, have kids, and they end up Mafiosos? I get now what Pauly meant about being afraid of Marco's mother. In the space of, what, ten — fifteen —minutes I discovered I have that capacity for unparalleled protectiveness.

That's why I've followed Massimo's instructions. I haven't said a word except to say I was physically all right to Sinead. She reinforced Massimo's message to remain silent. I've already faced a barrage of questions. Male, female, FBI, ATF, NYPD. I haven't told them a single thing about me. They took my purse which I dropped when Marco and I were knocked to the ground. I don't even remember carrying it. I must have clutched it to my chest while we ran. They know who I am now.

They know where I live, so I'm certain they're turning over the place right now. They'll find nothing. Marco hasn't spent any time there. They won't find a single fingerprint of his. Not just because he touched nothing the one time he walked me to my door but because I dust regularly. I don't enjoy seeing fingerprints on anything. Occupational hazard, I suppose. Or maybe it's a compulsive behavior that serves me well for work.

My mind's wandering as I'm shuffled into an elevator then down a hallway. I'm still being observant, but I'm distracting myself from thinking about Marco being handcuffed somewhere. One woman escorting me opens a door to a room I can tell has two-way mirrored windows. It surprises me to see Massimo, Luca, and Sinead all inside. Luca's not an attorney, so I'm not sure about him. I didn't expect to see Massimo and Sinead together.

"Gabriele's waiting for Marco."

I meet Massimo's gaze as he lifts a tremendous weight off my chest. He turns away from me and looks up to a corner. I'd already noticed the camera up there.

"Turn it off, Sawyer. The audio recording too. Ms. Scotto and I are going to speak to our client. Mr. Mancinelli will wait outside."

So, Luca's the muscle. It's odd hearing Massimo call his son Mr. Mancinelli, but I suppose this is a rather formal occasion. It's not every day the FBI hauls me in to question me about my Mafia boyfriend.

Luca walks past me, meeting my gaze for only a moment. I can only imagine what people will think with him standing outside the door. I doubt too many people will approach him and suggest he goes somewhere else. I don't know what the Mancinellis put in their food to make the men grow so large. By the way Marco's body engulfed me today and what I notice as Luca walks by, these men are far taller and broader than any I've seen in a single family. Intimidating as fuck to most people. Reassuring as fuck to me right now.

Massimo turns back to me and nods.

"Sinead told me you've said nothing. Thank you."

I glance back up at the camera and then to the two-way window. I'm not convinced we aren't being recorded.

"You're smart to be suspicious, but I know we aren't being recorded. They wouldn't ignore my request."

Request. That's laughable. It was a command, and one I think whoever Sawyer is knows not to disobey.

"Can you tell us what happened?"

Massimo pulls out chairs for Sinead and me before he moves around to the other side.

"We walked to the restaurant, but when we got there, Pauly checked it and said something felt off. A moment later, we saw Vinny fighting one of the men who followed me. When I looked the other way, I didn't see Tony. Vinny knocked the guy out and was trying to get to us when Marco and Pauly took me inside. We went straight to the men's restroom, where Pauly locked us in. A few minutes went by. I think. I don't have a sense of time for what happened. Then a guy knocked on the door and spoke in Italian to Marco and Pauly. They said it was Luigi, but Marco wasn't sure if he could be trusted. He wouldn't tell me why. Pauly said he was trustworthy. Pauly went out first, and when Marco and I followed, Pauly had his arm around Luigi's throat and a gun to his head."

I pause as the fear rushes back to me. I'm picturing everything that happened. All I want is Marco right now. I'm trying not to panic since I know Massimo and Luca can physically protect me. I know Sinead will run laps around these agents. But Marco is the only person I'll feel safe with.

Sinead covers my hand and gives it a squeeze.

"This isn't the initiation into the family anyone wants for you, but you're amazing. You're stronger than most, and that's saying something about the men in this world."

"Family?"

Sinead's smile is gentle as she nods. Am I going to be forced into marrying Marco now? Do I know too much? Is it the only way to stay alive?

No. Pauly said I'm Nicoletta's future daughter. Marco and I have already talked about being all in for a long future. He told me that once his family knew we were together, they'd treat me as one of them. He didn't date before me. I'm certain he didn't introduce any women to his family. I inhale and calm down. I can keep going with my story.

"Luigi knew how to disarm the emergency exit alarm, so we went out the back. Marco heard something or sensed something. I don't know. He had his arm wrapped around me again with his chest to my back. That's how we went into the restaurant. He turned as we ran, and I know I heard a gun with a silencer. A second later, a bullet landed beside my left foot. Luigi and Pauly were back and forth, sometimes in front of us and sometimes behind us. Marco saw someone to our right that I didn't. He shot them, then he shot one of three officers who stepped into the alley in front of us. By then, Vinny and Tony were running toward us. The other two officers went down, but I don't know which of the four men shot them. We ran to the car and were so close before someone tackled Marco and me. Marco fought him, and I shot him."

"What?"

Massimo and Sinead speak as one. I nod.

"I don't know what came over me. That's the worst cliché, but it's true. The guy was hitting Marco, and I spotted Marco's gun near their heads. I grabbed it and put it to the man's head. I told him to stop, or I would shoot. I moved it to the outside of his shoulder and did. Marco forced my hands down before I killed him. Somehow, I wound up in the car, but Marco didn't. Vinny was already in there and tried to drive off. Then I called you and Gabe. That's when I realized Afonso was in the car too. You know what happened after that."

I will not cry. I will not fucking cry. If I start, I won't stop. If I'm joining this family, then I need to buck up, buttercup. That makes me think I seriously need psychiatric help. How can I not be more fazed by all of this than I am? I've shot a lot of shit in my life but never a person. I don't have an inkling of remorse.

Sinead's still smiling at me as she speaks. It doesn't match the question.

"Did the press see you shoot him?"

"I don't know. I didn't notice there was any at the time. I don't think they'd realized what was happening at the back of the building yet. But by the time I was in the car, and Vinny tried to leave, there was press gathering. They were taking photos of Marco as they arrested him."

Massimo nods, and his lips twitch too.

"They've done us a favor by calling the press. Now we have photographic and video evidence of everything. I'll subpoena all of it. It'll show no one Mirandaed the men. It'll show you didn't resist, so there was no reason to handcuff you. It'll show you leaving the restaurant with Sinead, no longer restrained. It'll show what an utter shitshow they made of this bust."

"Why did it happen?"

I flinch. That feels like an idiotic question to ask. I try to clarify.

"Why did it happen today?"

Massimo shrugs nonchalantly.

"We don't know yet. They thought the wind blew the right way. Maybe it was convenient. Maybe someone wants a promotion. It could have been any number of reasons. The thing that concerns me the most is that they did it with you present. There's no justification for that beyond witness intimidation.

They wanted to scare you into telling them what you know about our family."

"It'll be a fucking freezing day in hell before that happens."

I mutter my response, but I cringe when I realize I swore in front of Massimo. He doesn't react.

"I don't understand why those agents approached me. Why would one of them shove me?"

Sinead answers that.

"It was to start the intimidation. They wanted you to know you're being watched, but they didn't want you to know by whom."

"Can they assault me like that? I nearly tripped getting off the train. My foot nearly went in the gap."

"They'll say it didn't happen. If video captured it, they'll say he was just trying to get off the train before the doors closed. They'll come up with an excuse."

Marvelous. I want to know what caused them to act now. Why not last week? Why not next week? I'm sure Massimo knows but isn't telling me. I'm not sure Sinead does.

Marco must have inherited his mind reading skills from his father.

"Liz, we truly don't know why this happened today. I doubt Marco will be able to tell you the reason, but we will find out."

That sends a shiver down my spine. That's way more fucking ominous than the entire morning's events. That's the reaction from a father I expected. I never pictured him ranting or raving. I never imagined him lobbing threats. But those last four words held so much menace that I'd piss my pants if he directed them at me.

"Are they going to detain Marco for long?"

Massimo offers me a reassuring smile before answering.

"No. Salvatore is dealing with it, and Luca's here to make sure nothing gets forgotten."

I don't know where to look now. I focus on Sinead, who appears entirely unperturbed to hear the closest thing to an admission of bribery as we'll get from Massimo.

"Will I be free to go?"

Sinead glances at her watch.

"You already are. The paperwork probably processed about five minutes ago. But this is the safest place for you to be until Luca lets us know Marco is done."

Safest. An FBI interrogation room is the safest place for me to be against the FBI. Makes shocking sense. No one can talk to me or watch me in here. I have another question for Sinead.

"Will I get my purse back?"

"Yes. Make sure everything is in there before we leave. Look through absolutely everything to make sure you aren't leaving with more than you arrived with."

I open my mouth, then snap it shut when I realize what Sinead means. Bugs. Some type of listening or watching device. Would they really do that with so many Mancinellis here to look out for me? Probably. After all, they tried to bust Marco in broad daylight. They wanted the spectacle. They wanted the feather in their cap that they got a Mafia star. Something occurs to me.

"Who handles your family's PR?"

Massimo blinks then smiles.

"You mean who's issuing the press release demanding a public apology, and who's going to take an interview to martyr Marco. Normally, it would be Marco."

Well, shit.

"It'll be my sister, Paola. She's a political campaign manager and well-connected to the mayor and several Senators and Congresspeople from across the country. They all owe their positions to her because she's a brilliant strategist. Don't play chess against her. The news that Paola needs to address this won't go over well with any of them. It'll remind people she helped them get into office, a fact they prefer drift into the background."

"Will Marco have to stand beside her for it?"

"Yes. People need to see him battered and bruised."

Police brutality. Considering how Marco left the guy who jumped him, I don't know how that will work out. Then again, that guy probably won't want to admit Marco beat the snot out of him and I shot him. It'll only prove the failure that their mission was. I remember how Tony and Luigi looked. That was unnecessary roughness to say the least. But I don't know that they'll be up front and center.

I need to prepare myself to see Marco in whatever condition they left him. Any bruising and swelling will have set in since I left him on the sidewalk. My brow furrows as I meet Massimo's gaze.

"What happened to all the people in the restaurant? It was busy when we entered, but it was deserted when they took me back in to question me."

"They cleared everyone out while you were running down the alley."

"Were there agents already in there? Pauly sensed something was off."

"Probably. To the average person, they can blend in. Just like our bodyguards can. For those who know what to look for, they were a blaring siren."

"It would have been so different if Luigi had gotten there five minutes earlier."

Massimo just stares at me. One of those things I won't know. It shocks me as I consider how much I learned today. Out of necessity but still. But there'll always be a line he won't cross. Things I can and will never know. I look at Sinead. She doesn't appear surprised. More resigned I guess. No. That sounds morose. Accustomed.

I turn when there's a knock on the door. Luca opens it and sticks his head in. He looks at his father and nods. Massimo stands, so Sinead and I follow. Massimo follows Sinead and me out of the room. Luca walks in front of Sinead and me, exactly between us. I don't know how since he didn't watch us to position himself. I get the sense Massimo is the same.

When Marco steps into the hallway followed by Gabe, it takes everything in me not to shove Luca out of the way and run to him. He has no such reserve.

"*Muoviti.*" Move.

Luca steps aside just in time to not have his brother knock him down. He opens his arms to me, and I rush into them. He holds me, and everything is right in the world again. I feel like I can breathe. My chest hurt the entire time I was in that interrogation room. His hand presses my head to his chest, and I close my eyes.

He whispers so softly to me I wonder if I imagine it.

"*Mia piccolina.*" My little girl.

"Daddy."

It's more like a puff of air than a word. But from the way he tightens his arms around me, I know he heard me. Neither of us kisses the other. I think we're both keenly aware we're in the open now, and anyone could watch us. I'm also scared to touch his face. His lips are split. His left eye is swollen. He has bruises on both cheekbones.

"Uncle Massi."

I turn at Sinead's voice, never having heard the nickname. I don't get the family connection that she would call him uncle. Huh? I'll ask Marco or Chelle later. She hands her phone to Massimo, who swipes his finger up a few times before tapping the screen twice. He gives it back to Sinead, and his expression is finally grim.

"Auntie Paola's on the way."

Gabe's declaration earns him a nod from Massimo. Auntie? Am I just not remembering shit? Marco's father steps forward, and I try to move out of the way. But Marco's arm turns into a steel band. He at least lets me shift, so father and son can embrace without squashing me.

"*Ti amo, scimmietta.*" I love you, little monkey.

I understand the I love you part. Marco looks down at me as Massimo leans back but doesn't let go. His arm is still around his son's back, but his other hand rests on my shoulder.

"It means little monkey. Marco was always into everything. He was climbing on things he shouldn't. He was constantly chattering. And he would wrap himself around my leg until I'd walk around the house with him like that. The name stuck."

That's the sweetest thing I've ever heard. I picture toddler Marco, and it finally makes me truly smile.

"*Bellissima cuore.*" Beautiful sweetheart.

I can understand that. Marco kisses my forehead, and I close my eyes again. When I sigh, it feels like all the air leaves my body, and there's nothing but bones. I feel like I can barely stay on my feet. Massimo backs away, and Marco envelopes me again.

"We have to get through a little more, then we're going home, *piccolina.*"

Home. Where is that? Does he mean his place? I don't even want to think about what condition mine will be in. Will they have searched his?

"If you want to go to your place, we will. If you want to come to mine, we will. But home is where we are together, little one."

Hold it together. Now is not the time to burst into tears. I nod against his chest before I pull back. Gabriele, Sinead, Luca, and Massimo are whispering together. I can tell they're trying to give us some privacy, but it's not possible. The hallway is too narrow, and there are desks and offices all around us.

"*Cucciolo.*"

I look over Marco's shoulder and notice a sophisticated woman with dark hair and hazel eyes is almost within reach. I remember her from the reception. She's Carmine's mom and Marco's aunt. Paola Mancinelli Ciccone is a name I've heard before on the news, but I never paid much attention. This woman is every bit Salvatore and Massimo Mancinelli's younger sister. She's in a suit with her hair pulled back. Her jewelry is understated but speaks of style and wealth. Her glasses give her an edgy look that seems to reenforce that she's here with a purpose.

"*Cucciolo, come stai?*"

Once again, I try to move out of the way, but Marco's arm won't budge. He hugs his aunt, who carefully kisses his cheek.

"What did they do to my little cub? Who?"

Little cub? My guess is that's what *cucciolo* means. This woman who looks like she chews men up and spits them out for lunch sounds like a worried mama. She turns to me.

"Are you all right? Did any of them hurt you?"

"I'm okay, Mrs. C—"

"Paola."

She cuts me off before I finish her name.

"Thank you."

She turns to her brother after she lets go of Marco.

"Are they charging either of them?"

"No. Sal made some calls."

"Yes. To me. Our brother is too nice for the people I spoke to. The DA is up for reelection. At least, he was. I pulled out of his campaign. He's effed. The Commissioner already knew I was gunning for him next by the time I called. Jimenez must have been texting Braxton while I was chewing him a new one. The NYPD is working on a public apology. It looks like the FBI is being rather hospitable. I'll remember that the next time I speak to Director Hollands. He made a wise choice. The ATF is throwing a tantrum. Director Wattling wants to make a name for himself on this one. I'll bury him. The only name he'll have is on his career tombstone."

She turns back to Marco and pats his chest.

"Didja eat?"

She grins and winks at me. That's the stereotypical Italian — Sicilian —mother. No wonder she calls her nephew little cub. She is in politics. The way she flips the switch from being a shark to a minnow is remarkable. One moment she's out for blood. The next, I feel like I could bake cookies with her.

"No, Auntie Paola. We didn't make it that far."

"Let's fix that. Gabriele, I can practically hear your stomach from here."

"My wife was too busy saving this *idiota's* ass to make me breakfast."

Luca snorts.

"Saving him. That's why she was too busy. Okay."

Gabriele looks utterly unrepentant, and Sinead looks bored. Was Luca hinting that they were— Oh. He was.

"Luca, don't be crude."

"Yes, Auntie Paola."

I suck my lips in to keep from smiling. He looks duly chastened. The Mancinelli family's underboss got in trouble with his aunt for making a rude joke. Not only that, he looks guilty as sin. Chelle mentioned at the reception that she thought she'd entered the Twilight Zone when she met the family. They are so fucking normal that it's unnerving. I think it's how they survive. It's not just guns and whatever. It's their loyalty and love for one another. It must help them get through the grisly shit.

And that reminds me where we are and why. How are they just bantering like they aren't being watched by practically every set of eyes on this floor? Everyone must be wondering why we're hanging out. I'm wondering that.

"We need to wait for the right press to arrive. When they're in place, we'll head out. Someone will let Auntie Paola know when they're ready."

Marco has finally released me but only to take my hand. We've laced our fingers together, and we're leaning against each other's arm. I glance around, realizing it doesn't really matter that we didn't kiss. He held me for so long people couldn't miss it. Now we're holding hands.

"Reading my mind as always."

He leans to whisper in my ear.

"I'm going to give you that kiss when we're alone. I'm going to do a lot more than that, *piccolina*. Decide what fantasy you want to act out tonight. I plan to make you forget today at least for a few hours."

I perk up as our gazes lock. Maybe letting my mind run wild with sexual ideas will help me get through the impromptu — no —strategic press conference we're headed to. I'm scared to be in front of those people when I walk out. Even if I move aside, I'm going to have to watch and listen to people attack Marco and his family. If I can distract myself just a little, then my fear will ease. And I won't be likely to sink my claws into anyone who says a disparaging thing about my boyfriend. My hackles are rising thinking about it.

"We'll forget together, Daddy. Once we're alone, please stay with me. I—"

Finally, the dam cracks. A single tear slides down my

cheek. I force myself back under control, but Marco sees it. The back of his fingers stroke my cheek.

"You won't be out of my reach, *mio tesoro*. I'll lose my mind if I'm apart from you again today. I can't cry here for obvious reasons, but don't think I wouldn't if I could. You're so damn brave, Beth. I'm so proud of you."

"We just need to get through this press conference."

Chapter Fifteen

Marco

Well, that was a shitshow and a half. Auntie Paola led the way out since she orchestrated the press conference, arranging for the reporters most favorable to us to have the best spots. Carmine and Matteo made sure of that. Papa, Luca, Gabe, and I shielded Beth and Sinead. They stood behind us, and for the most part, no one could see them.

Auntie Paola spun this shit like it was pure gold. I've always known she could work miracles for even the most fucked-up candidates, but I never realized how easy it is to fall under her spell. By the end, I was believing half the shit she said. She didn't flagrantly lie, but she sure did find some remarkable ways to make the truth work for us.

It wasn't until we had to get into the cars that things flew off the handles. Reporters recognized Sinead first. There was a horrendous article printed about her when she first started representing Gabe for a crime he didn't commit. They retracted it, but seeing her among us opened the flood gates. I

thought Gabe was going to murder one guy right there on the spot. It was Sinead's hand on his arm that restrained him. I couldn't blame him. I was ready to go apeshit a minute later when they went after Beth.

They wanted to know who she was. How she was connected to the family. Whether she was already somehow related to us. What it was like to date a mobster— we're the fucking Mafia, ass wipes. How is that so motherfucking hard? Whether she was going to leave me.

That one made her look directly at the reporter and raise her chin. It was a dare if ever I saw one. The guy backed down. But it only meant someone else took his place. They wanted to know if she came from a Mafia family. Whether she already had ties to known crime families. One even went so far as to ask if she set me up. That made Auntie Paola, Sinead, and Beth stare at the woman, who scooted back into the crowd.

Blessedly, it's over. We're finally in a car alone, and it's quiet. I opted for a town car only for the sake of the privacy glass. We have SUVs surrounding us that the others are riding in. But we have the space to ourselves. The moment the door shut, we were fumbling with our clothes. She keeps kissing around my mouth not wanting to hurt me. But it's driving me nuts.

"Ahhh."

She moans as she slides down my cock. I fist her hair and hold her in place. I plunder her mouth, my tongue touching every satiny bit it can reach. I want to taste every inch of her, and I will tonight. We aren't moving except for our mouths. It's one of those times where we just need to be connected for a few minutes. A little calm during our storm of emotions.

My free hand slaps her ass hard. I pull my mouth back from hers, but my hands hold her in place.

"Right now, I need to feel you and know you're truly okay. I need to know we're okay. I'm feeling possessive as fuck, Beth. I'm angry at the world for coming near you. I'm angry that anyone thought they could use you to get to me. I'm angry that I couldn't be with you during this. But I'm not angry at you. However..."

She bites her bottom lip and nods.

"We are going to have a reckoning. You didn't have to prove you'll shoot someone for me. You put yourself at risk, and I can't overlook that no matter how badly I want to spoil you and take care of you."

"You're right, Daddy. And whatever punishment is coming is your way of taking care of me. What I did was— I don't know what to call it. Impetuous, yes. But more than that. Selfish. Thoughtless. Childish. I lashed out without thinking about the consequences. I did what I wanted. I'm sorry, Marco."

"Those aren't the reasons I'm upset. I would have done the same thing. The difference is I'm equipped to deal with what could happen next. I have the training, the connections, and the means to protect myself, even if I wound up in prison. You don't. You endangered yourself, and that I won't tolerate. Even if you did it for a good reason."

She presses her lips between her teeth, closes her eyes, and nods.

"We will deal with that later. Right now, I'm going to make love to the woman I love."

The backseat of a car isn't the greatest place to make that declaration, but it can't wait. Today's— adventure —solidified what I was already feeling. It made all those emotions come together with a clarity and brightness I didn't expect. I was three-quarters of the way there before this. Now I'm certain of it. It's not just the heat of the moment or the haze of passion.

Everything about Beth today made me realize there is no more perfect a woman for me than her. She's everything I need and more than I deserve. Being apart from her was agony. Not knowing what was happening to her. Gabe tried to reassure me, but I told him to shut the fuck up since he'd be just like me if the situation were reversed. The moment I saw her, the world went back on its axis. The moment she was in my arms, I knew my life is bound to hers until my last breath.

Her eyes snap open at my declaration. I'm not sure how she's going to take it. She cups my jaw in both hands, lifting my chin.

"I love you, Daddy. I want to make love to you, too."

"Vanilla?"

"Yes, please."

I cup her tits together and kiss the top of them before swiping my tongue down her cleavage. My thumbs rub over her nipples until I feel them peak beneath her lacy bra. We've both ignored the crap on our clothes. Dirt. Dried blood. I don't care. I unbutton her shirt until I can get to her nipples. I alternate sucking both of them, building the pressure from licking to devouring.

She holds them up, pressing them together like I did. My hands move to her ass, gliding over her silky skin, along her hips, and down her thighs, then back up again. Over and over. She didn't have panties to take off yesterday, so there were none to put on. Nothing was in the way once I got her skirt up to her waist and my pants open.

"*Piccolina*, I think you can throw out all your pants along with your panties. When I want your pussy, I'm going to have it. Nothing in the way."

"Yes, Daddy."

I'm not sure she knows what she's agreeing to before she swoops in for another kiss. She's riding my cock and making the most erotic sounds that are getting me way too close to coming.

"This is vanilla, but your orgasms belong to me. Who decides if you get to come?"

"You, Daddy."

"Who's going to make you come?"

"Only you. Daddy, shh."

I chuckle as I go back to kissing her. She wants us to kiss more than she wants our dirty talk. I'm happy to oblige for now. She's being so gentle with my lips. I'm the one who's being more ardent, not because I feel more than she does, but because I'm no longer feeling the pain of my split lips. Her kisses are curative.

We move together for I don't know how long. I know she's gotten close then slowed down. She hasn't asked to come. Neither of us wants this over. She's edging herself right now. She alternates between sliding up and down my cock, her tits bouncing, and rocking her hips, making her tits sway. How magnificent they are.

"Marco, I can't hold out much longer. I tried because I want to come with you, but I can't. May I come?"

"Yes, baby girl."

"You— you said you were feeling possessive. Me too. I want your cum, Daddy. I want you to fill me with it. I want to feel it spilling out of me. I want it on my tits too. I want to see you mark me with it. That cum is only for me."

"It is. And one day, we're going to make babies with it. For now, we're going to keep practicing. Hold on."

She wraps her arms around my neck, and I shift us until she's lying on the backseat. I keep my thrusts slow, not pulling back more than a couple inches before sinking balls deep and staying there for a few seconds. I do this over and over until I feel her pussy tighten around me. I push her shirt up to see her belly flutter as she comes.

I groan as I shoot my load. Just as my orgasm wanes, and

I'm certain I don't have much cum left to spend, I pull out. I jerk myself twice while my jiz lands between her tits that she's pushing together again. I slide back into her, needing the connection to last a little longer. I draw her up and onto my lap as I once again sit. She curls around me. I never told her about my dad calling me little monkey when she chose chimpanzee as her safe word. I'll think of her cuddling into me more like a koala.

She reaches between us and unbuttons my shirt until we're skin to skin. I rest my hands on her ass again as we bask in our afterglow. Traffic is a nightmare, and I've never been more grateful. But eventually, we pull up to her place in Brooklyn. We settle our clothes as best we can. When Dante showed up with a car for us, he had a bag with fresh clothes for me. Mama. She must have pulled some stuff from the closet in my childhood bedroom. I still keep a few pieces of clothes there just in case.

When we get to her door, I notice the frame is still fully intact. It doesn't look like anyone attempted a forceful entry. I stick out my hand for her keys, and she gets behind me. It shocks both of us that the place hasn't been touched. I already know from Enzo that no one's been near my place. When I got my phone back before we left the FBI, I had a shit ton of texts to scroll through. The one that stands out to me came five minutes before we got to the restaurant. I never felt my phone buzz.

LUIGI

Feds are coming. They're following you and plan a bust today. Stay home.

He tried to warn me. If only I'd seen it. Pauly was right about Luigi's loyalty. It leaves the unsettled question of who set him up as the feds patsy?

"All I want is a shower, then something to eat. Is that okay with you?"

Beth's voice pulls me back from my thoughts as I sweep her place. I check along all the baseboards and under all the drawers and in all the cabinets. There are no bugs here. They might not have forced their way in, but I didn't trust that someone hadn't been here.

"Of course. Do you want me to join you?"

She looks at me as though I've lost my mind. I'll take that as a yes. I follow her into her bedroom and into the bathroom. We both gladly dropped our filthy clothes into the hamper. Well, I drop my shirt, socks, and boxer briefs into them. Back to my usual. The suit will need dry cleaning. She adjusts the water and steps in. I'm right behind her. I wrap my arm around her belly as I press my cock between her ass cheeks.

"You held me like this earlier. Is that what they trained you guys to do? That way the woman can keep up and is shielded?"

"No. Though I suppose that would be a good idea to share. I did it because I wasn't letting a damn thing come between us. I couldn't shield your front and your back, but I could cover most of you if I leaned over you. I wasn't going to risk getting separated."

"I love you so much."

She turns around and is so careful when she goes up on her toes to cup my cheeks and press a kiss to my lips.

"I love you."

She repeats herself now that we can see each other.

"Beth, I hate that today happened. I hate that this part of my life touched you. But I know without a doubt just how strong my feelings are for you. We'll go at your speed, but I want you to know that when you're ready, I want to talk about getting married."

I try to temper it and be a little vague. It was just this

morning that she thought she wanted to end things. It didn't last much longer than a shower, but I can't forget she had that moment of feeling overwhelmed. I don't have the words to describe where we're at now if that was too much.

"Marco, forget this morning before we left your place. I woke up thinking about how I want to make my life with you. I plead a moment of temporary insanity. That panic came and went. It had before we set off. I have never been so scared in my life. But I wasn't scared for me. I was scared for you. They might have hurt me, but I was convinced they were going to kill you. I asked your dad at least twice if they were really going to bring you in. I was terrified they'd say something like you resisted arrest or tried to go for an officer's gun. Anything that would justify them shooting you. That blinding fear started the moment you turned around to shoot the first time. I realized how exposed you were. When that guy fought you, all of that fear turned into rage. Something gave me the restraint to only shoot him in the shoulder. It wasn't just you holding my wrists. But if he'd swung again, I would have killed him. I do not doubt that for a moment. If anything should have overwhelmed me and made me have doubts, it was everything that happened at the restaurant. All it did was solidify the fact that it is us against the world. You and me— and your family. We aren't separate anymore. It's us from now on."

"God, I love you."

"I love you."

Our kiss is so incredibly tender until it's not. As always, the flicker turns into a flame. My ribs are bruised, and my legs are killing me from running and now standing. But I'm not passing up the opportunity to finally have shower sex with my girl-friend. I lift her, and she wraps her legs around my waist just before I thrust into her. I press her back against the wall, giving me some relief from bearing all her weight. If the car was gentle, this is frantic. Her nails scrape over my scalp and back. My fingers are going to leave marks on her ass.

My mark. Mine. Mine. *Mine.*

"I am yours, Daddy."

I must have spoken aloud. Or maybe it's our telepathy. I understood her each time we exchanged a look. We didn't need words earlier. Right now, they're just nice to hear.

We're done nearly as fast as we started. I lower her to her feet, and we take turns washing each other's hair and bodies. I might insist we never shower alone again.

"I know what fantasy I wish we could enact. But it would require going to the club, and I'm too scared to leave here tonight."

Tears well in her eyes as she admits her ongoing fear.

"What do you want, *piccolina?*"

"I want to be bound and suspended in the air. I want to be entirely at your mercy. Blindfolded, gagged. I'll even take the ear plugs."

That's an enormous sign of trust since she told me from the get-go that those are a hard limit.

"I don't want to know what you're going to do to me. I don't want to know whether you're going to make me wait or start immediately. I want you to leave me long enough each time to grow nervous. I want to take my punishment like that too."

"You want to submit entirely to me tonight."

"Yes. I want to give you absolute control. I want to know that it's my decision to do that. That no one took control from me. But I also want to give it to you because I trust you to always take care of me. Because I know you need to have it as much as I need to relinquish it. After my punishment, I know I won't get to come. I want to do whatever you desire to get you off. Clamps, plugs, any kind of impact play, heat, cold. Whatever you need."

"You want to be a sex slave for tonight."

"I guess that's what I described. Or basically a sex doll. I don't know. But that's not how I see it. I see it as showing you that my trust is absolute and that my love is unconditional."

The images her words conjure. Lab.Oratory is pretty hardcore in a lot of spaces. The rooms might be cute, and the amenities are top of the line. But the things that go on there are not for novices to explore alone. Knowing that, I know Beth means what she says. She understands what she's offering me. That sentiment is worth more than anything we can physically do. That said, I know we need this. I won't take her there ever again. Not now that I know the feds are aware of my membership and hinted that they knew about hers. We'll find somewhere else or build something in our place wherever that is.

I picture her place and mine. Is there anywhere I could suspend her from? Is there anything high enough and sturdy enough? My mind is ticking in overtime. Gabriele owns several hardware stores, so I could get what I need fast. But then there would be the question of why. Or worse, Gabe's kinky ass would guess. All the men of my generation have the same proclivities, apparently. We don't discuss it. We just know.

Fuck. Nothing is coming to mind. Do I try to get a guest pass at one of the other clubs? No. Definitely not. I'm not taking Beth anywhere public like that even if they're exclusive and supposedly private. I can't picture a hotel that isn't some seedy pay-by-the-hour place that might have what I'm looking for. Fucking-a.

My libido is in overdrive imagining what she suggested, but more than anything, I want to give her this. I told her to pick a fantasy. She's confided in me what she wants and needs.

"Daddy, I can hear the gears spinning. That fantasy doesn't have to be tonight. Some day. I— um —I have a few things here."

Her face flushes deep red. I try not to see red.

"The vibrators are ones I've only ever used on myself. The other stuff I got because I hoped we'd..."

She's not sure where to look. I'm looking at a body that I still want to taste every inch of.

"What do you have, *piccolina*?"

"Shibari rope."

She really likes the idea of being restrained.

"Marco, this isn't like my thing. I mean, bondage and restraints have always been good in the past. But with you—after you put me on the Saint Andrew's Cross the first night. It's been on my mind a lot."

I run my hands over her tits.

"I'd love to see these in diamond holsters. Watch them turn pink as your nipples expand. Such an invitation to suck and spank them. Maybe I'll bind your wrists at your back then your calves and ankles. I'd leave your thighs free, so they can spread wide enough for me to fuck your pretty little cunt before I fuck your tight little ass."

Her chest rises and falls faster, and I notice her nipples have turned into little nubs. She likes my suggestions.

"What else do you have for us, little girl?"

"A ball gag, so my neighbors can't hear me when you make me come."

"Anything else?"

She nods. Just how much shopping did my girlfriend do before we were even a couple?

"Marco, it was an impulse one night when I was lonely because you had to cancel for work. I hate the idea of using certain toys and implements at the club, even if I know they sterilize them. I thought I might bring them with me some time."

"Would you rather show me?"

She nods. I turn off the water and reach for a towel for her then for me. I wrap it around my waist before rubbing hers up and down her body. I let my fingers play with her clit.

"Marco."

She moans my name as she tries to reach beneath my towel.

"Not yet. Let's see what you have. And we still have your punishment to discuss."

She freezes as she looks at me. It's not fear. It's regret.

"What's wrong? What just made you retreat?"

"I'm going to show you all these things, and I'm certain you're going to get off. But I won't. If you even touch me, it'll be to edge me."

"What makes you think that?"

"I'm pretty damn sure you're going to tell me pleasure doesn't follow punishment."

"Why are you so sure of that?"

"Because it wouldn't be punishment otherwise. You want me to understand how dangerous my actions were, and that you didn't voice an empty threat when you warned me."

"Normally, I'd say you're right. But today was unlike any I've ever had. I thought I was going to die and leave you unprotected. It terrified me that you'd be shot, or they'd hurt you while taking you from me. The punishment is a given, but so is the pleasure. I don't want to leave you with only memories of pain from tonight after everything that happened."

"Okay. I also have a waist harness. The kind that has the attached garters and the wrist cuffs that hook onto the garters. I got one more bondage thing. It has the throat cuff, wrist cuffs, and ankle cuffs all on connected chains. It came with a spreader."

"To connect to the wrists and ankles. Does it have a leash?"

"Yes."

"I won't use it, Beth. That's a hard limit for me with you."

"With me?"

Fuck. I know how that sounds.

"It wasn't in the past. I may tug your hair, and we might do breath play, but I won't lead you around like pet play or a slave. I can't with you. Just the thought makes it feel all wrong."

She wraps her arms around me, her hands clasping at my lower back.

"We've avoided anything more than the basics about our past partners, and I'm glad about that. I don't want to know, and I don't want to have to tell you. But I know you've used leashes before, and I've worn them. I'm certain you've called women sluts, whores, cunts, and a few other things. I've been called those. Slapping my face has also been a hard limit. I didn't think to mention it because I've never once gotten the sense you would do that or fish hook my mouth. I like the praise kink. The other stuff was fine, but it never did for me what your praise does. I like how we are, Daddy."

She gives me a peck as she bounces onto her toes. She lets go and steps around me, but I grasp her wrists and pull her back.

"I like how we are too, *cuore*."

She leads me out to her dresser and pulls open a drawer full of items still in their packaging. I lift out the last harness she described and unwrap it. I examine how it's put together before I summon her over. I attach the neck cuff, along with wrist ones, then I guide her to the bed in silence. She climbs on and moves her hands to her lower back without me having to instruct her. But rather than attach the spreader, I leave her kneeling there. I fetch my belt and hold it up. She nods her consent.

"Beth, I need you to talk to me during this. I need to know if I'm too rough. Safe word or tell me to lighten it. If you take it because it's a punishment, and it does more than just hurt, I don't know that I'll forgive myself enough to do anything like this again. I can't handle the idea of harming you."

"I will. I never want to break your trust. Period. But especially not about something as intimate as this. Something that is just between the two of us. I never want to make you regret anything about being with me. And I don't want you to regret anything you do with me. I won't put you in that position, *amore mio.*"

And now my heart is a melted puddle on the floor. To hear her call me her love, and for it to be in Italian the first time— that's everything to me. It almost makes me want to abandon the spanking. But I love her, and I want her to feel absolved of her mistake while understanding just how dire it was. I still can't believe she shot the guy. I wanted to. I would have if he'd gotten any closer to Beth. It was just so unexpected.

I sit on the bed, and she shifts to lie across my lap. I consider folding the belt in half, but at this angle, I don't know that I'd have as much control as wrapping most of it around my fist.

"Five, Beth. No more. And that's total, not each side."

"Yes, Daddy."

I felt her disagreement the moment I said the number. I won't harm her, but I won't be gentle either.

"Are you ready?"

"Yes."

I raise my right hand and bring it down with a crack across both cheeks. I land a second one just an inch lower than the first only a second later. The next two are immediate and hit her horizontal crack. It'll be uncomfortable to sit for a couple of days. The last one is across the very top of her thighs. It's far lighter than the previous four. I don't have the heart to spank her anywhere I already have. Her ass is bright pink already. I uncoil the belt, then rub, and squeeze.

I help her sit up, her ass between my thighs as I make sure the towel drapes open. I hold her and rub her back.

"Thank you, Marco. It hurts like a motherfucker, but I feel better."

We sit together for five minutes as the burn lessens in her ass. When she feels better, I help her onto her feet.

"There's one more thing in the drawer. It's specifically for you."

I furrow my brow as I walk back to the dresser. I spot what I hadn't noticed before. I hold it up and grin.

"Are you trying to tell me something?"

"No. I got it before we even had sex. And you definitely don't finish too fast. I just thought it might be fun to try."

"Onto the bed. Kneel, legs apart."

She hurries to do as I say as I rip the packaging off the cock rooster. It's an ejaculator delay. I don't get the name since it's redundant, but it's a cock sleeve with a ribbed outside tip and textures along the side to stimulate Beth's pussy while I fuck her. The base will fit around my cock snuggly enough to be a ring that slows how soon I'll be able to come. Considering how badly I want to drive my dick into her until she's screaming my name, this might not be a bad thing. I don't know how long I'd last with all these things to choose from and the picture she's painted in my mind about suspending her.

She's watching me, and her smile is the sexiest smirk I've ever seen. Fucking hell. She was smart to get this. But I'll edge her with it until I can't hold back. I slip the ankle cuffs onto her, then attach her wrists and ankles to the spreader bar. The chain from her throat cuff also connects.

"Daddy, I want to suck you."

Who am I to say no? I help her turn, so I can put one foot on the bed and guide her mouth to my cock.

"I want you to fuck my mouth not just let me suck you off."

I nod, too eager to say anything. Her mouth opens, and I slide in. I press the back of her head forward as I flex my hips. The temptation to thrust over and over, pushing her lips to my pubic bone is fucking intense. She'd choke, and I don't want that. I don't want to hear that with her. I keep the pressure light and my movements shallow. I let her decide what she can take. But my head falls back, and I groan as I feel the tip slide along the back of her throat. Fuck. I need that cock ring.

I won't last if she keeps doing this. She gives amazing head, and I'm ready to come already. I pull out and grab the rooster. I slide it on before getting onto the bed. It's easy for me to lift her and position her how I want, so she can ride me. The bar bangs across my shins, but I don't care. I grasp her hips and bounce her on my dick as my left thumb rubs her clit. I don't let up until I know she's close. I know how to read her expressions and her body. I lift her off, and she wails. I spin her around then thrust into her, making her scream. Maybe I should have grabbed the ball gag. My legs bracket hers as I use the chain running down her back to pull her to my chest and pin her there as I flex my hips over and over.

We go around and around as I edge her. The cock ring is doing the trick. I feel like I can keep going forever. But I know she's going to get overly sensitive if I don't be careful. I let her come once about halfway through our little game of sorts. The last time I lift her off me, I pull off the rooster and toss it aside. I reposition her the way we started. She slides down me, and I tip her forward, so I can suck her breast.

"May I come, Daddy?... Please, Marco. I can't take it anymore."

"I know. Come in five. Four. Three. Two. Now."

My count is slow as I thrust into her over and over. She screams out my name as I call out hers. I may have blacked out there for a moment. I hurry to unfasten the restraints, so she can straighten her legs and move her shoulders. She flops forward onto me as we pant.

"You're amazing, *tesoro*."

"So are you, *amore mio*."

I'm just about to tell her what it does to me to hear her call me that. But my phone buzzes three times on the dresser where I placed it when we passed it on the way to the bathroom. It stops. Then rings three more times.

"You've got to be fucking kidding me right now."

Chapter Sixteen

Beth

"What is it?"

I follow Marco's pissed off stare to his phone on the dresser. It rang three times, then stopped. It keeps doing that pattern as Marco stands up. I watch his chiseled ass muscles flex with each step. His body is a temple I'll gladly worship at until I die.

"*Cosa vuoi?*" What do you want?

Sounds like Marco isn't thrilled to speak to whoever is on the other end. He remains quiet, but I can't hear anything. Even if I could, it's probably in Italian. Clearly, he doesn't want me to know what's happening since he answered in Italian. It's mostly a one-sided conversation with him listening until he hangs up.

"Why do you speak Italian and not Sicilian?"

I don't know why I blurted that question, but it tumbles out. I guess it's something else I don't know about him and want to.

"I do speak Sicilian, but rarely. Most of the families we're connected to have Sicilian roots, but over the years, Italian became the common language because it allowed us to communicate with people from other regions. It's the default now."

I nod. Makes sense.

"We need to go to Uncle Sal's. Something's come up, and I'm not comfortable with you staying here without me. I don't want you at my place alone, either."

I stare at him. I don't want to go out and be around other people. I like the little bubble we created here. He walks over to me and perches on the edge of the bed.

"I have to go out tonight, and I don't want you as unprotected here as you will be. Even with the guards outside your door and outside your building, I don't want you alone here."

"Outside my door?"

I look past him and into the living room. We left the bedroom door open. Did those men hear us? I'm fucking mortified.

"I had three men with us to walk to a restaurant and look what happened. Did you really think I would take you anywhere and not have guards posted outside the door?"

"I didn't think about it."

"Well, I did. I spoke to Luca while you talked to Auntie Paola after the press conference. He knows I want the detail tripled and around the clock. No one is coming near you again. But I still won't be at ease with you somewhere like either of our places. Uncle Sal's property is in a gated community behind its own gate. The walls are high, and he has armed men patrolling it twenty-four seven."

Scary and reassuring at the same time.

"I'm sure you won't tell me where you're going, but can you tell me if you'll be alone?"

"I won't be. The other wives will be there with you, too."

Other wives. I'm not one of them. But he's watching me, and the expression he's giving me tells me not to argue with the obvious.

"Does that mean you're all going to do whatever this is?"

"I don't know yet."

I believe that.

"Is this about today or something else?"

He remains silent. I can assume it's about today, but who the fuck knows what else he's been dealing with?

"Do you know if you'll be back tonight?"

He doesn't answer. I have other questions, but clearly it's pointless. This is what I signed up for. These are the lies he told me he'd tell. Either by word or omission. He scoops me onto his lap, and I shift uncomfortably. Fuck. My sore ass meeting his rock-solid thigh doesn't feel good. He cocks an eyebrow at me as if to say "see." That was the point of the punishment. I wanted it, and I took it.

"You know I would answer your questions if I could. There will be times when you ask me things I can't answer. I truly won't know the answer. And there are times you'll ask things I just can't tell you. Part of me hopes you'll keep asking. That you'll wonder and care. That you won't just resign yourself to me keeping things from you. But the other part of me fears you'll stop asking because you'll resent me never telling you the truth."

"I will always wonder and care. But it is frustrating to know there's no point."

"I'm sorry."

"It's not you, Marco. You've warned me since the start. I knew from Chelle. It's just different when it's happening to you."

"I promise I will tell you as much as I think is safe. Right now, I don't know enough to decide, so I'm erring on the side of caution. I will always do my best to say goodbye before I leave, even if it's just a call."

"I'd ask if you're warning me that there's always a chance you won't come home. But after today, I'll never wonder that again."

He cups my cheek and kisses me with so much love and tenderness that I melt into him. I wish this kiss could carry on forever, so neither of us has to accept he's going to drop me off with virtual strangers and leave. At least my sister will be there. Thank God for that.

But it's over way too soon. He's putting on the fresh clothes that appeared in a bag before we left the FBI. I'm wearing jeans and a nice shirt. I'd rather be in yoga pants and oversized -shirt, or better yet, one of Marco's. But I try to appear presentable.

We're quiet in the car to Queens. I nestle against him, his arms wrapped around me as I sit next to him. Halfway there, we both get fed up with the angle. I don't know if it's because it's a town car, and it kinda feels like the old days of cabs where no one wore a seatbelt, or if it's being with Marco, but I never question sitting on his lap. I snuggle with him as we both look out the window. I'm so comfortable I would fall asleep if I wasn't so anxious about being around his entire family. On top of that, he'll be leaving me with them to do heaven only knows what.

When we arrive, the door opens, and Chelle darts out. I let go of Marco and run to my sister. We crash into each other, and we'd fall over if Marco and Enzo didn't keep us on our feet. We cling to each other much longer than most would consider necessary. It slams into me how close I came to never seeing my sister again. Marco and I haven't talked about what to tell my parents. Neither has called, so maybe they haven't heard about the press conference.

Chelle tucks hair back from my face as she looks me over, my arms still around her. We lean in again, hugging more than we have since our brother died. No one tries to hurry us. I noticed Enzo and Marco hugging, but they're giving us time.

"Lizzie, I was so scared. And angry. Enzo practically had to tie me to a chair to keep me from going down there. I wanted to know what they were doing to my big sister."

"When I saw Sinead, I wondered why you weren't there, too. But I realized you're not a defense attorney."

"That had nothing to do with it. Enzo knew I was too furious. I didn't trust myself not to lose my shit and make things worse. I knew you needed time with Marco, so I didn't go to your place. But that took restraint I didn't think I had. That was harder than not going to Federal Plaza."

Now I feel guilty.

"Lizzie, stop. Don't feel guilty. Not about not calling me or Mom and Dad. They know what happened. I talked to them. You and Marco needed to be alone to deal with this. It's the first time for you. I needed it after the car accident, but we couldn't have it right away. I'm glad you did."

"We got lucky, and neither of us was seriously hurt."

"But you could have been, and that's why I was too enraged to go anywhere near the authorities. I would have been the one arrested."

I glance over at Marco.

"I've always felt protective of you, and not just because you're younger than me or because Sam died. When I learned what happened to you and how badly you could have been hurt or died, I discovered a newfound level of it. But what I felt today when I thought Marco was going to die— I didn't recognize myself."

"I know what you mean. How I feel about Enzo has heightened all my emotions. Seeing that press conference made me realize how important all my family is to me, and there is nothing I won't do to protect it. I get my in-laws in an entirely new way. In a fucked-up way, I feel even closer to them, knowing I wouldn't think twice about killing someone to save you."

"Same."

We hug again, and it brings me a different kind of relief from what Marco gave me. My sister and I walk into the house arm-in-arm. But I soon feel like I need to straighten my posture and get my manners together. They're all there, even two little girls watching something on their device.

Nicoletta pushes past Luca and Enzo to get to Marco. He lifts her off her feet as she hugs her son. I need to call my parents. She's speaking in such rapid Italian I don't know if anyone can understand her. He puts her back on her feet, but neither of them lets go. I guess no one completely gets used to the threats and danger. They aren't impervious to the fear and relief.

When Nicoletta eventually lets go of Marco, she turns to me. She's slower as she approaches me, but she offers me a hug. I accept. The moment she wraps me in her arms, I burst into tears. What the hell? I feel safe with Marco. But I feel comforted with Nicoletta. I can't stop sobbing. Marco's hovering, but she's waving him away. I reach out a hand to him, and he grips it like he fears I'll float away. I'm not ready to let go of his mom yet. She's cooing to me and rubbing my back. It's the next best thing to my own mom.

I hear male voices, but I can't tell what they're saying even though I know they're speaking English. I think they're planning. I turn my head to look at Marco, and I can see the men at the other end of the living room. He should be there not holding my hand while I have a meltdown. I step back and wipe away my tears. I try to use both hands, but Marco won't let go.

"I'm okay now."

He nods, but he won't let go. I smile at Nicoletta who slips away. Marco yanks me to him, and I press my right hand to his heart as my left arm wraps around him.

"Truly, Daddy. I'm okay now. I had a moment because your mom felt like a mom should. But I'm back to normal."

I whispered to him, and he brings his lips to my ear.

"She's awesome, and I know what you mean. I'll never ever outgrow my mom's hugs. But that doesn't mean I enjoy seeing you upset. And it's totally normal not to feel normal right now."

"Thank you. Between your mom and you, I'm not upset anymore. You need to be over there, don't you?"

"Yeah."

He doesn't let go.

"Marco?"

"Just let me hold you a little longer."

I realize just how much it bothered him to see me crying so hard.

"You can hold me for forever, but I won't break. I know I didn't turn to you, but I needed your mom in that moment."

"Beth, I'm not upset about that. I'm glad you have my mom. It makes me feel better knowing that. I hate that I'm the reason you needed her."

"You are not the reason. You were born into this, and I know now that my grandfather left. But I can tell why you can't. Why you won't. I will never fault you for putting your family ahead of yourself. It was vainglorious people with chips on their shoulders who did this. I don't have to understand every law of physics to know that bullet landed next to my foot when it did because someone shot at you first. That told me the other officers would have shot at you, too. And they wouldn't shoot to miss. They started it, and you protected me. They are the reason. Not you. Not ever *you*."

It isn't him as an individual. It's the fucked-up world he belongs to. One I don't think a single member of his family would remain in if they could escape while keeping everyone they love safe. I admit I was a bit judgy when I learned what kind of family Laura married into when she became a Kutsenko. I shouldn't have been because now I'm exactly like her. Because my sister is just like her.

There's something about these men and these families... You can overlook what happens when you're not there. You can make peace with who they have to be. You can love them for how they'll do anything for the people they've sworn to protect.

I don't know if there's some kind of initiation into manhood like a bar mitzvah for Mafiosos. I don't know if the other syndicate families have something. Maybe the pledge doesn't have to be said out loud, but it's there.

"I pray you never change your mind, *piccolina*."

We're still whispering to each other, but it's wistful too. I pat his chest as I give him a squeeze. I need to show him I can handle this. I need to stand on my own two feet so he can concentrate. I let go of him and turn toward the living room. Something dawns on me.

"Are those girls your cousins?"

"Yeah. Uncle Salvatore and Aunt Sylvia's daughters. Pia is the older one, and Natalia is the younger one."

"Aren't they going to ask questions about your face?"

"They know we all box. They'll think I lost. One of the guys will cover for me. We keep away if there are any other injuries, but if we can blame boxing, we do."

I wonder how old the girls will be when they realize their family is built on lies and love. They look around nine and eleven, maybe ten and twelve. I'd guess there's about two years between them. They laugh at something they're watching. When they look up to call out to someone, they notice Marco. Both girls run over, and I brace myself for knowing Marco's going to lie to their faces.

"Are you Liz? Are you Chelle's sister?"

The questions come out, and I don't know who asked which.

"Yes, to both."

"Chelle's so cool. I like her. She's so much more fun than Enzo. Are you more fun than Marco?"

It's Natalia who speaks up. Pia elbows her.

"What? It's true. At least I'm not the one who told Enzo that. You hurt his feelings."

Both girls turn to look at me. They really want an answer.

"Yes. Marco and Enzo are boys. They're always boring."

I wink, and both girls grin at me.

"What were you watching? It looked way more interesting than anything Marco's going to talk about over there."

I jut my chin to where their father, uncles, and cousins stand. Pia grins.

"Totally."

I turn my head and give Marco a peck on the cheek before the girls lead me away. I know he's watching me for a moment, then he's following us. I get a pinch on the ass before he walks over to the men. Natalia looks up at me.

"Do you know everyone yet?"

"Not really. I remember you two from Chelle and Enzo's wedding."

"This is Mama. You look like you already know Auntie Nicoletta."

We stop in front of a woman even more elegant than Paola. She looks like she stepped off a European runway. Glamorous.

But her home feels like Martha Stewart should retire. Everywhere looks so comfortable. It feels like a home not a house. Though, from the outside, I think it's more a castle than anything else.

"Hello. I'm Sylvia."

Her accent is still thick, even though I know she's been here for nearly fifteen years, I think. Maybe a little less since Pia isn't a teenager yet. Then again, what do I know? Maybe she and Salvatore were married a while. He's definitely older than his wife by a decade. There was so much going on at the reception that I didn't get to spend much time with the Mancinellis. I wasn't sure yet where I would fit, so I'd stuck with my family and friends.

Sylvia and I shake hands. Her smile is so welcoming that it puts me at ease as I face the rest of the family. Natalia continues the introductions.

"This is Auntie Carlotta. She's Matteo's mom and Auntie Nicoletta's best friend. See that man over there? The one next to Marco. He's Uncle Domenico. He's Auntie Carlotta's husband. He's best friends with Uncle Massimo. He's Papa, Uncle Massimo, and Auntie Paola's second cousin. Sort of. Like they are, but not like Carmine, Maria, Marco, Luca, and Enzo are my cousins. He was adopted. The other guy standing next to Marco is Matteo. Marco is two-and-a-half hours older than Matteo. They used to share cribs. They've been best friends since they were three and could pick. You'll see him a lot. But maybe not as much now that he's married to my actual — like blood —cousin Maria. She's Uncle Massimo and Auntie Nicoletta's youngest. Marco is number two. Enzo is the last boy, and Luca was the first. Boy and kid. Um. Oh yeah, Carmine is next to the super big guy, Gabriele. He's Auntie Paola and Uncle Cesare's only kid. Uncle Cesare isn't here, but Auntie Paola is. She's over there with Auntie Nicoletta and Serafina.

Sera's Carmine's wife. She owns two bakeries and is even better than Auntie Carlotta who was the best baker until Serafina came. Sinead is the one laughing at us. She's married to Gabe, the huge one. Um. Oh! The short lady is Olivia. She's married to Luca and is Petra's mom. Petra's a baby and still sleeps a lot. Maria's the one with the really long dark hair. You know Enzo and Chelle."

The child came up for air twice.

I'm trying to keep up waving and smiling to all the women. The men only glance over when they hear their names. Fucking ears like dogs. Natalia wasn't speaking that loudly. Pia rolls her eyes at her younger sister.

"Don't worry. I'll make you a family tree like I did for the others."

The others must be the women who married into the family. I'll take it.

"Girls, go set the table for dinner."

It's only then that I realize Marco and I have been running on fumes all day. We haven't eaten. We planned to after we had sex at my place. That didn't happen. I remember Paola asking if we'd eaten and teasing Gabe, but nothing came of it for us. My sister appears and hands me three chocolate chip cookies. The big kind like from a bakery.

"Don't let the guys see, or you'll have nothing but crumbs."

"Thanks. These look amazing."

But I'm not sure if I'm allowed to eat in the living room. This isn't my home.

"*Mangia, mangia.*"

Sylvia laughs as she speaks. That's the second joke today about the stereotypes. Paola's "didja eat" and Sylvia telling me to eat makes them seem so totally normal. Not like women waiting for their men to go off to— battle? Blow shit up? Steal shit? Beat people up? I glance at Marco and accept that I really am okay with what he must do. Not because he hasn't told me the details. I definitely don't want to know them. But because I hadn't exaggerated earlier or the time I told him he's a good man. I guess morally gray is my new favorite color. Seems like I'm redecorating my home in it.

Chapter Seventeen

Marco

I've left Beth in my mother's and aunts' capable hands. I've walked down the hall with the other men to Uncle Salvatore's office. It's a converted den since there aren't many other rooms spacious enough to contain all of us. There's nine of us. That's three more than on an offensive or defensive line in American football. There are sofas and armchairs spread around to make a semicircle in front of Uncle Salvatore's desk, which faces the windows. Of course. His back isn't to the door either. Could the windows make him an easier target? Sure. Can anyone sneak up? No. I mean, they could try. But really?

Uncle Salvatore's drumming his arpeggio on his chair arm. This is one of those times where it's not reassuring me. Could everyone hurry the fuck up and sit already? My hope for a night alone with Beth, even though it's still only late afternoon, went to shit. I don't like leaving her with people she doesn't know, even if her sister is here. If I have to be in here, then I don't want to wait to find out who the fuck did this, either.

Uncle Salvatore sits forward and looks at me. Wonder-fucking-ful. What now?

"Auntie Paola made some more calls this afternoon."

Usually, the women stay far away from Mafia business. We try to shelter them for many reasons, but most of all, we don't want any blood on their hands— which would be inevitable if they saw the risks we take. There'd be no tenuous balance of power among the families. Our mothers, wives, and sisters would annihilate anyone for moving even a single hair on our heads. The world might be more peaceful run by women, but only because they'd resolve things much faster with their scorched earth tactics.

Uncle Salvatore has plenty of his own connections, but it's obvious Auntie Paola has resources at her disposal that are just as effective, if not more in this situation. I want to know who and what.

"What'd she learn?"

"You can thank *Tres J's* for this."

Motherfucking sons of a cum dumpster bitch. Fuck that balance of power. I will kill Javier, Jorge, and Joaquin. Those motherfuckers.

Carmine shakes his head before he speaks.

"Calm your ass down. I talked to Mama already. They're the ones who set up Luigi and bribed the ATF to make a move. The FBI didn't want to be left out. But they didn't tell either agency when to make their move. According to Javier, they told their CI with the FBI to back off Liz. The dumbasses found out the three guys were following Liz and found out two of them touched her. I guess the assholes didn't listen to the advice *Tres J's* CI gave them."

Papa chimes in.

"They'll leave the three to you, as is your right. But apparently, their CI wasn't long for this world. He's been taken care of. Not because *Tres J's* feel badly that Liz got involved. They're pissed the bust was a bust. The shit timing and execution means we know now. There's no element of surprise for the Diazes anymore."

As is my right. My right to defend my woman. My right to have a vendetta, which will be short-lived. Six months. That's how long those men have left to kiss their families goodbye. Too soon, and it's too obvious. Too late, and they don't live in fear. I'll drop some hints in the meantime. Let them think I might come after their women.

"Explain to me how this worked out. Luigi and Enzo were only gone a month ago. How'd the Diazes find out what happened with the Rizzos and Grassos? How'd they get the FBI and ATF to move so fast?"

Carmine speaks up again.

"Enrique set some guy up in the Rizzos a while back when he thought— feared —Luca would marry Cecelia. He wanted to know what was going on with an alliance between New York and Chicago. I guess he didn't pull the guy."

"How did he get someone in with them?"

No one welcomes new people to their organization unless they come from the old country and are fully vetted. It's not like we hand out invites to join the club. Our Made Men, the highest-ranking men who aren't *capos,* are all Italians. Mostly Sicilians. Associates are the men we allow in who aren't Italian of any kind. They're few and far between in the Mancinelli branch or any other. Below that are our *soldati*— soldiers —the guys who do the street hustles and odd jobs. They're still mostly Italians. We might pay an outsider to knock off a corner store or garage that isn't paying us on time. But anything more than that stays in our community.

It's no different in any other city with *Cosa Nostra.* So that brings me back to how'd they get someone in? I want Carmine's intel.

"The guy can fake an Italian Chicago accent well enough to date one of Edoardo's *capo's* daughters. The guy has big ears and a silver tongue. Probably a big dick, too. I guess the woman's big on pillow talk, so Enrique's guy told the Diazes everything the woman knew about her family's business. Way more than she should have known. She's a nosy fucker."

Our fathers "let" us swear when we're in here. But swear in front of the women in our family? Hard limit. Especially Auntie Carlotta.

Enzo runs his hand through his hair.

"It means at least the Rizzos know what I did. The Grassos probably do too. I was hoping for at least another month or two before they put together all the pieces. I'm the most newly married. One of you is taking the next trip."

"Papa always made me clean up after you, little brother."

Luca smirks, and Enzo makes an obscene gesture with his fist. I ignore them since I have more questions.

"Anyway. Enrique's guy found out shit from Edoardo's people. He told Enrique, and Enrique told *Tres J's*? Or did this guy report to *Tres J's*? Did Enrique assign this to his nephews, or did they take it upon themselves?"

I want to know just how big a bomb I need when I retaliate. And when I say bomb, I mean bomb. I didn't study electrical engineering for nothing. Uncle Salvatore leans back in his chair as he frowns at me.

"We don't know yet. Auntie Paola is waiting for a couple calls back. She's got a client in Chicago who's making inquiries to find out who Enrique's man told. This contact wants to be sure the Rizzos' secrets aren't going further than the Diazes."

"Call Enrique."

I don't usually issue orders to my uncle. But I don't want to wait around for a game of telephone. I also don't love having my aunt in the middle of this. Even if politics is her profession, and she mingles with her own set of dirty people, I don't want her caught in the middle for my sake.

Uncle Salvatore stares at me. It would scare the shit out of me when I was a teenager and just moving from Uncle Sal being my fun uncle who let me drive his golf cart way too fast to being my don. It made me anxious when I became a *capo*. Now I'm too fucking pissed to be anything but angry. I stare back.

"*Attento, ragazzino.*" Watch it, little boy.

The worst day of Uncle Salvatore's life— at least until men took Aunt Sylvia —was the day he found out what Carmine, Luca, and Gabriele did that risked a bratva then-girlfriend-now-wife's life. It was the day he had to be a don first and an uncle second.

I didn't know the man could be so angry. Angry at what my brother, cousin, and friend did. Angry that it put him in a position to punish them. He doled it out to his little brother's son and his little sister's son. To his long-time best friend's son. He wound up breaking Luca's arm and almost shattering Carmine's nose. They deserved it, and Uncle Salvatore had to keep up appearances. He had to show our men and the rest of the world that he hadn't lost control over our family. But he will not talk about that day.

I don't need to put him in that position, and I sure as shit don't want to be on the receiving end. I also don't want to do that to Papa. He had no choice but to accept what his older brother did to his oldest child. As *consigliere*, he had to advise Uncle Salvatore that there was no choice but to punish the three of them. As a father, he had to watch.

If Luca hadn't been involved, it would have fallen to his shoulders as underboss to carry out the beating. If my older brother never has a son, then I'll be his underboss. Then my son, if I have one, would become the underboss when he's old enough and eventually don after me. I don't want to be in Papa's or Uncle Salvatore's position. That makes me wonder if Beth realizes any sons we might have are likely to enter this life.

We don't know what the future holds. None of us want another generation in the Mafia, but is there really another choice? It's not like Luca could abdicate to another family on his death bed. That would leave the rest of us and our children and grandchildren in another family's crosshairs. I'm going to have to explain my position as *capo dei capi* to Beth. There's no way out of that. I'm going to explain what that means for our future.

"*Sì, Zio.*" Yes, Uncle.

Uncle Salvatore gives me one last long look. A reminder. Then he looks at Carmine.

"Find out where each of them is."

Carmine sighs.

"I already know. They're at the hospital. Margherita had surgery today. There were complications. Their priest is there, and even Laura and her parents went."

Fuck. Margherita is Enrique's sister-in-law. She married Luis, Enrique's younger brother, and they had two sons— Pablo and Juan. Juan fucked around and found out that Maks doesn't issue empty threats to anyone who gets too close to his wife and twins. Pablo is Luca's equivalent. If Laura and her family set aside their hostility toward the Diazes, it must be dire. Juan was Laura's oldest friend. They grew up next door. The Doyles and Diazes alternated hosting Sunday dinner for nearly thirty years. Now they won't even look in each other's direction. Margherita's on her deathbed.

Fuck my life.

Everyone looks at me.

"I know. We can't strike them if their aunt is dying today."

I meant it a little more sincerely than it sounded. She's a nice woman who used to bring tres leches cake to our games if it was someone's birthday. That's right. *Our* games. We not only played little league and peewee sports with our enemies when we were kids, we were often on the same fucking teams. Given how history repeats itself, one day my niece, Petra, might play on the same team as Konstantin or Mila or Lev Kutsenko.

Uncle Salvatore's frown is even grimmer than usual.

"We can't do anything that might kill them, but we can fuck some shit up. They knew their aunt was going into surgery, and they treated today as business as usual. They can't have it both ways. We don't involve Enrique right now. Let him be an older brother to Luis. Let Pablo be a son. But fuck *Tres J's* and Alejandro."

As though our fucking family tree isn't an actual orchard. Enrique also has two younger sisters. One sister is the mother of *Tres J's*, and the other is Alejandro's. *Tres J's* grew up in Colombia until they were teenagers. They saw some fucked-up shit there. They're fucking psychopaths. Some might call me a sociopath, but they're bona fide disturbed. Alejandro travels to Colombia a lot with his *Tío* Luis. The shit people hear about the streets of Bogota? They can thank Alejandro for probably half of it.

Leaving Enrique and Pablo out of it. That's as close to sympathy as my uncle gets for anyone outside our family. Even among our community's families, he's not that generous.

I have the tickle of an idea.

"Luca, when's their next shipment of carfentanil coming across the border?"

"Good memory. It's supposed to be tonight."

"Have they paid?"

I look over at Enzo. He keeps tabs on the other syndicate's cash flows and investments.

"Half."

I shift my gaze back to Luca.

"Let's take all of it."

It means a trip to New Mexico. There are only three legal crossings to Mexico from that state, and they're all in Chihuahua. That doesn't mean there aren't several other crossings. Enrique likes New Mexico because it isn't as obvious as California or Texas, or even as obvious as Arizona. Border Patrol's still a pain in the ass, but they're nowhere near as aggressive as in the other three states.

Papa glances toward the door then meets my gaze.

"Are you going?"

"Yes."

I don't want to leave Beth, but she knows I'm going somewhere tonight. She's as prepared for that as she's going to be. If I have to be away, then I may as well make the most of it. Luca pulls out his phone and must be sending a text to our pilots. He glances up at me.

"What do you want to do with it once we have it?"

"Drop it back off in China."

"What?"

At least four voices bark the same word.

"We know the chemicals likely came from China. It was mixed and made in Mexico, and one of the cartels there sold it to Enrique. He'll lose his product and have the Mexicans still wanting him to pay the outstanding half. We give it to the Triad, and they can sell it a second time. Except now they have a complete product."

"I'm not handling that shit."

Gabriele crosses his arms. This shit is so lethal that looking at it could kill you. I don't blame him.

"None of us are going near it. We are going near the Mexicans and Colombians running it across the border. We are going to borrow Alejandro's new plane and his pilot. They'll fly it to China. If something happens along the way, and they don't make it all the way to China, oh well. It can wind up with the Triad— and they can owe us a favor —or the bottom of the Pacific. Either way, the Diazes don't have their shit. The only thing I'd feel guilty about are the fish it would kill."

Carmine grins.

"This might just kill Alejandro."

The guy wouldn't fly commercial if it was the only way out of hell. With all the trips he now makes back and forth to Colombia, he's very particular about customizing his personal jet. He recently lost one— I grin back at my cousin —so he'll be extra sensitive about losing his replacement.

Alejandro might not be our primary target, but what hurts one, hurts them all. *Tres J's* are the ones who head up the Colombian Cartel's narco-trafficking. This will put a serious dent in their business. Not only will the product be gone, but they'll have problems with their Mexican partners. Considering Mexico produces its own ingredients for carfentanil, they don't technically need the Diazes as middlemen to get chemicals from China to make the shit. And the Diazes could just import the chemicals to the U.S. and have it made here. But this kind of triangular trade is better business.

Luca looks up from his phone.

"Okay. Our guys can be gassed up and ready in an hour. How do we want to handle Alejandro's jet?"

Carmine gets out his phone.

"I still have someone who can get it out of the hangar for us, but we need their pilot."

I watch as he puts his phone to his ear, waiting for someone to answer.

"Benny, it's me. We need his new jet... Yeah, I know. I paid you well last time. I'll pay you even better this time... I don't give a shit what your plans are with your girlfriend. It's my money or my bullet. Which do you prefer? ... Uh-huh. I figured. What's the pilot's name? Do you have an address for him? Or could you get it?"

Carmine goes quiet for a moment but switches the call to speaker as he taps on his phone. He must be pulling up his encrypted notes app. I listen as his guy rambles off a name and address for the pilot.

"Great. Thanks. Have it ready to go in an hour."

"An hour? It'll take me that long just to get to the airfield."

"No, Benny. It won't. You'll fucking sprout wings if you have to. I said an hour."

We can have a little wiggle room on this, but he doesn't need to know that. One of our pilots and a few of our guys will make sure the plane makes it to New Mexico. After that, we don't give a shit what happens to the plane once Alejandro's pilot is behind the yoke. We'll make sure the pilot is all strapped in and convinced not to make any detours. If he gets a whiff of something from a small leak, then too bad.

Even if he crashes in the U.S., it wouldn't be horrible. The plane is registered to Alejandro since even we can't totally circumvent the FAA. A plane goes down full of the most dangerous drug in the world, and it's obvious it belongs to the Diazes is just like Christmas in July for us.

Uncle Salvatore looks over at Luca.

"Send Alonzo and David."

Alonzo is Afonso's brother. Afonso was up to driving this morning, but he was shot not too long ago while guarding Chelle. He's not in any condition to rough someone up or force them onto a plane and then to fly it. I'm not sure what their parents were thinking with the rhyming names. They're not twins, but they look enough alike that they could be. Confusing as fuck if you don't know them well.

Luca makes the call as the rest of us plan for when we land in New Mexico. There is a strip in the southwest corner where there's not a vehicle or pedestrian barrier along "The Wall." It's marked on maps as *"other fence."* In other words, so fucking desolate that few people pass through. There are mountains, and that's about it. The terrain will make it difficult but not impossible.

Gabe looks at me, and I'm rolling my eyes.

"I'll make sure you're only away from your wife for one night."

"Back before breakfast, Marco. Sinead has a doctor's appointment tomorrow I will *not* miss."

That makes everyone pause and look at him.

"No, it's not serious. And no, we don't have an announcement. But we'd like to sooner rather than later, so I'm not missing her appointment."

"Fine. Do you really think I want to leave Beth for that long after what happened today? We're in, and we're out."

Please don't let me have just tempted fate.

It doesn't matter what time of year it is. It's fucking cold at this elevation at night. I'm blowing on my hands as we wait in the dark for the mules to come past. I wouldn't want to be them, running drugs across the border for a living or to pay to get into the States. The ground is fucking freezing under my belly as we all lie in wait. We have our NVGs on, so the world is an eerie shade of green. Since most of our missions leave from Uncle Salvatore's house, we all keep a set of tactical gear there. I took Beth up to my room— we all have rooms at our parents', and aunts and uncles' houses —while I got changed.

She watched, wide-eyed, as I got dressed. I told her what I could. I was going out of state. I would hopefully be gone just tonight. If I was going to be gone longer than that, Papa would tell her. I was going with the other guys, so I wouldn't be alone. She wouldn't be alone either, since all the wives agreed to spend the night there.

She didn't ask a single question, which makes me proud and worried at the same time. I'm glad she's holding it together and taking this in stride. This is only the first— not the last — time she'll see me leave like that. But it worries me she didn't open up. The only wife she knows well enough to confide in is her sister, and Chelle hasn't been through this either. Yeah, Enzo had to travel while they dated. But she never watched him leave dressed in all black with a pistol strapped to his thigh. That's how we all looked when we left. Our moms said their goodbyes after our dads. The wives and Beth were the last ones we hugged and kissed before we walked out to our SUVs.

While I wait and try to keep my fingers from going numb, my mind fixates on what could have happened to Beth today. I hadn't let myself fully picture it. Now I do. I envision her lying dead in the alley, her body riddled with bullets. Or just one through the forehead or the back of her skull or her heart. That ATF agent fired first. I just fired better. That was who shot the bullet that landed near Beth's foot. Yes, we were evading them. But no, there was no reason to shoot at that point.

I don't think Beth saw the man I shot to the right of us. He was ready to pull the trigger when I hit him. As he fell back, his gun discharged straight into the air. Better that than Beth. At that point, I knew all three of the officers who stepped in front of us were going to shoot first, ask questions later. I decided on a proactive approach and shot one, knowing Luigi and Pauly would get the other two. Turns out, Vinny and Tony got them too.

It's been a long ass time since I've been in a shoot-out with law enforcement. It hasn't been nearly long enough since I've been in a shoot-out. The last one was not so long ago. About a year-and-a-half. It was while Luca and Olivia were dating. It was unexpected, and Gabe took two bullets. It's not like we exactly send out calendar invites for when we're going to try to kill our rivals or they're going to try to kill us. It was that none of us went into that situation thinking so many bullets were going to fly.

"Marco, over there."

I hear Carmine's voice through my earpiece. I glance at him and see him point east. I see vague movement. He passes down the heat-seeking binoculars. I flip up my NVGs, so I can look through them. Five SUVs made for rugged terrain not comfort head our way. They're also not made to withstand the fire power we have with us. The benefits of flying are that we have an entire hold for our arsenal.

Carmine and I are our explosives experts since he's a structural engineer, and I'm an electrical engineer. Matteo will help us strategize if there's time and a blueprint since my best friend is an architect. Luca's our rifles expert. He's the best shot with one, while Gabe's best with handguns. Best among us. My sister is the best of any of us with anything— handguns, rifles, bows and arrows, knives. She's a regular G.I. Jane.

It makes me wonder about Beth. She said she's a competitive shooter. I haven't been trap shooting, but I understand the rules. I wonder if she shoots skeet or sporting clays or five stand. I only know the names of the first two. Sick and twisted as it is, maybe these are something we can do together as a couple. I know Matteo takes Maria to the range.

I hand the binoculars over to Matteo, who looks before

passing them down the line, so everyone else can get a read on what's approaching. They make their way back to Carmine, who has a controller in his hands. They come into view with just our NVGs on a minute later.

"In three. Two. One."

He counts down before hitting a button. We cover our heads and ears. We're all wearing an earpiece in one ear and an earplug in the other. A small roadside bomb detonates, and rocks slide down to block a portion of the road. It forces the four-vehicle convoy to stop. Men get out, and that's my signal. I have my SAW set up in front of me. It's a gas-operated machine gun with a disintegrating metallic link-fed belt for the bullets. It's the type seen in movies with a service member lying on their belly rapid firing on an approaching enemy. I'm not in fatigues, but I am camouflaged in all black.

Before any of them can figure out they're about to die, they're dead. They never had a chance to see where the bullets were coming from or who was shooting. I'd counted the heat spots, so I know I got all of them. Their own damn fault for all getting out of the vehicles. The fifth SUV was half a mile behind the others when I watched them approach. They tasked the men in that vehicle with making sure no one followed them. We didn't. We got here first.

They're now the ones who are going to do the loading for us once we get the cargo to the plane. My brothers, cousin, friends, and I are on the move. We pour down the hill we hid on, rifles pointing at the last vehicle. Matteo takes out the left tires. We don't need that one since none of the product will be in it.

Carmine's voice carries through the now quiet air.

"*¡Fuera!*" Get out.

We slow our approach, fanning out to cover all the doors and liftgate. Carmine gives them another order.

"Vamos, gilipollas." Let's go, assholes.

Luca shoots between the driver's feet to let them know we aren't particularly patient. He calls out to them.

"Uno de vosotros conduce cada vehículo. Intenta atropellarnos o salirte de la carretera, y te mataremos como hicimos con los demás." One of you drives each vehicle. Try to hit us or turn off the road, and we will kill you like we did the others.

We all speak Spanish, so there's nothing we won't understand when they inevitably try to escape. They put their hands up without being told. A little common sense. As they each move to a vehicle in their convoy, ours pull forward. They weren't far from the road but invisible without their headlights on. Carlo, Dante, and Frederico are each behind the wheel. After the shit with being unsure about Luigi's loyalty, we're keeping shit tight. These three have been guarding Uncle Salvatore and Papa since they were in high school together.

It doesn't take us long to get things moving. It's a thirty-minute drive to the planes. Only one of them tried to pull off the road. Carlo rammed the driver's side. It was a convincing tactic. We didn't have another problem after that. We keep gas masks in our tactical gear bags, so we each put one on before we get out at the open strip we used as a runway. We're not taking any chances inhaling even a speck of carfentanil. None of us have touched their SUVs or any of the men either.

With our guns pointed at their heads, they're busy little worker bees, loading the drugs onto the plane. They're wearing masks with respirators, but not ones as protective as our gas masks. They cover their bodies from head to toe, and they're all wearing beanies. But they left their eyes and cheeks exposed. Dumb motherfuckers. One of them's dead before he even pulls out the first crate. The other three are way more careful, approaching each crate with care. We lose a second one just as they load the last container into the hold of Alejandro's plane.

That's how fucking dangerous this shit is. Exposure alone will kill you. Never mind ingestion.

It'll be about a four-and-a-half-hour flight from here to San Diego, then it's out over the ocean. We have someone who'll be monitoring their flight route. They'll need to refuel in Hawaii, which we've arranged for. If the pilot tries to put down anywhere before Hawaii, we'll know. Carmine makes one brief call, and poof. The plane is in a million pieces. The pilot knows that.

It's only a few minutes later before we watch the plane taxi, then take off. We watch as it disappears into the night sky. I allow myself one breath of relief. That part went off without a hitch, but there is still so much that can go wrong. I don't want to tempt fate by thinking about it. But I like contingency plans. I like planning for worst-case scenarios. I've faced way too many in my life to not believe in Murphy's Law.

"You ready to go home?"

I turn toward Enzo when he comes to stand beside me.

"Beth and I have to talk to her parents. Considering how things went when you met them, I'm not sure what to expect when I do."

"Let's hope I broke them in."

"Chelle said she spoke to them, so they know about today. I'm surprised they weren't waiting for us when we got to Uncle Sal's."

"Chelle convinced them not to come. She said there would be things we needed to do that couldn't get done with them there. She was right. We couldn't have gotten ready there for one."

We couldn't have met in Uncle Salvatore's office for as long as we did. We couldn't have walked out of the house in our tactical gear. We couldn't leave them there for Mama, Papa, and the others to distract. Well, we could have. We could have done all those things, but it wouldn't have been wise. However, there's nothing stopping me from having to face them. Having to admit yet another one of their children is going to live with life-threatening danger every day.

I'm not in such a rush to do that. But I want nothing more than to get home to Beth. To make sure she's okay. I promised Gabe we'd be home in time for Sinead's doctor's appointment. It's a little after one a.m. It's a five-and-a-half-hour flight plus a two-hour time difference. We need to hurry. I breathe a second sigh of relief as our own plane takes off. Once we're at our cruising altitude, we turn our phones back on. In hushed voices, we each call the woman we love to tell her we're on the way home.

I'm exhausted as I climb into the SUV waiting for us. I want a hot shower with Beth and to fall into bed with her. I want to dredge up enough energy to make love to her then fall asleep inside her. But I don't even have time to get the words "Honey, I'm home" out of my mouth before I realize something is very wrong.

Chapter Eighteen

Beth

I turn as the front door opens, and the men pour inside. I notice the others, but it's Marco I focus on. He's exhausted, but he looks untouched. I glance at my parents, who're sitting between me and Chelle on the sofa. I'm perched on the arm, as I shift my gaze to Chelle. We might be looking over our parents' heads, but I sense they know Chelle and I are trying to communicate silently. She and I stand and walk toward the men. Enzo gets to her before Marco gets to me. I watch how he engulfs her in his embrace and devours her. No one else cares since women are greeting husbands, and parents are greeting their children. I hang back and let Massimo and Nicoletta hug Marco.

Then it's my turn. He sweeps me into his arms, pressing me against his front. His hand is in my hair, not fisting it but cupping my skull. His other hand presses against my lower back. I raise my chin to accept his kiss, and for a moment, everything is how it should be. But that lasts only a few seconds before I pull back.

"Marco, my parents are here. The feds went after them."

I whisper to him as his gaze meets mine. The hand in my hair slides around to cup my face. His thumb strokes under my eye. I'm certain he sees the dark circles there. I don't think I would have slept even if the night had been uneventful. But my parents arrived half an hour after the guys left. We've all been sitting up since then.

"What happened?"

"They got warrants for my parents' home and offices. The FBI went to each of their offices at 4:50, just as people were finishing up for the day. Of course, Mom and Dad came into the city because of it. It meant the FBI separated them. While they were there, the ATF went to their home. I don't even know how the ATF can have any jurisdiction to search them. But they claim my parents still have ties to the mob. Obviously, my grandfather was on their lists. It's not like it's hard to figure out his living descendants. They're claiming my parents are active members of the O'Rourkes."

"The weapons your parents have. Are they all legally registered?"

"Yes. Everything is on the up-and-up. They have nothing to hide. The officers found nothing. Apparently, they bagged nothing at the offices. They didn't take my parents' computers or anything. They took the guns from the house, but the ones there haven't been discharged in a while. They're ones I compete with. I don't store mine at my place in Brooklyn. Your men took the ones from when those guys attacked their home. We never got those back."

"You won't. They've been disposed of. Nothing is left to link your parents to anything from that day."

That means there are no bodies left either. It's not just the guns they made disappear when men tried to shoot Enzo, Chelle, and my parents in my parents' New Jersey home.

"As soon, as the FBI let them go, they came here. They didn't even go back to their house."

"How do you know they took nothing but the guns, *piccolina*?"

I'm not sure when he started holding both my hands, but he's running his thumbs over the backs of them. That and finally hearing him call me little one is keeping me from full on losing my shit. I want to because his shoulders are broad enough to carry the weight of all this. At least, I want them to be. I want to believe they are. But I don't want him to actually have to. I want to prove I won't fall apart again. I've kept it together since my parents arrived and told us everything. Everything is such a fucking jumble of thoughts and emotions right now.

"Salvatore said he's had men outside my parents' home since the attack. His men didn't see the agents leaving with anything but the weapons. There were no boxes or bags. My parents didn't see anything taken from their offices. According to my parents and Salvatore's men, the agents went in, made a colossal mess, scared my parents and the people in their offices, made the neighbors notice, then left. They didn't even question my parents."

I glance back at them as Marco and I continue to speak quietly in the foyer.

"How is this legal? I mean, how'd they get a warrant? Leaving empty handed proves there was no probable cause, right? If they're doing this to intimidate your family, isn't this pushing the envelope for using federal funds or something?"

"They'll call it the beginning of an ongoing investigation. The fact they took the weapons will be their argument for continuing to harass your parents. They can't get to Enzo or me directly or even through you and Chelle, so they're going after your parents. They're hoping family discord will make you and them flip. They know Enzo and Chelle are married, so they can't force Chelle to testify against Enzo. They could push her to testify about the rest of the family. They're also dragging the O'Rourkes in, hoping they'll pressure you and your parents to narc on us. If you do, then it'll take the focus off them."

"Now I get why they say it can take years to build a case. They have a lot of maneuvering to do to keep it from looking like entrapment and witness tampering and planting evidence."

"Yes."

I wait for him to say more, but he's now looking over my shoulder. I assume he's watching my parents. But he pulls me in for another embrace. He tucks his chin and whispers to me.

"I'm going to have to go out today. I need to make it look like a workday like usual. You do too. But I don't know if I'll be home tonight. I want you to stay here another night, okay?"

"Yes, Daddy."

I have questions. But I can't ask them. When he says he needs to make it look like a usual workday, that tells me it's anything but. I want to cling to him and tell him we all need to hide until the feds get tired of looking for us. I want to tell him to stay here, so the O'Rourkes don't do anything to him for dragging them into this. I'm certain they'll find a way to blame Marco and Enzo in particular because of Chelle and me.

"Let's go talk to everyone else. Then I'm going to have to talk to my uncles and Papa."

"Do you need me to do anything? Do you want me to make you some breakfast? Are you going to have time to sleep?"

I guess I am asking questions.

"My mom and aunts will start cooking soon. I'm surprised I didn't arrive to a full breakfast already."

"But—"

"Beth, having your family involved is unusual. But having

the government breathing down our necks isn't. We don't stop our lives because of it. We all still have to eat. I'd love to crawl into bed with you, but I can't. I napped on the flight. I want you to have three guards and someone from my family, but you need to go into the office. You have to appear like none of this rattled you or your family. If we hide, then they'll claim your family is up to something. They'll think we're weak if my family doesn't go about business as normal. No one can ever see this faze us."

It all makes sense, but it's all so fucking complicated.

"Salvatore said he'll arrange extra security for all the women and that he'll have discreet details for my parents."

"Good. Let's have breakfast, take a shower together, then head out."

"A shower together?"

"You think I'm starting my day without filling you with my cum? Not a chance, little one. I'm going to listen to you moan my name. And you're going to feel how much I missed you."

"How do you keep everything you have to do in your mind when you're always thinking about sex?"

"I can multitask. Now, let's eat our breakfast, so I can eat you out."

He gives me a nudge toward the dining room where people are gathering. There is more to our relationship than sex. There wasn't supposed to be, but there is. However, a little dirty talk and hopefully a good fuck will calm me down a bit. That or day drinking.

"Mr. and Mrs. Decker, Feng Shui would have a more minimalist approach."

I look at my clients as we walk through their under-construction home in Westchester. I'd just gotten to the office and was sitting down to work on designs for them when they called and announced they "hoped" I'd join them at the site. I've worked with them on three homes now. I know it meant expected. Carmine was about as thrilled with the change of plans as I was. Now I'm standing in the master bedroom trying to convince them they can't have a fucking rumpus room and say it's Feng Shui.

Alicia Decker, with her fake nails and fake tits, is wife number three out of what will probably be five before Craig Decker dies. She points around the room as she speaks.

"Having the elliptical and treadmill in here will motivate us. And we need the seventy-five-inch TV to give us something to watch while we work out."

They won't work out, but it wouldn't surprise me if Mr. Decker doesn't love watching porn on a TV that big. Fucking up close and personal to every dick he wishes was his and every clit he thinks he could work.

Fine. Whatever. Have your shit in your room and call it whatever you want. Right now, I want to finish this walk-through, head back to my office, and remind myself that clients like them are paying off my grad school loans.

"Are you set on the canary yellow accent wall behind the TV?"

Supposedly, it'll make them think of the sun when they wake up to the freakishly bright paint every morning in winter. I didn't even know they made the shade until they brought a sample with them today.

Mr. Decker pats his wife's ass as he grins.

"Definitely."

I think he's still thinking about what he's going to watch on the TV mounted to that wall. Believe it or not, but Craig isn't an older man with a younger wife. Oh, no. He likes his sugar mamas. He likes them old enough to practically be his granny. He outlived the first two wives, and he'll probably outlive Alicia. He's in his early forties, and she's gotta be in her mid-seventies, maybe even early eighties. I can't tell from all the work she's had done.

I mosey them out of the bedroom and back downstairs. They have to look at practically every doorknob and outlet on the way. Come on. Fucking-a. They're not bad people, but I know what they like and don't like. I did a house for them on the Cape and in the Hamptons. I don't need to waste this time. Billable hours, Beth.

I think of myself as that now. Only one person calls me that when the rest of the world calls me Liz or Elizabeth. But in my head, I'm Beth now.

"Well, I think that's all for today. Thank you, Liz. We appreciate you coming all the way out here on such short notice."

I try not to grimace.

"It's not a problem, Mrs. Decker."

They made sure I knew I'm not welcome to use their first names the first time we met. I watch them head to their car and drive off. Carmine steps out of the town car parked in the driveway and heads toward me.

"They look like douches."

I laugh.

"Pretty much. Thanks for waiting for me. I know this has to be super boring."

"It's okay, Liz. Marco trusts me with you, and that matters. Sitting in the car is no big deal if it lets him get on with his day."

I nod. I'm not sure what to say since I don't know what

Marco's day involves. He kissed me goodbye when he dropped me off at my office. Carmine and the other men were in two town cars that pulled up behind ours. There were four men in them, but Carmine and a guy named Giuseppe escorted me into the building. Forty-five minutes later, and I was in the house with the Deckers.

"Can you at least get some of your work done?"

"Yeah. I got plenty taken care of."

I know he heads the construction company their family owns. Matteo is their architect, so my guess is they work together a lot. Marco's told me a little of their family history and how Carmine and Gabe were personas non grata for a long time, but I guess they've all resolved their differences. Now Carmine and Matteo don't mind the time spent with each other. Since Matteo and Marco are best friends and used to spend almost all their time together before Matteo married Maria, Carmine and Marco now hang out more than they used to. I don't get any hints of hostility between them, so I guess they're letting bygones be bygones.

I slide into the car after Carmine opens the door for me. It threw me a bit when he rode in the front seat on the way out here, but he explained that he's my bodyguard today. Not my boyfriend's cousin. If he sits in the back, he can't see the vehicle cameras they have installed, and he can't look out the windshield. It would mean he's less prepared to protect me. It was a rather grim reminder of why I have guards, but it also reassured me enough to face coming all the way out here to Larchmont, one of the most expensive towns in Westchester County.

I sit back as we make our way into the city with the guards in the second town car following us. I close my eyes, and I'm asleep before I know it. I wanted to doze on the way to the site, but I had shit to review before meeting with the clients. Now I let myself go until I hear someone rap on the window. I look up and see Carmine waiting outside the car. I pull the door handle, and he opens it for me.

"Good nap?"

"Yeah. It was a long night."

"You handled it well. You and Chelle did. Uncle Sal and Uncle Massi said your whole family dealt with it better than anyone could have expected."

"Thanks."

What else is there to say to it? My brother Steve still doesn't know what's going on, but he will soon. My parents are in hedge fund management and venture capitalism. As a stockbroker, my brother's world overlaps with my parents. They've sent each other clients. It wouldn't surprise me if he hasn't talked to them already after hearing about it through some grapevine. At some point, my parents are going to have to come clean with him about our past. Chelle and I also need to give him at least some clue about our husbands. Yes. I'm ready to think of Marco as mine. It'd be better if our brother hears it from us than rumors or accusations at work.

"Beth!"

I turn to my right and watch Marco hurry toward me. I glance at Carmine, who appears just as surprised as I am to see him.

"Hi. What're you doing here?"

He leans forward and kisses my cheek. He nods to Carmine.

"Do you have an office or a cubicle?"

"An office. Why?"

"Can we go in and talk? Otherwise, we can get back into the car."

"Um." I dart my eyes to my building. "We can go inside."

It's going to be weird having my boyfriend walk in with me. Is Carmine coming too?

"Do you need me?"

Clearly, Carmine's wondering the same thing I am.

"No. But can you come up? I still need you to guard Beth."

Carmine shuts my car door, and I walk between the two colossi as we enter the lobby then get onto the elevator. Carmine remains in the hallway as Marco opens the door for me. I smile at the receptionist, who eyes Marco like she wants to jump over the desk and jump his bones. Back off, Betty. My gaze bores into her until she senses me. She quickly finds something on her desk to read. Smart cookie.

Marco's just shut the door behind us when my phone rings. I know the sound. My brother must have telepathy.

"Hey, Stevie."

"Lizzie, what the hell's going on? Neither Mom nor Dad are answering their phone. Chelle said she couldn't talk. I'm getting texts left and right from people telling me the feds raided both our parents' offices last night because of them. I saw the press conference, and I could see you even if you were mostly hidden."

I wince. Then I put the call on speakerphone and hold my finger up to my lips.

"Stevie, remember how Marco came to get me from the club? We've been seeing each other ever since. I saw the way you looked at the Four Families at the reception. You know who all of them are, don't you?"

That's how I think of the syndicates now. I know I can't call them all the mob or the Mafia. It's easier to just lump them together with that title.

"Yeah."

He's hedging.

"Do you remember how Grandpa had that four-leaf clover on his chest?"

"Yeah."

That one sounds like he doesn't want to know what's coming next. I don't blame him.

"You know how he always said it was for Mom and our aunts? And that it was great that Mom and Dad had four kids because we each got a leaf?"

"I remember. Liz, spit it out."

"That tattoo had nothing to do with us or Mom or anyone in our immediate family. It was about a connection he had to an organization he tried to leave in the past. Don't say it."

I look at Marco. I point around my office, make a sign of something small with my thumb and index finger, then point to my ear. I shrug. His expression is grim, and that's why I wondered. He doesn't want me saying more on the phone because he's worried they might have bugged my office.

"Liz, what are you talking about? The O—"

"Steve, let's have this conversation in person. I don't want to explain it all like this."

"I want to know now, Liz."

"Well, I can't tell you. After what happened last night, I think we need to talk in person."

There's a long pause as I think the penny drops for him.

"Fine. When?"

I glance at my watch. I wish I could say right now, but I have to work one of these days. That actually gives me an idea. I mouth "lunch" to Marco. He nods.

"Can we meet for lunch?"

Marco steps next to me and whispers.

"I'll have one of the SUVs come. We can pick him up."

I nod as I look back at my phone as Steve answers.

"Sure."

"Okay. I'll come to you. I'll text you when I'm outside the building. I'll be in a black SUV, and Marco will be with me."

"Liz, this is family stuff."

"Which means Marco."

"Both of my sisters are going to marry into the fucking mob."

I clench my jaw. It amazes me how fast I am to want to correct him. But the whole point of meeting in person is to avoid things like that being blurted out.

"The Mancinellis are not the mob. Believe me."

"Fine. Can you be here at eleven-thirty?"

"Sure."

That's in twenty minutes. I'd hoped for a late lunch, like around one. It'll take almost that long, if not longer, to get to his office from mine. I watch Marco texting someone, so I'm certain he's arranging for the bigger vehicle.

"All right. See you in a bit, Liz."

"Bye."

I hang up and look at Marco before shifting my gaze to the wall that separates my office from the larger suite outside it. I drum my fingers on my desk for a moment before I look back to Marco.

"Matteo designs your family's projects. Carmine builds them. Can I decorate them?"

His brow furrows.

"Do you mean do some projects with the company?"

"No. I mean, can I be the company's interior designer? Can I work with Matteo on interior layout?"

"As in full time? Do you want to quit your job?"

"Not particularly, but I know Chelle's taking on some nonprofit projects your uncle wants to do. Sinead works along-side Gabe on the more— um —innocuous cases."

In other words, the cases that don't directly tie Mafia men

to the Mafia. It's not like she's handling speeding tickets. She actually has a grand larceny case. The guy is low level Mafia, and the alleged crime is unrelated to the Mancinellis. That's as much as she could tell me last night.

Olivia was in marketing for some big firm before she married Luca. Now she does the marketing for his car rental franchises and the casinos the family owns. Serafina has her bakeries, and Maria is a radiologist. If I'm going to be one of the wives, then that would make four out of the six of us working for the family.

Laura is Sylvia's equivalent for the Kutsenkos. She handles all their above-board corporate deals. Christina heads the Kutsenko Partners' construction division. Anastasia is Laura's paralegal and a law student. Sumiko is their accountant for their legal businesses. Heather does high school theater curriculum design, and Katerina is a school nurse. Four out of those six wives are connected to the bratva businesses. I learned all that from Chelle last night too.

"Beth, you don't have to quit your job."

"I know I don't have to. If we get married, it would make life easier if I can't show up to the office."

"What do you mean 'if,' *piccolina*? I haven't proposed yet, but I thought we agreed."

"You haven't proposed, and my mom's family connection is causing even more problems for your family."

"Your family connections are irrelevant to our relationship. If you can accept mine, then why wouldn't I accept yours? I haven't proposed because we can't seem to get a minute alone that isn't immediately followed by some shitastrophe. I'm not getting down on bended knee between gunshots, Beth. I'm going to do it properly. But I thought we already agreed our future is together."

"I know what I want, and I know what you've said. But until it happens, I won't assume anything."

He stares into my eyes, and I'm ready to drown in the whiskey pools. I'm certain he sees straight inside me.

"I know you're not pushing me away. I think you're scared and rightfully so. I think you're feeling adrift and need me to ground you. I think you want a spanking, so your helplessness has a purpose, and I can reassure you I have control over at least us."

I step closer to him, and he wraps me in his arms, both hands going to my ass. He squeezes, pressing my pussy against his dick. I burrow against his chest and inhale his cologne. I know it, and it soothes me. I want to quit if I know I can have a place with Mancinelli Developers. I want to work from home, so I can feel safe during the day. I want to be in a home office right now, so I can have that spanking. But we're in my actual office, and we're about to be in an SUV that doesn't have privacy glass.

"Can I have that spanking tonight, Daddy?"

"Of course, little one. And I'm still going to do it properly."

"I know. But properly doesn't have to be on one knee. Properly can just be you asking me because it's what we both want."

"If you say so."

He laughs as though he's indulging me. He is. I know he'll do his best, and that'll make it perfect. Even if it's not perfect. The contradiction seems so fitting for us. Or maybe it will be spot on. I don't know. My mind is babbling to itself because it's keeping me from facing the next step into the real world.

"We need to get going, or we'll be late."

I nod, but I don't let go yet. I tilt my head back, and he offers me a kiss. It's a breath of life. I step back, stiffen my spine, and follow him out. Carmine falls into place, walking ahead of me until we get outside. The SUV is where the town car was, and we're soon on our way. I spot Steve before we stop at the curb. Carmine gets out and greets him. Marco rolls down the window far enough for him to see me wave for him to come to the car. I slide into the middle seat, so my brother and my boyfriend can squash me. Marco offered to get into the third row, but I want him next to me. The moment the door closes, I launch into things. I know my brother. It's better to get ahead of his questions.

"Steve, Grandpa was a distant relation to the O'Rourke family. He was in the mob until he met Granny. He was pretty high up there, but he got out. I don't know all the ins and outs of it. But I know they still had some influence over him until he died. The feds must know this. We think they're targeting Mom and Dad to draw the O'Rourkes in. They hope Mom, Dad, and I— and maybe even Chelle —will turn over the Mancinellis to keep the O'Rourkes away."

I vomit the information because there doesn't seem to be much point in trying to tiptoe through the daisies. I recognize Pauly as the driver. His face is bruised, and he has stitches near his chin. But otherwise, he looks fine. Since I know Marco trusts him more than most, I feel comfortable speaking freely. Neither Marco nor Carmine stop me.

Steve peers around me at Marco and then at the back of Carmine's head since he's in the front passenger seat.

"Grandpa was in the mob, and so are my in-laws."

"No to the second part. The Mancinellis are *the* Mafia. I know we always thought mob and mafia meant the same. But they're not. Our family is now connected to the *Cosa Nostra* to be exact. The Irish are the mob."

"When are you going to marry my sister?"

"I'll do it tonight if she wants."

My head whips around to Marco after my eyes almost fall out of my head staring at Steve. So much for a proper proposal.

"*Cuore*, that isn't how I'm asking, so you can stop thinking it is."

His hand rests heavily on my thigh. Its weight and heat make me think this isn't just a show of affection. This is Marco taking control, and it makes me want to squirm. I definitely shouldn't be getting wet with my brother sitting next to me and my boyfriend's cousin in the front seat. But I can't help it.

I turn to look at him and mouth "Yes, Daddy" as I nod. His hand gets heavier, and his fingers press into my inner thigh without being inappropriate.

"You two haven't been together any longer than Chelle and Enzo were together before they announced they wanted to get married. What's the deal with your family? Nothing about you seems impulsive, but you and your brother seem to fall in love easily."

"Hardly. Enzo has never been in love with anyone other than Chelle, and I've never been in love with anyone but Beth. I've never met another woman I'd want to be in love with. You and I are not so different. You make immediate and sometimes irreversible decisions at work all day. So do I. But that doesn't mean either of us is impulsive. I've spent every moment my mind can spare thinking about Beth and our future since Enzo and Chelle's reception. Your sister is fun loving and can be spontaneous. But you grew up with her. I'm sure you knew what her bedroom was like and what her apartment is like. I was just in her office. They're way too meticulous for someone impulsive. She isn't thinking about a future with me on a whim."

I don't know about meticulous. I like things just-so. That's all.

Steve shifts his gaze to me, and I smile at him. I don't know what else to say. I just outed a huge family secret. Two family secrets. Neither Marco nor Carmine stopped me from saying the Mancinellis are the Mafia— are *Cosa Nostra*. I know that isn't something they just drop with anyone. Now my brother knows for sure. Fuck. I hope I didn't just fuck up.

"Liz may be the competitive shooter in the family, and our brother might have been in the military when he died, but Chelle and I learned to shoot too. I hunt every year. I have the patience to sit in a tree stand for hours. Hurt my sister, and you will find out just how long I can focus on one thing."

Marco reaches across me and offers Steve his hand.

"I know you said something similar to Enzo at the reception. I won't take it any less seriously than he did."

"Good. Liz, where are we eating? I'm starving."

"You're always hungry. You eat more now than you did when you were seventeen."

"And I weigh the same as I did then, too. Where are we headed?"

Marco speaks up since I actually don't know.

"Donatelli's. It's a family favorite. Our uncle's childhood best friend owns the place, and our uncle would eat there every day if my aunt weren't such an amazing cook who insists he's home to do the dishes every night."

Marco tilts his head toward Carmine as he speaks about their shared uncle. After spending so many hours with his family last night, I can believe that. The part about Sylvia's cooking *and* her rule that Salvatore does the dishes.

Carmine twists and joins the conversation as they discuss investments and how the market is doing right now. I could join in since I'm not ignorant on the topic, but I'm too tired. Marco wraps his arm around my shoulders, and I lean against him. I'm about to drift off when the vehicle stops.

"Wait."

Marco speaks to Steve over my head. I know the protocol that no one gets out of a vehicle unless the driver or guard opens the door, so I don't move. Carmine and Pauly get out, and a moment later Carmine opens Steve's door, and Pauly opens Marco's. Steve's not sure what to make of Carmine standing outside the vehicle, looking like he could be the chauffeur.

"Steve, get out. Carmine's my bodyguard today. But he's watching out for you and Marco. He's not going anywhere until you move."

I follow Marco out of the car since he's on the side with the curb. Steve walks around to us, looking in every direction before he looks down at me. It registers with me that he's wearing just as nicely a tailored suit at the other men. Carmine moves behind us while Pauly leads. Steve seems to just know that he should walk exactly at my right side like Marco is on my left.

I'm completely surrounded tightly enough that only someone taller than the guys could see me. My brother fits in shockingly well. I slide my hand into Marco's and wrap my other one around Steve's forearm. I give it a squeeze. He was always the mellow one in the family. Maybe that's why I was so blunt. I knew he'd take it all in stride.

Once we're at the table and have menus, I feel better than I have all morning. Salvatore is here so often and loves the place so much that the owner created a section specifically for the Mancinelli family. They've angled the table, so everyone has their back to a wall. Pauly's standing by the backdoor, and a guy from the kitchen who isn't dressed like restaurant staff is now positioned at the front door. The other guards followed us in a town car, and I think they're outside the building.

Among Marco, Steve, and Carmine, they've ordered the entire right side of the menu. I'll be lucky if the kitchen has anything left for me. I'm four bites into my manicotti when the bells over the front door jingle. I don't pay attention until Marco and Carmine both stand.

"Get behind us."

Marco pulls my chair out, and Steve stands too. Carmine and Marco shift, so my brother and I are behind both of them. It forces Steve and me to move until our backs brush the wall. We look at each other, neither understanding what's happening other than it's something bad.

Chapter Nineteen

Marco

What the fuck is he doing alive?

The last any of us knew, Robert Simms was on his deathbed. Actually, we thought the Triad beat him to death. The photo they sent us made it look like he was beyond recovery. Yet here he stands in the flesh. He looks like shit. I can see some fresh scars, and he looks like he's aged.

The man is a mercenary all of us have used. He's not loyal to a single family. He's loyal to the money. For years, we all figured he kept it tucked under a mattress. After the shit with Pasha Kutsenko, he probably actually does now. He's always been like a ghost. People rarely saw him, and most of us didn't know what he looked like. But shit with Pasha and his wife flushed him out.

The fucker's still elusive though, and he has more than nine lives. What the hell is he doing here? There's no way he believes he's meeting with Uncle Salvatore. The guy doesn't do business meetings. He uses burner phones for everything. I know he isn't here for Mikey's pasta primavera. Now I'm not getting my calzone. That alone pisses me off. The crust. The melted cheese. I'm ready to put a bullet through Simms's head thinking about my missed lunch.

"Simms."

I'm not offering anything more than that. I'm watching everything from the way he breathes to where his eyes focus. They haven't left us since he walked in, which means he already knows who's here. He's not expecting any surprises. That makes me worry about our guys outside. It's not like we've gotten a family photo with him or like we hang out with him. The men wouldn't have recognized him, but that wouldn't have stopped him from putting a bullet through *their* heads.

"Hiya, Marky."

I have never gone by the name. Mama said I came out of the womb too serious to ever consider a diminutive of my name.

Carmine remains silent next to me, but we both have our guns pointing at him. Pauly and the guy, who works for Mikey but doubles as security when our family is here, have theirs trained on Simms too. My cousin and I are shielding Beth and Steve, but they'll hear whatever this *disgratziat'*— disgraceful is the proper translation, but I mean bastard —has to say.

"You can stand in front of your *bella figa* with the DSL, but I know she's there. I've seen her plenty of times."

He's goading me. He just called Beth a beautiful cunt with dick sucking lips. He knows everything in me wants to shoot him. But I don't trust him not to have other people here. Ones who'll shoot me the moment I pull the trigger. Ones who'll kill Beth.

She's not moving more than to breathe. I can feel her against my back. I know Carmine's covering Steve as best he can. The guy isn't as broad or tall as Carmine, but he's close. Beth is practically invisible to Simms despite what he says, but

Steve's still a target. I wouldn't put it past Simms to shoot him to lure her out.

"Is this a little solo project or did someone hire you?"

"Does it matter?"

I laugh.

"It will when I kill you. I need to know whether this'll be done, or if I'll still have someone to visit."

Beth sucks in a breath. She knows I killed the last time I drew my gun. But now she's going to have a front row view since she isn't trying to put one foot in front of the other.

"You won't do that. Then you'd leave your *gnocca* for me to enjoy a *bocchino* before I take her *alla pecora*."

Once again, he insults Beth. *Gnocca*— vagina —a shit term to mean a hot chick. *Bocchino*— little mouthful —a blowjob. *Alla pecora*— like a sheep —doggy style. He's throwing out all the profane slang he must know.

I don't need to look at Carmine to know he's just as pissed as I am. It's not like we haven't used words like that— but never toward women. *Never.* Our mothers would skin us alive, and our fathers would beat us till our last breath. It's always been to insult men. There's a world of difference.

"Congrats on your Italian. Rosetta or Babbel? Get to why you're here."

"That's simple. Your new sister-in-law fucked me out of a shit ton of money. Killing her doesn't punish her, but killing her sister will. Getting their brother is just the cherry on top. You and fuckface are the whipped cream. I gotta kill you both to get to them."

He's had his gun trained on us the entire time, just like ours have been on him. But there's one of him and two of us. Mutually assured destruction. Unless he has someone else who can shoot Carmine or me— whoever's left standing. That makes me want to look around, and he knows it. He knows I want to survey the scene, but that means shifting my attention from him. It makes us vulnerable, but it also admits he has control of the situation since I don't know everything that's happening.

Neither Carmine nor I respond. What's there to say? I'm not giving up anything to him, so I can wait him out. The only problem is, standing, I can't hit my tracker on my belt, and neither can Carmine. To move our hand would signal him. To not move our hand means we can't alert our family.

"Carmine, you usually have plenty to say. Strong, silent type doesn't suit you."

My cousin laughs. But it's not with humor. I know the sound. It's the one he gives men just before he puts them in excruciating pain.

"You assume one of us will shoot you, then you'll shoot the other, and whoever you have waiting in the wings will shoot whichever one of us is left. But who's to say we both won't shoot you at the same time?"

"Because your men aren't outside anymore. At least, they're not breathing outside. You might kill me— though no one else has —but you won't get the bitch or her brother out alive."

That makes me think he wants to take all of us. He has other people here because he knows he can't manage all four of us by himself. If he intended to kill all of us, he would have sniped one guard at a time and come in guns blazing. He would have made it a solo mission and possibly succeeded. It wouldn't be the first time he took out that many people on his own.

Carmine laughs again.

"Then why are you stalling, *faccia de cazzo*? You can *fangul*." Testicle face. Fuck yourself.

"I'm not stalling. I'm giving Elizabeth Russo— five-feet-six, one-hundred-and-fifty-pounds, favorite color the cinnabar shade of red, and doesn't like caramel —a chance to adequately fear me. Steven Russo— five-feet-eleven-and-three-quarters, two-hundred-and-five-pounds, gets an almond milk latte every Thursday morning, and has a cheating girlfriend— is that cherry on top, so I definitely want him to fear watching his sister die."

How the fuck he knows these things is beyond me, but it means he's been studying both of them for a while. Likely since Laura came into the picture. He probably did a full dossier on Chelle since she's Laura's best friend. From there, he probably spider webbed out to do Chelle's entire family.

I hear noise coming from the back entrance where Pauly is. I can't turn to look, but I already know what's happening. Simms's people are moving in. He wasn't trying to scare Beth and Steve by making them wait. He was stalling. Something isn't going right with his plan. Standing around chatting like this invited failure for him. Before Carmine and I can make any move, we need to know how many people we're facing. I haven't heard a single peep come out of the kitchen since Simms entered. But I know Mikey has a full arsenal back there. You don't entertain the New York City don and not have protection for these kinds of situations.

Mikey has never paid a penny of protection money to my family in his life. He grew up with Papa, Uncle Salvatore, and Auntie Paola. He and Uncle Salvatore have been friends for nearly as long as Matteo and me. Their desks were next to each other in first grade. They drove the nuns crazy. People know not to come near this place. That doesn't mean Mikey's naïve. He has the guns and the people who know how to use them. That's why I haven't been scrambling to find a way out of this.

A woman pushes Pauly into the main dining area with a gun to the back of his head. I take one look at her, and I'm not worried Pauly can't get that gun from her. Five men follow them in, each with a handgun. I'm certain they all have at least one knife somewhere. Carmine and I have ours in our pockets.

Neither of us has left home without it since we each turned twelve. Fucked-up rite of passage into manhood. Here you go. Carry this because you're still a boy in our eyes, but the rest of world thinks you're fair game. Good luck.

I know some of them. They've done jobs for us when we've outsourced to Simms. A couple we've hired directly. I wait to hear the front door's bells jangle, but there's nothing. I hear no sound coming from the kitchen, so I doubt that door's opened. That's the one they're most likely to take us out through since it dumps into the alley. The emergency exit Pauly was near is also a backdoor based on layout, but it opens to a side street. There has to be at least one— if not two —people at the kitchen door, keeping an eye on however they plan to leave.

The thing that concerns me most is each of Simms's worker bees has a vintage military mailbag. More than ammo is in them from the way they hang. Why do they need that?

It becomes obvious the moment a guy walks over to Simms and flips his bag open. Fucking hell.

Carmine sees it at the same time as Pauly and me. Pauly spins, his elbow into the woman's outstretched elbow, his other fist to her jaw. Carmine and I flip the table to make a barrier for us. I reach back for Beth.

"Hold on to my belt. Steve, do the same to Carmine. Don't let go."

Thank God for our size. Carmine and I lift the table from the bottom. Our left shoulder goes against it as we raise it high enough to shield our heads. Our guns remain in our right hands. I feel Beth tuck her hand into my belt while the other grasps my suit coat. We barrel forward, Carmine and I both knowing to steer toward Pauly, so he can get behind our soon-to-be battering ram.

"I'm good."

Pauly's panting, so the woman must have put up some

fight. But I'm certain she's dead. He wouldn't leave her alive. We're not looking to take anyone with us. We just need to get to the door before any of them can get out their masks and smoke canisters. The moment those go off, we can count ourselves as taken. We won't be able to see or breathe, so being outnumbered truly will put us at a disadvantage.

"Beth, reach around to my buckle. Under the prong is a tiny bump. Press it."

I feel her fumble, but then the buckle shifts away from my stomach.

"I think I got it."

Rounds are fired from the kitchen, but I can't tell if that's Mikey and his staff or someone who came in from the alley. I'm not taking the time to look around. I just need to get Beth outside. We plow into someone and knock them over.

"Watch your feet, Beth."

She scrambles, but I feel her trip. I glance back as she stumbles over the person; she grabs the woman's gun. She pries it from the stunned mercenary's hand and shoots. My girlfriend puts a bullet in the woman straight between the eyes. She spins back to me and darts forward until she can grab my belt again. I can tell when she turns because her back bumps into mine. She's still reaching back to hold on to me, but I know she's now protecting my back.

"Steve, right."

She calls out to her brother who's moved around Carmine to help carry the table. I turn my head just long enough to see him drive his fist into a man's face as he yanks the gun from his opponent. He shoots the guy in the abdomen. It's not a kill shot unless the guy bleeds out. I'm about to shift my attention when Beth twists and puts a bullet through the guy's throat.

When her brother yells "cannister," this time he shoots to kill. But it's too late. The bullet goes through the masked attacker's shirt, but they'd already pulled the pin. I realize— just as Steve does —that there's a bulletproof vest that prevented his round from penetrating. His next round goes into the person's throat just like Beth's.

Most people aren't wired to shoot with ease, even when put in situations like this. They freeze. They run. They refuse. I don't know if their parents played some type of subliminal message to each of them during infancy or it's genetic. But Chelle, Steve, and Beth have no qualms about killing to protect their family. Their oldest brother served in the military. Love, loyalty, and duty are the bedrock of their family, too. Beth's not just marrying into mine. I'm marrying into hers. I'm fucking proud and fucking reassured.

The smoke bomb lands, and soon it fills the dining room with heavy clouds of tear gas. The coughing is nearly immediate. The impulse to rub your eyes almost consumes you.

"Beth, leave the gun. Pull your shirt over your eyes. Let me lead you."

Each word is a struggle to get out as another canister explodes. It's too much. We can't orient ourselves as the mercenaries move around us. We can't breathe or see. We drop the table, and I move to curl around Beth, shielding her from the smoke as best I can. But I know it's no use. I'm more likely to smother her. I pull her to the floor and wrap my body over hers as Carmine, Pauly, and Steve continue to shoot.

It's a lost battle. Hands grab my arms and try to yank me to my feet. I use my dead weight to remain with Beth until I see the barrel of a rifle almost touching her head. I try to jerk forward, but the two sets of hands drag me back. Beth's head pops up. The attacker doesn't expect Beth to swat the muzzle away or that Beth still has a gun. She pulls the trigger, catching the person through the side of their skull.

But the moment they're gone, three more replace them.

They pry the gun from her just as they've done to me. I can't see well enough to know what's happening to Carmine, Steve, and Pauly. I have no idea what's happening in the kitchen. Where are our reinforcements?

It's getting hard to think as I cough and splutter, my eyes feeling like they're on fire. I relent and don't resist once they have Beth on her feet. I'm not giving them an extra reason to shoot me, so I wind up leaving Beth alone. We're shuffled into the kitchen where I see Mikey with blood pouring from his shoulder as he presses his hand to his wound. Three people corner the rest of the staff. Mikey nods as I go past. He and the members of his staff who are *soldati* will take care of those three once we're safely past them.

My lungs suck in the fresh air as I'm shoved through the door and into the alley. Beth's coughing so hard she's weaving with each step. I drive an elbow into whoever is behind me on the right. I reach for my girlfriend, but a hand wraps around my wrist.

"Get the fuck off me."

I wrap my arm around the man's and break the hold. We box, and we grapple to train. There are few holds we can't get out of. It's a matter of timing and good judgement as to whether you fight or cooperate. Right now, it's the latter, so I sling my arm around Beth's waist and pull her against me.

"How touching. Halfway to dead, and you still have some chivalry left."

"*Fanculo.*" Fuck off.

I splutter the word, so it doesn't quite have the bite I would like. But Simms can suck it. He's not wheezing because he had a mask.

"Drop your phones."

I notice Beth doesn't have hers anymore, but the rest of us

do. We toss them together on the ground just before Beth screams.

"Steve!"

Beth tries to rip herself from my hold as someone pistol whips her brother, sending him crashing to the ground. She fights me to get to her sibling, and I can't fault her. Her strength and determination don't surprise me. But there's nothing she can do. As long as they don't kill him, he's better off left behind.

"What the fuck? Now we have dead weight to toss in the truck."

Simms snaps at the attacker who nailed Steve's temple. Guess he's not getting left behind. I didn't think they would since he could identify most of them. But I can still be a perpetual optimist, can't I? The glass isn't fucking half full or half empty. It's just fucking half.

We're all hauled into the back of a delivery truck. It has no logo or writing on it, but I memorize the license plate. Delaware. Interesting. I wonder what vehicle they stole it off. As we enter, I stand near it as I offer to help Beth into the back. Carmine and I get Steve in too. Pauly and Carmine sense I'm up to something, so they crowd my back. I noticed the registration year sticker is peeling, so I tug it off just before I pull myself onto the truck. Who knows? Maybe we'll get lucky, and they'll get pulled over for expired tags. Right now, I'll accept dealing with cops for the sake of getting Beth to safety.

None of them frisked us, assuming our lost guns were our only weapons. Simms is getting lazy. Carmine, Pauly, and I all have our knives. I wish Beth still had her purse. I gave her pepper spray before we left for work this morning. They also didn't restrain us. With our hands and feet free, we stand a fighting chance— pun not intended.

I'm stripping off my belt just like Pauly and Carmine. It's my cousin who speaks without looking at me.

"Did Liz activate your tracker?"

"Yeah. Did you two hit yours?"

"Yeah."

Both men answer, so there are three alerts going to my family. That'll get their attention. Any tracker going off gets their attention, but there's no way it was an accident that all of them are sending out texts while traveling together. The three of us wind our belts a couple times around our hand, buckle out. We can swing it like a miniature mace, or we can wrap it around someone's neck. I have my knife in the other before I slide down to sit next to Beth as the truck moves. As much as I wanted to hold her, I had to take the time to prepare what few weapons I have.

"Are you hurt, *piccolina?*"

She's stopped coughing, but her eyes are still watering just like mine. She shakes her head as she huddles against her drawn in legs. She rests her cheek on her knees as she watches me. We've positioned her, so she's in the corner. Steve's next to her, but she's the most protected. I'm to her left, so I'm less likely to hit her if I swing the belt with my left hand. Pauly and Carmine are giving us a modicum of privacy by sitting a few feet away from us on either side. I place my open switchblade on the floor beside my leg as I open my arms to her. She falls into them. I stroke her hair and kiss the top of her head.

She whispers to me as she tilts her head to look up at me.

"This is different from last time. Are you mad I shot them?"

"Little one, I'm so fucking proud of you I could burst. I hate that you're sucked into this. I hate anyone came near you. I hate anyone threatened you. But goddamn, I'm impressed by you. I love you."

"I love you, too."

Those four words are the sweetest I'll ever hear until she says I do.

"Do you have any idea where we're going?"

She asked what we're all wondering.

"I don't. Simms has always flown under the radar. He's never been easy to track down in person. He could be reached by burner or through his network, but until a year or so ago, we never saw him in person. I don't know where his lair is."

It could be anywhere in the tri-state area. It could be anywhere in the five boroughs. As we sit together, I try to picture where we might be. I can estimate we're going about fifteen miles an hour but with lots of stops and starts. We haven't left Manhattan yet. We pulled straight out of the alley and made a left. I lost track a little while talking to Beth, but I'm trying to remember what I might have subconsciously picked up. I look over at Carmine while we're stopped for a moment. He shrugs. He doesn't know where we are either.

We're riding in silence for thirty minutes— I still have my watch —before the sound of the road changes beneath us. We're going over a bridge, but none of them are that long in New York, so that doesn't tell me which one. Some have tolls, but there aren't booths anymore, so we don't slow down.

Beth leans against me with her eyes closed just like the rest of us. The tear gas still stings and will for a little longer since we had no way to decontaminate ourselves. As long as we all keep our clothes away from our face now, it should get better. I stroke her shoulder as I let my sense of sound and sensation try to give me a mental map.

It's not that long before it feels like we're passing over another bridge. I can't be sure that we passed over one let alone two, but I think so. I open my eyes and look at my cousin.

"Triboro?"

"That's what I'm thinking. Randall Island up to the Bronx."

What the fuck is in the Bronx that he wants to take us to? Is it one of his safe houses? Does he plan to toss us in the East River? We're back to riding in silence as traffic picks up. You can be stuck in a traffic jam at any time of day. Don't people have fucking jobs? Why are they all on the road? Why can't they be civilized New Yorkers and take the subway? Granted, I drive myself or use a driver most days. The subway smells funny.

Smells funny.

"Car, City Island. That smell that's drifting in. Remember when our dads used to bring us out here?"

There's a tiny nautical museum on the island that my dad and uncle used to take us to when we were really little. Carmine and I both loved boats and still enjoy sailing. The museum isn't that big, so it was perfect for two little boys. Just enough to keep our attention, and just big enough to make us tired. We'd stop at one of the local fish places for lunch. I must have been about nine, and Carmine was seven the last time we came. But we used to do it at least one Saturday a month. Papa and Uncle Cesare would take us after a soccer match or baseball game while the others went to Donatelli's.

Steve came round just as we crossed the second part of the Triboro Bridge. He's using his pocket square to staunch the blood from where the gun's muzzle cut his face. He looks between Carmine and me.

"What's on City Island?"

"Not a whole lot except for some excellent fish restaurants."

The truck rolls to a stop, and there's stuff clattering around us. Then we inch forward. The engine turns off, and we hear doors slamming. Carmine, Pauly, and I prepare to launch ourselves at whoever opens the rolling door. But nothing happens. Not true. It's just no one opens the door. A few minutes later, the truck sways.

Pauly looks at me in disbelief.

"That motherfucker is taking us to Hart Island."

It's a cemetery island. That's it. There are two car ferries left in New York. One to Governors Island, and one to Hart Island. Does he plan to bury us alive? Or will he shoot us before he drops us into someone else's grave?

Chapter Twenty

Beth

I thought Chelle getting into a car accident that could have killed Enzo and her was horrible. I thought men shooting up my parents' home while they were meeting Enzo was the worst that could happen. Why did I tempt fate by thinking that?

I'm from north Jersey. I've barely heard of City Island or Hart Island. I know the bridges and the Bronx. But I didn't come into the city much as a kid. I live in Brooklyn and work in Manhattan. I have clients all over the place— except the Bronx. I have no objection to it. I would go if my firm did. But they don't. Since I don't pick the clients, I don't know if no one from the Bronx comes to us or the owners turn away people from there. This shitshow isn't the only reason I want to quit my job. I'm not a big fan of the women who own the company. Our CFO is the CEO's brother and COO's husband. He's the token man to not make the place too much of a stereotype.

That brings me around to what I was thinking about earlier.

"Marco, what we were talking about earlier. I think this confirms why I should quit. How am I going to explain just not showing back up to work after lunch? I had meetings today. My bosses are going to be blowing up my phone then up my ass."

Assuming we survive.

This seems like as good a time as any. We're on a ferry, so it's not like anyone is still trying to guess where we're going. I don't expect Carmine to chime in.

"You could take over my firm."

I lift my head to look at him.

"I started an interior design firm straight out of college. But it didn't take long to realize clients weren't looking for a man— a man my size —a man with my last name— to make their homes showroom quality. My current COO is moving to LA because her wife got a job out there. I admit I've checked out your work. It's beyond excellent. If you want the job, it's yours."

"I do. I thought I might work with Matteo, but this is a great opportunity. Thank you."

"You might work with Matteo if you want. But my firm doesn't work with Mancinelli Developers. We purposely don't mingle. My name doesn't even appear on any letterhead, even though I'm the CEO."

That actually makes me kinda sad. The letterhead part is because of his family name. A lot of family stuff came up last night as we waited. Paola explained more about her past, so I would get her relationship with Cesare since it's so different from all the others. She told me about how Carmine didn't take his father's last name until he was an adult. He'd been Carmine Mancinelli his entire life until then. She'd refused to marry Cesare until after Carmine's birth, even though their fathers insisted they wed. She thought ensuring his name was Mancinelli would protect him. Now he's Carmine Mancinelli

Ciccone. It wouldn't be hard to find out that Carmine Ciccone is a Mancinelli.

The other part that is sad is that he probably does little with Matteo because of the rift between Carmine and all the others. I learned Carmine was the black sheep of the family until around the time Luca and Olivia got together. The guys have repaired the damage done over twenty years of no one understanding Carmine, and him not wanting to let anyone in.

"If I take this position, I'll be a—"

The truck lurches. Maybe it isn't so bad it interrupted me. I was about to say I'll be a Mancinelli. That name would be on my business card. Despite what Marco says, I'm trying not to put the cart before the horse.

"You will be a Mancinelli, but if you'd rather keep your maiden name, then that might be helpful."

Marco gives my shoulder a squeeze. Fucking mind reader.

"I'll take your name as soon as it becomes my name. We'll figure out letterhead after that."

After we get out of this truck and off this island. If we truly are on Hart Island, then there's only one reason we are. I hadn't penciled in dying today in my calendar. I'd rather not.

The engine turns on, and there's more clattering before we're moving again. It's only a few minutes before the engine turns off again.

"Isn't Hart Island really tiny? I can't imagine there are too many cars coming on and off that ferry. Won't people see us? Won't it seem strange to have a delivery truck in a cemetery?"

"They may not open the door until it's dark. They could claim they're delivering flowers and wreaths. Who knows what? Or Simms could have paid off people here to turn a blind eye. We won't know until they open the door."

He's right. I lean back against him, even though I can feel how tense he is compared to before we arrived wherever we are. He's coiled like a rattler ready to strike. You can't tell, but you'll know when he sticks his fangs into you.

I didn't have to ask why the guys curled their belts around their hands. Now that Steve's forehead isn't bleeding anymore, he's done the same thing. He might not have the experience boxing or grappling Marco, Carmine, and Pauly do, but he wrestled through college with a nearly undefeated track record over the eight years. He's still in excellent shape.

Carmine reaches out a hand and pats my hand where it rests on my knee before giving it a squeeze. Any other man would lose that hand.

"Assuming our trackers are still pinging, it's not a bad thing that we're on an island. It means our family will have an easier time finding us. The space to search is finite. The longer they leave us wondering in here, the more time it gives the others to get here."

I nod. I can see the sense in that, but that doesn't mean it doesn't blow being in here. Now that the engine isn't generating heat, it's getting cold. Better than it being stifling in summer, but it's going to get uncomfortable fast. Though, with the heat Marco generates, I should be toasty as long as he stays at my side.

I don't know how long goes by. We sit mostly in silence as we just wait. Every once in a while Marco and his cousin and friend speak in what I assume is Sicilian, so I truly have no idea what they're saying. I think they might be running ideas by each other to plan for when the door eventually opens. I mean, they wouldn't drive us into the ocean, would they?

My head bobs a few times, and Marco keeps setting it back against his shoulder. He eventually just rests his hand on it to keep it in place. But the moment I settle again, the door rolls up.

"Out."

It's a woman barking the order. My eyes fly open, and I scramble away from Marco. Fuck. He should have been ready. I look at him as he comes to his feet in one lithe movement. I guess I wasn't in his way. He and the others charge forward. I watch Marco's foot connect with the underside of her chin, snapping her head back. I know their usual rule about never hurting women, but here it's equal opportunity defense against our kidnappers.

The people waiting around on the ground are unprepared for the men in the truck to surge forward, leaping from it and tackling them. I watch Steve using his wrestling skills just like I used to see when I'd go to his high school matches. He's choking a guy out without needing his belt. I watch Carmine's knife blade slice through the air before cutting the throat of the man beneath him. Pauly has his belt wrapped around the neck of the woman who opened the door.

Marco's got his belt around a man's neck, and the man's back flush to his chest. He has his knife in the other hand. He's not backing away, using the man as a hostage. No. He's propelling them both forward, using the unfortunate fucker as a battle shield. His knife goes into a woman's sternum before he pushes the man to the ground, puts his foot between the guy's shoulder blades and tugs on the belt.

It's all happening so fast. I don't know how to take everything in. I sweep my gaze around the scene, looking for the man Marco called Simms. He's nowhere I can see. I inch closer to the open door, keeping my back to the wall. My new position makes it easier to see the cemetery and the water surrounding it. It's obvious the truck wasn't the only vehicle they brought across to the island. Only three people would have fit in the cab, and nearly as many people are here as there were at the restaurant. Easily a dozen. Simms must be expecting more Mancinellis. He's luring them here.

I spot a shovel and a duffle bag near an empty grave. I scan the people fighting. Marco and the others won't be able to defend themselves forever. There are more attackers than defenders. No one is watching me, so I slip off the back of the truck and sprint to the grave. I'm about to grab the shovel when I spot a shotgun inside the bag.

How'd these motherfuckers... Fucking son of a bitch. This is my best gun. I pull the bag apart and spot three more of my competitive shotguns. How'd they get these if the ATF confiscated them? Did they plan to line us up in front of a firing squad and be all ironic by killing us with my weapons?

There are cartridges in the bag along with my guns. I squat and check to see which are loaded. Hot damn. Someone was dumb enough to travel with them all loaded and ready to fire. I'm so accustomed to handling these, I take next to no time to see. I go back to the first one— my best one. It's a twenty-eight gauge, so this is no toy. It's made specifically for competitive shooting. I'm usually exploding clay pigeons, but the shells loaded right now are meant to take down a human. I line up all the weapons, then take aim. I'm about twenty yards from the first person who's near a tree. The power of the ammunition pushes the woman into the tree before her dead body lands on the ground.

I switch to another shotgun that holds five shells. I take out three women standing near the truck's cab before moving on to the next then the next. I work my way through each of my loaded shotguns. If they're here, then they knew they could die. If they're here, it's because they planned to hurt us at the least, kill us most likely.

Maybe later I'll consider how easy it was to disassociate these bodies from the people they were. They're just targets that were far easier to hit than clays flying through the air.

They weren't moving, and I could see them before I even aimed.

It's not like these shotguns are silent. Not like the handguns the Mancinellis and their men carry. It's no secret I'm firing them. But no one expected it to be me. They're looking around. It buys me the time I need.

"Brava, brava."

I watch Simms step out from behind a tree. Chicken shit. He knows how many shells each gun held and that I now need to reload. The way he's approaching me makes me think he didn't pack this bag. I'd fired from a semi-kneeling position, down on only one. It's not how I'd shoot in a competition, but I can do it.

There's one more gun in the bag. It's actually one of Steve's hunting rifles. Completely different from a shotgun, but I know how to use it just as well as any other gun. I put my left hand up as though I'm surrendering while my right hand puts down the shotgun.

"Smart girl. Now let's just—"

I snatch the rifle before he realizes what I'm doing. He's approaching me without a gun drawn because he believes I can't reload a shotgun before he can draw his 9mm. Smug bastard. *Stronzo.* Isn't that what Marco's called guys? Assholes.

I bring the rifle up and take aim.

"Stop, and I'll let Marco decide what to do with you. Take another step, and I will put every round in you."

"Enough."

For a moment, I think he's speaking to me. But his remaining mercenaries— of which there are only a few of now —back away.

"Marco, I knew your woman was an excellent shot when she's playing. I didn't think she'd have the balls to kill."

"I fell in love with her. Of course, she can. You're the dumbass for underestimating her."

My boyfriend looks at me and smiles. Such a fucked-up time to see he truly is proud of me. But my attention swings back to Simms when he reaches for his gun, thinking I'm distracted. I pull the trigger and put one in his thigh.

"I will keep shooting."

I shoot his right arm, ensuring he won't go for his gun again. I wait for him to make the next move. He wobbles but staggers a step forward. I shoot him in his left ribs. I purposely miss his lungs. He puts his hand to the wound, as though that's the one he's going to have to worry about.

"Your choice. Head or heart?"

I sense the movement to my left. I squeeze the trigger, confident the bullet will land in the center of his forehead. No time for Simms to pick. I pivot on my knee and fire the next round as I realize one of his men was far closer than I sensed. He goes down with a shot through the chest. I move quickly since I'm used to having to shift positions depending on where the clay pigeon is released from.

Simms is lying face up, eyes unseeing to the heavens. I wave the muzzle at the ones still standing, gesturing them away from Marco, Steve, Carmine, and Pauly. My boyfriend walks to me and holds out his hand. I'm happy to relinquish the rifle. I don't flinch when he shoots the last of them.

It's only then that I really see everything. Not just the carnage I left. I honestly don't really care about that. It's the truck they transported us in. But it's also the four midsize SUVs that Simms's people came in. It was like he needed a platoon to fight our squad. I look at my boyfriend, Carmine, and Pauly. Simms truly feared them if he thought he needed this many people to go up against the three of them. He didn't expect Steve and me joining in the fight. I bend over and rummage in the bag. I pull out three bowie knives. Who the fuck knows what they intended to do with these.

"Do any of you hunt?"

The three boys from Queens look at me like I've finally gone and lost my mind.

"Then I don't want to know how you gained the skills you're about to use. We gut them."

I hand one knife to Steve and the other to Pauly. I head to the guy I shot after Simms. Steve's already headed to one woman. I kneel and use the knife to cut through the shirt. Then I use both hands to press the blade into the body from the sternum to the jeans. God, I hated this part of hunting. I usually had gloves. I pry open the abdomen as best I can without touching much. I pray I don't regret exposing myself to someone else's bodily fluids. Marco's standing over my shoulder, probably horrified, as I cut loose most of the organs. I've never done this on a human, but I've done it on deer. Same concept.

"Help me roll him."

Marco hasn't said a word, letting me work. I haven't looked at him to see what he thinks about his girlfriend going all Jeffrey Dahmer— minus the cannibalism —on this guy. Marco moves around to help, shaking the body to make everything tumble out.

"They'll sink if we do this. Then we toss the organs in too. But we have to puncture all the lungs since they'll float. I know we can't leave anything behind."

I look over to where Carmine and Pauly are working on a guy too. Steve's a far more experienced hunter than I am, so he's moving faster than any of us. We're carving the last body when we hear the ferry whistle. Fuck.

There isn't time to get the corpses into the water along with their organs.

"What're we going to do?"

I'm finally feeling panicky. Marco tilts his head toward the truck.

"In there."

I run to a woman and stand behind her head. I grab her sweatshirt at the shoulders and drag her. It would take me twice as long to struggle with a guy than with any of the women here. I do what I can to help, but my guys are stronger and faster. They haul the bodies into the truck. It looks like a fucking black market for organs with shit strewn across the grass. I grab a shovel, and Carmine finds two more. It's like mucking out horse stalls, except it's hearts, kidneys, lungs, and intestines— among other slimy, gross shit —being flung into the truck.

Fortunately, the ferry docks on the other side of the island. We won't go unnoticed for long, but it's not like they're pulling in right next to us.

"Get in the SUV, Beth."

Marco points while Carmine pulls the truck's rolling door down with a clang. I run to the closest one. We searched pockets as we worked and found the keys to all the vehicles. That's all good and well, but our clothes. We're all covered in blood. Now what?

"Car, my belt pulsed."

I don't know what that means. I'm almost to the first SUV's back passenger side door when Pauly calls out. I look at Marco, and he's not hurrying with another shovelful. I don't understand.

"Beth, it's all right. Our belt buckle will pulse when the tracker is deactivated remotely. Our family's here."

Chapter Twenty-One

Marco

I watch as three of our SUVs skid to a stop in a semi-circle around our battleground. Out of the center one pours Papa, Uncle Salvatore, Uncle Domenico, and Uncle Cesare. The one to the right has Gabe, Matteo, Luca, Enzo, and Emilio slamming doors. The third contains six of our men. A fourth pulls up a moment later, and I know that's filled with our guys too. Twenty men to rescue four of us. But that's not what holds my attention.

My best friend's older brother is here. The man who was once my older brother's best friend. The man who sliced Luca's face when they were fifteen and left him with a scar that runs down his cheek, along his neck, to below his collar. Emilio is not a welcomed member of the family. Uncle Salvatore banished him to Jersey. Uncle Dom, Auntie Carlotta, and Matteo see him, but he's only allowed near us during Christmas or during missions so dire that we need all hands.

Papa and Uncle Cesare run to us. Uncle Cesare lifts

Carmine off the ground. That's no small feat since my cousin is two-ten, easily. Papa nearly pulls me off my feet as he yanks me into his embrace.

"*Scimmietta.*" Little monkey.

Beth is safe, and all is right in the world again. My dad is here.

"Papa."

I wrap my arms around him just as tightly as he does me. He gives an extra squeeze before pulling back and looking around. The moment he sees Beth, he runs to her. He doesn't crush her quite as much with her hug as he did with mine, but it's just as enthusiastic. I watch her hug him back, her cheek against his chest. I can tell she takes comfort in his presence, and I love knowing my dad's accepted her as his daughter. It means he has just like Mama. Well, they'd accepted her already. They accept her without reservation.

I make my way over as Papa lets go. He moves to hug Carmine as Uncle Cesare hugs Beth and me at the same time. It's not long before the rest of the family hugs us too. Uncle Sal goes first, so he can step aside and speak to Pauly. He'll get the rundown from him while Carmine, Beth, Steve, and I assure everyone else that we're alive and well.

Emilio stands off to the side, Matteo stuck halfway between him and the rest of the family. I stare at the man I'd once considered more of an older brother than a cousin however many times removed. Now he's a virtual stranger. I jerk my chin. I can at least acknowledge my thanks that he came, even if he wasn't needed.

I look at Luca, who's watching me. My expression is blank, but he understands. It was the right thing to do even if Luca may never forgive Emilio. Until Emilio can admit why he did what he did, and Luca can make peace with him, he'll never be welcomed back into the fold. The only five people who know the truth are Emilio, Luca, Carmine— who was eleven and there —Luca's wife, Olivia, and Carmine's wife, Serafina.

I shift my focus to my best friend. He doesn't know what to do, so he just shrugs when he meets my gaze. I don't envy him. He loves Emilio because he's his brother. That will never change because family will always be more important than anything else. But he doesn't like his brother. The fight with Luca was the worst thing Emilio did, but it wasn't the only shitty thing he did. If the situation were reversed, we'd all drop everything to save Emilio. Once we were sure he was breathing, he'd be right back in exile.

"Marco?"

I look down at Beth, who's come back to stand beside me after reassuring every man in my family at least five times over that she's okay. She also introduced Steve to everyone.

"*Piccolina*, what do you need from me?"

That could sound so horrible, but I mean it from the bottom of my heart. I'll do whatever I can right now. I can't imagine what she's thinking or feeling. I don't know if she even is thinking or feeling yet.

"To know you're safe. That no one else is going to try to murder you today."

I almost make a quip— at least not for now —but that won't help things. I open my arms to her, and she gladly steps closer to me. I rest my cheek on the top of her head. Simms is dead. That's one threat eliminated.

I found out Alejandro's plane is now part of Wing-hung's fleet. He's the leader of the Wo Shing Wo, one of the Triad. We thought he'd killed Simms from the photo we saw of the beating Wing-hung or one of his men doled out. With Alejandro's plane in China, the Diazes know to back off. That's a second threat that's at least alleviated for now.

But there's still the issue of who inside the FBI and ATF is really gunning for us. They're always trying to build cases against us, but nothing sticks. We make sure we pay all our legal taxes on time. The rest of the money is so damn well-hidden Sherlock Holmes, Miss Marple, and a bloodhound couldn't find it. We aren't going down for tax evasion like fucking Al Capone. We keep our records meticulously encrypted, so they aren't getting us on RICO— Racketeer Influenced and Corrupt Organization Act —like they did John Gotti. My uncle is the real "Teflon Don." You live, you learn. And that chaps their motherfucking asses.

"We're both safe, *cuore*. We're going to go home, take a shower, and sleep for three days."

"Sleep, Daddy?"

She playfully pouts. Despite what she's endured today alone, she's doing her best to remain strong. Even making jokes to convince me she's fine. She won't be. That's a given. I was a fucking wreck the first time I killed more than one person in a day. I threw up four times and didn't sleep for two weeks. Then again, she's thirty-three, and I was sixteen.

"Just enough so we have energy to fuck like bunnies."

She waggles her eyebrows at me before we share a brief but tender kiss. I need one day with nothing blowing up, so I can propose to her. Maybe we'll have a longer engagement than anyone else in our family. Maybe we won't. But we're in this together for good. You don't go through a day like today without either being bonded for life or disintegrating into dust. I don't think we're the latter.

"Seriously though. What's going to happen here? We got everything in the truck, but there's DNA everywhere. It's obvious there was a blood bath here. You can't exactly scrub blood out of grass."

"The six guys who arrived with my family are scrubbers, actually. They're fully capable of joining a fight when they need to, but their job is to clean up afterwards. They'll work their magic once we're gone. No one will think a blade of grass was disturbed by the time they're done."

We have teams that go in after us when we have situations that get out of control and get messy. They repair things and dispose of things that we can't afford anyone finding. They're worker bees who build the hive or the worker ants that build the sand hill. They don't get noticed, and we all prefer it that way. But they're diligent. Beth looks around and nods. She won't ask more questions. I could tell her what I just thought, but I can't tell her more specifics.

Uncle Domenico signals it's time for us to go. Enzo and Matteo are going to take the truck to our garage. They'll deal with the bodies there, and we have men who can dispose of the truck, so no one ever finds it. Uncle Domenico, Uncle Cesare, Carmine, Luca, Gabe, and Emilio climb into an SUV. My guess is Emilio and Gabe are in the third row, and Luca is driving. They're as far apart as they can get. Beth, Steve, Pauly and I climb into another SUV with Papa and Uncle Salvatore.

Papa's driving, and I have a flashback to four kids riding in Papa's minivan— yes, he drove one because it was the least assuming car a Mafioso could have —while he got us Happy Meals. Luca would trade me half his cheeseburger for half my nuggets. Maria would have taken a finger off if anyone got too close. Youngest child and only girl— she was tough. Enzo was just happy to be left in peace. Middle child life.

As Beth and I lean against each other, both exhausted, I think about how I'd gladly exchange my electric BMW i5 for a Volvo EM90 electric minivan. Yes, I'm into sustainability even if I spend some of my days destroying shit. I'm still an electrical engineer and love the science behind these cars. I'd let my kids get the apple slices *and* the fries. We only got fries when Papa was absolutely certain Mama wouldn't find out. At least not until we'd all woken up after passing out in the car after games.

The ride to Queens is blessedly quiet. I'm so drained right now I barely have the energy to breathe. I'm just so grateful I'm still able to. I laced my fingers with Beth's as she sits in front of her brother, who's in the third row with Pauly. She checks over her shoulder periodically, and Steve keeps squeezing it. When we get to my parents' house— which is as big as Uncle Salvatore and Aunt Sylvia's —we go through another reunion with the moms and aunts like we did after the shooting.

Then I'm finally alone with Beth. She watches as I take a large trash bag from beneath my bathroom sink, putting each item of my clothing in it, holding it out to her in between for her to do the same. It'll get burned. All of it. We left our shoes downstairs, and I had to explain that they would be disposed of, too. There's no salvaging either pair.

Once we're in the shower, we can't keep our hands off each other for a breathless kiss that makes my head spin. From the way she clings to my arms, I think she feels the same.

"Daddy, I was so scared they were going to kill you, and I'd have to watch. That there'd be nothing I could do to stop them."

"I know, little one. The same thing terrified me."

"I want to have faith that whatever Matteo and Enzo are doing and whatever those scrubbers are doing is enough. But I'm scared, Marco. Really scared. What if someone finds out what we did?"

"We do everything we can to make sure that never happens. I hate admitting we're experts, but we are."

We're scrubbing our own bodies clean as we talk. I wash her hair, and she sighs. She lets the hot water rain down on her as I lather my hair. Once I've thoroughly checked that she has nothing left in her hair or under her nails, she wraps her arms around my waist.

"Marco, is this over?"

My heart lurches for a moment. I panic for just a second, fearing she means us. But I realize she means this situation.

"I don't know. The guys who were responsible for the FBI and ATF attack have been dealt with. They're too high up in their family for anything permanent, but they know we know. Simms is gone, and his anger stemmed from something entirely separate. Law enforcement will always be after us in some way or another. That's the one that I still worry about."

"Your dad and Sinead helped me last time, but what if they can't? I remained silent, but they can compel me to testify."

She reaches between us and strokes me as she speaks. She surprises me when she steps back and kneels down. I thought we were still talking.

"You know there's only one way to ensure I never have to tell a soul anything about you."

She licks the tip of my cock before running her tongue from the base to the head. She swirls it over the hole. I'm loving this, but I'm also taking her hints. However, she could knock me over with a feather the next time she speaks.

"Marco, will you marry me? I'm down on bended knee."

She wraps her mouth around my dick and slides it down until I brush the back of her throat. I choke my answer.

"Yes."

Her head bobs as she sucks me off. She crossed her wrists at the small of her back as she works me. I grasp her hair, tempted to pull her off, so we can talk. But holy fucking shit. It feels divine. But when I'm close, I scoop her under her arms and lift her until she wraps her legs around my waist. I back her against the shower wall and pound into her.

"Little girl, I am going to marry you. But right now, I'm

going to make you scream my name as I fill you with my cum. I don't give a shit who hears us. I said yes. You're as good as my wife now. My cock is yours. Your pussy is mine to do with as I please. And right now, it pleases me to make my fiancée come over and over. *My* fiancée is going to take *my* cum because she's *mine.* You might have beaten me to the proposal— one that I will *never* forget —but I'm in charge of what happens now."

"Fuck. Yes, Daddy."

"You feel so fucking right, Beth. Everything about you. The way it feels to hold your hand. To hug you. To kiss you. To be inside you. I will love you for the rest of my life."

"Same, *amore mio.* I want you to be the last thing I see before I fall asleep and the first I see when I wake. I want to know I'm who you're coming home to every day. I want to know that one day, all that cum you put in me is going to make us a family. I want to see you become the papa you were always meant to be in this family."

"I want to leave you sore every morning, so every step you take reminds you of how right we are together. I want you to know every time you're in my arms there is no righter place for me. I want you to know that I'm so fucking proud of you I could burst. And who you are is who I want to be the mom of our family."

Our kiss is fierce. We can't get enough as we make love. This isn't gentle, slow loving. It's passionate mating for life. We move together as my fingers bite into her ass, surely leaving marks to remind us both that she's mine. Her hands roam over me, her nails leaving scratches on my back to mark her territory. I've never allowed that before Beth. But I'll gladly see lines up and down my back until the day I die.

"I'm close, Daddy. May I come?"

"Yes. You asked for this first one, my sweet *piccolina.* But you don't have to ask for the rest. I'm going to make you come over and over before I fuck you so hard I can't keep from exploding."

"Fuck me hard now."

She digs her heels into my lower back, and I oblige. She doesn't scream, but she moans my name every time I feel her pussy contract around me. It's a battle of self-control not to finish too soon.

"Marco, come. Please. I need to make you come."

She needs to know I'm enjoying this as much as her, that I need to fuck her as badly as she needs to fuck me. She needs to know she's the one who gives me my orgasms just as much as I need to know I give her hers.

"*Piccolina!*"

I don't exactly bellow, but neither am I quiet as I erupt in her. We hold each other, panting. When I feel my knees shake, I turn around and ease down to the tile floor. We sit there as the water falls over us.

"I love you, Marco. Truly. I kept thinking over and over that I'd be damned if someone was stealing my future with you. I'd be damned if anyone was going to take you from me. I love my brother and worried about him. But there wasn't any limit to what I would have done to protect you."

"I love you, too. You know I feel the same. It's not that I ever underestimated you. Not your depth of feeling or your commitment to us. But not everyone can do what you did. We teach women born into this world how to take care of themselves from as early an age as the boys. They're supposed to be untouchable, but not everyone plays by those rules. We pray situations don't come about like what you and your sister have faced, but they do. Unfortunately, way too often for my generation. You're as dedicated to family as I am. I think that's why we've known we're soulmates since the beginning. Honor, loyalty, and duty to family. I'll always protect you as best I can.

I know my family will always protect me. But to know there's a woman in this world who loves me like you do, one who will stop at nothing to protect me— that's priceless."

"May God have mercy on anyone's soul who comes near you or our children because I won't. Family has always been important to me. That's how I grew up. But losing Sam made me understand just how integral family is to me. Falling in love with you and being welcomed into your family amplifies that because there are more people to love, but there's also danger I never expected. I hate that what's happened has happened. I don't enjoy thinking I kill without remorse. But it's given me the strength to stand by you."

"No. It's shown you that you have the strength."

She smiles at me as she nods. She gives me a peck before we both look at the shower door. We know we have to go. Neither of us wants to. But both our stomachs were rumbling when we came up here. Yet another day with missed meals. I know my uncle will want to hear Carmine's and my version after having talked to Pauly. I want to check on Steve and Beth's parents, who arrived just before Beth and I came upstairs.

I help her to her feet before turning off the water. She hands me a towel. Once I'm dry, I wrap it around my waist. She turns toward the door, but I don't follow her. She watches me retrieve bleach from beneath the sink. I'm efficient as I scrub down the entire shower, not splashing anything on my mother's towels. I didn't survive today for my mother to kill me over nine-hundred thread count towels. Beth observes me disinfecting the shower to kill any DNA we might not have rinsed away.

Chelle already left clothes on the bed for Beth. Enzo probably told her Beth would need them. Or maybe it was Mama. I'm certain Chelle and Maria are eager to see their husbands even if they know they were safe the entire time. Enzo and Matteo should be back soon. Then it'll be time for the meeting. Once we're dressed, we head back downstairs. I hear people in the kitchen and the dining room. Thank God. It's only a moment later that Beth and I have heaping plates.

"Liz?"

Papa hands over her purse. Mikey or someone else must have brought it over. She thanks him and checks the contents. She looks up at me and nods. Everything is there with nothing extra. She checks her phone and winces. She's expressionless as she listens to voicemails. When she hangs up, she looks at Carmine.

"Can I have a corner office?"

Chapter Twenty-Two

Beth

I didn't lose my job, but I'm about a hair's breadth from being fired. I had five livid messages from my boss, reaming me out for not returning to work after lunch. I get why she's so pissed. I missed three client meetings and a walk through. I was also going to try to swing by the retail space in the building Matteo designed. Obviously, none of that happened. I've been a model employee since the day I started. I work from home rather than take sick days. I take the most persnickety clients. And I have the highest billable hours.

I know that being seen at the press conference and having my name linked to the Mancinellis pissed them off. They must know Marco came to my office today, and that I left with him. Disappearing with my boyfriend looks super bad. She warned I'm on probation.

"You can have a corner office and pick your salary. Redecorate the entire place in zebra print. Like I said, I've seen your work. The firm will be in even better hands than it has been.

I'm a silent owner, and I prefer it that way. It allows me to focus on the projects I have with Matteo for Mancinelli Developers. That's more than enough to keep me busy."

I assumed they didn't work together much because he said he likes to keep his design firm separate from the family business. I thought that was partly because of the rift I heard about. But it makes sense now. Both are legit businesses, but it shelters his more to make it look like it's unaffiliated with the entire family, not just Carmine. I know he's a structural engineer and oversees most of their construction sites. I just didn't think he and Matteo would look at it as working together so much as Matteo handing off blueprints. Well, you know what happens when you assume. But apparently I'm the only ass.

"Thank you. I'll leave the zebra prints to night clubs. We can negotiate salary later."

I grin, but Carmine shakes his head. My smile falls.

"Seriously, Liz. You're worth whatever price you ask. The business is thriving. We can afford it, especially considering the clients I know you can bring in. Take whatever you think you deserve and add a zero."

Carmine thrusts out his hand, and I'm back to grinning. I accept and shake.

"My W-4 and direct deposit form will be on your desk in the morning."

"Welcome aboard. When can you start?"

I can't believe I'm having this conversation over a plate of tortellini arrabbiata— which is seriously the most delicious dish I've ever tasted.

"I'll put in my two weeks in the morning."

"Car, she can't start for at least two months."

I turn toward Marco, my brow furrowed.

"You're going to have to wait until we're back from our honeymoon."

My face feels like it's radiating heat. I'm not upset that he announced it. It's what he's going to say when people assume he proposed. My mom beams at me, but his mother looks confused. Nicoletta tilts her head as she narrows her eyes at her son. Fucking hell. She knows we got engaged while we were just upstairs. I'm pretty fucking sure she knows it happened while we were having shower sex in Marco's childhood bathroom in her home. I want to cringe.

Instead, I accept Marco's kiss which verges on indecent in front of our parents. He grins unrepentantly at his mom. I take a sip of water, but I nearly choke when he speaks.

"Beth asked, and I said yes. It was very sweet."

Fortunately for me, we're sitting, or I might have fallen over. His hand squeezes my thigh. I snap my legs shut. I'll get him back for this later, and he knows it. I'm not sure how. But I will. Maybe we will have a power switch tonight, and I'll tie him up.

"Congratulations! Another sister. Hallelujah."

Maria claps as she smirks at Marco. If they were kids, I think she'd stick her tongue out at him. I can totally picture her as a little girl. I bet she was a total tomboy and determined to keep up with her brothers and cousins. I'm pretty fucking positive she was the true ringleader most of the time. From what I can tell, you won't find a sweeter person than Marco's little sister. But I also think you couldn't find a better person to get in trouble with.

"Lizzie, two sisters marrying two brothers."

Chelle winks at me, and I can't help but laugh at our inside joke. Back when boy bands were the thing, we stumbled across New Kids on the Block from the '80s. Neither of us wanted Jonathan or Jordan Knight. We both wanted Joey McIntire—never mind the obvious age gap. Since we couldn't both have him, we looked at Donny and Mark Wahlberg. We would have gladly gotten between Marky Mark and his Calvins. Alas, no two brothers for two sisters in that band. But we definitely thought about it. Now we get our tween dream.

Marco stares down at me, and all I can do is shake my head. Chelle and I pinky swore we'd never share our plan. That only makes me laugh harder. When she laughs too, I know we're thinking the same thing. Considering how much time the Mancinellis spend together, I'm excited to know I'll see my sister more often than I have since I left for college. I moved to Brooklyn after college and stayed during grad school. Chelle moved away for college and law school before getting a place in Manhattan.

When I look up at Maria, I see her watching us. From the twinkle in her eye, I have a sneaking suspicion she'll be feeding us plenty of ammunition against her brothers, one of whom is her husband's best friend. When I look at the other younger women at the table, I realize how fortunate I'll be to have more sisters and cousins who can help me get used to this new life. As I look at the older women, they all seem to ignore my antics with Chelle and Maria, but I can tell they're happy we're all getting along already.

It's not long before Enzo and Matteo return, both inhaling two plates of food each after greeting their wives and mothers. I expect Marco to head to his father's study with the other guys while I wait with the womenfolk.

"Beth, can you come with us, please?"

"Okay."

I glance at Chelle who shrugs and goes back to playing with her new and my soon-to-be niece, Petra. I take Marco's hand and follow him into the office. Cesare is the last to enter, so he closes the door behind him. They clearly designed the room as a library since this is probably a Prohibition Era or slightly older home. It's spacious for all the men crammed in here. Marco guides me to a loveseat. None of the men sit until I do. I've noticed that about them. They don't sit until the women do. In several situations, they've stood when a woman has. Old world charm that I hope our generation passes on to the next.

Salvatore sits in an armchair near his brother's desk. It's obviously Massimo's domain, but Salvatore still has a presence. The two brothers could practically be twins, except Salvatore's hair is a little closer to black. Considering how much Massimo's sons look like him, I have a good idea of what Salvatore must have looked like as a young man. I think he was in his mid-thirties when he became don, so not terribly much older than Marco is now. As my gaze sweeps around the room, there isn't a man from either generation I couldn't picture leading their family and their branch. They're imposing and impressive. Salvatore's voice focuses me back on the present.

"Liz, we could talk to just Carmine and Marco. But we'd like to hear from you. You might have noticed something the men missed. It's not that we don't trust your brother. We do. He proved himself today from what Pauly told me. But for everyone's safety, it's better that he not be part of this meeting."

Because they could force him to testify, just like I could be until Marco and I marry.

"I understand. Do you want me to start from the beginning?"

"Yes, please."

Marco laces his fingers with mine while I look at Salvatore and replay aloud the afternoon and evening in my mind. I close my eyes for most of it, so I can picture everything. Now that it's over, and I'm safe, I realize just how truly fucked-up it was. How truly capable I am of setting aside what most people would consider morality to do what I felt I had to in the moment.

When I finish my story, I look at Massimo and Cesare. Both

men look a little green, hearing about the danger their sons faced. I'm certain it isn't the first time they've heard the play-by-play, but maybe I told it differently as an outsider or as a woman. Either way, they both look like they could be ill. I'm positive it's not from the part where I told them about gutting the attackers like fresh venison.

Salvatore observed me— assessed me — or at least it felt that way —the entire time I spoke. His expression was inscrutable. The man could go to Monte Carlo, Atlantic City, and Vegas and win every poker game. Now that I'm finished he leans forward, and I get an almost paternal sense from him. Maybe an uncle.

"Liz, there's nothing easy about families like ours. We try to be as normal as we can when we're together, but you've already seen that can be cut short without notice. All the women who've joined our family have faced some type of— challenge, if you will —but you've certainly faced the most violent. You've seen more in a few short weeks than even most *Cosa Nostra* women born into this. Your strength is commendable, and I can't thank you enough for your dedication to protecting my nephews. I don't know what I would do if I lost either of them. You've certainly impressed my men, which is no small feat considering how jaded they've been since the womb. Marco has always been the most reserved in the family. He is the strong, silent type in any situation that doesn't involve teasing his siblings, cousins, or friends. Despite all this mishigas, he's more relaxed than any of us have ever seen him. You've brought that out in him. If you're willing to take on Eeyore and all that comes with this family, we welcome you. I welcome you as my newest niece. You're an improvement on any of my nephews."

Did the world just flip upside down? First of all, I don't expect an Italian don to use the Yiddish word for craziness. But this is New York. Everyone speaks at least four words of it.

Second, I never would have thought Marco was the most reserved. I thought that was Luca. Enzo's the laid back one. Third, he thinks of me as his niece. I just thought of him like an uncle. I belong.

"Thank you, Salvatore. This has certainly tested me, but being with Marco far outweighs any obstacle anyone throws at us. I wish I hadn't been pushed into this and interfered with your business. But everyone has made me feel part of this family since the start."

"You never interfered, Liz. You being here right now isn't interfering with anything. You being caught in all of this is something I won't accept, but it wasn't interference. We're all glad you are here. All of this would have happened regardless of whether you were in our lives. You didn't cause this. But you have helped my family survive."

"I appreciate that. You're a little intimidating. It's nice to know I belong."

Marco snorts.

"You think he's intimidating. Wait until you really get to know Natalia. Take every intimidating expression Uncle Sal has and pack it into a ten-year-old who thinks you need to grow up. Luca better have a son, or she'll be our don after him."

Salvatore beams with pride as Marco describes his cousin who's young enough to be his daughter. Enzo chimes in.

"She doesn't get that from Uncle Sal. That's Aunt Sylvia. If Uncle Sal is the head of the family, then Aunt Sylvia is the hand that turns it."

I hold my breath as I dart my gaze from Enzo to Salvatore, who only smiles even wider.

"That's why I fell in love with her before I even said hello."

Okay. This family teases each other. A lot. Like more than you could ever imagine given what they do. But even by most standards, I think they bust each other's balls more than most.

Marco's arm is around my shoulder, and he nudges my other with his shoulder.

"Just wait until you hear Mama and Auntie Carlotta go after Papa and Uncle Dom. You'll see where we all learned it from. They'll serve you a slice a pie while cutting you down at the knees. You won't even see it coming."

Carmine rolls his eyes.

"My aunts will never pick on Liz like they do us. They think all our wives are angels sent down from above because they agreed to shackle themselves to us for life. And Natalia might get a little of it from Aunt Sylvia, but most of it came from Mama. Aunt genetics are real. Mama is Auntie Nicoletta and Auntie Carlotta on roids. You all know I'm right. Right, Papa?"

Carmine looks over at Cesare, and I'm not sure what the man will say since he and Paola are separated. Is this going to open the door for Cesare to show how much he's estranged from his wife?

"Your mama runs circles around her brothers in heels with a smile. If she'd been a man, it wouldn't have mattered that she was the youngest. She'd be sitting in Massi's seat, and her big brother would have offered it to her. She's far smarter than either of these two *gaguzzes* put together, and they both went to Harvard Law."

"*Gaguzz?*"

I whisper to Marco because I'm certain I've never heard that one before. He's not so subtle when he answers.

"Meathead."

Watching Massimo, I'm pretty sure he would have given his brother-in-law an obscene gesture. But it would have been out of love. Cesare and Paola's marriage might be a disaster, but it's obvious Cesare is as much a part of this family as Salvatore and Massimo.

"If you Jabronis are—"

The room erupts in laughter as Domenico chimes in. Luca speaks first.

"Okay, Hulk Hogan. You gonna flex those twenty-two-inch pythons?"

"He'd have to hit the gym more than he hits his wife's manicotti."

For a moment, I thought Massimo was insinuating something way different. But when Domenico smirks and pats his stomach, I realize he really does mean food.

"Don't blame me that your wife forgot how to cook once your kids left home. My wife still likes me."

"Is that what you tell yourself? The woman has a kind heart. She couldn't stand to see you waste away. You can't even boil water. And you call yourself Sicilian."

Massimo dishes it right back at him. It's obvious these men grew up together as close as Marco and his brothers and cousins did. Toss Matteo and Gabe in there, and there're ten Frick or Fracks. I know Cesare came into the picture later, and it wasn't under good circumstances since he got Paola pregnant at nineteen, but it's clear the other men consider him one of them.

Marco pulls his arm away from me and stands. I follow him when he offers me his hand.

"You're all worse than old women at a fish market. Can you stop cackling long enough for Beth and me to say goodnight? I can barely keep my eyes open after all the food Mama cooked for *me*, Papa."

"Really? You want to throw down, *scimmietta*. Meet me at the gym tomorrow, and we'll see who walks out and who crawls out. I could bench Gabe if I wanted. You might be lucky to lift Pia."

I know firsthand Marco can lift a lot more than just Pia. My mind flashes an image of us in the shower not so long ago. He squeezes my fingers, and I know he's thinking about the same thing. Marco turns toward the door just as someone knocks. Massimo answers.

"*Entra.*" Come in.

It surprises me to see my brother open the door and step inside. He looks around as he approaches Marco and me. I can tell he's checking on me. He knows I'm okay, but he still worries. How do I know? Because I'm doing the same thing to him.

"I'm sorry to interrupt, but I think all of you need to hear this. I got a call this afternoon, but since we were busy, it went to voicemail."

He pulls out a phone that isn't his and taps the screen a few times. It rings once before his voicemail answers, and he enters his code. He puts it on speaker.

"Hey, Steve. This is Shane O'Rourke. I'm giving you a heads up that you and your sister need to stay away from the Mancinellis today. Michelle's already made a shit choice, but she's protected as Enzo's wife. Elizabeth needs to get far, far away from Marco. Shits been in the works for months that *Tres J's* almost fucked-up with their bottom feeder connections. Now that it's started, the feds won't back off. This is the only courtesy call you'll get, and it's for your grandfather's sake. We promised to watch out for your family, but there's nothing we can do if you side with the Mancinellis. You can call if you want, but I won't say more than this. You've been warned. If your family's in the crosshairs, we won't rescue you."

The message ends, and I stare at the phone in my brother's hand. What the fuck?

Chapter Twenty-Three

Marco

I listen as Steve's voicemail asks what he wants to do with the message. He saves it while all eyes are on him. He's watching me. Our gazes meet, and we come to a meeting of the minds. Beth comes first. If that means destroying everything connected to the O'Rourkes, Steve will do what he can. He shifts his gaze to Enzo.

"Chelle said you're an accountant, but you're also a licensed trader. She mentioned you have a degree in computer science. When I asked if you use that to design accounting software, she clammed up. You're a hacker."

There isn't remotely a question in his voice. No one responds.

"Get me securely into the O'Rourkes accounts. They're clients. I have their information, but I need to access it without triggering any alerts. Those boys are going to wake up as broke as their family was when they got to America. Your family, on the other hand, is about to be thirty million richer."

Beth steps away from me and stands in front of her brother. "They're clients?"

"Yeah. New ones. I didn't know about Grandpa yet, but I knew our families had history. They approached me about a month ago. I agreed to take them on, knowing who they are. I have other clients who have invested in their public traded entities. Since becoming my clients, I've seen their entire portfolio. The *entire* portfolio. Granted Finn probably has cash in his attic and his basement. Doom's Day prepper when it comes to money. He won't let them keep all their money in one bank."

We know. Oh, how we know. That fucker is an accountant with hacking skills too. He tried to fuck over the Kutsenkos by fucking Gabe and Carmine over first. He tried to pin the blame on them for the shit that ignited the feud with Simms.

"Steve, you could go to jail for this."

He gazes down at his sister. While I don't know exactly the words he'll pick, I already know what he'll say.

"Shane might claim there's nothing they can do to stop the feds, but that's bullshit. If they can get the feds to act on their command, then they can get them to stop on their command. They don't want to. That's why he warned me. The O'Rourkes aren't new. They've watched every guy in the Mancinelli family get married except for Marco. And that's like two days away from happening, anyway."

Tomorrow morning if it were solely up to me.

"Liz, protecting our family might have been part of the agreement Liam O'Rourke made with Grandpa way back when, but they obviously meant they'd protect us from outsiders. Not from them. They know you're with Marco. From what everyone's been telling me while you've been in here, the moment Marco introduced you, it's been inevitable that you'll get married. The O'Rourkes know this. They know telling me to keep you away won't do bupkis. They might protect me because I've already made them a shit ton of money in a few weeks, but they aren't trying to protect you. What I gaveth them, I'll taketh away."

He's not exactly God, but he's about to be the Devil.

"So you think the O'Rourkes are siccing the feds on the Mancinellis, and my life be damned."

"Pretty much."

Beth looks up at me. The rage inside of me is looking for an outlet, but I won't let Beth see it. It'll terrify her. But when our gazes lock, I know she can read me as well as anyone in my family. She knows what I'm feeling, even if I'm doing my best to hide it. She looks back at her brother.

"If Enzo can get you in, can you do more than wire the money out of their accounts?"

"Yes. I can make sure the stock value of every holding they have plummets. People will sell within an hour of the opening bell. But I'll need some help to make that happen fast."

He looks over at Uncle Salvatore and Papa.

"It's already morning in Asia. Do you have any connections to journalists in Tokyo or Beijing?"

Papa nods.

"Yes, but not directly."

"However you can do it, we need a headline in the financial papers to run about how their biotech company falsified approval from the FDA on the drug that's supposed to come out in six weeks. In Ireland, we need a headline that reads they're pulling their whiskey production from there and bringing it to the U.S. And in the rest of Europe, you need to run an exposé on how their agricultural imports have all been tested and found to have been grown with GMOs. If you can time the European ones for when their markets open, it'll drive the Asian ones to catch up. Once the Europeans see the Asians dropping the bio stock, they'll do the same. The Irish will go scorched earth on them over the whiskey alone. They talk a big game over there about how they're as Irish as they've ever been, they just happen to live in America."

Matteo's watching me instead of Steve, deciding on how he'll react based on how I do. He'll support me one way or another, as long as what I say doesn't fuck shit up for everyone. That doesn't mean he doesn't have questions.

"So when they get up and discover their cash is gone, and their companies are worthless, they have enough intelligence to scrape together to figure out it was you. Then what? They'll put a hit on you."

"I know. I hope they do. They've been involved in risking both my sisters' lives. Dillan and I can have a little chat one to one. If neither of us walks away, then at least neither of us walks away."

"Stevie, no!"

Beth lurches forward and grabs her brother's shirt. I recognize it as one of Luca's.

"Lizzie, our family has more secrets than the Vatican. There's shit I haven't told you about me that needs to come out. I'd rather tell you and Chelle in private then tell Mom and Dad, but I don't think that's going to work."

He looks over at Papa and Uncle Salvatore.

"Do you know?"

Both of them look as mystified as I feel. They shake their head in unison, and it's rather uncanny. It's Uncle Cesare who answers.

"I didn't, but I think I do now."

We all turn toward him. He's in insurance. He never came on missions until Carmine started dating Sera, and there were threats to them. He's been invaluable to us as a pencil pusher. Or at least by looking like one. He's made us and saved us millions.

We wait, but Uncle Cesare offers nothing. All eyes swing back to Steve as he clenches his right fist. He looks at Beth, and it's enough to make her lean against me for moral support. She's dreading what she's about to hear.

"Beth, what I did today wasn't because I'm an experienced hunter. It wasn't even because nothing was going to stop me from protecting you. That first man I shot. I didn't know whether Marco and Carmine would want him later. That's why I didn't shoot to kill. He's not the first man I've shot. Today wasn't the first time I've killed someone."

"What are you not saying, Steve? Spit it out."

"At Maks and Laura's reception, I got into a conversation with Grigori Kutsenko and Radomir Andreyev."

"I know. I remember. I was there for most of it. You talked about an overnight fishing trip you were taking in a few weeks. You mentioned you take a week off work for the opening of deer season. I guess they're hunters too."

Fuck. This cannot be going in the direction I think it is. I look at Uncle Cesare. How the fuck did he guess anything?

"Lizzie, I didn't realize it at the beginning of the conversation, but they weren't talking about shooting deer or bears. That wasn't the kind of hunting they alluded to. I didn't even know it until a couple months later when I got a call from Anton asking if I wanted to go on a hunting trip with them. I asked Chelle what she thought, and she asked Laura. Neither thought it was a big deal, so I went. It didn't take a genius to figure out what kind of family Laura married into. I already knew from working on Wall Street. The trip went well, and I impressed them with my skills. Not just my shooting but how I could field dress the animal and butcher it when it was time. I've done it so many times that the blood and guts don't faze me. I'm efficient too. They liked how I left the place cleaner than when I arrived."

"Steven, are you telling me they recruited you?"

"I'm not a *bratok*."

"What's that?"

"A foot soldier. I think your new family calls them a *soldato*. The Russians also call them *patsan* or *brodyaga*. I don't know the exact translations, but they carry out— stuff. I wasn't initiated in or anything like that."

"Then what are you trying to get at? I'm getting impatient."

So am I.

"On the way back into the city, we talked about Sam. I guess Maks's father was Grigori's younger brother and died in the Second Chechen War. We had something in common. He and Radomir were there when it happened. I told them I couldn't imagine going through that. Not only seeing it but the rage that had to have come with it. I was so angry for so long after Sam died. I made an offhand remark about how I wouldn't have thought twice about killing anyone I thought even had a hint of a connection to my brother's death. They got quiet for a while, and I thought I offended them. When the conversation started up again, I got the distinct impression that it took a while, but they punished the men who caused Grigori's brother's death. That it was people from their own side. That's when I realized the real hunting they'd meant at the reception. I looked Radomir straight in the eye and told him in no uncertain terms that with my experience I would have laid in wait, shot them, gutted them, burned their bodies, and left their organs out for the wolves. They believed me."

Beth takes a step back and bumps into me.

"You're a mercenary like those people today."

She's not recoiling from him. She wants to look him in the eye without tilting her head back.

"Yes. I work exclusively for them. In three years, I've done ten jobs for them. It was situations where they needed someone who could blend in with the Wall Street types and had no accent."

"Those were not righteous causes, Steve."

"You don't know that. They didn't just give me a description, location, and time. I studied these men. I learned them to make sure I picked the right way to do it. To do it without getting caught. These men were threats to Laura's family. Not their businesses. Their family."

"And they paid you for it."

"No. I didn't take any money for any of it. If something happened to Laura, it would devastate Chelle. If something had happened to someone in Laura's family, it would have devastated her. Which meant it would have devastated Chelle. We lost enough when we lost Sam. I wasn't about to watch my sister grieve all over again. Liz, I don't know how you're going to feel in the morning or in a few days or weeks or months or even years. I don't think you'll regret what you had to do today, but you might. I haven't lost a minute of sleep over what I did in the past, and I won't tonight. In an us-or-them, I will always pick us."

I look around the room, and I think all of us, but Beth guessed where Steve's story was going. Or maybe not. She asked if they'd recruited him, and she guessed he was a mercenary.

Beth says nothing, and we all wait. She rakes her teeth over her bottom lip before she steps into her brother's arms.

"I doubt Mom thought any of us would use the skills she taught us at the range, but she made sure we had them for this very reason. You wouldn't have become a hunter if Mom hadn't taught all of us to shoot. I never imagined our Mom had an ulterior motive for any of it, but I'm glad she did."

"Me too, Lizzie. I never want to see you in that kind of danger again. I never want to watch my sister die. If the

O'Rourkes were behind any of what happened today, I won't back down."

He's looking at me now. His gaze is defiant. He gives his sister an extra squeeze as he continues speaking.

"I know I can't take out any of them. But I have no qualms about killing people important to them and their organization. The moment any of them failed to protect Chelle, they broke their family's oath to Grandpa. None of us ever owed them loyalty, and I sure as hell don't respect them for breaking that promise to Grandpa. It doesn't matter to me that the men who made the agreement are both dead. Dillan and his men knew the deal, and they fucked up."

Beth goes onto her toes to kiss her brother's cheek before she looks around.

"I think I've heard all I'm allowed to. I think there's stuff you need to discuss without me. Just make sure my brother and fiancé come home in one piece. You do *not* want to deal with me if they don't."

She steps into my arms and gives me a peck and a hug. Then she's leaving the office, closing the door behind her. I look at Uncle Cesare.

"How'd you guess?"

"I've had some interesting claims dropped on my desk by some birdies in the life and catastrophic injury departments. People who were once Ivankov bratva but had falling outs with the Kutsenkos. Angry people. When I've talked about this with Sal, Massi, and Dom, we figured it was Simms. It was his caliber work. Better than any of the people he hired. The moment Steve said he went hunting with Radomir and Grigori, I knew those kills were his work. He just confirmed it."

Steve nods when Uncle Cesare finishes. Then he turns to me.

"I trust you and Enzo. I know you'll both protect my sisters with your lives. I won't get in the way of whatever you decide to do. But I'm going too."

This isn't my decision to make. It's not Enzo's either. I look at Uncle Salvatore, and Steve turns to look at my uncle, the don.

"Steve, when's the last time you took a job for the bratva?"

"About eight months ago."

"Have they approached you since?"

"Once, but it was while I was on vacation with the woman who's soon-to-be my ex-girlfriend."

Oh, that's right. Simms mentioned Steve's girlfriend is cheating on him. If he's gathered intel before doing a job, then he knows Simms did too. The dead fucker wouldn't have gotten it wrong, and I don't think he was lying.

"Would you take a job again if they did?"

Steve stares at my uncle, they assess each other before Steve finally answers.

"If it's protecting any of their wives or children, in a heart-beat. If it's because of a general threat or one to any of the men, they can figure it out themselves. My loyalty is to my sisters."

Which means to us.

"*Zio, lo facciamo diventare un partner.*" Uncle, we make him a partner.

They all know I mean an associate, but the word in Italian is *associato*. It's too close to English. I don't need to put that offi-cial term out there yet. My uncle looks at Papa as his *consigliere*, his chief advisor. Papa nods. Then my uncle looks at my brother. We're all young enough that Steve will still be alive when Luca becomes don. Uncle Salvatore wants to be sure his underboss agrees to one day being Steve's don. My brother nods. Then he looks at me. As *capo dei capi*, I'd techni-cally be in charge of him. If shit goes sideways, then our men will look at me to lay the blame. Uncle Salvatore nods to me. He approves of my idea.

Throughout this, Steve has stood watching our silent family communication. Scientists might not be able to prove telepathy is real, but we can. Uncle Salvatore stands up and approaches Steve.

"Your brother suggested we make you an associate. Do you know what that is?"

"Yes. Before I started working for them, Niko gave me a crash course on the syndicate hierarchies. I'm not Sicilian enough to be a Made Man."

Uncle Salvatore shakes his head.

"Technically, you are. Even if you're only twenty-five percent Sicilian, that would be a reasonable argument to say you're Sicilian enough to be Made. But I won't force the obligations on you that go along with that. Being an associate offers you our protection, our trust, and our loyalty without you having to give us your life."

We won't own him. A Made Man isn't a part-time job. It's a commitment for life that *Cosa Nostra* comes first. For most associates, there's no difference besides not being Italian. But allowing Steve to become an associate gives him those things Uncle Salvatore listed: our protection, trust, and loyalty without him having to commit to serving our branch beyond an odd job here or there to protect the women.

"Thank you. I mean that. I didn't appreciate finding out just how out of the loop I was on so much happening with my family. I know it wasn't a matter of trust so much as trying to protect me. I couldn't remain angry given the secret I have— had. I'll tell my parents, and I'd never ask Liz to keep it from Chelle. I take your trust seriously since it's rarely given. But also thank you for letting me be a part of this. The O'Rourkes deserve everything coming to them. Losing their money, their businesses, and a few of their men seems completely fitting."

He didn't bat an eye when Uncle Salvatore called me his brother. We don't use the qualifier in-law in our family. It's brother, sister, auntie, uncle, Mama, and Papa. Once you marry in, you're in for life. And that isn't some cheesy Hollywood line. It's because we never turn our backs on family.

Carmine and the others have remained quiet throughout the conversation. It's been a lot to absorb. But my cousin's been on his computer the entire time. I know he could repeat every word said, but he's been focused on something. I'm certain he's gathering info. He's our intel guy.

"It's Director Hollands from the FBI and Agent Spiegel from the ATF. They're supposed to just be brothers-in-law. They're a hell of a lot more than that." Carmine cocks an eyebrow as he looks around. "They're lovers."

Too bad for whoever's sister they caught in the middle. He scrolls something before looking back up at us and continuing.

"Cormac and Seamus made a deal with Hollands not to reveal their affair to his wife who happens to be a Deputy DNI. Ain't that some shit?"

So, the cuckolded wife is a Deputy Director at the Department of National Intelligence. One of the FBI's oversight bodies. She could blow up both their careers, but especially her husband's. Those two men must be paying the O'Rourkes some big hush money. And no wonder they aren't backing down.

They both want to make names for themselves in case something goes wrong, and they have to rely on their service reputations. They probably staged that whole fucked-up mess with the press, hoping they could make an arrest stick before the O'Rourkes could get their bribe money back. Because Finn will demand the cash if they don't do what they're paid for. The man counts their money like Uncle Scrooge in *Ducktails*.

I bet they're also figuring that taking me down despite being warned to back off from Beth will outweigh trapping her in the middle. From Shane's message, they aren't trying too hard to stop them. They're probably gambling on Steve intervening, either by keeping her away or hinting at the threat to make me push her away.

What I doubt anyone counted on was Simms. I wouldn't put it past the fucker to have known about the O'Rourkes' plan and have acted today to fuck them over too. He is— was — pretty pissed they didn't do a better job of keeping his payroll going when the jobs he was doing for them dried up.

I mull something over before looking at my uncle.

"Mikey won't have told anyone what happened. Uncle Cesare, you won't say anything when Mikey comes to you with the insurance claim. But Uncle Sal, have you told Maks, Enrique, or Dillan about Simms?"

"No. I don't feel any need to make that courtesy call. They can figure it out when he doesn't answer their calls."

"Good. Then Dillan and his family probably don't know about what happened today. They have no idea that we know. They're banking on Steve keeping that message to himself and us chasing our tails to find our why the feds have such a hard on for me. They want us to keep thinking it was all *Tres J's*. If we're going to get everything done that Steve suggested, we need to start now." I glance at my watch. "It's eleven a.m. in Tokyo and ten a.m. in Beijing. The morning is almost gone there."

Enzo moves to sit next to Carmine on a loveseat that always looks like it'll collapse under any two of us but hasn't yet. He had his laptop with him when he walked into the office. Now he and Carmine plonk away on their keyboards, periodically pointing to something on each other's screens or their own. The rest of us are quiet for ten minutes before Enzo looks up.

"We're in, Steve. Here."

My brother hands our soon-to-be brother-in-law his computer. That's a cosmic sign of respect and trust. Enzo won't even let the rest of us check our emails on his computer since it's linked to all our accounting, legal or otherwise. They swap places, and Enzo pulls over an armchair to sit beside Steve. My new brother keeps glancing at Carmine's screen to reference something. As the minutes tick by, exhaustion envelops me. I wish I was curled up in bed with Beth instead of killing time in here. I shut my eyes; the others chat while we wait.

"Done."

Steve's pronouncement makes me sit up. I glance at my watch. I must have dozed off. We have twelve hours until the U.S. stock market opens. They'll start getting calls from Asia and Europe within the next few hours.

He hands the computer back to Enzo as Carmine shuts his. Steve looks over at my uncles and Papa.

"If this is all you want me to be a part of, that's cool. But I'm not done."

There's a smidge of defiance in his tone as he looks at Uncle Salvatore.

"None of us are. Do you want to look at what we have? Or do you want to go to your place and get yours?"

Rifles.

"Let me see the options, then I can decide. And I want to tell my parents the truth. If I leave here with you or within thirty minutes of you, they'll know I'm into something. I'd rather they know I'm not acting alone."

Papa's been silent like the others once we got serious. Now he glances toward the door before settling his attention on Steve.

"We tell them as much as we do any of the women. We're going out. We don't know when we'll be back. It might be quick, or we might have to go to our place. If your mom grew up with any active mob ties, she knows what that means."

The garage. The place where we deal with less cooperative informants or where we punish people. All the syndicates have them. We suspect the Kutsenkos have a warehouse. We think the O'Rourkes have a storage facility. And we're pretty sure the Diazes use the basement of one of their bodegas. One of the unwritten commandments of syndicate life is don't snoop around our place, and we won't blow up yours.

"Thank you."

Luca frowns. I know he won't want to leave Olivia and Petra. I guess the cold they thought their daughter was getting was actually the first signs of teething. Apparently, nights are extra rough for my niece, which means her parents aren't sleeping much. Olivia's nursing, so she has to get up. But when Petra doesn't need to eat, Luca is on call. He looks over at me and nods. He doesn't want to go, but he will for me and for Beth. He speaks to all of us as our underboss.

"We go as a team of seven. We go to McGinty's. None of them are working tonight, but their men will be there drinking. It's a clean job. In and out. No damage to that place."

That'll send a louder message than trashing the bar too. It's not about inconveniencing them and making them clean up a mess before they reopen. It's about them knowing they're weak, and we know it. In fact, we're going to make them weaker.

I hear Matteo on the phone calling the guy at our real garage who manages our fleet of cars. He's getting two SUVs sent over. Once he's off the phone, we formulate our plan and assign roles. Next to Papa's office is another door that remains locked at all times because they don't want Pia and Natalia to open it when they're here. Behind the wood door is a reinforced steel one that leads to a panic room. It's also our armory. Steve finds a couple things he likes, and we put the rifles in cases and ammunition in bags.

Gabe owns a couple hardware stores, so we have legit businesses to get the things we need for homemade explosives. Carmine heads our construction division, so he has easy access to our demolition explosives for bigger jobs. Right now, I collect the homemade ones I keep stocked. I don't need my degree to set the fuses, but it helps to make them more complicated than a typical fertilizer bomb. It takes a bomb tech or someone else with my knowledge of electrical engineering to diffuse them without blowing themselves up first.

I may have paid for my MBA— just like everyone in my generation paid for their grad degrees —but Mama and Papa paid good money for me to officially learn how to blow shit up and to indulge my love of electric engines in cars. At least, that's what Mama complains about every time she dusts my diploma.

None of us care enough to hang our diplomas on the walls at our places, so they fill a wall in here. There are eight from Ivy League or Top Tier schools. Mama and Papa didn't buy any of us a degree. We earned our spots at those schools, and we earned those degrees. There isn't a dumb one in the bunch.

Steve just joined us back at the SUVs three blocks from McGinty's. He did a little recon for us since none of us can go in there without it setting off all the alarms. I know from past brawls in there, they have two alarm buttons under the bar that alert the O'Rourkes' leadership. There's one in the back office, and three in the kitchen. Fuckers obviously expect as much trouble as they get. It's been six years since that fight, so they might have added more.

"There's a waitress and a female bartender, but the rest are men. There're twelve around tables, four at the bar, and four between the two pool tables. Plus two dudes behind the bar. I waited around to see if anyone came out of the restrooms or the kitchen. They didn't."

I'm taking the lead on this since this is about retribution for what happened to my fiancée.

"What'd the bartender say about you drinking alone."

"That I just found out my girlfriend's fucking some asshole who isn't me. I got the drink for free. Left a five-dollar tip. Generous without being memorable."

That sucks. It's actually an explanation not an excuse. He could have gone in and looked around, said he didn't see his friend, and was going to step outside to call them. Then just not gone back in. Getting the drink is less memorable than the walk in-walk out, but what he told the bartender really just sucks because it's true.

"All right. Let's go."

Gabe, Carmine, and Luca are going around back to make sure no one can leave. Steve is guarding the front door. We'll be speaking Italian into earpieces. Since he can't understand the language, it's not safe for him to come in. Matteo, Enzo, and I are going in through the front.

Basically, we're going to kettle them by coming around from both sides and forcing them to remain in one place where we want them. But we have to be in an out before Finn, who manages the bar most nights, can get there after someone inevitably triggers the alarm. None of them live in this neighborhood, so we should finish before any of them can arrive, but who wants to tempt fate? Not I. I have a hot fiancée I plan to make love to before the sun rises. We move into place, and I give the signal. Carmine goes in through the back to get the women out. But once they're safe outside, he'll stand with Luca and Gabe. Anyone who makes it to the back door will get shot as they open it.

I lead my trio in through the front door, guns already drawn. I take in everything as my gaze sweeps the interior. I see that only one person has moved since Steve came out. There are only three at the pool tables. The guy must be in the restroom.

I hear Enzo through my earpiece since we're not standing together anymore.

"*Bagno.*" Bathroom.

He noticed the same thing I did. The guys out back will know to expect someone to flee in a few seconds.

"*Uno.*"

That was Carmine. One man down. It was probably the one in the restroom. He probably took him out as he leads the women to the back door. These women are likely mobster's daughters or sisters or nieces. The O'Rourkes are just like any other syndicate. We keep it all in the community. These women know to get out while they can. Even if it's an attacker leading them to safety, they go.

It's Carmine again in my earpiece.

"*Sicuro.*" Safe.

The waitress and bartender are out. I'm keeping track of all of this as I squeeze off one bullet after another. We don't just spray bullets everywhere. We aren't here to fuck up the place. Enzo, Matteo, and I are methodical in how we work our way forward like birds migrating south for the winter. We're in an inverted V, and I'm at the vertex. Matteo is to my right, and Enzo is to my left. We divide and conquer, each taking a third with the bar divided into columns.

Each of our 9mm pistols had fifteen bullets in the clip when we started. Enough for any of us to clear the bar since we each carry two. I sense more than see Enzo pivot to shoot a guy who just popped up from behind the bar. As Enzo turns, a guy aims at him from beneath a pool table. He's dead before he realizes I saw him. Stay the fuck away from my baby brother.

Matteo's hushed voice fills my ear.

"We're missing one."

"I know. It was a blond. He was near the pool table."

I didn't see anyone try to run out, but it's possible I missed the movement while focusing on a different target.

"*Due.*" Two.

It's Gabe. Someone must have tried to escape out the back.

"*Biondo?*" Blond?

"*Sì.*"

Good. All accounted for.

"*Doppio controllo.*" Double-check.

We can't leave until we're sure they're all dead. Our cleaners will be here soon, and they don't need any surprises. We don't need anyone trailing blood down the street or calling Dillan or one of his cousins. They'll leave the bodies, but they'll make sure we don't leave any casings or other ballistics evidence behind. I pull out my phone and wake the screen. I already have the text typed out. I hit send. Our team is five blocks past where we left the SUVs. They'll be here within minutes. Within half an hour, from the outside, it'll look like they just closed up early.

We're all wearing gloves in case we need to touch something. I walk around the back of the bar, stepping over the two bartenders. I look in one of their fridges and spot what I want. Cheap fuckers.

I'm leaving a calling card. A bottle of donkey piss prosecco. I wouldn't water my weeds with this shit. No one said these Irish had taste.

"We're good."

Matteo comes to stand next to me as I come out from

behind the bar. All said and done, it was over in five minutes. Probably not even. They were all armed with more than just a knife. They had the means to defend themselves, but they weren't ready. Some had their backs to the door. Dumb mother-fuckers. That's what you get. You're the first ones dead.

We head outside once the cleaners start work. Steve hasn't moved from the spot where we left him. We have one more stop before we can go back to my parents' place. We pack into our vehicles and ride in silence until we get to an establishment in Queens. Just having hair as dark as ours is enough to raise eyebrows around here. Luca's driving the other SUV while I drive the one I'm in. We pull into an alley and turn off our headlights. We leave the engines idling. No one says anything as Steve slips out with his rifle.

From the driver's seat I have a clear view as he makes his way to the fire escape along the side of an apartment building. He scales it with ease, jumping to pull down the ladder, then pulling himself up to the first rung. Then he's running up to the third floor on silent feet. I know because my window is open, and I don't hear a single sound on the metal. He's pretty much overhead at this point. It's cramped, but he settles onto his belly.

We're all in tactical gear, but Steve has an action camera affixed to a helmet. I pull out the app on my phone that receives his transmission. I watch him adjust his position, so he must be looking through his rifle's scope. He moves his head, so I have a view through it. I can see Lorcan Cullen getting a blowjob from a stripper in his office. He manages this club, and he's a total bag of shit. He's sixty-eight years old and a former NRA member. He's Finn's godfather along with Sean and Shane's, Finn's younger twin brothers. While Steve worked his magic to destroy all the O'Rourkes' investments, Carmine did a little digging to find out who Steve's girlfriend's been cheating with. Whaddya know? This fucker is her sugar daddy.

Besides being gross as fuck, turns out Lorcan has been one of Steve's clients since Steve got his license eight years ago. Steve suspects they hooked up during a client dinner in a restroom. He remembers his ex-girlfriend disappearing for a while, supposedly in line for the restroom. When he thought back, he remembered Lorcan took forever at the bar. He claimed he'd had to step outside to take a call. Now Steve thinks they were fucking somewhere. That was four months ago. But he admitted, for all he knew, she could have been with Lorcan before dating him. It could have all been manipulation.

The camera shifts a little, but I can still see through the scope. He moved it down to the brim of the helmet, so he could use the scope without me losing my prime-time viewing. Lorcan's pushing the girl off his dick, wrapping his hand around it to stroke it. From his expression, he's just about to come. Then he jerks, then does nothing.

Wow.

Steve is a better sniper than any of us could have imagined. No wonder the Kutsenkos hired him. He hit Lorcan in the pterion. It's just above the ear and the weakest part of the skull where three different bones meet. There's an artery—the middle meningeal artery —that runs underneath it. That bullet did a lot more than just rupture it and cause an epidural hematoma. The caliber of the weapon likely exploded the circle of Willis, which supplies much of the blood to the brain. It might not have been instantaneous death despite him going still, but he definitely didn't survive it.

I watch Steve climb back down the fire escape before getting into the car. He closes the door softly once he's in the seat behind me. We pull out and call it a night. We're exhausted by the time we get to my parents' home. But I'd call the night a success.

I slip into my bedroom and spot Beth fast asleep. I pause to watch her for a moment. She can never find out how blithely I entered that bar and shot those men. It wasn't like this afternoon where they attacked us first. It wasn't even a fight. These were executions. That's the monster this life has made me. That's what makes all of us morally black just like society believes. But in our world, morality is absolute, even if the outside world thinks ours is situational.

Either you honor the rules, or you don't. When you do, you have the chance to live. When you don't, you can pretty much guarantee your own death. It's why Luca, Carmine, and Gabe surviving what they did to Anastasia Kutsenko is unbelievable. If they weren't part of the don's family, they would be dead. The O'Rourkes done fucked up. And now they'll understand that I'm no different from any other man in the underworld. Come near the woman I love, and I will burn your world down.

I slip into the shower and run the shampoo through my hair. I'm unprepared for soft hands to skim over my skin from behind. The shower pouf rubs across my back then around to my belly as Beth wraps her arms around me, pressing her body to mine. I rinse my face and hair before turning around.

"*Piccolina*."

"Daddy."

We say nothing else as I lift her left leg to my hip. I maneuver between her legs and thrust into her. She grips my shoulders, squeezing each time I surge into her. Some of our most meaningful conversations happen while we're having sex because there's nothing more intimate than making your body one with someone else. But this time, neither of us says a word until we come together.

"I love you."

We grin at each other when we speak at the same time. I'm glad I already put my discarded clothes in a trash bag. They were gross. Blood splatters far more than you'd expect. Before I can grab it once we're out of the shower, she snags the bleach from beneath the sink. I reach for it, but she twists away. She lets her towel drop to the floor before bending over to pour a small amount onto the tiles. She's thorough, pouring out a little more when she needs it. She starts from as high as she can reach, which is above anywhere the water sprayed, until she reaches the floor. There isn't a single inch that doesn't get scrubbed at least three times.

When she's done, she rinses the sponge and puts it and the bleach away. She turns to the sink and washes her hands. She hangs up her bath towel as I watch her. Neither of us speaks. After I hang up my towel, she offers me her hand and leads me into the bedroom. We climb into bed, and she drapes her arm and leg over me as I stroke her back. Cleaning the bathroom was acceptance. She knew what I did tonight, and she didn't shy away from it. Cleaning the bathroom was another way she'll protect me. How did I get so lucky?

"This isn't over, is it?"

"No. It ties the score for now. But it doesn't end it."

"You've punished Alejandro and Shane. You've punished both families. But what about the agents?"

"I don't know yet."

That's the best I can offer, and she seems content with that. She tilts her head back to kiss me. We cling to each other until we're breathless. I fall asleep with the love of my life in my arms. I'll live to fight another day.

Epilogue

Beth

It's been nearly a month since the day Simms kidnapped us, and I went all Rambo on his mercenaries. I woke up the next morning with Marco spooned around me. I didn't want to get up. It was too perfect. We'd just finished having sex when Matteo knocked on the door. It was very much back to reality then. Within fifteen minutes, Marco was gone. I didn't see him for four days. Fortunately, I already knew this could happen. And doubly fortunate, I was already staying with Massimo and Nicoletta. I wasn't alone. It's going to take me a while to get used to Marco being gone with no means of communication.

Chelle and I hung out with our parents and Steve while Marco was away. It was good for us to be together. We have a veritable army surrounding us, so no one was coming near us. Mom and Dad told us more about the parts of our family history they wished we'd never learn. But it was good to understand just how deeply entrenched our family was in the mob for generations. It turns out, my dad's side of the family was

Cosa Nostra before they left Sicily. They'd escaped that life by coming to America. Oh, the irony that the great-grandson of an immigrant who fled the Mafia is now an associate by choice.

My parents accepted that far better than I imagined. But the mob is not in my mom's good book right now. I'd almost feel bad for the O'Rourkes if they cross her path. But I don't because I'd shoot them too.

"We're here, *piccolina*."

I look out the town car's window and smile. We're back where it all started. I check my mask is in place. No one can tell who I am under it. Marco's mask disguises him just as well since it covers all but his eyes. Pauly opens the car door and winks at me. He's lucky Marco didn't notice. Or rather, lucky Marco chose to ignore it. I suck my lips in not to grin. I trust Pauly unequivocally. Once he closes the door, he falls in behind us. Luigi leads the way. It surprised me when Luigi started being my guard while Marco was gone. But whatever shit happened between him and the don's family is resolved. I guess he got a royal pardon.

We enter through the side door, and Marco leads me straight to the room we used those nights we met here for the first three weeks. We don't stop to look around. Neither of us goes into the locker room. He nods to an owner as we make our way to the stairs. When we get to the door, I'm not sure what to expect Pauly and Luigi to do or where to go. When they post outside the door, I want to refuse to go inside. I'm mortified they'll hear us.

"These are the soundproof rooms, remember?"

Marco closes the door behind us, and I take off my mask. I nod, but I'm still looking over my shoulder with unease.

"Beth, I would not take you somewhere I know my men can hear me pleasuring you. This is between us and only us. Now strip."

The last two words sound different from all the ones before them. They're a command. I don't hesitate to obey. Then I'm walking toward the Saint Andrew's Cross. Marco helps me onto it, fastening my wrists and ankles, making it impossible for me to do anything but wait for Marco's next move. He kisses my belly as he swipes his fingers between my pussy lips, letting the tips dip into me. He presses my clit for a second before pulling his hand away. He sniffs then licks them. I'm forced to watch him walk over to the chair then move it to sit before me.

We stare at one another, neither wanting to speak first. What fun would that make this game? After a few minutes, Marco opens the large purse I brought. He pulls out several accoutrements. He gathers what he wants and prowls over to me. He latches onto my left nipple sucking hard, drawing on it until it elongates enough for him to put a clamp on it. He repeats the process with my right one. Then he drops to one knee and sucks my clit. I see the chain hanging down my belly. It's only a matter of seconds before there's a clamp on my clit. A clitty clamp. Sounds so much cuter than it feels.

He licks my pussy as his hands wrap around my ass cheeks and spread them until his fingers can press the jeweled plug already in my ass. He twists it while thrusting his tongue into my cunt. I moan, and it spurs him on to keep tormenting me. While he keeps working my pussy, he turns on an egg-shaped vibrator and slips it inside me. It rests against my g spot and makes me tremble. Holy fuck. I close my eyes as I focus on not squirting or coming. My toes wiggle, and my hands fist and unfist. Fuck.

I open my eyes as Marco presses gentle kisses to the inside of my thighs then my belly. His hand rests protectively—possessively —perfectly over my belly. He's had to travel during the past two weekends for legit business. I suggested I start my new job with Carmine's firm, but he still firmly resists. He insists we're going on a honeymoon soon. But we haven't set a wedding date. We consider ourselves engaged, but I'm not wearing a ring.

"Beth, the first time we were in here, I knew I wanted you for more than a good fuck. That scared the shit out of me because I already knew I wanted you for forever. I swore up and down for years that I wouldn't even remotely consider that. One argument with you, and you changed my mind. I've always known soulmates exist, but I was never interested in looking for mine. I should have known that's not how the universe works. I love you."

"I love you."

I wait for him to stand, but he doesn't. It can't be that comfortable to have one knee on the linoleum. But he's waiting me out again. He can tell I'm growing impatient. My clit pulses with a need for relief.

"Daddy."

"Yes, *piccolina*."

"I need you."

"Need me to do what? Spend the rest of my life with you?"

"Yes."

"Grow old with you?"

"Yes."

"Make babies with you?"

"Yes."

Each of my answers is getting more and more desperate. He's teasing me when all I want is to come.

"Will you marry me?"

"Yes."

I didn't say that just because that's what the response has been to all the other questions. I said it because I mean it. I want him to know I will. That nothing has changed, and nothing will. But I'm utterly unprepared for him to hold up his fist and open it palm up.

"Marco?"

"Yes."

"Is that a ring for me?"

"Yes."

"Can I have it?"

"Yes."

He stands and releases my left hand before he slides the ring on. It's the most exquisite thing I've ever seen. He has ridiculously good taste in everything, but one look at this, and I know my sister helped him. It's my dream ring, which is something I never told him about.

"I would have given this to you sooner, but the stones I purchased while I was away got tied up in customs. Then the jeweler's father died. I had to wait for him to set them."

"Daddy, good things come to those who wait."

I can't believe it. I cup his cheek and lean forward as best I can to kiss him. I have my eyes closed, but I can tell he's reaching around for something as we kiss. Then the clamps are gone, and a wand vibrator is against my clit. His mouth goes to my nipple. I scream. The sensations are so overwhelming. The fullness in my ass. The pulsing fullness in my pussy. The streaks of pain in my nipples and clit. The urgency from the vibration on my clit. I explode.

"Tsk, tsk, *piccolina*. You didn't ask. I think Daddy is going to have to punish you for that. Mmm. Maybe no more orgasms for at least fifteen minutes."

He releases me from the cross, and I walk with him to where there's a pulley system attached to the ceiling and the wall. He gathers the rope and positions me how he wants. He begins to create a diamond harness around my back and chest.

"How does this feel?"

"It's good. My joints are fine."

He's not cutting off any circulation to them. We keep talking as he binds me, both ensuring I'll be safe once he hoists me in the air. When he's got me secured to the hook, he slips a blindfold over my eyes and a ball gag in my mouth. He has earplugs in his hand. He's still wary of that, but I said I wanted to try. I trust him implicitly. Since I won't be able to safe word, he's insisted I prove I can snap throughout the process.

"Are you ready, *piccolina*?"

I can only nod before he slips the earplugs in. He's slow as the pulley lifts me off my feet. I twirl a little but not much. I inch off the floor and lean forward. I can't tell how high he brings me until he secures the ropes, and I feel his lips on my nipple from underneath. He's over six feet tall. Maybe he's stooping, but probably not that much. But if something should happen to the rope or the pulley, I know he can catch me. He will catch me.

He grasps my hair when I try to look down, as though I can see through the blindfold. He gives me a harsh kiss beside the gag, then he's gone. I make myself breathe through the immediate panic. I can't hear him. I have no idea of what's happening around me.

This is what I wanted. I want to surrender control entirely to him. That's why I agreed to the earplugs— insisted upon them. This is my fantasy, and he's sharing it with me. I have unwavering faith in his promise to take care of me, so a couple breaths later, I'm calm again. Then it's curiosity that takes hold.

How long is he going to let me hang here? What's he doing while he waits?

I don't know how much time passes, but I feel a vibration along the rope before I'm lowered. A little. Then I'm stopped again. A paddle lands against my right nipple from below. They're sticking out thanks to the harness. He alternates sides.

I want to kick my feet, but my legs are bound together. I moan and writhes. That earns me a paddling on the ass. Then it's over, and I'm being lifted again.

This goes around and around, but I have no sense of time. Up, down, and up again. A wand vibrator to my clit again. Nipple clamps. A flogger across my ass. He twirls the butt plug and toys with it each time. I'm so aroused that my pussy burns with need. I'm certain he can see the sweat on my brow. I'm sucking in lungfuls of air through my nostrils. Just when I don't think I can take much more, just when I've decided to snap, he lowers me to the floor. He removes the earplugs first.

"Your trust in me makes everything in this world endurable."

He then removes the gag and the blindfold.

"Are you all right, little one?"

"Yes, Daddy."

He unwinds all the rope, then rubs my arms and legs. I move them to get the circulation flowing again. I wince a couple times, but I assure Marco I'm okay. I can tell he's on the edge of panicking and dragging me out of here.

"Daddy, that was so perfect. You remembered."

"Of course, I did. I'll give you everything you need."

"And I needed this. I needed this time with you. I needed to know I can show you just how certain I am that you're the only one for me."

"And I take that seriously. I know the earplugs weren't easy for you."

"They weren't. But it was all worth it. What's your fantasy, *amore mio*?"

"Oh, *cuore*, I have many. Let me show you one of them."

He carries me to the bed. He instructs me to lie just how he wants me as he strips. The map of Italy so prominent on his chest. I'm the only woman in this club to have ever seen it. He told me that even when he came into these private rooms, he didn't strip off his tank top. He remained clothed. I'm certain the women found that sexy as fuck. I know being naked while he was dressed just minutes ago was erotic as hell. But he did it because he didn't trust any of them the way he trusts me.

"Marco, you've given me the sun, the moon, the stars."

"You're the star that will always guide me home."

He thrusts into me as we kiss. Nothing has been more perfect than this moment. The moment I truly know my happily ever after began.

Are you ready for the next family? Dillan O'Rourke will meet his match with a woman with a paste no one expects. *Mob Boss* will here at the end of March. Stay tuned on Sabine's Facebook for preorder information and ARC information.

Thank you for reading Mafia Star

Sabine Barclay, a nom de plume also writing Historical Romance as Celeste Barclay, lives near the Southern California coast with her husband and sons. She loves her days at the beach soaking up way too much sun, a good Netflix binge, and a strong hot chai. Her heroines are independent women who can defend themselves but love their Alpha heroes who want nothing more than to protect their soulmates in her Mafia Romances. She's Gen Y/Oregon Trail and loves creating engrossing contemporary romances that will make your toes curl and your granny blush.

Subscribe to Sabine's bimonthly newsletter to receive exclusive insider perks.

www.sabinebarclay.com

Join the fun and get exclusive insider giveaways, sneak peeks,
and new release announcements in
<u>Sabine Barclay's Facebook Dubious Dames Group</u>

Do you also enjoy steamy Historical Romance? Discover
Sabine's books written as Celeste Barclay.

The Mancinelli Brotherhood

Luca

This asshole is pissing me off. We've been going around in circles for five minutes, and the longer we stand out here, the greater the likelihood someone will spot us. I have a sixth sense about these things. It's why I'm still alive at the ripe old age of thirty-one.

"Espinoza, enough already. Either sell to us or don't, but we set the price. Your tequila is good, but it isn't nectar from the gods."

I'm watching Carlos Espinoza, some lackey for the Mexican Culiacán Cartel, try to maneuver me into paying more than the agreed upon price. I know it's so he can skim off the top.

"It's as close as you're going to get. You've upped the order, so the price per case goes up."

My uncle, Salvatore Mancinelli, is the New York don. He negotiated this deal, and I warned him it was a bad idea. But what do I know as his underboss and heir? I'm not backing down.

"Haven't you ever heard of a bulk discount? The more I order the better the price should be. No one else around here is buying from you. You know we're your only choice in three out of five boroughs. You aren't going to the Bronx because you won't get more than pennies there. You aren't going to Queens because you don't want to run into the Colombians. You aren't going to Manhattan because then you face the bratva along with us. And what are you going to do in Staten Island? Sell to us anyway? We control Staten Island and Brooklyn when it comes to liquor stores, so take the money and go."

"Luca, there are plenty of liquor stores in Brooklyn that aren't owned by Italians. I'll go there."

We aren't friends. He's patronizing me by using my first name. Fuck him and the horse he rode in on. I have other solutions for this shit.

"And I'll just take what I want from them for free. That's not a half bad idea. The deal's over. Take your shit with the worm in it and go."

"Motherfucking racist. Not all tequila has a worm in it."

"You're selling Mezcal. It's known for the fucking worm. I wouldn't start calling me names, you *penche hijo de puta*." Fucking son of a bitch.

He has twenty-five crates of stolen tequila that he's trying to offload because he knows he can't sell it at his own liquor store.

"What did you call me?"

Carlos takes what he thinks is a menacing step forward, and his two bodyguards do the same. Not smart. Neither of my two bodyguards nor I react, but the three men in each of my cars open their doors. They won't do more than that. It's just a reminder that the Culiacán can try, but the *Cosa Nostra* still run New York City.

"This is the third and final time I say this. Sell or leave."

Every head turns toward the liquor store's back door as it opens. A gorgeous blonde steps out, and I wish I had the time to appreciate her beauty, but she's about to die. Carlos and his men draw their guns and pivot toward her. My men pull their weapons too, but we keep them pointed at the Mexicans. The woman stands like a deer in the headlights for a second before ducking behind the industrial garbage dumpster like a frightened rabbit. Three shots hit the metal almost at the same moment. That's all it takes for my men and me. The two bodyguards standing with me aim for a guard each, and I set my sights on Carlos. We squeeze our triggers, and the men fall.

Screeching tires tell me Carlos's driver takes off. I hear more gunshots as at least one soldier in my cars tries to shoot the escaping vehicle. Glass shatters, but the sedan keeps going. I hear more tires squeal as one of my SUVs takes off and chases the guy. I holster my gun and wave my men to do the same.

I inch forward toward the trash can, but I see the shadow shift. The woman bolts from the other side. She's still the frightened rabbit, but I'm the fox pursuing her. She's fast, I'll give her that. But she has to be at least a foot shorter than me. My legs are a lot longer and cover a lot more ground with each stride.

She weaves among the cars, most likely believing it's harder to hit a moving object. She isn't wrong, but I have no intention of shooting her. I push myself harder and pounce as she darts out and tries to cross the last stretch of parking lot to reach a better lit area near a bus stop. I lunge.

"Stop running, *piccolina*. I won't hurt you."

I wrap my arms around her and pull her back against my chest, but I'm quick to spin her around and put space between us as I grasp her arms. Of course, she fights me.

"If I wanted you dead, I would have shot at you, too."

"It doesn't mean you won't kill me after."

She's breathless as she continues to struggle. I almost let go to take a step back, insulted at what she implied. But I can't blame her. If I were a woman, I'd be terrified of the same thing.

"I'm not going to rape you. I'm going to talk to you."

"Talk? You are not a man who talks if you just killed a guy."

"To keep him and his men from killing you. I told you, if I wanted you dead, I would have shot at you too. And I wouldn't have missed."

She stops struggling against me, but her eyes continue to dart from one place to another, trying to find somewhere to flee. I know I can keep her in place with only one hand, so I release her left arm. I still have a firm hold on her right one, but I haven't held it nearly as tightly as I could.

"I'm Luca. I know you figured out you interrupted something you shouldn't have. Did that man know who you are?"

"Yes."

"What about his driver? Would he know you?"

"Yes."

"Do you have a name?"

"Yes."

"*Piccolina*, we won't get very far if yes is all you can say. Are you willing to answer me with more than one word?"

"No."

I knew that was coming, and I grin. I can't help it. I wasn't wrong about her being gorgeous, but I doubt she wants to know that's what I think. At least, not if I want her to know I won't assault her.

"Fine. I have more than twenty questions I can ask that you can answer with one word. Do you work at the store?"

"Sometimes."

Ah, an improvement.

"Did Carlos know you were still working?"

"No."

"Do you have a car, or do you take the subway or bus?"

She raises her chin and remains silent. Smart but counterproductive.

"The subway or the bus will get you killed. You're too easy to find and follow. Do you have a car?"

"Yes."

"Can you stay with someone instead of going home?"

She refuses to answer.

"If that man knew you and you sometimes work in the store, then he knew where you live. If he found that out, so will someone in his cartel."

"I know. Let me go. The longer I stand here, the more likely someone is to come back for me."

"No one will touch you while I'm here."

"Arrogant. If he shot at me, he would have shot at you."

"And he would have died, anyway. What's your name?"

"Jane."

"Look, I know you won't get in one of my cars and let me drive you somewhere. In most cases, I would say that's a smart move. But you did nothing wrong tonight except for leave work at the wrong time. I know that, and you know that. But the Culiacán won't see it that way, *piccolina.*"

She freezes for no more than five seconds before she trembles so much that I can see it. I don't know what drives me next, but it's the same instinct that's made me call her little girl three times. I pull her to my chest and tuck her head against it. I stroke her hair down to her shoulders, rubbing my hand up and down her back. This is the most inopportune moment to notice she isn't wearing a bra. I will my body not to react.

"What does that mean?"

Her voice is barely more than a whisper, but I know what she's asking.

"It means little girl."

"I should be insulted, but the way you say it…"

"It has nothing to do with your height. I know you're not a child."

God, do I know she's not. She feels amazing. Her tits are soft as they press against me, and I can see she has the most delectable ass. I'd love nothing more than to cup it and squeeze until she goes up on her toes and begs for me to wrap her legs around my waist and fuck her. For fuck's sake. Stop, you disgusting asshole. That is not what you need to be thinking about.

"Why didn't you shoot me? Whatever you were talking about, if it was with a Cartel member, then it wasn't completely legal. Carlos didn't want me alive to talk about seeing you together. Why are you letting me live?"

"I told you. You did nothing wrong but try to leave work. He should have checked the building before starting the meeting. That was on him. The only thing I take issue with is you leaving by yourself and walking into a dimly lit parking lot. I suspect you do that often, and that's too dangerous. Jane Doe, I don't hurt women."

Mafia Sinner

Mafia Beauty

Mafia Angel

Mafia Redeemer

Mafia Star

The Ivankov Brotherhood

Bratva Darling

BOOK ONE SNEAK PEEK

LAURA

As I sit across from the four Kutsenko brothers, I press my lips together to keep from drooling. No four men should be so strikingly handsome. Not all from the same family, anyway. I fight a valiant battle against letting my gaze drift toward the eldest, Maksim, whose ice-blue eyes bore into me. After years of negotiating billion-dollar investment contracts while facing countless ruthless businessmen, I've learned to keep my expression studiously blank. But it's a true struggle today. Instead, I focus my attention on the squirrelly lawyer sitting across the conference table. While he's disingenuous with each comment, he's a good negotiator. But I'm better. How cliché am I?

While I feel Maksim watching me, I focus on Dmitry Yakovitch as he continues to argue the merits of the venture capitalist company I represent, RK Capital Group, merging with Kutsenko Partners. What he means is the merits of Kutsenko Partners acquiring RK Capital Group, then stripping it and making it another money-laundering shell corporation. While most people in New York have little awareness of the Russian mafia, I do. The Kutsenko brothers' names appear on no titles or deeds anywhere in New York City, but it wasn't difficult to determine which shell companies likely belong to them. Their assumption that I'm unfamiliar with them is proving beneficial to me as they continue to whisper amongst themselves in Russian. I think they may even believe they're convincing me that they don't speak much English.

The senior partners of RK Capital Group know who I'm negotiating with, though they may not know I'm aware of these Russians' more nefarious operations. They've given me the go-ahead to agree to a merger with an eventual acquisition, but only for the right price. A price to the tune of twenty billion dollars. Considering an investment firm like Goldman Sachs is worth nearly one-hundred-and-twenty billion dollars, my clients' asking price appears reasonable.

"Mr. Yakovitch, I shall stop you now." I raise my left hand, pen caught between my index and middle fingers. When I have his attention, I lean back in my chair and casually twirl the pen over my index finger and thumb. "Fifty billion is my clients' asking price. You know that. Your clients know that. RK doesn't oppose the merger. What they oppose is the insulting offer you've made. It's nearly noon, and I'm hungry, Mr. Yakovitch. I have a delicious ham sandwich waiting for me. I even have three chocolate chip cookies waiting for me. If we aren't going to make any progress, I shall let you go, so I can move onto my eagerly anticipated lunch."

I cant my head just enough for me to appear as though my gaze rests solely on the opposing attorney's face, but I can see each Kutsenko brothers' reaction. My face battles yet again against showing my emotions as I fight not to smirk. Their muted but surprised expressions confirm what I already know.

"Please tell your clients to make a reasonable counteroffer, or I will conclude this meeting and enjoy my ham sandwich and cookies."

Dmitry glares at me before turning to Maksim and his three brothers. In rapid Russian, he doesn't interpret my suggestion. Oh no. There's no need for that. I can't catch every word because his voice is too low. But I catch something along the lines of "The bitch refuses to budge. What now? A fucking ham sandwich. More like a stick up her ass."

Maksim swivels his chair to look at his brothers. In Russian, he says, "Fifty billion is ridiculous. She's not so stupid or naïve not to know that. My guess is they'll settle for twenty billion. We offer fifteen."

"That's barely better than what we already offered," Aleksei, the second-oldest brother, argues. "She'll be eating the fucking sandwich and dipping her cookies in milk before we walk out the door. We need the buildings."

"We offer twenty, Maks," Bogdan, the youngest, insists.

As I watch the brothers discuss, their voices barely lowered, I pull my lunch sack from the black leather satchel by my feet and set it beside my laptop. It's a ridiculously pink floral bag with an embroidered monogram, the L and D overlapping. It's an empty prop, but they don't know that. I watch as five sets of eyes narrow. I offer a smile that would appear innocent in any setting other than this meeting. It's patronizing, and I know it.

Bratva Sweetheart

Bratva Treasure

Bratva Beauty

Bratva Angel

Bratva Jewel

www.ingramcontent.com/pod-product-compliance
Lightning Source LLC
Chambersburg PA
CBHW030229120726
47903CB00005B/1424